KU-112-135

THE
DARK-EYED
GIRLS

Also by Judith Lennox

THE SECRET YEARS
THE WINTER HOUSE
SOME OLD LOVER'S GHOST
FOOTPRINTS ON THE SAND
THE SHADOW CHILD

Judith Lennox

THE DARK-EYED GIRLS

BCA

LONDON NEW YORK SYDNEY TORONTO

This edition published 2000
By BCA
By arrangement with Macmillan
A imprint of Macmillan Publishers

CN 3994

Copyright © Judith Lennox 2000

The right of Judith Lennox to be identified as the
author of this work has been asserted by her in accordance
with the Copyright, Designs and Patents Act 1988.

All rights reserved. No part of this publication may be
reproduced, stored in or introduced into a retrieval system, or
transmitted, in any form, or by any means (electronic, mechanical,
photocopying, recording or otherwise) without the prior written
permission of the publisher. Any person who does any unauthorized
act in relation to this publication may be liable to criminal
prosecution and civil claims for damages.

Typeset by SetSystems Ltd, Saffron Walden, Essex

Printed and bound in Germany by
GGP Media, Pössneck

To Danielle, remembering those times

PART ONE

The Further Shore

1960–1969

Chapter One

Liv searched among the pebbles for pieces of coloured glass. When she was very little, she had believed they were jewels: emeralds, sapphires, diamonds, and – a rare find – a red stone, like a ruby. Her father, Fin, had explained to her that they were glass, polished by the sea. Liv imagined the waves scooping up broken bottles and shattered window-panes and rubbing them with a cloth, until they acquired the soft lustre of the string of pearls Thea wore round her neck.

Ahead of her, Fin and Thea walked along the beach. The pebbles crunched as they walked, and their heads were bent. Fin's overcoat billowed out into a great, dark cape, and Thea's silk scarf rippled like a pale pennant in the breeze. Gulls swooped and shrieked, echoing the angry rise and fall of their voices. Their hands were dug into the pockets of their coats and, as they walked, their paths diverged, Fin tending towards the sea, Thea heading almost imperceptibly back to land. Liv looked at neither her parents nor at the waves, but kept her gaze fixed on the narrow swathe of stones, searching for rubies and diamonds.

A year later, leaving the coast, travelling inland, it rained the length of their journey. Like tears, thought Thea, absently watching the drops slide down the window of the bus. She glanced at her daughter, sitting beside her. 'Nearly there,' said Thea encouragingly, smiling.

Liv did not smile back. Neither did she speak; in the eight months since her father had left home, Liv had increasingly rationed her conversation, and her dark brown eyes had acquired a shuttered appearance. Once more Thea attempted reassurance. 'We don't have to stay if we don't like it, darling.' Though where on earth they would go if Fernhill didn't work out, she had absolutely no idea.

It was still raining when they reached their stop. The horse-chestnuts dripped, and the silky petals of the poppies on the verge had been bruised by the storm. The wheels of the bus made curls of brown water as it drew away, leaving mother and daughter alone at the side of the road. Thea recalled Diana's instructions. 'Turn right at the bus stop, away from the village. We're just over the brow of the hill.'

Thea's head was bowed as she walked, and her legs ached. The fierce, crackling energy that had sustained her throughout this last awful year seemed to have deserted her. She tried to remember when she had last seen Diana. At Rachel's christening, of course, but that must have been ten years ago. They had met since, surely. She rubbed her wet forehead with wet fingertips.

At the top of the hill she paused, gazing breathless at the patchwork of field, stream and knoll that marked the Cambridge-shire and Hertfordshire border. Alongside the road was a wall, into which were set gates of splendidly wrought iron. Thea read the lettering on the gates: Fernhill Grange, and saw the large, red-brick house, set in landscaped gardens. 'Goodness,' she said, taken by surprise, unable for a moment to imagine the bossy, jolly Diana Marlowe of her memory the chatelaine of such an imposing country house. But Diana, Thea reminded herself as she opened the gate, had come from a good family, and had married well. Henry Wyborne was now a Member of Parliament. And, besides, Diana had the knack of always falling on her feet.

They squelched up the driveway. At the front door Thea paused, looking down at her daughter. 'I had no idea it would be so splendid,' she said. Gently, she reached down and coaxed Liv's wet black fringe out of her eyes.

*

Over tea and cakes, Diana reminded her, 'You came to the reunion in 'fifty-three, Thea. That was the last time.'

'Seven years ago? So long?'

'You should have come last year.' Diana smiled. 'It was terrific fun. Bunty Naylor was there – you remember Bunty, she was a scream. That time she...'

Diana continued to reminisce. Thea half listened, her gaze flitting round the large, comfortable room. The two little girls were kneeling on the window-seat. Rachel chattered; Liv, as was her habit these days, remained mute. Rachel was only a few months older than Liv. Thea remembered the christening: Rachel, the perfect baby, her dark eyes peering out serenely from beneath a froth of old lace. Now, ten years later, Rachel was still perfect. Taller than Liv, she was – there was no other word for it – beautiful, her hair a rich, wavy chestnut, her eyes a clear, calm brown. She radiated health and confidence. Thea's gaze moved from Rachel, in her crisp, bright cotton dress, to Liv. There were darns in the elbows of her cardigan, and her hunted, haunted eyes were shadowed by the overlong fringe. Thea had to swallow down her sudden rush of bitterness and love.

'Thea?'

Thea's head jerked up. Diana was staring at her. She tried to pull herself together. 'Sorry, Diana. It's just that – well, it all seems so long ago.' She twisted her strong pale hands together. 'The war, I mean. The FANYs. That frightful place where we were stationed.'

What she wanted to say was, I don't think I'm that person any more. I can hardly remember that person.

Diana said sympathetically, 'Of course. You've had the most ghastly time, haven't you? Don't take any notice of me, darling, I just chatter on. I always did, didn't I?' She paused and, looking at their daughters, said softly, 'Our dark-eyed girls, Thea.'

Thea bit her lip, pressing her nails into the palms of her hands. She heard Diana say, 'Rachel, why don't you show Olivia your bedroom?' and was able to wait just long enough for the door to close behind the two girls before the first choking sob escaped her.

Once she started she couldn't stop, not until Diana gently folded her fingers around a glass, and said, 'Works much better than tea, I always think.' Thea took a large shuddering gulp of whisky, and sat back in the chair, her eyes closed. After a long while she opened them and whispered, 'Sorry.'

'Don't be ridiculous, Thea. Why shouldn't you howl?'

'It seems an imposition—'

'Nonsense. That's what friends are for.' Thea had forgotten how kind Diana was. Bossy and sometimes slightly ridiculous, but always kind.

'You haven't heard anything . . .?'

Thea shook her head. 'It's been eight months. And he left a note on the kitchen table.' *So sorry. You'll be better off without me. I won't insult you by offering explanations or begging forgiveness. Love, Fin.*

'He won't come back,' she said firmly. 'My marriage is over. Coming here – it'll be the best thing. A clean break.' She took a deep breath. 'Tell me about the cottage, Diana.'

'It's frightfully small.' Diana looked dubious. 'But rather sweet. There's a drawing room and a kitchen and two bedrooms, so it should be fine for . . .' The words tailed off.

Thea completed Diana's sentence. 'For just the two of us.' Once there had been three, now there were two. She was almost used to it. 'Is there a bathroom?'

Diana grimaced. 'There's a lavatory, but it's outdoors and rather grim. And the Seagroves used a tin bath.'

Mrs Seagrove, the previous tenant of the cottage, had been Diana's daily help. She had recently gone to live with her daughter in Derby.

'The rent . . .' Thea forced herself to swallow her pride. The Wybornes' opulent room exuded money.

'It's very reasonable, I believe.'

Thea gave a small, private sigh of relief. Then Diana added tentatively, 'It might be easier, Thea, if . . .'

'Yes?'

'It might be easier for you if you let people assume that you are a widow. Fernhill's a small village, and rather old-fashioned in some ways. And the cottage is owned by the Church. The vicar is a terribly good friend of ours, and...' Diana's voice trailed away.

Thea was unsure whether her sudden flare of anger was directed at Diana, or at Fin. She said coldly, 'I won't embarrass you, Diana.'

'I didn't mean—' Diana was pink.

Thea felt suddenly ashamed. 'I'm sorry. I shouldn't have said that. You've been so kind. And you're right, of course.'

Diana glanced at her watch. 'We could go and look at the cottage, if you like. Mrs Nelson will keep an eye on the girls. We'll take the car – why on earth you didn't let me meet you at the railway station, Thea, instead of getting soaked to the skin...'

'And this is my collection of dolls,' said Rachel, opening yet another cupboard door. 'Daddy buys me one whenever he goes abroad.'

Liv stared at the dolls: Miss Holland, Miss Italy, Miss Japan in her pink kimono. Rachel said, 'This is my newest one,' and held out to Liv Miss France, who was wearing a Breton coif. Liv touched the doll gingerly, afraid of disturbing her rigid perfection.

'We could play Ludo,' said Rachel. There was a hint of desperation in her voice that Liv recognized, and understood. She knew that she was being boring, she knew that she had hardly spoken a word since Rachel had taken her upstairs, and had shown her the toys and ornaments and books and clothes in her vast bedroom. She knew that she should make friends with Rachel, that if they were to live at Fernhill, her mother would expect her to make friends with Rachel. Yet the pink and white splendour of the room, and Rachel's own self-assured prettiness, overwhelmed her, deepening the feeling that had seized her since her father had gone away: that everything familiar had been kicked aside, that nothing could be depended on.

'Or shall we play in the garden?' Rachel peered out of the window. 'It's almost stopped raining.'

Liv nodded. They went outdoors. There, they tramped across wet lawns and knelt beside the pond, with its waterlilies and fat goldfish. They played on the swing, and ran between long lines of rosebushes. Red tulips bloomed confidently in vast flower-beds; magnolia trees dropped waxy petals to the close-cropped grass. It reminded Liv of the municipal gardens by the sea front at Great Yarmouth.

Rachel took Liv to see her pony. 'Do you ride?' she asked. Liv shook her head.

'I love riding,' said Rachel. 'Though I hate gymkhanas.'

'Because of all the people?'

'People?'

'Like going to a new school. Walking into the classroom ... not knowing anyone ... people staring at you.' The words, and Liv's fears, pent up for too long, tumbled out.

'I'll be your friend,' said Rachel, kindly. 'And so will Katherine.'

'Who's Katherine?'

'She's my best friend. What's your best friend called?'

'I haven't got one.' Afraid of sounding pathetic, Liv explained, 'I've been to lots and lots of different schools. And sometimes I didn't go to school – sometimes Dad taught me at home.'

Rachel's eyes widened. 'Lucky you. Not having to go to school.'

'But I'll have to go now, I suppose.'

'Because your daddy's gone away?'

Liv nodded miserably.

'Perhaps he'll come back.'

She said logically, 'I don't see how he can come back if we're living here. He won't know where to go.'

Rachel frowned. 'We could do a spell.'

Liv stared at her. 'A spell?'

'To make him come back.'

'A *real* spell?'

'Katherine knows how to. She's got a book. We did a spell to make Miss Emblatt ill so Katherine wouldn't get into trouble about her needlework, and she sprained her ankle. And when Katherine wanted a new bicycle we did another spell.'

'Did she get one?'

'No. So we're going to try again. My daddy says, if at first you don't succeed, then try and try again.' Rachel giggled. 'That's the trouble with gymkhanas.' She smoothed her pony's mane. 'I never win, and can't be bothered trying again. Prizes and cups and rosettes ... I can't see the point, can you?'

'I suppose,' said Liv, 'that it shows you can do something better than everyone else.'

'That's what Daddy says. But I don't *mind*, you see. I don't *care* whether I can do things best.' Rachel seemed untroubled. 'Daddy says it's not the winning, it's the taking part. Then he laughs and says, "Well, actually, darling, it's the winning that's important."'

The sun had come out at last, and the wet fields and the distant roofs of the houses gleamed. Liv circled slowly, shading her eyes from the light.

'What are you looking for?'

'The sea.' Liv squinted. 'I'm trying to see the sea.'

'It's an awfully long way away. Daddy drove us there in the summer, and it took *hours*. But if you do this –' Rachel outstretched her arms ' – you might be able to see it. It makes everything sort of tilt.'

Rachel began to spin round and round. Liv, too, straightened her arms, and turned, slowly at first, then faster and faster. In the whirl of dizzying colour as field, garden, house and tree blurred together, she could believe that she saw, far away, a thin strip of silver sea.

Then, like spinning tops losing momentum, they lost their

balance and collapsed to the ground, a tangle of arms and legs, breathless with giddiness and laughter.

'What do you think?' Diana had asked, 'Is it too frightful?' and Thea had been able to reply, honestly, that the cottage wasn't frightful at all. It was tiny, but Thea didn't mind that because it would be cheap to heat and, besides, they'd rattle about less.

Now, alone at last (Diana had driven back to the Grange to fetch the girls) she moved silently around the little house, pacing through the rooms, imagining it her own. In the garden, the lavatory (well scrubbed, its wooden walls almost obliterated by seaside scenes cut from magazines) stood next to the coal bunker. The well in the centre of the small lawn rewarded Thea's efforts with a thin stream of ice-cold water. The garden was long and narrow and unexpectedly magical, with twisting paths and tiny courtyards. Thea wove through tangled dog-roses and early honeysuckles. Closing her eyes, she breathed in their scent. Tall trees met overhead, enclosing her in a dark green cave where the first shoots of bluebell and wild garlic pushed through the earth. At the end of the garden, a stream ran through a steeply banked ditch. Beyond, the view opened out to fields.

The journey, and her tears that afternoon, had left Thea exhausted, so she sat down on a fallen log, revelling in the silence, the peace. The jangling, relentless anger that had consumed her since Fin's departure had begun at last to ebb. She thought, I shall remember him just once more, and then I shall forget him. She thought of the day they had met. It had been during the Blitz; she had just joined up – twenty-one years old, her first time away from home – and she had been travelling to her first posting. The train had been crowded; she had been crushed into the middle of the carriage, her face the height of the soldiers' coat buttons, sandwiched between damp khaki uniforms that gave off a smell of wet dog, and at such a pitch of excitement and terror at the prospect of her new life that she had begun to feel faint. Then, just when shame had seemed inevitable, strong hands had swept her up, a voice had said, 'Room for a little one,' and she had spent the rest of the journey sitting in the luggage rack.

His name, he had told her, was Finley Fairbrother. Far too many syllables, he had said, just call me Fin. He had black curling hair and eyes as dark as peat pools, and, like the other men in the carriage, he had been in uniform. Thea still remembered how the string of the luggage rack had dug into her stockinged legs. She still remembered how his eyes had hypnotized her.

Fin had changed her. He had spied some streak of eccentricity in the vicar's daughter, and had teased it out. Thea had never been able to go back to the conventional creature she had once been. They had met intermittently throughout the war years. He told her about the places he had seen, the things he had done. His life, with its adventure and colour and travelling, seemed an antidote to the greyness of wartime Britain. Thea had lost her virginity in a dingy hotel room in Paddington, with the wreckage of the city scattered around them, and the two of them the only constants in a world falling apart.

Friends had warned her about Fin. 'Of course, he's utterly sweet and gorgeous, but he's not a *stayer*, darling. He's not the sort of man you *marry*.' Yet she had, of course, married him. In 1947, Fin had returned from the Far East; the wedding had taken place the following year. Throughout the first few years of their married life, they had travelled continuously, living nowhere for more than a few months at a time. It had been a wonderful, exciting, unsettling time; they had herded sheep on a Welsh hillside, had made pots in a London basement, had taught at a school in Lincolnshire. Nothing had lasted, but there had always been new adventures and new horizons to look forward to, so at first Thea had been untroubled. It had been Fin's originality and energy and carefreeness that had first attracted her.

Yet she began to realize that she was missing something: a home. The vague feeling of unease intensified when she discovered that she was pregnant. The thought of hauling a newborn baby from one unsuitable house to another appalled her. They rented a house in Oxford, where Olivia was born. Thea liked the house, and adored her tiny, dark-eyed daughter. She hoped the baby would settle Fin. Instead, when Liv was six months old, he went away, leaving a note on the kitchen table that said, 'Back in a few days. All love.' He was absent a fortnight. Returning, he begged forgiveness, and they moved house and made another new start. The following year he disappeared again, for a month. Travelling, he explained on his return. Just travelling.

So had the pattern of their lives continued. Partings and reunions, different jobs, different houses, a tightening spiral. They had moved steadily away from the centre of England, reaching, at last, the Suffolk coast, as though, in the sea, Fin had seen his escape. The pink, pebbledashed house they had rented struggled to contain their unhappiness. On grey shingle beaches, Fin had looked out to the horizon. Thea had sensed his desperation; in her, anger boiled and bubbled. 'It's not that I don't love you', he had said, and she had screamed at him, pummelling him with her fists. It had not surprised her to wake the following morning and find him gone. A month had passed – two – three. Thea could not quite recall the exact moment when she had accepted the permanence of his absence.

Her anger and defiance had prevented her at first from facing up to the practical difficulties of their situation. Then, when in the same week one letter had arrived from the bank and another from their landlord, telling her that the lease on the house would run out at the end of the month, she had been forced to search for solutions. During her peripatetic years with Fin, Thea had lost touch with most of her friends. Her parents had been dead for a decade. There were a few disapproving cousins she hadn't seen in years, but, Thea resolved, she would rather sleep in a ditch. Then she thought of Diana. Diana, whose friendship had helped her survive her first few months in the FANYs; Diana, whose life – army, love, marriage, daughter – so closely mirrored her own. Diana, who had fallen in love with Henry Wyborne, a hero of Dunkirk. During the war, they had confided to each other their hopes and fears. Since then, Diana's regular letters, with their reassuring narrative of domestic detail, had comforted

Thea during the fraught years of her marriage. Desperate, Thea wrote to Diana.

She remembered their conversation earlier that afternoon. 'I should visit the school, perhaps,' she had said, and Diana had screwed up her face and replied, 'The village school? Outside lavs and they don't know their times tables. Olivia must go to Lady Margaret's in Cambridge, with Rachel. I had a word with the Head. There are scholarships.'

Uprooting herself, transplanting herself and Liv from the shifting, silvery remoteness of the East Anglian coast, confirmed the end of her marriage. And Lady Margaret's School – a place, Thea guessed, of uniforms and rules – might provide Liv with the security she so desperately needed. Might also provide a counterweight to the impulsiveness and romanticism that Thea sometimes feared Liv had inherited from her father.

They moved into the cottage a week later. Liv took the exam for Lady Margaret's School and passed, and Thea gritted her teeth and muttered thanks when presented by Diana with a bundle of secondhand school uniform. In the summer the pupils at Lady Margaret's wore red candy-striped dresses and red cardigans, which suited small, dark Liv.

Thea took a job at the village newsagent. The work was undemanding and oddly soothing; she liked the sugary scent of the dolly mixtures as she measured out quarters for school-children, and she liked the shiny magazines, with their recipes and knitting patterns and comforting little stories about the young princes and princess. Working at the newsagent's enabled Thea to get to know people in the village. Once a week she attended an evening class at a local school, where she made huge, bright, boldly patterned pots. In the village, her widowhood was assumed. It had occurred to Thea, of course, that Fin quite likely *was* dead. He had never been particularly careful of his own safety.

They had been living in Fernhill for three months when Thea met Richard Thorneycroft. Mr Thorneycroft came to the counter in the newsagent's and handed Thea a sixpence and a card to put up in the window. 'A fortnight,' he barked, and left. Mrs Jessop, who owned the shop, said, 'Won't get no one, not if we put it up for a year. Mabel Bryant tried, and so did Dot Pearce, and she couldn't stand him for more than a week, though she's the patience of a saint.' She lowered her voice. 'Lost his wife and kiddie in the Blitz, see. Terrible shame, but that's no excuse for bad manners, I always say.'

Thea read the card. It said, 'Housekeeper needed, three hours per day. Must be quiet and hardworking. Idiots need not apply.'

Later that day, she knocked at Mr Thorneycroft's door. 'My name's Thea Fairbrother,' she said. 'I've come about the house-keeping job.'

He peered at her. He was tall and thin, and wore battered tweeds. In his right hand he gripped a walking stick. 'You'd better come in, then.'

She followed him into the house. It was Queen Anne, Thea guessed, one of the nicer houses in the village, though its dusty austerity did not do justice to its quiet beauty.

'What would my duties be?'

'Light housework. A girl comes twice a week to mop the floors. Shopping. Three hours each morning, four shillings an hour.'

'Two hours each afternoon, five shillings an hour. I have to fit this in between my other job and my daughter's school hours, Mr Thorneycroft.'

He frowned, but said, 'Beggars can't be choosers, I suppose.'

During her first month as Mr Thorneycroft's housekeeper, Thea was greeted each morning at the shop by Mrs Jessop saying, 'Left the old bugger, then, have you?' to which Thea would shake her head. 'I like working there,' she'd say, and she meant it. She liked the house, which was quiet and graceful and reminded her of the Dorset vicarage in which she had spent her childhood. Her new employer's tongue was no sharper than her father's, nor that of her commanding officer in the FANYs. She respected Mr Thorneycroft: he had a tenacity that, in the end, Fin had lacked.

A landmine in southern Italy had left him with a right leg two inches shorter than the left, yet he never complained, though Thea suspected that he must often be in pain.

Mr Thorneycroft was writing a book about the Dardanelles campaign. His study was a gloomy treasure-cave of books and records. The first time Thea cleaned it, he stood at the door, making sure she left nothing out of place. She picked up a framed picture to dust it. It was a sketch, in crayon and ink, of flower-scattered cliffs leading down to a turquoise sea. 'Where's this?' she said, expecting a dismissive reply.

But he said, 'Crete. I was there before the war.'

'It's lovely.'

He said, 'It was like paradise, I thought,' and limped away, leaving her to her housework.

That Liv settled quickly at school was largely due, Thea knew, to Rachel. Rachel had inherited the generosity of spirit that Thea still saw in Diana, and that enabled Thea to put up with Diana's bossiness and clumsy attempts at patronage. Rachel who so easily might have been the archetypal spoilt only child miraculously was not. She attended her ballet lessons, music lessons and riding lessons with a sunny lack of interest that secretly amused Thea. Rachel remained contentedly somewhere in the middle of her form at Lady Margaret's, not because she lacked intelligence but because she had no ambition. Rachel, Thea concluded, literally wanted for nothing. Sometimes Thea found herself wondering what would happen if Rachel ever found out what it was like to long for something.

Rachel shared everything with Liv: books, clothes, paints and crayons. She also shared Katherine. Katherine Constant was lanky, fierce and clever, with straight sandy hair that escaped in erratic shards from her spindly plaits, and brown eyes the colour of toffee. Thea wondered at the unlikely pairing, and eventually concluded that in Katherine Rachel found the enthusiasm and intensity that she herself lacked. There was a hunger, a scornful impatience in Katherine's dark gaze that initially startled Thea. Then, one afternoon, she had taken Liv to Katherine's home in a nearby village. She had seen the large, ugly, untidy house from which Katherine's father, a doctor, ran his general practice, and she had met exhausted Mrs Constant and Katherine's three brothers. There was Michael, the eldest, Simon, Katherine's twin, and Philip, the youngest. Complications following an attack of measles when he was a baby had left Philip both mentally and physically handicapped. Thea would have liked to have said to Katherine, 'Be patient, and what you want will come to you', but Katherine, she sensed, despised patience. She would have liked to have given Katherine the hugs that Thea guessed she rarely received at home, and did so sometimes, but felt Katherine's bony frame flexing beneath her arm, as if even that fleeting stillness alarmed her.

As the months passed, Thea and Liv made the cottage their own. They decorated plain walls and empty mantelpieces with seed cases and skeleton leaves gathered on country walks, and with pebbles and shells collected during their years beside the sea. They made curtains and blinds to cover the small-paned windows, and loose covers and cushions to brighten their old sofas and dining chairs. Thea could trace the story of Olivia's childhood in the sitting room's patchwork curtains: a scrap of an infant's romper suit in one corner, a square from a flowered summer dress in another. In the garden, geraniums and lobelias sprang from Thea's pink and orange pots; inside the house, plates and bowls painted with gods and goddesses – Pomona, Diana, Apollo – bore heaps of windfall apples and plums.

Two years after they moved to Fernhill, the landlord built a bathroom on to the back of the cottage. Thea and Liv gave a party to celebrate the dismantling of the outside privy. They drank cider and Tizer and lit a bonfire, on which they burned the wooden planks and seat and the curling cut-outs of tropical beaches. Diana and Rachel and the Constant twins came to the party, as well as Thea's friends from her pottery class and Mrs Jessop from the shop.

In 1964, the Conservatives lost the general election. Hiding her indifference, Thea consoled Diana. 'At least Henry kept his seat.'

'But a Labour government – too dreadful.'

Privately, Thea suspected that things would jog along much as before. She went to the window and leaned her palms on the sill, looking outside to where the three girls strolled across the lawn in the sunshine, their arms linked. She heard a peal of laughter. And she thought, I haven't done too badly, have I? Wherever you are, Fin, I haven't done too badly. We've a home, and I've work. And Olivia is laughing.

Chapter Two

Katherine had seen the advertisement in the local newspaper. 'Extras,' it had said, 'wanted for film to be made in local area.' She had shown the newspaper to Liv and Rachel. 'A *film*! We might be famous!' She had brushed aside any objections. Liv and Rachel had a free period last thing on Wednesday; Katherine herself had Latin with Miss Paul, who was an old dear. It would be easy.

Liv fantasized about the audition: the film director would be tall and dark, with a foreign accent, perhaps. He would pick her out of a crowd of people. 'She is the one,' he'd say. 'She must be my muse.'

They were late, so they had to run. They took off their red berets and ties and hid them in their bags, and rolled up the waistbands of their skirts to shorten the hems. Katherine had brought mascara and eye-liner and Miner's foundation, in an orangy-brown shade, the colour, Liv thought, of her mother's clay pots before they hardened. Rachel had a pale pink lipstick and a bottle of Patou's Joy, which they squirted on their necks and wrists as they walked. It was February, and there was frost on the shadowed bits at the inside of the pavement, and Liv's fingers, as she paused fleetingly to daub a persistent and depressing spot, were numb with cold. She wasn't sure the foundation helped: she was rather afraid that it just gave her face a mottled appearance – blue nose, pale skin except for tawny dabs of makeup.

The queue from the church hall where the auditions were to be held spilled out into the street. There were about ten times as many women as men, mostly girls like themselves in their late teens. Some were combing out their long, straight

18

hair, the sort of hair Liv longed for and never achieved, no matter how much Creme Silk she poured on her thick, dark curls. Most of the girls were wearing ordinary clothes rather than school uniforms.

'I heard someone say,' muttered Katherine, 'that it's *War and Peace*.'

'They'd want men . . . for battles.'

'I asked Simon, but he thought it would be boring.'

Liv often thought that Simon was Katherine in reverse: pale eyes and dark hair to Katherine's dark eyes and pale hair, indolent where Katherine was always busy. She imagined that they had lain face to face in the womb, making of each other a mirror image.

The following October, Katherine and Simon would go to Oxford. Liv had also applied to university, largely because she could not think what else to do, and she had chosen Lancaster on impulse, because it sounded exciting and new and rugged and cold and hilly. She imagined herself striding across moorlands, or battling to lectures through snowstorms. She longed for remoteness and bleakness and for something – a cause, a person, or an art – to absorb her entirely. She needed to find a resolution to the boredom that increasingly dogged her. Her small bedroom was crammed with the results of her latest enthusiasms – tapestry, paper sculpture, smocking, paper-making – many half finished. Nothing lasted, nothing satisfied.

Rachel said, 'Did I tell you? I'm going to Paris in September. Daddy's fixed it up.'

'*Paris*,' said Katherine enviously.

'Finishing school, though. Learning how to make soufflés, and how to write thank-you letters.'

They were slowly shuffling up the small run of steps into the hall. Rachel glanced at Liv and Katherine. 'You won't forget me, will you?'

'Why on earth should we forget you?'

The ends of Rachel's red cashmere scarf flapped in the breeze. 'When you go away to university. All those new people. So exciting. You'll phone, won't you? I'm afraid I might feel . . . left behind.'

'We're blood sisters,' said Liv. 'Remember?'

'Our spells.' Rachel smiled. 'I'd forgotten.'

Liv remembered the spell they had cast to make her father come home: the moonlight shifting through the willows at the end of the garden, and the scent of bonfire smoke.

They went into the hall. Two men and a woman sat at a desk, clipboards in hand, and a second man cupped his hands around his mouth and called for quiet.

'It's been such a good turnout that I only need one more, for a particular scene.' He began to walk slowly around the room, peering at face after face. Katherine glared into the middle distance, and Liv gave a quick tug at her fringe to hide the spot. Her heart seemed to pause. She thought, If he chooses me . . . and imagined the photographs in the colour supplements: *Eighteen-year-old Olivia Fairbrother, the shining new star of 1968* . . .

He stopped opposite Rachel. 'You,' he said. 'Come with me.'

All the other girls went limp with despondency, and began to walk slowly out of the room. Liv heard Katherine mutter, '*Rachel*. Always *Rachel*.' Outside, sitting on the low wall that circled the church, Katherine searched in her pockets and brought out the remains of a tube of Polos: little pieces of red fluff from her cardigan clung to them, but they ate them anyway.

'It wasn't as though we wanted to be actresses,' said Liv comfortingly.

'*Anything*,' said Katherine fiercely, 'I'd do *anything* to get away from home! Sometimes I have this awful fear that I'll end up like Mum – a *housewife*.' She stared at Liv. 'At least your mother gets paid for looking after Mr Thorneycroft. My mother does it for free.'

'You can't expect to be paid for looking after your own children, can you? You do it for love, don't you?'

'*Love!*' said Katherine scornfully. 'You fall in love with some man, and get married in a drippy white dress, and you end up having endless dribbling babies, and scrubbing floors and cooking! Well, all I can say is, no, thank you!'

'But don't you think,' said Liv, 'that it would be different if they were *your* children, and *your* husband? That then you wouldn't mind?'

Katherine's eyes narrowed. 'My mother minds. She never says she does, but she does. I'm never going to be like her. Never, ever.' She looked up as Rachel came out of the church hall. 'So is it a starring role, Rachel? Your name in lights?'

'I said I couldn't do it.'

'*Rachel*—'

'They're filming at the end of March. But we're going to Chamonix so I can't.'

'But, *Rachel*—'

'It sounded awful, anyway. A musical comedy set in medieval England.' Rachel began to walk to the bus stop. Katherine, with one more exasperated sigh, followed her.

A few weeks later, Liv arranged to meet Katherine at a youth-club disco in a nearby village one Saturday evening. The hall in which it was held was cavernous and draughty, and the boys, who had acne and patchy little Zapata moustaches, skulked against the walls, furtively watching the girls, who danced alone, their handbags on the floor between them.

Liv perched on the wall outside, waiting for the Constant twins. It was past nine o'clock when they appeared. 'Sorry we're late,' said Katherine. 'Jamie Armstrong gave us a lift. He had to wait for his dad's car.'

Simon looked round the hall. 'Do any of these yokels actually *dance*?'

Katherine hissed, 'Where's the loo? I had to wash up the supper things so I haven't had time to do my makeup.'

In the cramped ladies' room, Katherine spat into her mascara and glared wide-eyed at the fly-bitten mirror, brushing furiously.

Liv glanced at her. She was wearing a minidress of layered grey-green chiffon.

'New dress?'

'Rachel lent it me. It's Mary Quant. Isn't it fabulous?'

'It's a pity she couldn't come.'

'Rachel? Go to a village disco?' Katherine's voice was sharp. 'Just think what one might *catch*. Just think who one might *meet*.'

'It's not her fault.'

'I know. It's Mummy and Daddy. But she should stand up to them.'

Liv thought of pointing out to Katherine that Rachel did as her parents asked because she loved them and didn't want to upset them, and that Rachel's parents were over-protective because they loved their daughter more than anything in the world, and that Rachel, using charm and good-humoured persuasion, always got whatever she wanted anyway. But she said instead, 'Anyway, her parents are having a party, and they wanted Rachel to be there.'

'Your *hair*,' said Katherine suddenly, staring at Liv.

'I dyed it. It's supposed to be chestnut.'

'Beetroot, more like.'

'I think I left it on too long.' Liv glanced at her reflection. 'Perhaps I could rinse it off in the basin.'

'Don't be daft.' Katherine applied pale lipstick. Her tawny brown eyes, outlined in black, stared out from a white face. 'It's dark in there. No one'll notice.'

They went back into the hall. Katherine slid into Jamie's arms. Simon Constant held out his hand to Liv. 'Liv?'

'Yes?'

'Don't look so surprised. I'm only asking you to dance.' When she was in his arms, he looked down at her. 'It's that nunnery, I suppose. Lady Margaret's School. So unnatural, keeping girls cooped up like that. All those seething hormones. Even poor old Kitty hasn't lost her cherry yet, though I know she's dying to.' He smiled. 'You're blushing, Liv.'

'It's hot.'

22

'Does it embarrass you, talking about sex?'

'Of course not.' The important thing was that he did not detect the depth of her ignorance. She knew, of course, about the mechanics of sex, Thea had explained all that to her ages ago, but how one went about it, what it felt like, and why people made such a fuss about it, was unclear to her. She had never, for instance, even kissed a boy. The boys who offered to kiss her were not the sort of boys she wanted to kiss. Liv wanted her first kiss to be breathtaking and rapturous, something she would remember for the rest of her life.

When the music ended and the lights came on, Simon's arms were still around her. Liv looked up. He was staring at her intently. He said, 'What happened to your hair?' Her hands fell away from him, and she reddened, mortified.

Katherine said, 'It's beetroot colour, isn't it, Simon?'

'Magenta. Rather rococo,' said Simon, grinning. He looked at his watch. 'Let's head off. Liv?'

'Where are you going?'

'Cambridge. Before the pubs shut.'

'I can't.'

'Just for an hour?'

'I promised Mum I'd catch the last bus.' She glanced at the clock.

'Don't be a bore, Liv.'

'If she says she can't, Simon, then she can't,' Katherine snapped. They drove off, still squabbling, with a skirl of wheels on gravel. Liv searched for her cardigan and carrier-bag, and ran down the road. Turning the corner, she saw the bus draw away from the stop. Though she waved and shouted, it disappeared into the darkness. She peered at the timetable. The twenty-to-ten was the last bus; there wouldn't be another until Sunday morning.

After the first blank panic had subsided, she began to walk. It was four miles to Fernhill. If she walked fast, she thought, she could be home in an hour, perhaps. Heading out of the village, she left the street-lamps and the lights of the houses behind. She fumbled in her bag for the torch Thea insisted she always carry. Its small, watery circle of light wavered on the road ahead of her. It had begun to drizzle. At least, she thought, the rain might wash out the wretched hair-dye. She tried not to think of Thea, who always pretended to be sleeping when she came home, but who always, Liv knew, waited up for her. She wished for the hundredth time that they had a telephone. Though she could imagine Thea's alarm if she explained her predicament. Walking home? On your *own*? In the *dark*?

She sang to herself to keep up her spirits. 'You can't hurry love' and 'Pretty Flamingo' and 'House of the Rising Sun'. When she had run out of songs, she thought of her favourite characters in books: Max de Winter in *Rebecca*, and Heathcliff, and Mr Darcy, of course. And all the handsome, brooding heroes of all the historical romances she had lately begun to feel embarrassed about still enjoying.

Her imagination comforted her, allowing her a refuge, yet she was uneasily aware that fantasy had not yet been replaced by real adventure, real love. She needed excitement and challenge; she needed to feel at the centre of things, instead of always at the periphery. Yet now, surrounded by leaves that rustled, and branches that creaked, and unidentifiable rustlings in the grass, she longed only to be home. Her legs ached and her chest felt tight, and every now and then she would mistake the thumping of her heart for footsteps, and would look back, certain that someone was following her. But the road was always empty.

Liv had been walking for about twenty minutes when a car passed her. There was a squeal of brakes, and then it reversed, snaking back towards her. The pounding of her heart speeded up as the window was wound down, and a young man peered out.

'I'm sorry to trouble you, but I'm a bit lost.' He put on the light inside the car. His metal-rimmed spectacles slipped down his nose as he peered at a map, and a lock of fair hair flopped over his forehead. He held out the map to Liv. 'Could you tell me where I am?'

She squinted in the darkness. 'Just there.'

'*Oh*. Miles off course,' he said cheerfully. He glanced at her. 'Where are you heading?'

'Fernhill.' She pointed to the dot on the map.

'It's on my way. Hop in.'

Liv stood motionless for a moment, paralysed with indecision and anxiety. She could almost hear Thea's voice. *Never accept lifts from strangers, Liv.* Yet this stranger had nice blue eyes and a pleasant voice and, besides, it was late and she was very tired. And if she took the lift she could be home in ten minutes instead of an hour.

As she opened the car door, she imagined the headlines in the newspapers. *Girl's Battered Body Found in Ditch.* Yet the footwell and the passenger seat were cluttered with books and maps and empty spectacle cases. The chaos reassured her a little: surely a rapist wouldn't own such a homely, untidy car.

He swept up the clutter from the front seat and flung it into the back. As he started up the engine, he said, 'Never been to this part of the country before. All these little villages – one looks much the same as another if you've never seen 'em before.'

'Where do you come from?' As soon as she had asked the question she regretted it. Too personal, she thought. He'd reach over and pat her thigh, and say, *How about if I take you there, little girl?*

But his hands remained on the steering-wheel, and he replied, 'Northumberland. Ever been there?'

'No. Never.'

'You should do. Loveliest place on earth.' He glanced at her. 'There's some fruit pastilles in the glove compartment. Want one?'

And never take sweets from strangers. 'No, thanks.'

'I know what you mean. Rather scratchy. Can't stand them myself, but I'm trying to give up smoking. Filthy habit – got into it at school, and—' He broke off, frowning. The car had begun to lurch. 'Drat,' he said. 'I think we may have a puncture.'

He braked, and drew to a halt at the side of the road. Liv bit her lip. Now he would lunge at her. Wildly, she stared outside.

The verges were treeless and empty, and there wasn't a house in sight. In the moonlight she could see the smooth shapes of the chalk knolls that dotted the landscape. She thought, If he touches me I shall scream. She knew that bad things could and did happen: her own father had gone away, and just think of poor Philip Constant. Only people like Rachel led charmed lives, where nothing ever went wrong.

But she heard him say, as he opened the driver's door, 'I'm frightfully sorry about this. I do apologize, but I won't be a tick. I'm quite nifty with punctures.'

Liv climbed out of the car. The boot opened and tools clunked. Liv heard him singing to himself, and was once more illogically reassured. When he had repaired the puncture, he held up to her a long iron nail.

'This was the blighter.' He frowned. 'My hands . . .' They were covered with oil.

She offered him her handkerchief. 'Seems a shame . . .' he said. The handkerchief was clean and white and embroidered in the corner with the letter O. 'Let me see . . .' He looked at her. 'Olga? Oonagh? Ophelia?'

She smiled. 'Olivia. Olivia Fairbrother.'

'My name's Hector Seton. I'd shake hands, but you'd get oily.'

They drove on. As they neared Rachel's house, Liv thought quickly. 'Could you drop me here, do you think, Mr Seton?' It might be difficult to explain to Thea the sound of a car drawing up outside the cottage.

Fernhill Grange was lit up like a fairytale castle. The Wybornes were giving a party. There was a marquee, and strings of coloured lights crisscrossing the garden. Couples meandered around the lawn, and in the distance, Liv heard music.

Then she saw Rachel. She was wearing a dress Liv had not seen before, of pale, shimmering stuff. Standing on tiptoe, one hand clutching the filigree iron gates, Liv called her name.

Years later, she thought how it must have been for Hector. The scent of spring flowers after a rainstorm, and the moonlight, and Rachel turning and smiling and walking towards them, a silvery flame in the darkness.

Katherine was in the back of Jamie Armstrong's car. Jamie said, 'God, that was fantastic,' and slid off her.

There was a second's pause, and then Katherine said, 'Yes, wasn't it?' and wriggled upright, pulling her clothing back into place.

'Cigarette?'

'Please.' He lit it for her. There was a long silence while they smoked. Then she said, 'I'd better get back soon or Mum will fuss,' and he said, in a relieved sort of way, 'Of course,' and they shuffled into the front seats.

When they reached the Constants' house, Jamie gave her a quick embarrassed peck on the cheek. 'Next weekend, perhaps?' Katherine smiled, and walked into the garden, shutting the gate very quietly behind her.

Indoors, she made her way through the clutter that always littered the hall. She did not go immediately to her room, but took a glass of milk from the fridge and sat in the living room, looking out at the moonlit garden. Though the Constants' house was substantial, it never seemed quite big enough for the six of them. Things – fishing-rods and football boots and Philip's toys – seemed to burst out from everywhere, so there was never a surface free of clutter. Just now, Katherine shared the sofa with two teddy bears, Simon's cricket sweater and her mother's knitting bag. It mystified Katherine that her mother worked in the home for fourteen hours each day, every day, and the house still looked like this. It just showed what an utter waste of time housework was.

She rinsed the glass in the kitchen, and went upstairs. Inside her small bedroom, the walls were covered with the posters Katherine begged from travel agents – the Eiffel Tower, the Tivoli fountain in Rome, the Empire State Building – or photographs of Caribbean beaches and Swiss mountains, cut from the

National Geographic magazine, which was, along with *Punch*, the staple of her father's waiting-room.

Undressing, Katherine looked down at herself, aware of a sudden pang of disappointment and bewilderment. She had thought that she would *look* different. She squinted in the mirror. She had expected – what? Radiance ... womanly mystery, perhaps? She giggled to herself, and her reflection stared back, her brandysnap eyes unaltered by the loss of her virginity, her pale skin framed by curtains of straight, sandy hair. For the hundredth time she wished that she had Rachel's wavy chestnut hair, Rachel's unfreckled, creamy complexion. Everything was so *easy* for Rachel.

Sitting down on the bed, hugging her knees, Katherine confronted her bewilderment. She simply could not understand what all the fuss was about. A few moments' discomfort and embarrassment, and people wrote *poems* about it! When Jamie had gasped and quivered and then rolled off her, she had almost said, 'Is that all?' but had just managed to hold her tongue. He, after all, had seemed to enjoy it; it must, therefore, have been her fault. All the books, all the songs, said that sex was glorious.

But along with the confusion, she was aware of triumph and relief. She had promised herself two things before she became eighteen in August. New clothes, and the loss of her virginity. She had saved eleven pounds from her Saturday job towards clothes (the rest she had put aside for her trip around the world; she had started her going-round-the-world fund when she was eight) but her unwanted virginity had hung around her neck like an albatross. Only very plain girls, or good girls like Rachel, or hopeless romantics like Liv were still virgins at eighteen. So she had crossed a bridge. That it hadn't been much fun was unimportant. It was having done it that mattered.

Hector Seton was waiting outside Liv's house when she came home from school on Tuesday.

'I wanted to give you this back.' He held out to her her

handkerchief, laundered and ironed. 'I asked at the post office . . . where you lived . . . the Fairbrothers . . .' He ran his fingers through his untidy hair. 'I wondered whether you'd a minute. There's something else . . .'

She offered him a cup of tea, and he followed her into the house. In the kitchen he paused, smiling, touching the strings of threaded shells that served as a window-blind. 'What a splendid idea. So much jollier than flowered chintz.'

Liv put the kettle on the hob. Hector said, 'That girl you introduced me to the other night . . .'

'Rachel?'

'Yes. Is she — does she — has she— The thing is, I can't stop thinking about her.'

'*Oh*.' Liv stared at him. So Hector Seton was in love with Rachel. It didn't surprise her in the least that someone could fall in love with someone so suddenly: it was always happening in books.

'I wondered whether there was anyone . . . whether she was engaged, for instance.'

'Rachel hasn't a boyfriend. Not,' Liv added quickly, 'that loads of boys haven't wanted to go out with her. She just hasn't met the right person.' She handed him a mug of tea. 'Shall we go into the garden?'

He opened the door for her. There was a small clearing half-way along, with two rickety chairs and a table.

'I say, this is rather stunning.' Hector admired the table.

'I made it.'

'Did you? Jolly clever.' He peered at the surface. Smooth pebbles of coloured glass were set into plaster.

'I found them on the beach. We used to live at the seaside. When I was little, I thought they were jewels.'

'I used to collect things from the beach at home. Fossils and shells and bits of driftwood. I filled almost an entire room with them.'

Liv remembered their conversation in the car. 'In Northumberland?'

Hector blinked, owl-eyed beneath his glasses. 'I haven't lived there for ages. I'm in London now. But I still think of it as home.' He looked at Liv. 'Rachel . . .'

'She liked you.'

His expression, his entire stance altered. He seemed lit up from inside. 'Really?'

'Yes. She said so.' Though that was not quite what Rachel had said. *I kept thinking, Liv, that I'd met him somewhere before. When I spoke to him, it was as though I'd known him for years. But I've thought and I've thought, and I don't think we've ever met.* She had seemed puzzled.

'Her parents . . . what are they like?'

'Auntie Diana's very kind. Mr Wyborne . . .' in her mind's eye, Liv pictured Rachel's clever, ambitious father '. . . he's a Member of Parliament.'

'Oh. *That* Henry Wyborne.' Glancing at her, he smiled. 'Scary?'

'A bit.'

There was a silence, and then Hector said, 'I have to see her again.' Not, Liv noticed, 'I'd like to see her again,' nor 'It would be nice to see her again.' But, 'I *have* to see her again.'

Katherine had made herself a large, messy revision chart, the three subjects divided into topics and marked in differently coloured felt-tips. There were only six weeks remaining on the chart, and so far, not one of the gaudy categories was crossed off. Her hands over her ears, Katherine stared at her copy of *The Aeneid*, trying to shut out the crying and the telephone's insistent ring, and, most of all, the shouting of her name. '*Tendebantque manus ripae ulterioris amore?*' she muttered: they reached out their hands in longing for the further shore.

Knuckles rapped on her bedroom door. 'Kitty!' More thumping. '*Kitty!*'

She flung open the door. 'What?'

'Ma wants you,' said Simon. 'The brat's being a pain in the neck, and the phone needs answering.'

'Why can't you?'

'Driving lesson,' said Simon smugly, and sauntered down the corridor, hands in pockets, whistling.

'I've *exams*!' she yelled.

He glanced back. 'Worth it if I pass. Then you won't have to rely on Jamie, will you, Kitty?' She felt herself go red. It was over a month since she had seen Jamie Armstrong. He had not phoned. She was almost relieved: she needed to concentrate on her schoolwork, and she was secretly glad to be spared the disagreeable tussle in the back of the car. Yet, walking home one afternoon, she had passed Jamie at the bus stop. He had not acknowledged her; he had continued to talk to his friends. She had caught a word or two of their conversation. *Tart*, she had heard. *Easy*. Katherine had walked on, willing herself not to blush. Yet just the memory of those two muttered words made her go cold inside.

Barbara Constant was in the kitchen with Philip, spooning food into his mouth. Philip was twelve now, but the brain damage he had suffered after a severe attack of measles as a baby had left him with the mental capacity of a much younger child. It had seemed to Katherine recently that as Philip grew bigger, her mother seemed to shrink, her hair greyer, her clothes untidier, her face wearier.

Barbara looked up when Katherine came into the room. 'He's rather tetchy – won't feed himself. He may be sickening for something. And the washing-up's not done, and the potatoes not scraped. And the phone's ringing nineteen to the dozen.'

'I've got homework,' said Katherine truculently. 'Can't Michael . . .?'

Yet she saw that Philip's face was blotched red with tears. When he held out his arms, Katherine hugged him, and his bright, bristly ginger hair rubbed against her cheek. He looked up at her, his eyes, the same warm brown as her own, focusing on her, looking for reassurance. He took a great, shuddering breath, and sat back in the chair as she gently patted his back.

Mrs Constant scooped up more dinner, but Philip batted the spoon out of her hand, spattering food on to the tiles.

'Dear *God*—' The words shook with tension. The telephone began to ring again.

Katherine said quickly, 'It's all right, let me.' She picked up the spoon and rinsed it under the tap.

Her mother left the room. It's always the same, Katherine thought, as she scraped up the last of the potato and stew. The boys mowed the lawn and washed the car, but the potato-peeling, the ironing, the table-laying, vacuuming and dusting, all these were Katherine's tasks. She had to fight to have any time to work, she thought resentfully.

But as she popped the spoon into Philip's mouth, she found herself acknowledging that her lack of revision was due more to lack of interest than to lack of time. Dismally, she admitted to herself that she loathed Latin, Greek and Ancient History. She wasn't even looking forward to going to Oxford. An all-girls' college would be just like school.

After she had wiped Philip's face, Katherine coaxed him from his chair to the battered old sofa, and sat, her arm around him, rocking him, singing to him. After a while, his eyes closed and he slept. Gently, she swept his fringe from his forehead. She remembered the day he had been born. She had tiptoed upstairs to see her new baby brother. She had wanted a sister – an ally in this male household – but she had quickly come to love him. He had been a bright, happy, healthy baby. And then, along with Michael, Simon and Katherine herself, he had caught measles. Katherine remembered being in bed, itching, miserable and bored. Her mother rushing from room to room with cold drinks and calamine lotion, and her father saying irritably, 'It's nothing to worry about, Barbara. Half the children in my surgery have measles just now.'

Katherine could not quite pinpoint the moment when the tenor of the house had changed from tiresomeness and tedium to anxiety and fear, but she could remember the arrival of the ambulance. The siren had woken her up, and she had cried for her mother. Only six years old, she had felt neglected and confused. She had been told that Philip had been taken to hospital, but when eventually he had come home again, she had believed for a while that her baby brother had been stolen and replaced by this unfamiliar, floppy-limbed, dull-eyed child. It had been years, literally years, before she had properly understood what had happened to him. She had been flicking through a medical textbook in her father's study, and she had read, 'Encephalitis is a rare complication of measles, and may lead to epilepsy, brain damage, deafness and blindness.' It was only then she had understood, with a finality that had made tears trail silently down her face, that Philip would never be able to say more than a handful of words, that he would always walk slowly and for no great distance, and that, most alarmingly, he would continue to suffer from fits.

Katherine tucked Philip's old comfort blanket around him, then rose and went to the sink, which was crammed with dirty saucepans and smeared tumblers. She was about to plunge her hands into the tepid water when she heard a tap on the window. She spun round, smiling when she saw Rachel and Liv. She ran outside.

They wound through gloomy laurels and dusty choisyas before reaching a small clearing, where they flung themselves full-length on the ground.

'Go on,' said Katherine, '*tell* us, Rachel.'

The previous evening, Rachel had been out on another date with Hector Seton.

'Did he kiss you?' asked Liv.

Rachel, who was sitting with her knees pulled up and her arms folded round them, nodded.

'What was it like?'

'Lovely. Just lovely.' Rachel fell silent, and Katherine was aware of a flicker of irritation. Perhaps Rachel felt about Hector Seton as she felt about her pony and her ballet lessons and her lovely clothes: they were something she took as her due and expressed thanks for, but she did not long for them in the way that Katherine longed for so many things.

Then Rachel said suddenly, 'I need you to help me. I have to think what to do.' Her serenity had gone, dropped like a mask. She picked a daisy, piercing it with her thumb. 'Hector wants to show me his house in Northumberland. He wants me to go there for a weekend.'

'Your parents?'

'Wouldn't let me, of course.'

'Have you asked?'

'There's no point. I told Hector I'd ask, but I haven't.'

There was a silence. Then Liv said, 'You could tell Auntie Diana that you're staying with me for the weekend.'

Rachel picked another daisy. 'I suppose I could.'

Katherine looked up, shocked. Rachel – good, obedient Rachel – was planning to lie to her parents.

She frowned. 'Liv's too close – they'd find out. Tell them you're staying with me. Yes. That's what you must do.'

Sunlight gleamed on the hills of Northumberland, and the air smelt sharp and sweet.

'Like it?' Hector turned to Rachel.

'It's glorious.'

'You should see it in winter. All black and white, like a pen-and-ink sketch.'

They had driven up from Cambridgeshire that morning. Rachel still winced when she thought of the lies she had told her mother. Now, she looked out through the passenger window at the stone walls that delineated the fields, and the sheep that dotted the purplish slopes. She had never been so far north before. She had travelled, of course, but to places like Cannes and St Moritz, never to the north of England.

They had driven for a few more miles when Hector said, 'There's my house. There's Bellingford. Behind those trees.'

High stone walls, pierced with narrow windows, rose from a fringe of beech trees.

'Hector, it's a castle!'

He smiled. 'Just a little one.'

They left the road, turning up a driveway edged with trees. More trees grew in a great dark curtain around the house, and beyond it soared the Cheviot hills. Braking in the courtyard, Hector did not immediately climb out of the car.

Rachel placed her hand on his. 'Darling?'

'I haven't been back since my father's funeral. I've never seen it empty.'

She squeezed his hand. 'It won't be empty. I'm here.'

Hector unlocked the front door, and Rachel followed him inside. She had an impression of gloom and solidity; the hallway had a musty, disused smell. When she shivered, Hector slipped off his jacket, and draped it round her shoulders.

'I should have warned you, the place is always like an ice box. The walls are six feet thick.'

A vast fireplace dominated one end of the room, and huge, dark, carved pieces of furniture loomed from the walls. The paintings on the wall were dimmed by a patina of age and time. Rachel placed her palm against the cold stone, and tried to imagine what it would be like to belong to such a place. You would know, she thought, every hill and every stream. Other people's memories, other people's loves and hates and betrayals would have sunk into the stone.

'How long has your family lived here, Hector?'

'Oh, centuries,' he said vaguely. 'One of the Plantagenets – a Henry, I can never remember which one – gave the land to one of my ancestors. Services rendered and all that.'

'Are there ghosts?'

He laughed, said, 'I've never seen one,' and took her hand. He led her through room after room. When he drew back the curtains, sunshine poured into the musty darkness, and motes of dust danced. Rachel peered at sepia photographs of heavy-jawed, unsmiling Setons, and ran her fingertips along oak tables whose centuries of polish had hardened into a dark crimson lacquer. In the tower, the stairs curled narrowly around the circular walls, clinging like ivy. The windows were cold arrow-slits, as though a knife had cut through the fabric of the building.

They picnicked in the courtyard. Sheltered by three high stone walls, the sunlight gathered, warming them. Hector had brought prawns, encased in their coral-coloured shells, and a piece of Brie, ripe and oozing. They washed the food down with champagne, Rachel's favourite drink: she liked the way the dry, sharp little bubbles bounced against the roof of her mouth.

They had almost finished the picnic when Hector, looking up at the house, said, 'I'm trying to decide what to do with it, you see. That's why I wanted to bring you to Bellingford, Rachel. I have to decide whether to come back and live here, or whether to let it moulder, or whether to sell it.'

She stared at him. 'Hector, you can't sell Bellingford!'

'It would be difficult – there's all sorts of trusts and things. But it would be the sensible thing to do.'

'It would be the *wrong* thing to do. It *belongs* to you, Hector. You're *part* of it.' Rachel looked around. 'It's just that it's so beautiful.'

'I'm pleased you think so, but there are death duties to be paid, and not much money in the bank. And I live in London, after all.'

'You could move. Though your job—'

'I hate my job.'

'Well, then.'

'Just look at it, though. It's a huge white elephant. What on earth would I do with it?'

'We could have a riding school. Or we could keep hens. Or,' Rachel giggled, 'we could have a tea shop.'

Hector became very still. *'We?'*

'I think so, don't you?' She felt shaken, knowing for the first time in her life what she wanted, and how much she wanted it.

She looked up at him. 'You did mean to ask me to marry you, didn't you, darling?'

He looked dazed. 'Of course – it's why I brought you here, but . . .'

'But what?'

'Rachel, we've only known each other a few months. And I'm twenty-six – eight years older than you. You may think you love me now, but how will you feel in a year's time, or in five years' time?'

'I'll feel just the same. I love you, Hector.' She looked up at him. 'And you? Will you still love me?'

'I shall love you in ten years' time, and in twenty,' he said simply. 'I loved you the first moment I saw you, Rachel, and I shall be yours till I die.' He drew her to him, and began to kiss her.

Coming home from her Saturday job, Liv saw the car parked outside the cottage. Diana Wyborne was sitting in the driver's seat. Liv's stomach lurched.

'Olivia?'

'Yes, Auntie Diana?' She felt herself smiling desperately, ingratiatingly.

'A word, please.' Diana Wyborne stepped out of the car. Clumsily, Liv fitted the key to the lock. She had shut the door behind them when Diana said, 'I am right, aren't I? Rachel is with that man.'

Liv's heart was hammering wildly. When she did not reply, Diana cried, 'At least have the courtesy to tell me I need not phone the police!' The words, raw and anguished, echoed in the small room.

'Rachel's with Hector.'

'Ah.' Just a small exhalation of breath, like a sigh. There was a silence, then Diana said, 'And you girls, you knew about it?'

'Yes.'

Diana's face was white. 'No doubt it was Katherine's idea to tell me that Rachel was staying with her.'

'Mine,' Liv whispered. She stared at the floor.

'I see.' Diana fumbled in her handbag for cigarettes. 'Where have they gone?'

'To Northumberland. To Hector's house.' There was a silence, interrupted only by the flick of Diana Wyborne's lighter. Liv gathered up her courage. 'They're in love, Auntie Diana. Rachel and Hector are in love.'

'And I suppose,' hissed Diana, 'that you think that makes it all right?'

Faced with such anger, she had to force the words out. 'Yes. Yes, I do.'

Footsteps crunched on the gravel path. The front door opened. Thea said, 'Diana, what a nice surprise,' and then, looking from one to the other, 'Is something wrong?'

'Rachel has gone away for the weekend with a man.' Diana almost spat the words out. 'Your daughter arranged it.'

Thea blinked. 'Is this true, Liv?'

Miserably, Liv nodded. Diana added, 'And is fool enough to think that being *in love* excuses it.'

'Could we start at the beginning?' Thea filled the kettle. 'And a cup of tea would help, perhaps. Rachel has gone away,' she repeated, 'with . . .?'

'With Hector Seton, Mum.'

'Olivia introduced them.' Glaring at Liv, Diana flicked ash into the sink.

'Hector Seton? I don't know the name. Is he at the boys' school?'

Abysses opened for Liv, and chasms yawned. 'He's grown-up. He lives in London and works in a bank.'

'I wouldn't have let him near Rachel,' muttered Diana furiously, 'but he told me that he was one of the Northumberland Setons.'

Thea, eyeing Liv, said, 'And you met him *where?*'

Her mouth had gone dry. She mumbled, 'He gave me a lift.'

Thea was still clutching the kettle. 'A lift?'

'In his car. I missed the bus one night, and he was driving home and he offered me a lift.'

Now the expression in Thea's eyes echoed that in Diana's.

'He was very nice!' Liv said wildly. 'He didn't . . .' The words trailed away as Thea plonked the kettle heavily on the hob.

Diana cried, 'And when I telephoned Barbara Constant about Rachel's slippers, only to find out that Rachel wasn't there — well, you can imagine what I thought!'

Thea took a deep breath. 'It must have been very upsetting for you, Diana. But now that we've established that Rachel is safe—'

'What do you think they're doing?' hissed Diana scornfully. 'Picnicking? Bird-watching?'

'She's safe, and that's what matters most. And if Hector loves her, as Liv says, then no doubt—'

'*Love!*' Diana's voice rose in a shriek. 'Why does *love* excuse everything? You of all people, Thea, should know the folly of depending on *love!*'

There was a long, appalled silence. After a while, Thea said, her voice small and tight, 'I think you should go to your room, Liv.'

In her room, Liv slumped on the bed, feeling miserable and guilty. After a few moments she heard the front door slam, and the sound of a car engine starting up as Diana drove away. Hearing footsteps on the stairs, Liv sat up. Thea came into the room. 'Tell me what happened, Liv.'

So she told her. Missing the bus and meeting Hector and Hector seeing Rachel, and, six weeks later, Rachel, with that curiously intense look in her eyes, saying, 'I need you to help me.'

'I didn't think,' wailed Liv, 'that it would cause so much trouble!'

'You didn't think,' said Thea crisply, 'that anyone would find out.'

She bit her lip. 'What will happen?'

'Oh, I should imagine that Diana will rage and protest for a while longer and then she'll remember that Rachel is a grown woman and accept the situation.' Thea's eyes were unforgiving. 'But meanwhile, Liv, you are gated. Till half-term. You will not go out in the evenings, you will go to school and you will go to work on Saturdays. And that's all. Because I can't trust you, you see.' Thea's mouth was set in a thin line. 'Accepting a lift from a stranger. Dear God, it makes my blood run cold.'

Rachel and Hector drove back south on Sunday. At the gates of the Grange, Hector paused. 'May I come in? I should talk to your parents.'

Rachel began, 'Hector, I didn't——' and then she caught sight of her father walking down the drive towards them.

Henry Wyborne flung open the gate. Hector had gone to take her case out of the boot. Rachel said, 'Daddy——' and Henry Wyborne, ignoring her, said to Hector, 'I think you'd better go.'

'Daddy——'

'Rachel, be quiet.'

'Mr Wyborne, I'd like to speak to you.'

Rachel heard herself wail, 'Hector, I didn't tell my parents I was going away with you!' but her words were obliterated by her father's voice.

'As I said, you'd better go, because if you don't, I may do something I'd later regret.'

Hector went white. Rachel whispered, 'Please do as he says, please.' Hector, irresolute, turned and looked at her. She whispered again, 'Please, darling. For me.'

He said, 'If you need me . . .' and touched her face, pressing the tips of his fingers against her cheek. Then he climbed into the car and started up the engine.

Rachel picked up her case and walked up the drive to the house. The door was open; she saw her mother. Diana said, 'Rachel, how *could* you?' and burst into tears.

In the drawing room, Rachel sat down in an armchair. Her legs felt peculiar, aching and wobbly. 'How did you find out?'

'I telephoned Mrs Constant.' Diana blew her nose loudly. 'You'd left your slippers behind, and I wasn't sure whether Katherine would have any spare.'

'I'm sorry I lied to you. But you wouldn't have let me go if you'd known, and I had to go.' Rachel took a deep breath. 'Hector and I are going to get married, Mummy.'

'Don't be ridiculous, Rachel. *Married* – what nonsense! You hardly know him.'

She knotted her hands together, looking from one to the other, trying to make them understand. 'Mummy – Daddy – I *love* him.'

'You're only eighteen,' said Henry Wyborne coldly. 'Not old enough to know your own mind.'

'I'm not a child, Daddy.' Rachel's voice was quiet and dignified. 'I want to marry Hector.'

'Do you? I doubt if you'll feel the same in six months' time.'

'*You* knew, Daddy,' she pleaded. 'You knew you loved Mummy.'

He stood up. She watched him take a cigarette from the case on the sideboard and light it. 'I was twenty-six when I married – your mother was twenty-seven. Nine years older than you, Rachel. Those nine years make the devil of a difference.'

In her father's expression she saw no sympathy, only anger and obduracy. 'I'm old enough to marry, Daddy,' she whispered.

'We have given you everything, Rachel, and protected you from everything. What experience of the world do you have? What makes you think your judgement is better than mine?' Henry Wyborne's lip curled. 'You may think you're an adult, but let me tell you that I *know* that at eighteen you're not old enough to decide the course of the rest of your life.'

His voice was like ice, and what she saw in his eyes frightened her: a dark unchangeable hardness, a limiting of affection and understanding that she had never before encountered. She wanted to cry; she wanted, for the first time in her life, to shout at him. But instead she stumbled out of the room, running upstairs to her bedroom, slamming the door behind her.

In the small pink bathroom that adjoined her bedroom, Rachel ran the bathwater and stripped off her clothes, one by one. Then she sat on the cold tiles, pressing her face against her knees. She could still smell him on her skin. She whispered, 'Oh, *Hector*,' as tears trickled down her face then on to her legs.

After a while, she got up and stepped into the bath. She felt as though she was washing him away. Her eyes ached; rubbing them, she saw through the steam and the thick cloud of bubbles her collection of china rabbits and glass birds on the window-ledge. All this – the ornaments, the jars of bath salts with their flower motifs, the fluffy pink dressing-gown – seemed unrelated to her, to belong to a different Rachel, a Rachel she had half forgotten. She could not imagine being that Rachel again.

There was a tap on the door. Her mother called, 'Can I come in?'

'Yes, Mummy.'

Diana sat down in the Lloyd Loom chair. She said, 'Do you *have* to get married?'

It took a few moments for Rachel to understand what her mother was asking her. Then she reddened. 'No. It's not like that, Mummy.'

'You've shared a bed with him, though.'

She remembered the four-poster bed at Bellingford, hung with faded cretonne, and the way his body had fitted into hers. Rachel said defiantly, 'Yes. It was lovely.'

Diana's eyes sparked. 'Was he the first? Or have there been others?'

Rachel found herself breathless with anger. She said, 'How dare you? How dare you?' the choked words sharp and small, like arrows.

There was a short, tense silence, and then Diana muttered, 'I'm sorry, darling, I shouldn't have said that.'

Rachel clutched the sponge to her chest. 'He didn't know I'd lied to you. It wasn't his fault. And we didn't mean to make love, it just happened.'

'I think we'd better keep it from Daddy, though, hadn't we,

darling? Better to let him think Hector was a gentleman.' Diana dipped her hand into the water. 'Brrr! You're getting goose-pimples. Hurry up and get dried or you'll catch a chill.' She left the room.

Rachel remained in the cooling water. Her limbs felt heavy. The bubbles had dispersed, and she moved her hand slowly through the tepid water, watching the ripples as they swelled against the side of the bath. She seemed to hear doors shutting, gates clanging shut. She climbed out of the bath and, wrapping herself in her dressing-gown, went into her bedroom. For the first time, its pink and white luxury seemed both oppressive and demeaning, a pretty cage that trapped her. She stood for a while at the window, watching the rain, her gaze moving from the garden and the road, to the low, rolling fields, and then she lay on her bed, and fell asleep. She dreamed she was climbing up the pele tower at Bellingford. The stairs seemed to spiral up and up for ever.

In the evening, there was a knock at the door. Rachel opened it. Her father was holding a tray.

'Thought we should talk, pumpkin.' The old childhood nick-name reassured her.

He came into the room, and placed the tray on the table. 'Cocoa,' he said. 'I made it, I'm afraid. Hope it's not too frightful.'

'Where's Mrs Nelson?' Mrs Nelson was the Wybornes' housekeeper.

'Her daughter's producing another sprog, so she had to dash home. And Mummy's got one of her heads, so I'm holding the fort.'

'Oh, *Daddy*. I'm so sorry. I didn't mean to cause so much trouble.' Tears ached at the corners of her eyes.

'There, there.' He hugged her. Then he said, 'I had a word with Hector. He called. You were napping. He seems a decent chap. And he obviously cares a great deal about you, poppet.'

She began to hope again. 'He loves me.'

'Yes.' Henry put down his cup. 'But there are other consider-ations, darling.'

She whispered, 'Other considerations?'

'Yes.' He grimaced. 'Money, I'm afraid. Hector has inherited a sizeable estate, but there's death duties to pay and not much in the way of saleable assets.'

She must have looked bewildered, because he explained, 'Paintings, antiques, agricultural land. That's the sort of thing people sell when they have to pay off the tax man. Or they give the estate lock, stock and barrel to the National Trust. But Hector told me that you mean to live there, so that's not an option.'

She said wildly, 'I'd live anywhere, Daddy, if it means Hector and I can be together. In a bungalow – or on a council estate, anywhere.'

'But *I* don't want you to live "anywhere", darling.' He squeezed her hand. 'I've something put aside for you, Rachel, for when you marry, only we want to be sure you're doing the right thing. That's not unreasonable, is it? Both Mummy and I would like you to see a bit more of the world before you settle down. So we'd like you to agree to wait a year. After all, you've only known the chap a few months. A year isn't much to ask, is it, pumpkin? To please Mummy and me.'

'But I'll be able to see him?'

'We think it'd be better if you didn't.'

'But, Daddy—'

'All I'm suggesting is a year's separation. But no letters or phone calls. Better that way – a clean break – and kinder, don't you think? And if at the end of it you both feel the same, well, then, you may marry with our blessing.'

She cried, 'But what will Hector think? What will he think?'

'He'll understand. And it's the best solution, don't you agree, darling? It'll mean that Mummy and I won't worry, and Hector, if he really cares about you, will be prepared to wait.' Henry took the cup out of Rachel's clenched hands and placed it on the tray. 'Is it a bargain, then?'

She nodded mutely.

'Promise?' he said.

'I promise.' The words were just a whisper.

'Good,' he said briskly. 'Then Mummy and I have decided that the best thing would be for you to go to Madame Jolienne's now, instead of waiting for the autumn.'

She stared at him, bewildered. Madame Jolienne ran the finishing-school in Paris. 'But Lady Margaret's?'

'Only one term left, darling. We won't worry about those silly exams. They don't matter, do they?' Her father smiled. 'Better write to Hector and explain, then. Just a short note. I'll post it for you. You're a good girl, Rachel. You know that Mummy and I only want the best for you. Now, why not get an early night? You look exhausted, pumpkin.'

Early one morning Rachel was bundled off to Heathrow, and Paris. With Rachel's departure, it seemed to Liv that everything had changed. The bad feeling between Thea and Diana lingered, unresolved and unvoiced. Liv missed her long conversations with Rachel at the weekend or after school, lounging on the wicker chairs in the Wybornes' sunroom or curled up among the pictures and books in her own bedroom. She missed their walks, their cycle rides, their afternoons spent trying on each other's clothes, or experimenting with makeup.

In a thrift shop in Cambridge, she bought ragged velvet skirts, Victorian lace blouses and long strings of beads. In the village, people stared. With her earnings from her Saturday job, she bought shampoos and hair-dyes, eyeliners and lipsticks to draw on the blank canvas of her face. Nothing had quite the effect it promised: no matter what she put on her hair, it still tangled into a bird's nest, and her mascara always ran, trailing black tears down her cheeks.

The cottage had become small and cramped, and the friends and neighbours she had known for years now seemed irritating and dull. Worst of all, an invisible wall seemed to have grown up between herself and Thea. She seemed no longer capable of the uncritical love of her childhood. Now, she saw Thea with an older, colder eye. Part of her – a part she did not much like –

took in Thea's eccentric, home-made clothes, and her greying, straggling hair, which she cut with the kitchen scissors, and the narrowness of her life, and judged her harshly. In a small corner of her mind something unkind and condemnatory said, 'Well! No wonder he left you. You could at least *try*.'

She threw away her historical novels, and read Jack Kerouac and Vladimir Nabokov, Iris Murdoch and Margaret Drabble instead. Reading, she escaped. At school, each day lasted an age. School had become restricting and irrelevant, like an old garment she had grown out of. A seed of rebelliousness uncoiled inside her, and entire lessons passed by as she sat in the back row of class, doodling on a pad, her boredom a tangible, rather frightening thing. For the first time in her life she was in trouble at Lady Margaret's: for work not handed in, for lack of co-operation. She and Katherine formed a small, disaffected coterie, separate from the other girls.

When her form teacher wrote a letter to Thea, expressing concern at the falling standard of Liv's work, Liv gave sulky, uninformative replies to Thea's questions. Thea's patience made her feel both angry and guilty. Thea, struggling to understand, said kindly, 'You don't have to go to university if you don't want to, darling. You can stay here and get a job, if that's what you'd prefer.'

Liv hissed, 'Stay here? What on earth would I do in this dump? There's nothing to do, and everybody's so *boring*,' and retreated to the place at the end of the garden with the willows and the stream, the place where years ago they had cast their futile, childish spells. Hunched on a log, she covered her face with her hands. She hated school, she hated Fernhill, but most of all she hated herself. Her miseries were small. She was not starving in India. She was not a Vietnamese refugee.

After a while, she went back to the house. In the kitchen, she hugged Thea and mumbled apologies, then went up to her room, got out her books and worked for hours. University was her escape: she could not afford to fail. And then, at the beginning of

May, the unfolding events in Paris replayed themselves on television. The demonstrations and arrests at the Sorbonne, the barricades, the clashes between students and police. Liv, watching the flickering black and white pictures, felt a sudden stab of optimism. As though anything might happen. As though, if she were patient just a little longer, anything might happen to her.

Washing up that evening, she saw Hector Seton's sports car draw up outside the house. Thea was in the garden; Liv wiped her hands on her jeans and ran outside.

'Hector!'

'Liv. How are you? Don't fancy a spin, do you?'

'I can't. I'm gated.'

'Oh.' He ran his fingers through his unruly hair. 'I wanted to talk to you.'

'About Rachel?'

'Am I so transparent?'

She smiled. 'Well, yes, you are, actually.'

'She's in Paris, isn't she?'

'At a finishing-school run by someone called Madame Jolienne. It sounds awful.'

He looked at Liv. 'Her father told me that Rachel *chose* to go to Paris early. Was that true?'

'No, of course not.' She stared at him, shocked. Henry Wyborne had lied to Hector. Rachel's letters from Paris drooped with misery, and were blotted with her tears.

'Hector,' said Liv firmly, 'Rachel didn't *choose* to go to Paris. Her father made her go.'

He blinked. 'Do you know where she is?'

Rachel had written to her, *Daddy has made me promise not to contact Hector.*

She told him the address.

Rachel hated Paris. She could see that, under different circumstances, she might have felt otherwise, but just now, exiled and disgraced, she hated it. For the first time in her life she discovered what it was to feel lonely. She missed Fernhill; she missed Liv and Katherine. Most of all, she missed Hector.

She did not fit into the school, quickly discovering that though in the small milieux of Fernhill and Lady Margaret's, she might have been perceived as both special and privileged, here she had no such status. Compared to the other girls at Madame Jolienne's – the daughters of ambassadors, of displaced European princelings – she was small fry indeed. She could not trace her ancestry back four hundred years, she could not discourse with equal facility in five languages. A week at Madame Jolienne's taught her that she did not know how to dress, and that her beauty routine – a ribbon to tie back her hair, and a lick of lipstick – was derisory. The school year was into its third term by the time Rachel arrived. Many of the other students had known each other for years, fellow-pupils at expensive Swiss boarding-schools. Little cliques had formed, cliques that excluded Rachel.

The lessons – the litany of etiquette, and the composition of menus for vast, complicated dinner parties – seemed to her utterly futile. She learned how to climb out of a sports car without showing too much leg, and how to prepare Coquilles St Jacques. The mere phrase 'sports car', and, in her mind's eye, she was sitting beside Hector as they drove through the Northumberland countryside. The sight of the pale, gleaming scallops turned her stomach.

She took to skipping lessons, and wandering around Paris. *Flâneur*-ing, she called it to herself. Browsing among the *bouquinistes* on the Left Bank, wandering through the Tuileries, she was able to think of him without interruption. She longed for him. She had not thought it possible to miss a person so much. Her body ached for his. Sometimes she did not see how she could endure another month, another week, another day, another hour without him. The thought of not seeing him for a whole year made a knot of panic form beneath her ribs. Sometimes the enormity of her need frightened her. A self-contained, happy child, it was as though in becoming an adult the boundaries of her self had broken and blurred, sending her bleeding into the world.

She didn't notice at first much of what was taking place in Paris that May. But gradually the headlines on the billboards, and the excitable commentary on television and radio penetrated her consciousness. The word *révolution* seemed to hover in the air, whispered excitedly, expectantly or disapprovingly according to taste. People spoke of students demonstrating in the street, of street-fighting in the Latin Quarter. Slogans appeared on the walls: *The dream is reality*. Or, *The aggressor is not the one who rebels, but the one who upholds authority*. Rachel rather liked the slogans, and took to repeating them to herself as she disobeyed her teachers' injunctions to keep to the school building or to her lodgings. She began to read the newspapers, to listen to the news bulletins. Secretly, sometimes, she found herself longing for the storm to break: for the demonstrators to sweep through Paris, burning cars, tearing paving-stones from the streets, crashing through the wide boulevards and stately buildings like a tidal wave.

Once more, they were exhorted not to go out into the city. Walking from school to lodgings one evening, one of Rachel's fellow-students repeated, wide-eyed, the rumours of a demonstration taking place only a few streets away, in the Boul' Mich. The early-evening air was warm and close; as they reached her lodgings, unable to bear the prospect of a three-course dinner she did not feel like eating, followed by an evening in her cramped little room, Rachel said, 'I think I'll go out for a walk.'

'*Rachel*. Madame said—'

'I won't be long.' She headed down the street. She found herself drawn towards the Boulevard Saint-Michel. The whole of Paris seemed to be going there. Mingling with the crowds, she knew that in her neatly pressed cotton dress and pink cardigan, wearing court shoes, she stood out like a sore thumb. She longed for denims and a matelot top and a Greek bag, slung carelessly over one shoulder.

In the Boulevard Saint-Michel, the barricades, made of packing cases and flower-pots and crates, were topped with tricolour flags. A single voice started to sing the 'Marseillaise', and within a few moments the entire street was singing. As Rachel joined in, something seemed to stir in her, to come alive, something that had been dormant, almost dead since she had left England.

Then the police arrived. At first the crowd pushed forward, and then, as the police turned on the water-cannon, it sank back, then surged forward once more, with a roar of anger. Missiles soared through the air. The demonstrators prised up paving-stones and hurled them at the police. There was a deafening crack, not far away from Rachel, and she clamped her hands over her ears. '*Grenades*,' someone shouted. '*The police are throwing grenades.*'

She began to feel frightened. She saw that, part of the mob, she was not merely insignificant, as she was at Madame Jolienne's, she was anonymous. She was neither Henry Wyborne's daughter, nor Hector Seton's fiancée; she was nothing, and she mattered to no one. She began to try to make her way out of the heart of the crowd, towards the perimeter of the street. She'd be safer there, she reasoned, and she'd be able to make her way back to her lodgings. Bodies pushed against her, cries and curses echoed in her ears, as she wormed her way through the mass of people. Her stockings had laddered, and she was soaked by the water, and terrified by the grenades. Fragments of paving-stone fell around her like hailstones. She wanted to go home. She wanted to be standing on top of the pele tower at Bellingford, Hector's arm around her, looking out to the wide, empty hills.

After she had reached the pavement, she began, tortuously, to head away from the barricades. The crowd pressed against her, like a many-headed monster. Someone was bawling out the words of the 'Internationale', and a policeman, struck by a paving-stone, was screaming. She thought she heard, almost lost in the clamour, a voice call her name. *Hector*, she thought, and wondered whether, all those miles away, he knew somehow that she needed him. There were tears in her eyes; she wiped them away with her fingertips. A paving-stone landed a few feet away from her, and she pressed herself against the wall. Looking up, she thought she saw him. Tall, fair-haired, unmistakably English in his flannels and white shirt. When he vanished, she knew him to be a figment of her imagination. She wanted to weep; she ached with exhaustion. She had to fight the desire to curl up on the pavement, her arms wrapped around her knees, her fingers in her ears to shut out the noise.

So when the fragment of paving-stone struck her on the forehead, she almost welcomed the sudden onslaught of darkness. And the last thing she heard, before she blacked out, was Hector's voice saying her name.

On 15 May, Liv received a letter from Rachel. The envelope had a London postmark.

> We're going to be married, Liv! Hector and I! Daddy has given us permission – isn't it marvellous?
>
> I got caught up in a demonstration on the Left Bank, and then something hit me on the head, and I must have blacked out for a few minutes, and then – I couldn't believe it – he was there! Just like in one of your books, Liv! He'd seen what was happening in Paris on the news, and he was worried, so he came to find me. I wasn't really hurt at all, just a little scratch. And we agreed we couldn't live without each other, and that a year was too long to wait, and that Hector would go and tell Daddy what we'd decided. So we flew back to London, and Hector went to the House and spoke to Daddy. And Daddy was so worried about what had happened to me in Paris, and so grateful to Hector for rescuing me that he agreed that we could marry!!! Isn't it wonderful?

In July, to celebrate the end of her exams, Katherine went to London. Taking the tube from Liverpool Street station, she looked at the other girls in the carriage, envying them their clothes, their haircuts, their sleek, cool confidence. Walking through Chelsea, her savings from her Saturday job heavy in her pocket, Katherine felt light-hearted and free.

In the cavernous gloom of Biba, she chose a plum-coloured minidress and a pair of knee-high suede boots. She had the assistant pack her old clothes while she wore the new. Leaving the shop, she wondered what to buy for Rachel. What wedding present, thought Katherine, did one give to the girl who had everything? In the end, she slipped into an antique shop and bought a tiny jug with blue flowers on the spout. The small chip on the handle was hardly noticeable. Rachel would adore it.

Outside a hairdresser's in the King's Road, Katherine paused, reading the sign in the window. She pushed open the door. A bored-looking receptionist drawled, 'Yes?'

'I've come about the advertisement. The one saying you want models.'

The receptionist slid slowly off her stool. 'I'll fetch Jeremy.'

Jeremy wore a purple crushed-velvet suit and had long black hair and a drooping black moustache. He ran Katherine's sandy plait through his fingers, handling it, thought Katherine, as though it wasn't even attached to her. 'Oh *dear*,' he said. Beneath the moustache, his lip curled. 'Such *condition*. The *split ends*.'

She was taken to a basin to be shampooed, and returned to Jeremy with a towel wrapped round her head. He combed disdainfully through her long, wet locks. Then he picked up his scissors. Katherine gasped. 'You're cutting it all off!'

'My services at a ridiculously low rate in return for a free hand with your hair. That's the bargain.'

Jeremy cut, brushed and blow-dried; Katherine, biting her lip, looked away from the mirror.

After twenty minutes he said, 'There,' and stood back.

She looked up. A smooth bell of shiny red-blonde hair hung around her face. Her dark eyes were framed by a long fringe. She felt a thrill of excitement. 'It's wonderful!'

'An improvement on that dreadful plait, don't you think?'

Katherine felt like a butterfly that had sloughed off its

outworn chrysalis. The dress, the boots, the hair. Walking down the street, she kept glancing into shop windows, as if to reassure herself that the reflection she saw was hers. One more treat, she thought, and went into a coffee bar where she ordered herself lunch.

As she waited for her omelette, she looked around. There were gingham tablecloths, and banquettes upholstered in slippery orange plastic. On the walls were posters of Che Guevara and Jimi Hendrix, and advertisements for rock concerts and political meetings. Two young men sat at the adjacent table. Katherine studied them covertly. One was small and clean-shaven, with silky dark hair and mournful dark eyes – like a spaniel, she thought. The other had a moustache and frizzy red hair that stuck out in corkscrews around his head. They were both wearing loons and velvet jackets with badges – CND and star signs and 'Gandalf Lives!' – on their lapels.

The red-haired man took out a cigarette packet. 'Got a light, have you, love?'

Katherine realized that he was speaking to her. She fumbled in her bag for matches.

'Have one yourself, sweetheart.' Katherine accepted a cigarette. 'Don't mind if we join you, do you?' They did not wait for her reply, but slid into the seat opposite her.

They introduced themselves. The red-headed man was called Stuart, the dark one was Toby. Stuart was from Glasgow; Toby was a Londoner.

'Mmm. Breakfast,' said Toby, when plates of bacon and eggs arrived.

'Breakfast?' asked Katherine. It was three o'clock in the afternoon.

'Late night. We're starting up a magazine. We had our first editorial meeting last night,' explained Stuart.

'Magazine?'

'*Frodo's Finger*'ll be more incisive than *Black Dwarf*, and more daring than *Oz*,' said Toby optimistically. He smiled at Katherine. 'You wouldn't like to work for us, would you?'

She was about to repeat, 'Work for you?' but she caught herself. 'What sort of work?'

'Anything, really,' said Toby vaguely. 'When the magazine gets going, there'll be too much for us to do. I've got the contacts and I'll control the finances, and Stuart does the layout. We both write, of course. And Felix does the odd cartoon, but we could do with someone else . . . a girl, preferably . . . for – oh, this and that.' His dark, soulful eyes focused pleadingly on Katherine.

'Secretarial work,' said Stuart, inspired.

'Yes. And reception. For our offices.'

'Writing?' asked Katherine.

'Oh, of course.' Stuart stubbed out his cigarette. 'I must say, Katherine, you'd be *eminently* well qualified.' He was staring at her chest. 'Wouldn't she, Toby?'

'Eminently,' said Toby, and beamed at her.

Rachel and Hector were married at the beginning of August, on one of the hottest days of the year. The parish church in Fernhill heaved with Wyborne friends and relations. Wide-brimmed straw hats jostled for space. The colours of the ladies' outfits competed with each other: crimson and emerald and turquoise and canary yellow. Stephanotis and lilies erupted from every niche and corner, so that the air was thick with their scent. Henry Wyborne's posture, as he stood beside his daughter in the church, was militarily upright. Diana wept throughout the ceremony. Hector dropped the ring, which had to be retrieved by the best man from beneath a pew. Only Rachel, pale and beautiful in white silk, remained calm.

The reception was held at the Wybornes' house. Eyeing the marquee in the garden, Katherine muttered sourly to Liv that one expected elephants, or perhaps an acrobat or two. They queued for food at the buffet in the dining room. A voice at Katherine's shoulder said, 'Quails' eggs in aspic. Supposed to be a treat, I know, but . . .'

'They look,' said Katherine, 'like eyeballs.'

'They do, rather, don't they?'

She glanced over her shoulder at him. He was much older than her, but handsome, with light brown hair and a Roman nose, and chill grey eyes.

'I believe,' she said, defiantly scooping eggs on to her plate, 'that you should try everything at least once.'

'An admirable philosophy, so long as one excludes certain experiences.'

'Such as?' She anticipated a dull, grown-up lecture.

'Oh – cream sherry and boiled cabbage and people who always count the cost of things.' He smiled. 'May I help you with that? You seem rather laden.'

She let him take her plate, on which a mountain of food was built, and followed him into the adjacent room. The tables were crowded, diners spilling out on to the terrace. He said softly, 'Now, we can sit here and endure a dull conversation about the devaluation of the pound, or whether we should join the Common Market, or we can play hookey and find ourselves somewhere a little more private.'

'There's a summerhouse on the lawn.'

He slid a bottle of champagne and two glasses into the pockets of his jacket. 'You are full of good ideas, my dear Miss . . .?'

'Constant,' she said. Threading through the crowds, they went out into the garden. 'Katherine Constant.'

'My name's Jordan Aymes.'

The name was familiar, but she could not place it. He opened the door of the summerhouse. 'Katherine Constant . . .' he mused, as he uncorked the champagne bottle. 'Do people shorten it?'

'My twin brother calls me Kitty. But everyone else calls me Katherine.'

'Twin brother? Are you close? Do you share each other's thoughts, like twins are supposed to?'

'What an awful idea. Certainly not. I should hate Simon to know my thoughts, and I certainly wouldn't want to know his.'

'Quite. That sort of closeness must be so suffocating. Intimacy needs to be offset by distance and surprise, don't you think? Or the magic goes.'

He had not touched her, had not even shaken her hand, and yet she felt a small shiver run down her spine.

She looked down at her plate. 'Well, then – quails' eggs. I must eat them now, mustn't I?'

'I believe you must.'

She bit into one of the small, slippery things. It was nicer than she had expected it to be. She ate half a dozen quails' eggs, washing them down with champagne. When she had finished, Jordan Aymes said, 'You are an extraordinary woman, Katherine Constant,' and refilled her glass. 'Tell me about yourself.'

'There's nothing much to tell.'

'A dull start. Try again.'

'My father's a doctor. I've three brothers.'

'Older or younger?'

'One older, one younger.'

'And one just the same. So you're in the middle of the family.'

'Yes,' she said bitterly. 'The filling in the sandwich.' He raised an eyebrow. 'It's what you said about being suffocated,' she explained. 'Families are so suffocating. I can't wait to get away.'

'You still live at home?'

'At the moment.'

'I assumed—' He looked at her. 'How old are you, Katherine?'

'Seventeen,' she said.

'*Ah.*' A slight widening of the eyes, a small twist to the corners of his mouth.

'Eighteen next week,' she added quickly. 'Rachel and I were at school together.'

'At school . . .' He stood up. 'I think, then, that I should go and finish my meal in the dining room.'

'Why? Have I annoyed you?'

He smiled. 'It would be easier if you had.'

She was bewildered. 'I don't understand.'

'I'm thirty-three,' he said. 'Almost twice your age. There are limits, you see. Dear me, Katherine. I should like to put you on ice for a few years . . .' His lips brushed the back of her hand. 'But failing that, I shall bid you a regretful adieu, and wish you all good fortune in whatever life you choose to have.'

As he walked away, she remembered where she had seen his name. It had been in the newspapers: SHOCK RESULT IN BY-ELECTION AS TORY SEIZES SEAT IN LABOUR HEARTLAND. She sat down again, staring at his retreating back as she scooped up a dribble of mayonnaise from her plate with the tip of her finger.

The three girls walked through the rose garden behind the house. Their shadows mingled on the grass.

'Any second thoughts, Rachel?' asked Katherine. 'At the altar, as you chained yourself for life . . .'

Rachel was wearing her powder-blue going-away suit. 'None. Though . . .'

Katherine pounced. '"Though"?'

'Everything's changed, hasn't it? This isn't my home any more. Wyborne isn't my name any more. I'm Mrs Seton, yet I feel as though I should be going back to school next month.' Rachel looked quickly from one to the other. 'You'll come and visit me, won't you?'

'Of course we will,' said Katherine. She smiled. 'And now, I've got something to tell you both. Something exciting. I've got a job.'

'A job? *Katherine*. Where? Doing what?'

'In London. Working for a magazine.' She told them about Toby and Stuart.

'A summer job?'

'No. A proper job.'

'But what about Oxford?'

'It wouldn't suit me, would it? All those rules and regulations and having to get permission to do anything. I wouldn't last a fortnight.'

'Your parents?'

'The funny thing is that it was Mum who minded. Yet it was Dad who went to Oxford, not Mum – she just got married. She tried to make me change my mind. I wouldn't, of course. You are pleased for me, aren't you?'

'Course we are.' Rachel hugged her. 'When will you begin?'

'Monday. I'm going to London on Monday.'

'*Monday*. Not *telling* us, Katherine!'

Liv found herself standing slightly apart from the pair of them. They had become unfamiliar, she thought: Rachel, with her French pleat and expertly applied makeup, and Katherine, who had exchanged her discontent for a bob and a Biba dress and a transforming confidence and brightness. It was as though they had walked off ahead of her, leaving her standing at a crossroads, uncertain which way to turn. She, alone of the three of them, had not yet had a lover. She had no idea what she would do after university.

A voice called Rachel's name. Diana was coming down the gravel path towards them. 'I've been looking for you everywhere, darling! The car's here.'

Guests were assembling in the courtyard. Thea had borrowed Richard Thorneycroft's camera. The shutter whirred, and Rachel, Katherine and Liv, walking arm in arm across the lawn, were frozen in time. 'Our dark-eyed girls,' said Thea, smiling, remembering.

Katherine was swallowed up by the crowd. A small circle – Hector, Mr Wyborne, Mrs Wyborne, Hector's aunt Clare – gathered around Rachel. A trail of dark red rose-petals smeared the lawn. Rachel threw her bouquet into the air, and a plump bridesmaid in yellow satin caught it. The taxi carrying the newlyweds disappeared down the drive. Groups of guests huddled together on the lawn, but the day had acquired a weary, over-bright air, as though the festivities had gone on too long.

Liv walked back to the cottage. She needed to be by herself for a while. Indoors, she picked up the postcard from the mat, glimpsing a picture of blue skies and beaches and palm fronds. She felt flat and tired, and her dress stuck clammily to her back, so she made herself a glass of orange squash, letting the icy water run through her hands, splashing her hot face. The summer stretched out before her, long and bleak, a summer without Katherine, without Rachel.

Turning the postcard over, she read what was written on the back. She began to tremble, and she had to put the glass down on the draining-board. She walked out into the garden, to the stream and the willows. Only when she was sitting down on the old mossy log did she read the postcard a second time.

'Happy eighteenth birthday to my dear daughter, Olivia. Sorry if this is late. Your loving father, Finley Fairbrother.'

She had to press her knees together to stop them shaking. The early-evening sun fell through the thick canopy of leaves, dappling the ground like golden raindrops. She had to keep looking at the card and the signature to make sure she had not imagined them. Her tears blurred her father's handwriting.

Eight years ago, three little girls had come to this clearing to cast a spell. They had made a pyre out of sticks and dry leaves. Katherine had had matches and a penknife; Liv had made a quill pen out of a goose feather, and Rachel had brought Miss France, with her Breton coif and ric-racked skirts. They had nicked their fingertips with the penknife, holding hands, letting the blood run together. 'Blood sisters,' Katherine had whispered. Dipping the quill into the blood, Liv had written her father's name on a piece of paper. They had folded it three times and buried it in the centre of the pyre; then they had placed Miss France on top, and had struck a match. The twigs and leaves had caught fire, and then, in a sudden bright flare, Miss France's coif and dress had burst into flames. Her pink plastic limbs and her pink plastic face had twisted and melted. And somewhere in the heart of the fire, the name of Finley Fairbrother, written in blood, had burned bright.

She had expected her father to come home that night. She had lain awake, anticipating the footsteps on the path, the knock at the door. But he had not come, and as the weeks and months and years had passed, hope had faded. So she had woven stories around him, imagining him unjustly imprisoned, prevented from returning to his family, or embroiled in some secret, heroic mission where he must remain incognito. But eventually she had recognized those fantasies as what they were, just fantasies, something to put off the day when she must accept that, for whatever reason, he had chosen to live apart from her. She had not forgotten him, though, and he still occupied a place in her heart.

Once more, she looked down at the postcard. If she half closed her eyes, his signature seemed to brighten, so that it was written in scarlet once more, its twists and curls binding the three of them – Fin, Thea, herself – together.

Chapter Three

Katherine loved London. She thought of it as lots of different worlds colliding, like coloured beads on a string. She loved the busy streets, felted with dust beneath the bright sun, or gleaming after a rain shower. She loved the dignified squares, with their gardens of plane and laurel, like secret jade-green jewels. She loved the great department stores, Harrods and Harvey Nichols and Dickins and Jones. She never bought anything, but she enjoyed wandering through them, and thinking, *One day*.

Stuart and Toby disapproved of Harrods and Harvey Nichols. 'Temples of bourgeois consumerism, Katherine,' Stuart would say, in his thick, scathing Glaswegian accent. And Toby, who had been to public school, would agree.

Katherine also enjoyed working for *Frodo's Finger*. She was initially disappointed to discover that her role consisted more of typing and making cups of tea than writing, but she reminded herself that everyone had to start at the bottom, and set about making herself indispensable. As Stuart couldn't spell and as Toby suffered from perpetual nervous tension, indispensability, she discovered, wasn't difficult, and she was soon writing articles and arranging interviews. She enjoyed the busyness of it all: the phone ringing, and the endless stream of people who called at the office. She enjoyed taking complicated tube and bus journeys to parts of London she had never seen before, and she experienced a rare feeling of confidence and serenity when she heard Toby say to a potential advertiser, 'Oh, talk to Katherine. She does everything round here. We couldn't manage without her.'

Through Toby, she met Felix Corcoran. He had been at school with Toby. He was tall and thin, with curling nut-brown hair. His slightly slanting, greenish-hazel eyes and hollow, high-cheekboned face gave him the appearance, Katherine thought, of a gangly, disreputable elf. He wore denims that had frayed at the knees and ankles, and shirts missing buttons at the cuffs. In the winter, he wrapped up his gaunt frame in a vast grey army coat that, Katherine suspected, had seen action on the Russian front. In the evenings, he pulled pints at a nearby pub, the White Hart; by day, he divided his time between driving a van for a shop in the East End, and drawing cartoons for *Frodo's Finger*. When Katherine explained to Felix that she was looking for somewhere to live, he helped her find a bedsit. It was in a tall, ramshackle house in Earls Court, adjacent to a restaurant. At night, cats stole scraps of fish from the restaurant's dustbins, and consumed them, yowling with pleasure, in the tiny concrete courtyard behind the building.

Katherine's room was large and square, with draughty sash windows. Had it been half the size, and noisier and colder, she would still have loved it. She let the washing-up pile up until she ran out of plates, and she dashed off to the launderette when she ran out of clean clothes. She lived off sliced white bread, Marmite and apples, bought from the corner shop across the road. She spent most of her money on clothes and makeup, and the rest on books and posters for her room.

She got to know the other tenants in the lodging-house. Mrs Mandeville lived on the ground floor. Inviting Katherine into her dark, crowded rooms, she reminisced about the war. Mrs Mandeville supplemented the restaurant cats' diet with tins of Kit-E-Kat. Two girls called Denise and Heather shared a room on the first floor adjacent to Katherine's: they were typists, like Katherine, but they planned to become models. They showed Katherine how to glue individual false lashes to her lids – 'Like Twiggy,' explained Heather. Katherine hadn't the patience: jabbing her eye with tweezers, she had to wear a patch for a week, to Stuart and Toby's amusement. Afterwards, she reverted to her old habits of spitting into her mascara and wearing a great deal of Miner's navy blue liquid liner. Mr and Mrs Mossop, a young Australian married couple, lived in the room above Katherine's. Felix had the room next to the Mossops'.

Toby, Stuart and Felix became Katherine's friends. She went to the pub with them, watched TV with them, argued with them. It was an easy, undemanding relationship, and she was careful never to let it become any more than that. Every now and then Toby or Stuart would make an attempt to seduce her, which she would gently but firmly repel. She knew that sleeping with either of them might jeopardize her work, because it would certainly jeopardize their friendship with each other, which, she suspected, was only capable of bearing so much rivalry. As for Felix – well, it was Felix who showed her how to slip the lock to her bedsit when, yet again, she lost her keys. It was Felix who explained to her the workings of the temperamental gas-ring. It was Felix who taught her how to roll a joint, and how to drive his battered van. And it was Felix who, when Katherine realized her wages from *Frodo's Finger* were not enough to pay the rent, found her an evening job in the White Hart.

It was not that she was not attracted to Felix; sometimes, talking to him and smoking with him late into the night, she'd imagine waking in the morning, his head on the pillow beside hers. Yet something stopped her from putting her fantasy into practice. The men she went to bed with seemed somehow to belong to a different category from the men who were her friends. Though she had plenty of lovers, sex remained an awkward and unpleasurable business. Katherine was mystified. The rest of the world seemed to enjoy sex, so why didn't she? She read books and magazine articles about sex, but couldn't seem to apply the theoretical to the practical.

She had far too much pride to admit her problem either to blissfully married Rachel, or to naïve, romantic Liv. She thought of confiding in Denise and Heather, but could not bring herself to do so. Katherine resolved to keep her secret. She'd learn to enjoy it soon, she knew she would. Meanwhile, as one after another of her relationships fizzled out or ended in disaster, she came to the conclusion that she liked Felix far too much to risk going to bed with him.

Like the cold wind that blew along the concrete walkway that bisected Lancaster's campus, university seized Liv by the scruff of the neck, shook her and woke her up. She fell in love at first sight with her room in the halls of residence, with its bed and chair and desk and wardrobe, and bright orange rug and bright orange curtains. She made the room her own, attaching to the pinboard sketches and postcards and photographs: herself and Katherine and Rachel, walking arm in arm at Rachel's wedding; Thea, in a feathered home-made hat, her reading glasses slipping down her nose; and, of course, her father's postcard from Tahiti.

Her first night she lay awake, cold and homesick, listening to the roars and heavy footsteps of the male students as they rampaged through the corridors after the bars closed. The next day, Liv bought herself a hot-water bottle, a striped scarf and a thick pair of socks, and wore them in bed, when necessary. She enrolled for courses in history, English literature and cultural studies, and sat in draughty lecture halls, scribbling notes on a pad. At weekends she went to Lancaster or to Morecambe, happy to be near the sea again, remembering the pink house in which she had lived as a child.

She got to know the girls in her residence, and the people on her course; she joined the Theatre Group, the Film Society, and the History Group. She watched Situationist dramas and Absurdist plays; at folk clubs, her soul was stirred by protest songs and Irish rebel songs. She drank Guinness and cider, and woke up the next morning on a friend's floor, still wearing her duffel coat, with a headache of Vesuvian proportions. She spent an evening with a pale, etiolated boy she met on her literature course: on the altar of a Velvet Underground album he rolled a joint with sacramental care. She took a few experimental puffs, and sat in the half-dark, waiting for the rush of bliss, and the world through different eyes. Yet everything remained the same, and she had to counter her disappointment by reminding herself that here, at least, she had crossed a boundary.

Other boundaries remained. The fact of her virginity embarrassed her. The men she fell in love with did not fall in love with her; the men who pursued her she shied away from. Some seemed so gauche, so half formed, that though she might have liked them as the cousin or brother she had never had, she could not, no matter how hard she tried, fall in love with them. Others were brash and over-confident, and she found their noise and certainty off-putting. One by one, the other girls on her floor acquired lovers. She saw them in the mornings before the nine o'clock lecture, ostentatiously making two mugs of coffee and carrying them back to their rooms.

At the end of her first term, she confided in Katherine, who was scathing. 'You've always got your head in the clouds, Liv. Half the time you look as though if a boy speaks to you you'd jump out of your skin, and half the time you look as though you expect perfection. Men don't want girls like that. They want girls to be attainable.'

Liv asked Katherine how many lovers she had had. 'Five,' Katherine said. She looked smug.

In the spring term, Liv met Carl. He was tall and thin and had gentle blue-grey eyes, and shoulder-length dark-gold hair. He owned a battered guitar, on which he played, haltingly, 'Gilgarry Mountain' and 'Blowin' In The Wind'. Liv wasn't quite sure whether Carl thought of her as his girlfriend. Their relationship was a series of hesitations and feints, borne, she later thought, of a mutual lack of conviction. One spring afternoon they kissed for hours, sitting on the steps of the square. Parting from Carl, she was aware of a mixture of delight and relief and excitement. It had happened at last. She was in love.

Yet she did not see him for the next three days. When she called at his room, one of his friends told her that Carl had gone to visit his parents in Barrow. A few days later, she glimpsed him at a Film Society disco, dancing with a girl she recognized from her history-of-science course. Their bodies touched, shoulder, breast and hip, and his thin, pale hands played with the girl's long brown hair.

The following day she phoned Katherine, who invited her to stay for the weekend in London. Liv packed her rucksack and bought a coach ticket. At Victoria Coach Station, peering out of the window of the bus, Liv picked out Katherine from the crowd. She was wearing a white embroidered Afghan coat and her plum-coloured boots. They waved at each other madly.

They took the tube to Earls Court, and Katherine's bedsit. Katherine moved quickly among the chaos, putting on the kettle, spreading marge and Marmite on Mother's Pride to make sandwiches, holding a blouse or dress up against herself and glancing into the mirror as she talked. It seemed to Liv that her months in London had given Katherine a kind of gloss, a thin, brilliant glitter that made men's heads turn as she walked past.

There was a party that night at Toby's place in Chelsea. Toby was looking after the house while his parents were abroad. He had covered Heal's lamps with pink tissue paper ('for atmosphere') so that the rooms were like warm, rosy caves. Every now and then the tissue paper would smoulder and have to be hurriedly stamped out, leaving black marks on the Indian rugs. Oil paintings had been turned to face the wall, posters were taped to Regency Stripe wallpaper, and someone had painted a mural of swirling psychedelic patterns alongside the stairs. There were a great many empty bottles and Rizla packets, and full ashtrays and dirty glasses.

The party flowed through all four storeys of the house. There was music and dancing in the basement, and in the living room a boy wearing a caftan and beads played the sitar. People sat on the stairs, smoking and drinking; Liv almost tripped over a girl crouched over a pack of Tarot cards, telling fortunes. In the early hours of the morning, the guests began to drift away. Liv and Katherine lounged side by side on bean-bags on the floor as Toby made coffee in the wreckage of the kitchen.

'Best edition yet, don't you think?' Toby poured boiling water on to ground beans. 'My piece on Castro ... and the editorial.'

'Terrific.' Stuart was stretched out on a sofa, smoking.

'You don't *really* think revolution's the answer to everything, do you, Toby?'

Toby ripped open a packet of sugar. 'Yes, I do, actually, Felix.'

Felix was wearing a holey Ban the Bomb T-shirt and worn velvet jeans. Ash sprayed from the tip of his cigarette as he gestured to Toby. 'Helping the poor by sending them to the barricades ... They'd end up with bloody noses, or worse, don't you think?'

'So what do you think should be done?' Toby frowned. 'No teaspoons ...' He tipped the sugar bag in the approximate direction of the coffee cups. 'Or perhaps you think things should go on as they are. The workers pleading for enough cash to feed the kids while the boss lives in luxury.'

'Exploiting the workers runs in the family, doesn't it, Felix?' Stuart smiled. 'Your father owns a factory, doesn't he?'

Katherine said, '*Felix*. You never told me.'

'Just a wee one, eh, Felix?'

Liv thought Felix looked embarrassed. 'What does it make?'

'Wallpaper,' said Felix gloomily.

Stuart smirked. 'So you salve your conscience by doling out goodies to the deserving poor. A touch of the Marie Antoinettes, wouldn't you say? A slab of fruit cake here, a swiss roll there ...'

Felix grinned. 'We don't sell swiss roll. Far too decadent.'

'Far too *edible*,' said Toby.

'Swiss roll?' Liv sat up as Toby passed her a mug of coffee.

'I drive a van, you see, Liv,' explained Felix, 'for a wholefood co-operative in Bethnal Green. We buy food in bulk, decent stuff – fruit and veg and wholemeal bread and pulses – and sell it at reasonable prices.'

'To be bought by fashionable Chelsea housewives ...'

'Well, we can't *vet* the customers, can we, Stuart?'

'. . . while the lumpen proletariat prefer their Heinz beans and sliced white.'

'It's an attempt at practical help. You can't get much more practical than feeding people.'

'*Frodo's Finger* feeds *minds*,' said Stuart pompously. Felix snorted.

In the early hours of the morning, Katherine stayed behind to help Toby mail copies of the magazine, while Felix walked Liv home. The full moon silvered the tiles of the houses and greyed the evergreens in the gardens. The world slept, so that the curtained windows of the houses were like so many sleep-shut eyes. Even the pigeons in the eaves dozed, their heads tucked under their wings. Thin clouds veiled the face of the moon.

Felix asked Liv about her family. 'There's only my mother and me,' she explained. 'Though I suppose Katherine and Rachel have been my sort-of sisters.'

'Ah, the lovely Rachel,' said Felix dreamily. 'She and her husband visited at Christmas.'

Liv thought, *Everyone* falls in love with Rachel. 'Rachel's going to have a baby,' she said. 'In June.'

'Then you'll be a sort-of aunt.'

'Rachel's sure she's expecting a girl. Though I suppose Hector might like a son to inherit Bellingford. Lucky Rachel,' said Liv, with a sigh, 'living in a castle.'

'Do you think so?'

'Don't you? So romantic.'

'Things like that – houses and names – can be such a tie.'

She thought of the pink house by the sea. 'When I was little, we lived in lots of different places. I always thought it must be lovely to *belong* somewhere.'

'There's belonging,' he said, 'and there's being owned.'

At that moment she felt completely, unexpectedly happy. The moon had a particular brightness, and the city streets a louche, dusty beauty. She wondered whether she had fallen in love with Felix, and decided that she couldn't possibly have, so soon after Carl.

'I've always wished I had a proper family,' she said wistfully.

'A big, complicated family with lots of brothers and sisters and cousins and things. Is your family like that, Felix?'

'I've a father and a stepmother and a sister.'

She imagined a tall, thin, green-eyed girl: laughing, affectionate. 'What's your sister like?'

'Rose is quite, quite mad. She nurses wounded rabbits and talks to her pet snails.'

Liv giggled. '*No one* has pet snails.'

'Rose does. And slugs. The gardener poisons them because they eat the hostas, you see, so Rose rescues them and nurses them back to health.' He glanced at her. 'You look frozen.'

She shivered; she had not brought her coat, and the air was sharp and cold.

'Have my jacket.' He wrapped it around her shoulders, a tattered khaki kagoule that was much too big for her. 'And we could run.' His eyes glittered in the darkness. 'When I was little, my mother used to take me to London at half-term. For some reason, I was always scared of the dinosaurs in the Natural History Museum so I always used to run past it. If I made it by the time I'd counted twenty, I was all right.'

'And if you didn't?'

He grinned. 'A nasty encounter with tyrannosaurus rex, I suppose.' He took her hand in his. They began to run. She clutched his jacket around her neck. She heard him counting, 'One ... two ... three ...' and she struggled to keep up with his long strides. Streets and houses rushed by; stars blurred in a navy sky. Thirteen ... fourteen ... fifteen ... 'Come on, Liv, the stegosaurus ...' They had reached the corner of the road. Her heart pounded, but she felt exhilarated and free as he hauled her up the steps of the lodging-house. 'Nineteen ...' she gasped, and, helpless with laughter, let her head fall against his shoulder as he fitted his key to the lock.

Waking early in the morning, Rachel could see through the windows of their bedroom the distant Cheviot hills. She had witnessed their alterations as the months passed: summer green during the first weeks of her marriage, then hazed with purple as autumn encroached, and white with the first winter's snowfall. Now, in late spring, they were green again.

Like the hills, her body was changing. Before she even opened her eyes in the morning, she would place her palms on her belly, waiting for that first, reassuring movement. The trail of a sharp little elbow beneath the curved dome of her womb, or a sudden twist, like a fish curling through water. Her body had become unfamiliar, surprising her just as Bellingford itself surprised her, with sudden changes of shape and colouring, and odd little quirks and unexpected sights. Nine months after her marriage she still discovered each day something new at Bellingford: initials carved into a stone wall, only visible when the light fell in a particular way, or pale blue scyllas, pushing up through the soil in a quiet corner of the garden.

Seven and a half months into her pregnancy, the sudden flecking of silvery stretchmarks and the pangs of cramp at night took her similarly unaware.

'I look like a blancmange!' she said, peeling off her nightgown one morning, and seeing the vast white mounds of breasts and belly. 'You have married a blancmange, Hector!'

He kissed her. 'A very delicious blancmange.'

'A blancmange, nevertheless.' She sighed. 'I wish it was June. I wish she was here. Don't you?'

He came to stand behind her, folding his arms around her. 'Sometimes I wish . . .'

'What, darling?'

'That I'd had you to myself a bit longer, I suppose.'

'You don't *mind*, do you?'

'Of course I don't. How could I possibly mind?' His lips nuzzled the hollow of her neck and shoulder.

'We didn't exactly plan, did we?' Rachel smiled to herself, remembering the first few weeks of their marriage: the days they had spent in this room, in this bed . . .

Hector planted a kiss on Rachel's shoulder. 'Get dressed,

darling. You're all goose-bumps. I'll telephone the wretched heating contractors this morning.'

They were installing central-heating at Bellingford, a major undertaking. Henry Wyborne's wedding gift had enabled them to begin restoring the house. The tasks were endless: roofs to be retiled, chimneys to be lined, rotting joists and window-frames to be replaced, damp-proofing to be installed, walls and ceilings to be taken down and replastered. The garden, too, had become wild and overgrown.

Knotting his tie, Hector said to Rachel, 'We should think of a name.'

'Not yet.' Rachel would not explain even to Hector her suspicion that naming the baby was unlucky, that it would tempt fate. 'Not till she's born.'

Hector had bought Rachel a car and taught her to drive; a few members of what Hector called the county set had visited, but though they were pleasant enough, Rachel had made no close friends in Northumberland. Hector worked in a bank in Newcastle; their nearest neighbour lived half a mile away. Hector had bought Rachel a dog, a cocker spaniel called Charlie, and he telephoned several times a day so she didn't feel lonely. There was plenty to occupy her at Bellingford. Rachel became a dab hand with a paintbrush; at the weekends, she and Hector decorated the less ramshackle rooms. In the spring, she discovered an unexpected passion for gardening, and lost track of time as she grubbed away at the earth, clearing aside the undergrowth to reveal delicate snowdrops or golden crocuses. Once a week, she drove into Alnwick to shop, and to meet Hector for lunch. Sometimes, when Hector had to go to London on business, she accompanied him. Every month or so, she stayed for a weekend with her parents. Her mother worried. 'I don't like to think of you alone in that great house, darling. What if something should happen?' Rachel tried to reassure her. First labours were supposed to take ages, so she would have plenty of time to get to the hospital. Her mother, questioned more closely, agreed that Rachel herself had taken an entire day to make her way into the world.

Rachel wanted lots of children. Four, at least. Bellingford was the sort of place that needed children, and that children would adore. She imagined brightly coloured pictures and furnishings in the bedrooms, and small feet running along the quiet corridors. She had wanted to have the baby at home, in keeping with family tradition, but the doctor was reluctant, muttering about first babies, and Hector, too, was unenthusiastic. So, to please them both, she booked into a private clinic.

During the early months of pregnancy, the coming child had seemed unreal, something that made her sick in the mornings, and made her breasts sore and uncomfortable. Then, one evening, sitting by the fire, she had felt the baby move, a small fluttering, like a bird in a cage. She had begun to love it then, and to long for its arrival. She lurched between a wild, euphoric happiness, and a fear that something dreadful would happen, that the baby would be taken from her. At seven months pregnant, Rachel gave a small, private sigh of relief (at seven months, the books said, most babies could survive a premature birth). She had collected a vast hoard of baby clothes: tiny white nightgowns from Harrods, gorgeous sleeping suits and little coats from exclusive French children's shops, minute cardigans and mittens knitted by her mother and by Hector's aunt.

Hector unearthed from an attic a carved wooden crib, which had been in the Seton family for generations. Diana reminded Rachel of all her own baby things, stored in a room at Fernhill Grange. Rachel decorated the nursery, painting it a soft pale pink, and hanging pictures and mobiles. Hector said, 'What if it's a boy, a great, hulking, rugby-playing boy?' but Rachel hugged her arms around her swollen belly, and smiled to herself, and longed for the arrival of her daughter.

The seminar room was crowded. As Liv wound through people and furniture, her purse, precariously balanced on top of her books and notepads, began to slide to the floor. As she grabbed at it, books, purse and pencil-case shot out of her grasp, scattering in a flutter of paper and clatter of pens to all four corners of the room.

She stooped to gather up her belongings. Sheets of paper had skidded beneath the chairs and the desk. She heard someone say, 'Here, let me help.'

She looked up. He was dark-haired, in his mid-twenties, she guessed. 'I'd shake hands,' he said, 'but I don't think I can.' He was holding her textbook, file and notepad. 'My name's Stefan Galenski,' he said. 'I'm Dr Langley's research assistant. Dr Langley's unwell, so I'm helping out this term.'

She told him her name. When he smiled, his dark blue eyes crinkled at the corners. He quoted softly, ' "O! when mine eyes did see Olivia first, Methought she purg'd the air of pestilence . . ." '

It was half-way through the seminar before she had recovered her composure and was able to listen properly. Stefan Galenski's voice was rich and mellifluous and slightly accented. She darted glances at him, and sketched in the margins of her pad the gesture of a hand, the sudden flash of a smile. When, once, his eyes met hers, she looked down quickly as the blood rushed to her face.

The following week, she arrived early, slipping into the room amid a flurry of people. Stefan Galenski's seminars were not like Dr Langley's sober dissections of the topic. They were a wild, reckless rush of ideas, an exploration of original thought that left Liv breathless and exhilarated. Stefan paced the room, emphasizing his words with expansive, dramatic gestures. Every now and then a lock of hair would fall over his eyes, and he'd sweep it back impatiently. Liv noticed that the elbows of his corduroy jacket were threadbare, and she saw how his sudden smile curled the corners of his mouth, lighting up his features.

At the end of the seminar, a handful of students lingered, clustering round him. Slipping quickly out of the room, Liv was aware of a feeling of exclusion, and of disappointment in herself. She had said only a word or two during the discussion. She managed to contribute to other seminars, so why not to Stefan Galenski's? Two terms at university, she thought savagely, and still she had not managed to shake off her lack of sophistication, her intermittent and mortifying episodes of bashfulness.

A few evenings later, she was in the bar, waiting for a friend, when she noticed Stefan in the far corner of the room, almost lost in a crowd of people. She recognized them from her course: the girl with the Afghan coat, the boy with the auburn hair and gold wire glasses. She did not join them, convinced that he would not remember her, nondescript, tongue-tied Olivia. Yet she found her gaze returning frequently to him, and when their eyes met, he waved. Curled around her glass, her hands trembled, slopping beer on to the floor as he crossed the room to her.

'Liv,' he said, 'I tried to catch you after the seminar the other day, but you'd gone.' He smiled at her. 'I've invited a few of my students to my home on Saturday afternoon. You'll come, won't you? I live a few miles from Caton. Bit of a trek, I know, but there's a bus that'll take you most of the way.'

She didn't need to think. 'I'd love to.'

'I'd better explain to you how to get there.' He went through his pockets, and found a felt-tipped pen. 'Have you any paper?' She shook her head.

'Give me your hand, then.'

On the back, he drew a map. Caton and Quernmore, and the high road that wound between them. And a small square, with a tree beside it. 'That's my house,' he said. 'Holm Edge Farm.'

Blue felt-penned lines echoing the paler blue lines of her veins. The warmth of his hand holding hers, and the hills mapped in miniature on her skin, marking out the future contours of her life.

The bus wound wheezily through narrow roads that rose towards the distant fells. The tops of the fells were smudged with heather, or were bright with acid-green moss, and blotted by grey slabs and boulders. Hawthorn trees, contorted by the wind, crouched and twisted on the lower slopes.

Liv alighted from the bus near Crossgill. The narrow, winding Littledale road led up into the hills. The early May air was cool and clear, and the sky was a pure, cloudless blue. The breeze tugged at her hair. Perched on drystone walls, blackbirds sang, and violets quivered on the verges. A mile along the road, she began to look out for the track that led from the road to Stefan's house. Opening a five-bar gate, she found herself heading into a farmyard. A sheepdog barked at her and she retreated rapidly, ducking along a footpath lined with rowans. At the edge of a field she paused, watching the lambs, forgetting the time. Cutting back to the road, she sank up to her ankles in spongy, rain-drenched sphagnum moss. Rivulets of water ran down the hillside, a legacy of the previous night's rainstorm. Looking up, shading her eyes, she caught sight of the house on the fell, and the dark green tree beside it.

Sunlight glittered on the grey roof, and was caught and magnified by the window-panes. The farmhouse nestled in the curve of the hill, which rose up behind like a great, purplish wave. She thought how marvellous it would be to live in such a place, to see such beauty when one opened one's eyes in the morning, to spend one's days surrounded by such silence and splendour.

Glancing at her watch, she saw that she was almost an hour late. She hurried up the steep track to the gate. She could hear voices and laughter. Half a dozen students were sitting round a table set on the tussocky grass. Stefan was at its head. He spoke, and they laughed, and rays of sun fell through the barbed leaves of the holly tree, marking shifting bright papery cut-outs on the lawn.

Liv perched on the edge of a bench, half listening to the conversation.

''Sixty-eight represented the death-throes of bourgeois society.'

'The beginnings of the revolution.'

'Oh, come on, Andy,' this from a girl wearing a crocheted beret, 'I don't exactly *see* signs of collapse, do you? The police are still out in force at demos, and the university establishment still tells us what to learn, and when to learn.'

'But, Gillian . . .'

As their voices faded into the background, Liv's gaze drifted from the high fells to the fields, dotted with cotton-wool sheep, then back to the house. It was stone-built and slate-roofed. A battered Citroën was parked to one side, and there was a tumbledown barn to the other. Tucked into the slope of the hill, the long, low lines of the house echoed the tracery of drystone walls that crisscrossed the fields.

'Olivia?'

She started, hearing her name. Stefan Galenski said, 'I wondered what you thought?'

'About what?' There was a ripple of laughter from the other students. She said quickly, 'I'm sorry, I was admiring the view.'

'We were talking about the death of the author. But you're right, of course, it's rather a sterile topic for such a beautiful day.' Stefan rose. 'May I show you my house?'

She followed him across the grass to the front door. Inside, she blinked to accustom herself to the dim light. The windows were small rectangles cut into the thick stone walls, their sills cluttered with books and papers. The irregularities of the walls showed through the plaster, and in places the whitewash had peeled and yellowed. A large fireplace occupied most of one end of the room, and encased an iron stove. There were faded rag rugs on the flags, and more heaps of books grew from the surfaces of the table, chairs and cupboards. A narrow stone staircase led to the upper storey.

Alone with Stefan, she found her awkwardness slipping away. She heard him ask, 'Do you approve of my house, Liv?'

'It's wonderful. So –' she struggled for the right words '– so remote and enchanting. How long have you lived here?'

'I've been renting it for a few weeks, since the beginning of the month. I was on campus, but it was intolerable. The noise . . . the disruption. I couldn't work.' His eyes narrowed. 'It's so essential to be able to give everything – your whole heart and soul – to whatever you choose to do, don't you agree?'

'Yes,' she said, and her heart gave a small, painful lurch, as though someone had taken it in the palm of his hand and gently squeezed it. She blurted out, 'It's just that I can't seem to choose *what* to do!'

'There's plenty of time.'

'Everyone says that.'

'I'm sorry. I didn't mean to sound patronizing.'

'One of my best friends is married,' she explained, 'and expecting a child. The other has always known exactly what she wants, and just keeps going till she gets it. Now, if they can make up their minds, why can't I?'

He frowned. Then, suddenly, he reached out and took her hand. 'My map . . .'

She could almost feel the intensity of his gaze. She had not washed off the felt-pen lines, and they were still visible, though the blue had blurred and faded.

He led her to the window. 'Look,' he said. The fells rose up in front of her, grey and mauve, patched with bright green marshland. And as if of its own volition, her gaze slid away from the view to focus instead on his profile: his high forehead and slanted cheekbones, long, narrow, hawkish nose, and dark blue, heavy-lidded eyes.

'When I'm unhappy,' he said softly, 'I look out there. There used to be glaciers covering those hills, did you know that, Liv? High seas made of ice. One can find fossils of tiny sea-creatures in the stone. And if oceans can turn into mountains, then who knows what may happen?'

Two days later, she was standing in the aisles of the tiny campus supermarket, when she heard him say her name. She spun round. 'Stefan.'

'You haven't got far with your shopping, Liv.' He glanced at her empty basket.

'I'm trying to decide between fish fingers and tomato soup.'

'Neither. Both are vile. I've a better idea. I'll make you goulash.' When she hesitated, he glanced at her. 'You'll come, won't you, Liv? I need cheering up, you see.' He began to grab things from the shelf, flinging them into her basket as they walked.

'A bad day?'

'Terrible.' He grimaced. 'I'll tell you when we're in the car.'

He drove fast along the Quernmore road. Tall trees loomed out of the darkness as the Citroën swerved round corners and swooped up and down hills. 'There was a gale last night,' he explained, 'and it blew open the window of the room where I work. I didn't notice until this morning, and then I found my papers scattered to the four winds.'

'Your research?'

'Some of it's missing – half-way to Quernmore, I suspect – and some of the rest is soaked by the rain, and fit mostly for the bin.'

'Have you copies?'

'Some of it. Not everything.'

'How awful!'

He shrugged. 'I'll just have to salvage what I can.'

'I'll help you, if you like.'

He looked at her. 'How kind of you, Liv.'

She turned her face away, staring out of the window, glad of the poor light. She felt curiously knotted inside, as though she was fighting for breath. The altitude, she thought. She was used to the low-lying, the level plain. Not to such chill, sharp, refined air. Not to hills made out of seas.

'Living where I've chosen to,' said Stefan, as he turned a corner, 'you have to expect difficulties. It doesn't seem too high a price to pay. Holm Edge is so *elemental*. If I wanted central-heating and fitted carpets, and all the rest of that suffocating paraphernalia, then I wouldn't have chosen to live there.' He glanced at Liv. 'The house has been empty for the last couple of years – it's too remote for most people, I suppose. But I loved it the moment I saw it. Sometimes you just know, don't you?'

She threaded her hands together, squeezing the bones tightly. The countryside sped past, blurred by the speed of the car.

'Why is it called Holm Edge?'

'Holm means holly. There used to be holly trees all along the edge of the field. My predecessor felled all but one of them – and in consequence died a horrible death, of course.'

The car bumped and rattled up the narrow track to the farmhouse. 'Why "of course"?'

'It's bad luck to cut down a holly tree. Witches appear.' Stefan steered the car through the gateway, and parked in front of the house.

In the kitchen, he lit the fire to warm the room, and sliced onions and braised steak. While the goulash was simmering, he poured two glasses of wine, and fetched his papers from his study. 'We'll see what we can rescue.'

He began to sort the sheets of paper. Some were streaked with rainwater. Words – entire sentences – were illegible. The room fell quiet, the only sounds the crackle of the fire and the scratch of Liv's pen as she copied out the damaged text.

Over supper, Stefan told her about himself. His mother had been half French, half English. After the war, she had married a Canadian serviceman of Polish extraction.

'So I'm a mixture of four nationalities,' he pointed out. 'A hotch-potch. An *olla podrida*.' He grinned. 'A goulash.' Liv giggled.

After Stefan's father had been demobbed, the Galenskis had gone to live in Canada. Stefan had been born in 1946. A year later, his father had died of TB, contracted during the war. After her husband's death, his mother hadn't been able to settle. They had moved back to Europe, first to France and then to Britain. Stefan remembered a succession of different towns, different homes. A succession, too, of stepfathers. When he was twenty-one, his mother had died. He had remained in England since her death.

'I had to clear out her flat,' he said. 'There were so few things – half a dozen paperback books, the odd piece of jewellery. A handful of photographs. I found myself wondering whether she'd ever really had anything, or whether she'd mislaid her belongings as we'd travelled from place to place.'

Liv thought of the pink house by the sea. Stefan smiled. 'And now, if you've had enough to eat, Liv, we must make sure the witches don't return to the house tonight and mix up my papers again.'

'How?'

'We'll nail a holly bough over the chimney-piece. That'll do it. And then nothing bad will ever happen to us again.'

Katherine met Simon at Paddington station. Catching sight of him walking down the platform towards her, her heart gave a little jump of pleasure. Whatever their differences, he was her twin, her other half.

He hugged her, then stood back at arm's length. 'You look like a vamp from a Theda Bara film, Kitty.'

She was wearing pale foundation, chestnut-brown lipstick, and had circled her eyes with kohl. 'You look the same as ever, Simon.'

'Tweed jacket, shirt and tie,' he said self-mockingly. 'You know me. I like to keep up the bastions of tradition.'

She linked her arm through his as they walked to the tube. Queuing for tickets, she asked, 'How's Oxford?'

'Oh ... gilded spires ... punting on the river ... You don't know what you're missing.'

They stepped on to the escalator. 'I love it here,' she said firmly. 'I adore London.'

Heaps of litter gathered at the edges of the platform, and the train, when it arrived, was crowded; hemmed in by people.

Katherine saw the distaste on Simon's face. 'Rush-hour,' she mouthed, through the bodies that divided them.

He wore the same expression when she showed him her bedsit. For the first time she found herself seeing it as others might see it – the heaps of clothes on chair and bed, the unwashed dishes, the stale bread and sour milk – and felt slightly ashamed.

'It's a bit of a mess. I'd meant to clear up.'

She had intended to make omelettes for supper, but something hard and black was welded to the inside of the frying-pan, and there were, she discovered when she looked in the cupboard, no eggs. So they ate fish and chips sitting on a bench in Brompton Cemetery, then went to the White Hart to meet Toby and Stuart.

Toby had spread out on the table several sheets of paper. 'Felix has done some fabulous artwork,' he said. Figures curled and coiled around the bulbous lettering of the title page, which said, '*The Fight for a Free Scotland!*'

'Stuart's idea for our lead article,' Toby explained to Simon.

Simon snorted. Stuart leaned across the table towards him. 'You've something against the idea of freeing Scotland from the English yoke, then?'

Simon's pale eyes glittered. 'You make it sound like Stalin's Russia ... or Czechoslovakia after the tanks rolled in ...'

'There are similarities.'

'Go on.' A smile played around the corners of Simon's mouth. 'Name them.'

'The land's nae owned by the people but by bloated establishment plutocrats. The inhabitants of my city, Glasgow, live in the worst slums in Europe—'

'So you've escaped to England ... chosen to live among the enemy.'

Katherine, noticing the way Stuart's knuckles had whitened, told Simon to shut up, and waved to Felix, who was drying glasses behind the bar. 'Love the illustrations!'

He ducked under the bar to join them. 'Will you use them?'

'Usual rates,' said Toby.

'I thought,' drawled Simon, 'this was a *Red* sort of magazine.

Not capitalist. No sordid *money* transactions. "To each according to his needs," etcetera.'

'"Usual rates"' said Felix mildly, 'are a couple of pints and twenty Player's No. 6.'

Simon glanced dismissively at the leaves of paper on the table. 'How do you finance this rag?'

'Subscriptions,' said Stuart. 'Advertisements. Contributions from sympathizers.'

'Most of my allowance goes into it,' explained Toby.

'*Oh.*' Simon's eyes widened. 'You mean, Mummy and Daddy pay for this radical publication?'

'You wee shite . . .' Stuart rose from his seat, fists balled.

Felix stood between them. 'Not in my shift. If you want to pick a fight, Simon, then wait till tomorrow when I'm having a day off. Stuart, sit down or get out.'

Stuart grabbed his jacket and left the pub. Toby, to change the subject, said, 'Off on your hols, Felix?'

'I'm going home for a couple of days. It's my father's birthday.'

'I'll get some more drinks in.' Toby rummaged through his pockets for change.

When they were alone, Katherine said, '*Simon,*' and Simon said, 'I know. Sorry.'

'What's wrong?'

'Nothing's wrong. Why should anything be wrong?'

'Something's wrong. I know you. All that sloshing about in the amniotic fluid together.'

He grinned. Then he said, 'I think they're going to chuck me out of Oxford.'

She glanced at him sharply. 'I'll fail my exams, you see,' he said. 'Bound to. I haven't done a scrap of work.'

'You could do some. If they thought you were trying . . .'

'It'd be pointless. I hate medicine. Loathe it. All that flesh and blood. If I can't face the dead bodies, then how could I cope with the live ones?'

'You could read something else. One of the arts, perhaps.'

'And have to plough through endless dull old books? No

thank you.' He smiled, but his eyes were troubled. 'The galling thing is that I adore university life. The *social* life, that is.' He lit a cigarette, and said carelessly, 'Dad'll be disappointed. Yet another son who doesn't come up to scratch. It'll be down to Michael to fulfil the parental expectations.'

Katherine said, 'What about me? You're forgetting me, Simon,' but even as she spoke, she knew that daughters did not count, had never really counted with her father. Whatever she achieved, she would not, in her father's eyes, make up for the idle son, or the damaged son.

Chapter Four

The Corcorans lived in Norfolk, in a large, rambling, weather-boarded house called Wyatts, set among twisting lanes and gentle hills. Felix's grandfather, Silas Corcoran, had built the house at the end of the nineteenth century, with the profits from the wallpaper factory he had founded. Edward Lutyens had designed Wyatts, and Gertrude Jekyll had created the garden. Felix had been born in the large, light bedroom that looked out over the garden. He was familiar with all the winding passageways and many eccentric, irregularly shaped rooms. He knew the fields and meadows that surrounded the house; he had fished for tiddlers in the streams, and had built dens in the woods. With his father, he had visited the factory in Norwich, and had stared at the racks of hand-made blocks, and watched the paper rolling along conveyor belts, and gazed wide-eyed at the huge tubs of dye.

His mother had died in a car crash when Felix was nineteen. Seven months later his father, Bernard Corcoran, had married for a second time, to a woman twenty years younger than himself. Mia Heathcote had been thirty-five, tawny-haired, heedless and happy. In her company, Bernard had been able to forget his grief. If, as time passed, Bernard discovered, waking in the night, that grief still lingered in the shadows, then because he was a man of great loyalty and integrity, he kept the feeling well hidden.

Mia was a country girl. She must have ponies, she said, and she must have dogs. So now two horses and a donkey nuzzled the grass in the adjoining meadow, and half a dozen dogs, huge and untidy, sloped around the house. Under Mia's auspices, Wyatts was messier, verging on chaotic. Felix's younger sister, Rose, adored the horses and the dogs. They almost enabled her to tolerate Mia. Soon, a dozen hens, some Mandarin ducks and a fat Persian cat were added to the menagerie. But the realities of country life, with its casual, routine carnage – the fox hunts, the pheasant shoots and vermin traps – began to appal Rose as she entered her teenage years. It had seemed to Felix, returning from university at the end of each term, that Rose wept no less than she had during the dark days following their mother's death. It was just that her tears were now for fox cubs, or for veal calves sent off for slaughter. Rose's tears, and her unending, devouring need for him, filled Felix with such a mixture of pity and resentment and guilt that, shortly after graduation, he had left Wyatts for London, where he had now lived for over a year.

Rose was sitting on the gate, waiting for him, as he came round the bend in the road. She ran to meet him. 'Where have you *been*? I've been waiting *ages*.'

'The alternator's gone in the van, so I had to take the train.' He hugged her. 'What on earth are you wearing?' Rose's fragile fifteen-year-old frame was enveloped in a sack, to which feathers were attached.

'I'm trying to look like a crow, or a jackdaw. They keep shooting them, Felix. I found one last week, and its poor little wing was full of shot. This,' she fingered the sack, 'is my protest. I'm going to stand in the field when they go out shooting. Then I'll get in the newspapers. Or do you think,' she asked, with sudden doubt, 'that it looks silly?'

'I think it looks most impressive, but I'm afraid you'll end up full of buckshot.'

Rose hooked her arm through his as they walked down the drive. Half-way along, Felix paused, hearing a strange, high-pitched call. 'What on earth's that?'

'Peacocks. Mia bought them for Dad for his birthday. Aren't they lovely?' He caught a glimpse of blue-green iridescent feathers behind a rhododendron bush. 'Bryn and Maeve hate them, though, and snarl at them.' Bryn and Maeve were Mia's Irish wolfhounds.

'Where's Dad?'

'In the meadow, I think.' Rose shivered, clinging closer to Felix. It was a chilly day, and her skinny arms and legs were bare and mottled purple with cold.

'You look frozen, Rosy.'

'I don't mind.' She gazed up at him. 'It's so lovely to see you again, Felix. It's *ages* since you've been home.'

'I've been busy,' he said vaguely, guiltily.

'I missed you. Mia is so *awful*. I hate her.'

He sighed inwardly, but said aloud, 'Why don't you go and get changed while I see Dad? And then maybe I'll borrow his car and we'll go for a drive.'

'To the coast?'

'If you like.'

Rose's mournful eyes lit up, and she scurried off to the house. Felix found his father in the garden, putting up a fence.

'Damned birds were half-way to Burnham Market last night,' explained Bernard, as he hammered a stake into the ground. 'Ever tried getting two peacocks into an Austin Cambridge? Not easy, I can tell you. Thought I'd better make a pen.' He looked properly at Felix. 'Good to see you, old son. You look well.'

Felix thought his father looked tired. A week's work, and a night chasing peacocks round the countryside had taken their toll. But he said, 'I'm fine. Happy birthday, Dad.' He handed his father a parcel.

Bernard unwrapped the bottle of Scotch. 'Just the ticket. Thanks. We'll have a glass or two tonight.' He looked pleased. 'Have you seen Mia yet?'

'Just Rose.'

Bernard's smile faded. 'She's in trouble at school again, did she tell you?' Felix's heart sank. 'Perhaps you'd have a word. I've tried, but...' Since her mother's death, Rose had attended three different schools.

'What is it this time, Dad?'

Bernard stooped to select U-nails from a tin. 'The headmistress thinks she's a bad influence.'

'Dear God.' Felix felt angry. Rose could be tiresome, he knew, but surely anyone with any sense would perceive the unhappiness that lay beneath her clumsy acts of rebellion.

'She wants to leave school,' said Bernard.

'Permanently?'

'I've tried to dissuade her, of course, but you know what she's like when she gets a bee in her bonnet.'

'Yes.' Felix shrugged. 'I'll have a go, if you like, Dad.'

He'd ask her to wait for him after the seminar had ended, and she'd lean against the wall of the corridor, pretending to read a book until the other students dispersed. 'Well, Liv,' he'd say, 'where today?' And he'd drive her to the Trough of Bowland, where they'd watch the river crash between mossy banks, or they'd go to High Cross Moor and climb the Jubilee Tower and look down across the fell towards the coast, and the bright, distant sea. Sometimes, walking across the square or down the long, covered passageway that bisected the university, she'd look up and see him. He'd be far away, a little black matchstick man at first, but she'd know him instantly, and know, too, that he had seen her. In crowds, in the bustle of shops and lecture hall, they'd pick each other out in one quick glance. It was as though, she sometimes thought, an invisible rope joined them together: a single tug, and there he was, and the day would have sloughed off its everyday ordinariness. He was always on her mind, his image filling the blank lines of her lecture notes and the unturned pages of her books. Liv wondered sometimes whether that was what pulled them together: her concentration, her fascination. Whether her thoughts were his homing beacon.

She told Rachel about Stefan. 'I think I've got some awful disease. I can't eat properly, and I wake up very early in the morning, and I lie there, and I can almost see my heart beating.'

'Have you a temperature?'

'No.'

'Perhaps you're working too hard, Liv.'

'I'm hardly working at all. I go to the library and I'm supposed to be revising because I've exams next month, but I don't write a thing. I just think of Stefan.'

'Tell me about him.'

'He speaks three languages, and he's lived in lots and lots of different places. He's terribly clever, and he's writing a dissertation about how landscape influences myth. He never plans, he just gets up in the morning and thinks that it'd be a lovely day to go to the Lake District, so off he goes. He lives in a wonderful house on a hill, and he hasn't any of the things that ordinary people make such a fuss about, boring things like fridges and televisions, but he's planning to make an enormous vegetable garden – it's called a *potager*, I think – and he's going to keep hens and—' She broke off. 'Rachel? Rachel, are you there?'

'You're not *ill*, Liv,' said Rachel calmly. 'You've fallen in love, that's all.'

After she had put down the phone, she thought that Rachel must be mistaken. She couldn't be in love with Stefan because they had never even touched. Well, they had *touched*, of course – his hand had brushed against hers, opening the car door, or they had jostled against each other, walking along a busy corridor, little accidental meetings that had seemed charged with electricity – but he had never taken her hand, he had never put his arm around her waist. They had never kissed.

A sudden thought occurred to her, plunging her into despair. Perhaps she loved, and he didn't. Perhaps, once again, she was attracted to a man who did not return her affection. She felt desolate and mortified. Now, she took to walking with her hands stuffed resolutely in her jacket pockets, her gaze fixed on the ground so that she could not catch sight of him, so that she could not draw out of the ether a head of dark hair or the sleeve of a green corduroy jacket. She began to dread the next seminar, wondering whether she would look into his eyes and see pity, or amusement. Stefan had been kind to her, she thought, because he had felt sorry for her, tongue-tied at his seminars. Or he had been amused by her, the butter-fingered girl who had dropped her books. The intimacy, the spark that she had sensed between them had been, perhaps, of her own imagining.

But in the cultural studies department, she discovered a note stuck on Stefan's door: 'Stefan Galenski is unavailable at present. Please contact the department secretary for set work and for any urgent messages.' She knew that she would not contact the department secretary, because if she did, then what would she say? *I miss you. I want to be near you.*

She wrote letters to Katherine and Rachel, but spoke of Stefan only to Rachel. She could imagine only too well Katherine's dry, amused voice: 'In love again, Liv? That's *how* many times this year?' She herself saw, too clearly, the folly of it. She was in love with a man who was six years older than her, who was infinitely more travelled and experienced, and who was, to cap it all, one of her tutors, if only temporarily. In her letters to her mother she mentioned only her work, the weather, her desultory search for somewhere to live the following year. Rachel had been wrong, Liv told herself, she was not in love with Stefan Galenski, she was suffering from yet another humiliating and belated schoolgirl crush. Leaving home, she had not yet, it seemed, grown up.

A fortnight passed. She forced herself to concentrate on her work and to find lodgings for next term. She tramped around damp flats and dingy basements in Morecambe, trying not to think of a stone farmstead clinging to the curve of the hill. There seemed to be a hollow around her heart, or it was encased in ice perhaps, a thin, hard, colourless coating that quelled its natural rhythm? Everything seemed to link to him and to his absence: a song on the radio, or a fragment of poetry. The whir of a pheasant's wings as she walked through woodland brought back to her the time he had stopped the car to let a family of ducks cross the road. The bright emerald of a friend's cheesecloth skirt reminded her of the long, fringed scarf he flung around his neck.

The sun, shining into her room, woke her early one Saturday morning. She went to the launderette and shopped in the supermarket; back at her residence, she was making scrambled eggs for a late breakfast when the telephone rang. 'Liv, it's for you!' someone yelled. It galled her that her heart raced and her stomach squeezed.

She went to the phone. 'Yes?'

'Liv? It's Rachel.'

A small wash of disappointment, but she said, 'Rachel? Are you all right?'

'Yes.' A silence. 'I mean – no, not really.' Rachel's voice was oddly toneless, as though she had been crying.

'Rachel, what is it?'

'I must speak to you, Liv.'

Standing at the pay-phone, looking out of the window, Liv could see down to the grassy courtyard between the residence blocks. 'Go on, then.'

'Properly, I mean. I can't talk about it over the phone. I just can't. Something awful's happened.' The words were small, jerking gasps.

'Are you ill? The baby—'

'The baby's fine. It's not that.'

And then, looking out of the window, she saw him. Stefan was walking across the courtyard. Her heart seemed to stand still, and her hand clenched around the receiver.

'Liv?' Rachel's voice, small and weary, seemed to come from a long way away.

'Sorry, I didn't catch that, Rachel.' Stefan was heading towards the door of her residence block. He looked up and saw her, and she pressed her palm and forehead against the window, as if, reaching through the glass, she might touch him.

'I said, I must speak to you. There's something – could you come to Bellingford? Today?' Rachel's voice again, insistent and troubled. 'I know it's a lot to ask, but I really can't think what to do. I can't make my mind up about this by myself. I need you, Liv.'

'Is it Hector? Have you quarrelled?' From two storeys down, Stefan beckoned to her.

'No, no, it's not that. It's nothing to do with Hector. I haven't told Hector.'

'Rachel, I have to go—'

'But you'll come? You'll come today?'

She heard herself promise, and Rachel's gasp of relief. 'Thank you, Liv. Thank you. I'm sorry to be so silly.'

She put down the phone and ran downstairs. Out in the courtyard, she put up her hand to shade her eyes. From the sun, she thought. From Stefan.

He had been unwell, he explained to her, and then he had been obliged to attend a very dull conference. When he looked at her, when he said her name, she thought that it didn't matter why he liked her, and it didn't matter whether he felt sorry for her or was amused by her. He was here, so the ice around her heart dissolved, and she was complete again.

'I thought we could go to Glasson Dock,' he said. 'I thought we could catch crabs, and cook them for lunch.'

They had driven half-way to the estuary of the river Lune when she remembered Rachel. *I must speak to you. I need you, Liv. I'll go to Bellingford tomorrow, she thought. One day late won't matter. It won't matter at all.*

Glasson was perched on the edge of the estuary, looking out to a pale, flickering sea. Grey-brown water slid slowly between mudbanks slick with sun in the shallows of the estuary. Cranes stalked the docks like spiders. As the reeds on the banks shifted, they whispered, breaking the silence.

Always, looking back, the day seemed to glitter, to gleam, drenched in light. They walked across the lifting bridge, and looked out to the lighthouse and to the sea; they stripped off their sneakers and waded into the mud, looking for crabs. The mud sucked and pulled between their toes; when she almost lost her balance, he took her hand, steadying her. Her fingers remained linked through his, and her heart flew.

They didn't catch a single crab, so they bought sandwiches instead and lay on the grass, eating them. The sun dried them; mud caked and cracked on their flesh. 'Like the golem,' said Stefan sleepily. 'If we write the true name of God on a piece of paper and place it beneath our tongues, do you think that we'll be reborn?'

She told him about her father. The note on the kitchen table and, eight years later, the postcard. A picture of a beach in Tahiti. She had written to Finley Fairbrother, *poste restante*, at all the Tahitian towns she could find on the map. And to the British consul. There had been no reply. Fin had moved on.

Stefan's eyes were closed, one outflung arm cushioning his head. 'You're not angry with him? You don't hate him?'

'Hate him? Why should I hate him?'

'For abandoning you.'

'Mum said he was always a traveller. You can't change what you are, can you?'

He rolled on to his side, propping himself on his elbow, looking at her. 'If you'd been mine,' he said, 'I'd never have let you go.'

They walked up to the headland. He told her about his stepfathers. The one who had ignored him, the one who had shut him in a dark room, the one who had beaten him. He pulled down the collar of his shirt and showed her the faint pale mark where the buckle of the belt had caught him. She wanted to kiss away the scar. She imagined him, a dark, intense child, rattling the locked door of his prison.

At the end of the day, leaving him, walking back to her room late that evening, the familiar landscape seemed to have altered, the tangle of passageways and courtyards made strange by the remembered brightness of the day. Once or twice she took a wrong turning, and had to catch herself, to remind herself of her proper direction. When she heard footsteps, she glanced back, half expecting to see him. But a stranger hurried past her, shoulders hunched, his tread echoing against the high concrete ceiling of the walkway. She was aware of an odd sense of relief, a small clawing back of safety. She acknowledged that, with Stefan, she sometimes felt as though she were standing at the edge of the high fell, looking down, about to fall, to be consumed. She needed to remember who she was, what she was.

Tonight, the privacy of her single room seemed like a sanctuary. Someone had slid a note under her door. Liv opened it. There was a scribbled message. *Your mum phoned. She said to tell you that Rachel has had a baby girl, and that they're both well.*

Liv sat down on the edge of the bed. She was shaking. She thought, *Rachel*, and then, But it wasn't supposed to come for another three weeks. She thought of phoning Bellingford, or the Wybornes at Fernhill. She glanced at her watch, and saw that it was almost midnight. She would ring Hector tomorrow. Or she would catch the first train in the morning, and go to the hospital, and see Rachel and the baby, and explain why she had not visited today. Fragments of that odd, disturbing phone-call repeated themselves over and over in her mind, interspersed with scenes from the day. *Something awful has happened.* The reeds shifting slowly on the riverbank. *It's not the baby, Liv.* Lying on the grass beside Stefan, she had pressed the heels of her hands against her eyes to blot out the hot, pale sun . . .

She curled up in bed, wrapping the blankets around herself, drifting in and out of sleep. She was climbing a hill with Stefan, but when she looked down she saw that the grass was made of glass: translucent, green, and crystalline. She was in a small, windowless house; she knew that there was a baby hidden somewhere, but though she searched for it, she could not find it. She could hear the infant's cries through the stone.

The distant sound of the telephone woke her at nine o'clock. She lay in bed for a while, waiting for someone else to answer it, or for the caller to give up, but when the ringing persisted she climbed out of bed, pulled on her dressing-gown, and ran downstairs. The blue skies of the previous day had been replaced by steel-grey clouds that hung low on the horizon.

She picked up the receiver. She could not at first make out what Thea was saying because she was crying. The words tumbled over each other, falling, tangled, slippery with tears.

Then Thea said, 'Liv, the most terrible thing. I can hardly believe it. I am so sorry to have to tell you this. But Rachel is dead, my darling. Poor little Rachel is dead.'

The post-mortem showed that Rachel had died of an embolism. Liv looked the word up in the library. *A blood clot in the lung. A rare complication of childbirth.*

After a speedy four-hour labour, Rachel had given birth to a healthy daughter. Then, during the night, while she was resting, a bundle of cells had clumped together in her bloodstream, and had travelled through her veins to her lungs. It seemed to Liv so easy, so possible. Every now and then she would look down at herself, and wonder how her heart kept beating, how her lungs maintained their unthinking rise and fall.

The funeral was held at Fernhill. Diana, said Thea, had insisted that Rachel be buried at St Stephen's, rather than in Northumberland. Liv caught the train to Cambridge, and Thea met her at the railway station. She embraced her daughter, holding her for a very long time, as though Liv, too, might in the blink of an eyelid just vanish. At home, they were careful with each other, as if they were aware for the first time of their fragility, their impermanence.

The funeral service – the sombre clothes of the mourners, and the muted voices and solemn faces – seemed to Liv to be incongruous, to have nothing to do with bright, happy Rachel. Standing in the church where Rachel had been married only ten months before, she dug her nails into her palms, and tried to think of something ordinary, something dull, something distracting. If she thought of Rachel she would cry, and no one else was crying. Or not one of the three people closest to Rachel, and the entire congregation seemed impelled to take their lead from them. Henry Wyborne swayed slightly, out of rhythm with the hymn, as though the loss of his daughter had cast him rudderless and adrift on a stormy sea. Diana, white-faced and red-eyed, sang out the phrases with savage clarity. And Hector . . . Liv could hardly bear to look at Hector. The expression in his eyes frightened her.

Yet her own thoughts allowed her no refuge. Rachel's voice echoed: *I have to talk to you, Liv. Something awful's happened.* Her reply rang too clearly in her ears, making promises she had broken.

Later, in the churchyard, she drew Katherine aside.

'Rachel phoned me the day before she died.' She had to force the words out, a shameful confession.

'Yes.' Katherine lit a cigarette. 'Me, too.'

Liv's head jerked up. 'What did she say?'

Katherine's hands trembled, flicking the lighter. 'I didn't take the call, Felix did. I was out. But she wanted me to visit. She said she needed to talk to me.' She glanced at the mourners, now drifting slowly away from the grave. 'I can't bear this. I'm going.'

She walked out of the churchyard. Liv followed after her, down the narrow lane that led away from the village to the fields. The air was thick with the scent of hawthorn, and the hedgerows were frilled with Queen Anne's lace.

Liv asked the question that had haunted her for the past week. 'Did Rachel tell you what she wanted to talk to you about?'

Katherine's eyes were bleak. 'Felix said she wouldn't tell him. What did she say to you?'

'Much the same. That she needed to talk to me.'

'Surely you asked her?'

'Of course. And she said something awful had happened.'

'What?'

'That's the thing. I don't know. She wouldn't tell me over the phone. She wanted me to come to Bellingford.' They had reached the gate that barred the entrance to the field. 'I said I'd come. I said I'd come that day.' Liv's guilt was raw and painful. 'Only I didn't. I promised I'd go to Bellingford, and then I didn't. I thought it would be all right if I left it a day. But it wasn't, was it?'

Far below them, the dew-pond, caught in the palm of the valley, mirrored the cloudless sky.

'Rachel was upset, Katherine,' she said flatly. 'No – she was *frightened*.'

'The baby – she was going into labour.'

'She said it wasn't the baby. I asked her about the baby. The baby hadn't started then.'

'Then – Hector. Perhaps they'd quarrelled.'

'She said it was nothing to do with the baby, and nothing to do with Hector. So what on earth had happened? Why was she so distraught?'

Katherine was silent for a moment, and then she said, 'I didn't get Rachel's message until after I'd found out she was dead. That was the most awful thing.' Her fleeting smile did not touch her eyes. 'Or one of the many most awful things – it's so hard to choose, isn't it? I was out all night – I didn't get home till midday on Sunday, and I found a message from Mrs Mandeville under my door, telling me to phone home. Mum told me about Rachel. And then Felix came back from the pub. When he told me about Rachel's phone-call, I was so relieved. I thought Mum had made a mistake. How could Rachel be dead if she wanted me to go and see her? I kept making Felix tell me what she'd said, over and over again. I really thought that Mum had made a mistake.' Katherine flicked her cigarette stub to the grass, and ground it with her heel. 'And then he made me drink a glass of brandy, and he phoned Mum himself, and then I believed it.' She closed her eyes. Her voice was almost inaudible. 'Only I don't believe it, do you, Liv? I *can't* believe it.'

The pond had blurred, shifting through her tears. Liv whispered, 'Have you spoken to Hector?'

'Not yet. I will, of course, but, dear God, what shall I *say*?'

'The baby ... did she see the baby?'

'Yes. Mum said. Just once. She held her for a few moments. She was very tired.' Katherine's hands clenched. 'It's the waste of it I can't bear. The pointlessness. She was *nineteen*.' Her voice trembled with anger. 'She gave her life for them – for her husband and child. But that's what women are supposed to do, aren't they? To sacrifice their lives for their families.' She began to walk very fast up the hill, back to the village.

After a lunch that no one wanted to eat, when the first of the mourners were taking their leave, Liv found Hector in the front garden of the Wybornes' house. She wondered whether he was remembering the first time he had seen Rachel, dressed in silver, through the wrought-iron curlicues of the gate.

She saw him light another cigarette from the butt of the last, then look down at his hands, as though surprised by what they were doing. 'I'd given up,' he said suddenly. 'Because of the baby.'

She bit her lip. 'If there's anything I can do . . .' she muttered, but the words seemed to fall to the ground unnoticed, like the petals tumbling from the early roses.

Briefly, she told him about Rachel's phone-call. She wasn't sure whether he was listening. He seemed shuttered inside his own grief. She said, 'Do you know why she phoned me, Hector?' but he just shook his head, his eyes empty of everything except desolation.

Then he said, 'If I'd been at home – I should never have left her on her own.'

'You'd gone away?'

'I had to go to London on business. The baby wasn't due for another three weeks, so we thought it'd be all right. But I shouldn't have gone, should I?' He took a deep, shuddering breath. 'When I got back to Bellingford on Saturday, Rachel was in labour. I took her to the hospital. They said she was all right. They were a bit shirty, actually, said we could have waited. I thought they were going to send us home again. But the baby came quicker than they expected.' Closing his eyes, he rubbed his forehead with the tips of his fingers, and whispered once more, 'I shouldn't have left her on her own.'

She stroked his shoulder. His eyes were closed. 'I keep thinking,' he muttered, 'that perhaps the house . . . It was always so cold, you see – she used to wear her coat indoors sometimes. Perhaps the cold weakened her. And the building work, the noise and the dust, it can't have been good for her, can it? Or perhaps she had a fall – the place was cluttered with paint tins and things. She might have tripped, mightn't she, and not told me because she didn't want to worry me? Dear God,' his fists clenched, 'I wish I'd never taken her there, Liv. I wish I'd never taken her there.'

'Hector—'

He did not seem to hear her. 'I can't bear the house now,' he said. 'I used to love it, but now I hate it. Last week – those few days when I was on my own...' He took off his glasses and absently rubbed at the lenses with his handkerchief. Freed of their covering, his anguished eyes were naked and defenceless.

'I kept thinking I heard her. Kept thinking I'd turn a corner and see her. I'd wake in the night and know that she was beside me. I found myself wishing I'd never met her. Can you understand that, Liv? If I'd never met her then she'd still be alive.'

She put her arms around him. 'Hector,' she said gently, 'Rachel loved you. She wanted to be with you. I'd never seen her so happy as she was when she married you. And the baby – she was overjoyed about the baby. I know that what's happened is so utterly awful and ghastly, but there is the baby. You do have your daughter, Hector.'

He pulled away from her, and began to walk back to the house. Glancing fleetingly back over his shoulder at her, he said, 'The Wybornes are to bring up the baby. Didn't you know, Liv?'

Thea returned to Fernhill Grange the following afternoon. The housekeeper showed her into the drawing room. Henry Wyborne was standing at the windows, his hands clasped behind his back.

'I hope you'll forgive me for intruding, Henry.'

'Diana's asleep, Thea. She's taken a pill.'

'Then I'll speak to you, if I may.' Thea took a deep breath.

'Liv told me that you and Diana intend to bring up Rachel's child. That's not true, is it, Henry? Liv's mistaken, isn't she?'

'No mistake. Alice will live here.'

'Alice?'

'Rachel's favourite book, when she was a little girl, was *Alice in Wonderland*.' Henry looked away. 'Diana wanted to call her Rachel, but I said she should have a new name, a name of her own. So she's Alice Rachel.'

'Henry, you can't let Diana do this. It's not right. *Hector*—'

'Has given his consent.' Henry turned to face her. 'He's gone back to Northumberland.'

Thea felt winded. She sat down on one of the plush pink armchairs and struggled to collect her thoughts. She had never particularly liked Henry Wyborne, perceiving behind his charm and his handsome, imposing stature the ruthless ambition of a man who would have his own way, whatever the cost. She tolerated him for Diana's sake, but she had never liked him. Now she said levelly, 'Without his daughter?'

Henry did not reply, but his expression told her everything. Thea knotted her fingers together. 'Hector is in no fit state to take such an important decision,' she said. 'You must see that, Henry. If Hector has consented to this, then it's because he is mad with grief.'

'And Diana? And I?' His voice was harsh. 'Are we not wounded too?'

She said gently, 'Of course you are, Henry. I didn't mean to imply that your loss isn't also terrible. But surely you see that Hector *needs* the child. That without her he has nothing.'

He said again, 'And Diana?'

'Diana has you, Henry. You at least have each other. You've always had a good marriage.'

He turned away then and went to the cabinet. Whisky splashed into a glass, and over the mahogany surface of the cabinet on to the carpet. She guessed from his shaking hands and florid complexion that he was drunk, had been drunk, in all probability, for days.

'Thea...?' he said, indicating the bottle, but she shook her head. He came to sit beside her. He whispered, 'She blames him, Thea.'

'Diana blames Hector for Rachel's death?' Thea was appalled. 'Surely not.'

'She hates him. Can't stand to be in the same room as him. Says if he hadn't insisted on marrying her ... We tried to stop it, you know ...' Henry swallowed a large mouthful of Scotch. 'I tried to reason with her, but ...' When he looked up at Thea, she saw that there were tears in his eyes. 'What right have I to stop her taking what consolation she can?'

She thought, It will destroy Hector, but said nothing, because Henry Wyborne was weeping the choked, awkward tears of a man unused to displays of emotion. She took the glass out of his hands, and put her arms around him, and, when he apologized, said, 'Don't be ridiculous, Henry. Rachel was a dear, beautiful girl. We all loved her. None of us can begin to make sense of what has happened.'

He wiped his eyes and blew his nose. 'I'd always thought of myself as a lucky man.' He blinked. 'And one begins to believe that one is entitled to good luck. That one has earned it. When you first came here, Thea – when Fin left you – I suppose it made me think less of you. You'd chosen unwisely, I thought, you'd made your own bad fortune. What I had – Diana and Rachel, my work, this house – I felt that I somehow deserved.' He closed his eyes very tightly for a moment. 'But I didn't, did I? I was just lucky, for a while. I didn't deserve it at all.'

She said, 'But Hector ...'

Henry rose from the sofa. He walked back to the window. 'Hector's a single man now. No idea how to bring up an infant. Diana'll be good to the poor little thing, you know that, Thea. She'll love her. It might all be for the best, mightn't it?'

She whispered, 'Henry, this is *wrong*,' but he did not reply, and after a while she rose and left the room. She found herself almost running down the drive, as if to escape the pall of grief and bitterness that hung over the house.

She was walking down the hill when a car drew up beside her. Richard Thorneycroft wound down the driver's window.

'Can I give you a lift? You'll be soaked.'

She hadn't noticed that it was raining. She climbed into the passenger seat. He said awkwardly, 'Dreadful business – the Wyborne girl, I mean.'

'Yes,' said Thea. 'Dreadful.'

He let in the clutch. Rain beat against the windscreen. 'And funerals . . .' he said. 'So unutterably bloody.'

'They're so *cumulative*,' said Thea savagely. 'They always remind you of every other damned funeral.'

'Of course. Your husband.'

She knew that he was making an effort, but the anger and impotence she had felt while talking to Henry Wyborne persisted, and she said coldly, 'My husband isn't dead.'

'I assumed . . .'

'I know. Everyone *assumes*.'

He slowed as they neared the cottage. 'Would you like a drink?'

Her surprise at the unprecedented invitation was muted by the exhaustion engendered by the events of the week. She realized both that she was desperate for a drink, and that she could not yet face the bewilderment and desolation in her daughter's eyes. So she said, 'Yes. Yes, Richard, I'd like a drink. I'd like one very much.'

Liv went back to Lancaster. The essays she had not yet written, the revision she had not yet done testified to her week's absence. She sat at her desk, a book of poetry open in front of her, staring down at the page, but seeing only Rachel's baby, asleep in her crib at Fernhill Grange. She had touched her tiny crumpled cheek, and it had felt like velvet.

She closed the book and left the room, and walked across the campus to the cultural studies department. Standing outside Stefan's office, she thought, he won't be here, he'll be at Holm

Edge. When she rapped on the door with her knuckles, it sounded hollow. Walking back down the corridor, her footsteps echoed.

At the seminar on Wednesday, Stefan did not look up when she came into the room but went on correcting papers. He had not seen her, she thought. She contributed nothing to the discussion; she had not prepared any notes, she could not remember which notes it was that she was supposed to have prepared. At the end of the hour, packing her things into her Greek bag, her fingers fumbled, clumsy with nerves and tiredness. She saw that they had already surrounded him, his acolytes: Andy with his gold-rimmed glasses, Gillian with her crocheted beret. She saw how his face lit up when they spoke to him, and how his gestures and movement acquired their now-familiar expansiveness. She paused, waiting, her hands clutching her bag.

'Olivia. A word, please.'

The coldness of his voice shocked her. The ball of tension that had wedged itself beneath her ribs since Thea's phone-call tightened into a hard lump.

When the others had gone, he closed the door. 'You missed last week's seminar.'

Still no affection in his voice; she wondered whether she had imagined that day at Glasson Dock, or whether she had misinterpreted it, seeing love where there had been only acquaintance.

'I was busy,' she whispered.

'Students are supposed to notify their tutors when they can't attend a seminar.' Stefan had perched on the edge of the desk. His fingertips drummed against the wooden surface. 'Exams begin in two weeks' time. Are you so confident of your success that you feel able to pick and choose which classes to attend?'

His words dug into her, chipping away at recollections she had treasured: the man who had lain beside her on the grass and said, *If you'd been mine I'd never have let you go*.

'I couldn't – I had to go home—' She heard her own wail of despair.

His brows contracted. 'Family problems?' She nodded.

'Tell me.'

It was hard to get the words out. The words made it real. 'One of my friends – Rachel, my best friend – has died.'

His tense, taut body seemed to relax. 'I'm sorry,' he said.

'So you see,' she said bitterly, 'it wasn't that I didn't want to come.'

'My deplorable vanity.' The corners of his mouth curled. 'I thought we were friends, you see. And then . . . when you didn't turn up . . .'

She felt as though she were made of glass. Another cold wind, a small push, and she would shatter. She closed her eyes, and felt herself sway slightly.

'Here, sit down,' he said. He helped her into a chair. 'Stay there. I'll get you a drink of water.' His voice seemed to come from a long way away.

She pressed her knuckles against her face, and slowly the dizziness receded. He gave her the glass, and she opened her eyes. He was crouching in front of her, watching her. His fingertips stroked her face. She was aware of a drowning sense of relief. She had not been mistaken: he did love her. She heard him say gently, 'Would you like me to take you back to your room on campus? Or would you prefer to go to Holm Edge?'

She thought of her room. The books she had not read, the notes she had not revised. The photographs on the pinboard: herself, Katherine and Rachel, on Rachel's wedding-day. Her father's postcard from Tahiti. The dead friend, the absent father.

'Take me to Holm Edge, Stefan,' she whispered. 'Please take me to Holm Edge.'

He made her toast and tea, and afterwards they went for a walk. The wind buffeted her and she stumbled on the uneven ground, and Stefan held out his arm to her and she threaded her hand around it. Afterwards, back at the house, he built a log fire in the grate. He sat in the armchair, she at his feet, her back against his shins. His fingers played with her hair.

'Tell me about her,' he said. 'Tell me about Rachel.'

So she told him how, many years ago, Rachel had made a strange place a home. And how the three of them had knotted together, making something more than their sum. *Blood sisters.* The pyre, and the sunlight through the willows. And how, less than a year ago, they had parted, Katherine to London, and Rachel to Hector and Northumberland. And about the baby, and the tragedy of Rachel's sudden death.

'Rachel phoned me last weekend,' she said. 'Do you remember, Stefan, when you called at my residence? I was on the phone, talking to Rachel. She was upset – something had frightened her. She asked me to go to see her that day, and I said I would. But I didn't.'

'Why not?'

'Because of you.' Her voice was raw. 'Because I wanted to be with you.'

His hand, stroking her wind-tangled hair, paused. Now she felt neither embarrassment nor shame, only, somewhere in the pit of her stomach, a mixture of longing and relief.

'Come here,' he said. 'I want to hold you.'

She sat on his lap. When his arms encircled her, she felt safe and protected.

He said, 'Why did you want to be with me?'

'Because I love you.' Again, such an unexpectedly easy confession.

'You see,' he said, 'I wasn't sure.'

She turned to look at him. 'How could you not know? How could you not be sure? It must be written on my face – on everything I do . . .'

'Hush,' he said softly, drawing her down, so that her head nestled on his shoulder. She could feel the steady rise and fall of his breathing.

'When you didn't turn up for my class,' he said, 'I thought I must have been mistaken. I thought that you were like the others – plenty of the female students think that being seen with a tutor is a feather in their cap. Something to boast about to their friends. A sort of status symbol.'

'It wasn't like that at all.'

'I know, Liv.' She felt his lips press against the top of her head. 'I know that now.'

There was a silence. Curled in his arms, she could almost have slept. But instead she said, 'When I saw you, I forgot about Rachel. I thought it would be all right because I could go to her the next day. But it wasn't all right, was it? There wasn't a next day for Rachel.'

'Nothing you could have done would have made any difference. It wasn't your fault, Liv.'

'But it *feels* as though it is! I let her down, you see. And I keep wondering . . .'

'What?'

'Why she phoned. What had happened. Whether I could have made a difference. That's the thing, Stefan.' Her voice shook. 'I'm left with this enormous, terrible question I'll probably never have an answer for. I keep going over and over it in my head. She wasn't upset about the baby, and she wasn't upset about Hector. I wondered whether it was the house – it's a big, old place – whether she'd thought she'd seen something, heard something. But that doesn't make sense, does it? She'd have told me over the phone, wouldn't she? And then I thought that perhaps it was money – they hadn't much, and they were doing a lot of work on the house, so maybe they weren't managing and she was too ashamed to admit it. But that's not right, either. The Wybornes are wealthy – Rachel's father would have helped them if things had been difficult.'

He kissed her, quietening her. Her forehead, cheek, mouth. She pulled away, looking carefully at him.

'The others . . . Gillian . . . and that girl with the Afghan coat?'

'Are my students. Nothing more.' He cupped her face between his hands, turning her towards him. 'Never anything more. I love you, you see, Olivia. No one else.'

'But – *me*. *Why?*'

He smiled. 'Such a cliché, isn't it, to know the very first time? To know there's going to be one and no other.'

Again, she closed her eyes. His lips brushed against her eyelids, and he ran the back of his hand against her cheek, down to the hollow of her neck. Her body seemed to waken, to come alive at his touch. She heard him whisper:

> *'O! when mine eyes did see Olivia first*
> *Methought she purg'd the air of pestilence.*
> *That instant was I turned into a hart,*
> *And my desires, like fell and cruel hounds,*
> *E'er since pursued me.'*

The moment hung, paused in the balance. She could hear, in the silence, the whisper of the wind.

Then he said, 'Marry me, Olivia.'

PART TWO

The Holly Tree

1969–1974

Chapter Five

The wholefood co-operative that Felix worked for closed down at the beginning of September. 'Bloody silly idea, if you ask me,' said Stuart. 'Expecting people to eat rabbit food.'

They were in the public bar of the White Hart, hunched over pints. It was a grey, gloomy evening, as though the year had already given up on summer.

Felix asked, 'How's the magazine?'

'Oh. Fine,' said Toby vaguely. 'I think we're bumping along the bottom. They always say it takes a year to turn a business round, don't they? I'm sure we're through the worst.' Toby's bitten fingernails and chain-smoking belied his optimism. He looked around. 'Anyone seen Katherine? I was hoping she'd be here tonight. I was going to ask her to do the article on Nancy's commune.'

'Commune?' asked Felix.

'Somewhere in the sticks,' explained Toby. 'A friend of mine – nice woman – has started up a place. I said we'd do a piece. Katherine's idea, actually. She thought we should broaden the appeal of the magazine, have some human-interest stories. Nancy's looking for people to live there. Like-minded people.' He peered into his glass, which was empty. 'My round, isn't it?' He went to the bar.

'Communes are your sort of thing, aren't they, Felix?' Stuart stubbed out his cigarette.

'I admire anyone who doesn't make money the be-all and end-all of everything.' He was rather drunk, Felix thought, or he would not, he hoped, have sounded so pompous.

'You wouldn't *live* in a place like that, though.'

Stuart's cynicism irritated him. 'I'd give it a go.'

'Lots of sex,' Toby, returning, reminded Stuart. 'These places are all open relationships, aren't they? You can sleep with anyone you like.' He put the drinks on the table. 'Tell you what, you wouldn't write the piece for me, would you, Felix?'

'You couldn't stand it,' Stuart taunted. 'You'd be begging to be allowed back to civilization after a day.'

'Rubbish.'

'A bet, then,' said Stuart. 'A fiver on it. A fiver says you wouldn't last a week.'

'Done,' said Felix.

Waking the next morning with a sore head and a dry mouth, Felix did not at first recall the previous evening's conversation. Then he caught sight of the slip of paper beneath his door. He picked it up. He read, 'Felix, my friend's name is Nancy Barnes. The commune's address is The Old Rectory, Great Dransfield, Berkshire. Yours, Toby.'

The van had given up the ghost, so Felix hitch-hiked. A lorry gave him a lift as far as Newbury, and then he hitched rides in cars and vans.

He arrived at Great Dransfield in the mid-afternoon. The Old Rectory lay on the outskirts of the small, straggling village. The building was large and imposing – Victorian, he guessed. Into the greyish stone were set windows of a rather fanciful Gothic design. Virginia creeper snaked up the wall, its bright leaves offsetting the house's sombre appearance. Felix knocked at the front door.

There was no reply, so he followed the path that led round the side of the house. Clematis trailed overhead, forming an arched roof, and roses and buddleias, dusty and tired-looking so late in the season, encroached on it. Pushing open a rickety gate, moving aside the last few straggling branches, Felix stood for a while, looking out.

The garden went on for miles. Acres of lawn, then vegetable patches and orchards, and then a stream and a lake and a wood.

Sunlight glinted on distant water, and red apples dotted the boughs of the trees like rubies. Two children played beside the margins of the lake, their bare feet coated with chocolate-brown mud. A woman wearing a long skirt and a straw hat was tending the vegetable patch. Seeing Felix, she straightened, put down her hoe and walked towards him.

'Can I help you?'

'I'm looking for Nancy Barnes.'

'That's me.'

She was in her mid-thirties, he guessed. Tall and well built, her red, weatherbeaten face was innocent of makeup. She wore her brown hair in a plait, and her smile was pleasant and friendly.

'My name's Felix Corcoran,' he explained. 'I'm a friend of Toby Walsh's.'

'Toby said he'd send someone.' Nancy beamed at him. 'It's so good of you to come. So good of you to take an interest.'

He felt slightly ashamed, remembering the drunken bet in the pub. 'Toby thought you mightn't mind if I stayed a few days.'

'Of course. Stay as long as you like. How did you get here?'

'Hitching and walking.'

'You must be thirsty. I'll get you a drink, and then, if you like, I'll show you round.'

Felix followed Nancy to the kitchen. The herbal tea was dark and bitter, but the homemade bread and goats' cheese was delicious. He asked her about the house.

'My father left it to me. He bought it from the Church — modern vicars don't want to live in these draughty old places. It's far too big for one person, so I thought it would be a good idea to share it with others.'

'You're not married?' He remembered the urchins playing beside the stream. 'I thought . . . the children?'

'India and Justin are Claire's children. Claire's an old school-friend of mine. Her marriage broke up six months ago, and she had nowhere to go. That gave me the idea, really.'

'Of running a commune?'

'I prefer to call it a community.' Nancy's gentle brown eyes

111

focused on Felix. '*Commune* can sound a little ... half-baked, don't you think? The sort of thing smart city people make fun of.'

He had to look away, embarrassed, and take another mouthful of tea. 'How many people are staying here?'

'Well, there's Claire and the children, that's three. And Martin – he was a teacher at a prep school, but I think the boys gave him rather a hard time, so now he lives here. And there's Bryony and Lawrence and their baby. And Saffron and her friends.' She laughed. 'That sounds rather vague, I know, but Saffron has a great many friends. So,' she counted up on her fingers, 'there are nine or ten of us here most of the time.'

'And you're looking for more?'

'There are twelve bedrooms, so we could easily take another three or four. I believe the community will have to grow a little before it's truly self-sufficient.'

'Is that what you're aiming for? Self-sufficiency?'

'As far as possible.' She put down her cup. 'Come on, Felix, I'll show you round.'

They left the kitchen, climbing up the narrow basement stairs. 'We need to have a variety of skills,' Nancy explained, 'then everyone has something to offer, which is good both for the community and for the individual. It's so important for everyone to have a part to play. We share everything, all the work and our possessions. So much of what's wrong with society is caused by fear and insecurity, don't you think, Felix? People are afraid of losing what they've got, and that makes them greedy and selfish.' She smiled. 'Well, that's enough of the lecture. We'll start at the top and work down, shall we?'

More stairs. Nancy went on, 'Martin's a wonderful carpenter. And Claire does marvels in the garden, and helps me with the goats and hens. Bryony's very taken up with Zak, of course, but she does marvellous batik when she has the time. And Lawrence manages to keep my old van going. And everyone cooks and cleans, of course. Even the children help out – collecting eggs, picking peas, useful little tasks.'

He remembered the other name. 'And Saffron?'

They were standing at a large window that looked out over the garden. Nancy looked down. 'Ah, Saffron,' she said. 'Saffron doesn't *do* anything in particular.'

He followed her gaze. He saw the girl wandering through the orchard. She was wearing a long, indigo dress, and her feet were bare. Her fair, uncovered hair gleamed in the sun.

'Saffron just *is*,' said Nancy, softly.

Suppertime was bedlam. Felix was used to Wyatts, and the dogs barking and Rose sulking and Mia clanking saucepans and stirring pots, but this was in a different league. The children shouted and the baby howled and all the adults (except Martin, who didn't say a word) talked over the din. If the baby yelled louder, they talked louder. Several different arguments raged simultaneously.

He studied them as he ate. Martin was, Felix guessed, in his early forties. His greying hair framed a gaunt, intelligent face. Lawrence was much younger, twenty-five or so, his good looks marred by a sulky turn to the corners of his mouth. Bryony, his wife, sat beside him, the baby at her breast. There were dark circles around her eyes, and she ate furtively and quickly, echoing the colicky spasms of the suckling infant. Justin and India, Claire's children, were eight and nine respectively. Both had long, golden hair. India wore an embroidered blouse, far too large for her, and faded cotton shorts, but Justin was naked except for a daubing of mud. 'It's so important,' said Claire, to Nancy's tactful enquiry as to whether Justin might not feel cold, 'not to stunt a child's imagination. Justin's an Ancient Briton today, aren't you, darling?'

There was an empty seat at the table. The fair-haired girl, Saffron, whom Felix had glimpsed from the window, was absent. But when the meal was almost over, he looked up, and there she was, standing at the foot of the stairs.

'I've put some supper aside for you, Saffron,' said Nancy.

'I'm not hungry.' She was still wearing the indigo dress. Its hem, Felix noticed, was muddy and frayed.

'You must eat something – you're too thin – you'll fall ill again.'

'Just a little, then.'

Nancy heaped food on a plate. Saffron picked at it, walking slowly round the table. She noticed Felix. 'A new recruit?'

'Just a temporary one,' he said. Close to, he noticed that her eyes were not blue, as he had expected, but grey and fringed with thick, sooty lashes. Pale, feathery eyebrows arched over them, and her narrow, curving mouth was delicately drawn.

'This is Felix Corcoran. Felix, meet Saffron Williams. Felix is writing a piece on the community for Toby Walsh's magazine,' explained Nancy.

'So we'll be famous,' said Saffron calmly.

'*Frodo's Finger*,' said Felix, 'hasn't exactly a countrywide circulation.'

'Has Nancy showed you round?'

'Just the house,' said Nancy.

'Would you like to see the garden?'

'Your supper—' Nancy said, but Saffron was already half-way up the stairs.

Felix followed her. They had reached the back door when Saffron said confidingly, 'I make sure I'm late for supper. It puts me off my food to hear Bryony talking about her sore nipples, and to see those awful children eating like pigs.' She opened the french windows and they went out on to the terrace, on which stood a weaving loom, a large bowl full of blue dye in which hanks of wool were soaking, and a great many toys.

'Come on,' she said.

They walked through the orchard. The evening air was still and warm, and heavy with the scent of ripe apples and gone-to-seed grass. Felix ducked beneath drooping boughs; stinging nettles and the seedheads of dandelions caught at his ankles.

'This is my favourite place,' said Saffron softly.

Felix looked out at the lake. Reeds clustered around the banks like thin, pale pennants, and glittering dragonflies darted on the smooth water. Overhead, house martins performed their breathtaking aerial acrobatics. The sun was dipping down through the sky, a white-gold disc, and the lake flared, fleetingly catching fire.

He heard her say, 'What do you think?'

He thought that her long hair was the colour of the moonlight, and that her eyes had the fathomless depth of the lake. But he only said, 'It's beautiful. So beautiful,' and then he fell silent.

In the mornings, the watery sun streaming through the small, square windows of the cottage woke Liv. Tiptoeing downstairs to the bathroom, she'd wince as her bare feet touched the cold flags. Then she'd climb back into bed, and curl up beside Stefan, warming herself with his body. And her touch would rouse him, and they would make love.

By the end of June, Liv had known that she had failed her exams. It still frightened her to remember how she had stared at the question papers, her mind blank, the words fragmenting, refusing to form into sentences. 'At least I'm consistent,' she had said bitterly, when she had seen the uniformly disastrous results on the noticeboard.

She had also known that she was pregnant. They had not been careful; they had not made the slightest attempt to be careful. Once again, Stefan had asked her to marry him. This time, she did not suggest they wait, and there was not that sudden impulse to caution that had seized her at his first proposal. She flung her arms around him, loving the warmth and strength of his body, and whispered, 'Yes, Stefan. Yes.'

Marriage would allow her to wrest something from the wreckage of the previous year. Motherhood would mark her out as an adult, a woman. They were married by special licence with a couple of passers-by their only witnesses. Liv wrote to Thea, who caught the first train to Lancaster.

Liv took Thea to Holm Edge, and introduced her to Stefan. The weekend was civilized and difficult. She had thought that once Thea and Stefan met each other, then everything would be all right. How could they not like each other, these two people she loved most in the world? She said as much to Thea, on the day she caught the train back south.

'It's not that I don't like him, Liv.' Thea looked troubled.

'What, then?'

Thea sighed. 'Stefan's handsome and intelligent and charming. And it's plain that he loves you. It's just that—'

'What, Mum?' Liv could feel her lower lip beginning to stick out in a mulish way, as though she were fourteen.

'It's just that you've thrown so much away.' Thea looked sad, rather than angry. 'Your degree – your independence – the years of enjoying yourself—'

'I enjoy myself with Stefan. I've never enjoyed myself more. And I shall enjoy the baby.'

'Yes.' Thea tried to smile. 'I know you will, love.' She was silent for a moment, and then she said, 'It's because of Rachel, isn't it?'

She hadn't time to refute that because the train screeched into the station. But later, walking to the bus stop, Liv thought that Thea was wrong, that she had not married Stefan because of Rachel, that she managed quite well, these days, not even to think about Rachel. Rachel was part of a pattern of false starts, of failure and grief, that she had put behind her. Her marriage had allowed her to begin again. Moving from the university to Holm Edge, Liv had felt a weight fall from her shoulders.

The practical difficulties of living in Holm Edge now absorbed all her energy. It took her weeks to get the knack of the coal stove. Food would either be burned or raw; stoking it, she was enveloped by clouds of ash. Washing clothes meant either rinsing them by hand in the sink, or Stefan taking carrier-bags full of dirty linen to the launderette on the campus at Lancaster. Liv asked Thea to send up by train her old bicycle so that she could cycle the two miles to the shops in Caton. They had very little money – on leaving university, her grant had stopped, so there was only Stefan's research grant to live on. Stefan gave her ten pounds a week housekeeping money, but brought up by Thea, she was used to living simply.

She and Stefan bought their books in secondhand shops, and their clothes in street markets. They owned neither a television nor a telephone. Liv learned to make stews and soups, and they ate a great deal of lentils and spaghetti and potatoes. As her waist disappeared, she covered the widening gap with baggy jerseys borrowed from Stefan, or maternity smocks, made with an ancient Singer sewing-machine bought from an old lady in the village.

One of Stefan's fellow tutors cut down a tree in his garden, so they drove to Silverdale and filled the boot of the Citroën with logs for the fire. A local farmer promised them a pair of goslings later in the year. People were drawn to Stefan, to his enthusiasm and energy. A passing word extended into a half-hour's conversation, gifts were pressed on him, advice and help freely offered. No two days were the same. Sometimes he'd wake her with a kiss and bundle her into the car, and they'd speed down the track before dawn had broken. They'd drive to Kendal or Windermere, where they'd picnic and wade at the water's edge, or climb to the summit of the fells. Once, when she was tired, he piggybacked her downhill. Stefan himself never seemed to tire. He was an early riser, and often Liv would fall asleep to the sound of his footsteps in the room below, as he paced the floor in his search for inspiration for his paper.

He drew up the plans for the vegetable garden. It would be beautiful as well as functional, patterned and perfect like the intricate gardens of the Renaissance. They dug the first section in the autumn. The earth was thin and stony, and pebbles caught between the tines of the fork. Stefan had read somewhere that seaweed could be used to enrich poor soil, so they drove to the coast and wandered along the shore, filling carrier-bags with shiny brown bladderwrack. Back at Holm Edge, the seaweed hardened and dried, and flies buzzed around it. Stefan burnt it and coaxed a bootful of manure from the farmer in the valley. They planted their first crops that September.

In the evenings, Liv helped Stefan with his work, organizing his notes and copying out passages from the tall towers of books that crowded the living room. These evenings always ended in much the same way. She'd be hunched over the table, writing, and he'd stoop and press his lips against the back of her neck. Or he'd cover her hand with his own, the ball of his thumb stroking the hollow of her palm, and she'd turn to him, her body needing his, and he'd unbutton her blouse, cupping her full breasts, running his hand over the gentle swell of her stomach. Her thighs would ache, and her heart would pound. Sometimes they'd make love there and then, standing up, her back pressed against the desk, their clothes pooled on the floor around them. And sometimes he'd scoop her up in his arms and carry her to bed, and kiss and caress her until she cried out, hungry for him.

In the autumn, Katherine came to stay. Stefan met her at the station. Looking up from the kitchen window, Liv saw Katherine climb out of the passenger seat of the car and pick her way across the muddy garden.

'My shoes . . .' She was wearing grey suede platforms.

'I'll lend you some wellies.' Liv hugged her.

Katherine disentangled herself. 'I thought you'd be fatter.'

'I'm disgustingly fat. I have to use a safety pin to do up my jeans.'

She showed Katherine round the house: the kitchen, Stefan's study, their bedroom, and the little room, crammed with books, where they'd put up a camp-bed for Katherine, the room that one day would be for the baby. The small bathroom was tacked on to the side of the house. There was a cast-iron bath and a tall, clanking lavatory.

Katherine turned on a tap. 'At least there's running water.'

'Of course there is.' Liv felt irritated. 'The previous tenant had it put in just before he died.'

'What did he die of? Pneumonia?' Katherine was still wearing her Afghan coat. She had turned up the collar around her face.

'He shot himself.'

Katherine's eyes widened. 'Here?'

'In the garden.' Liv decided not to tell Katherine about the holly trees: she could imagine too well the look of urban amusement such rural superstition would provoke.

Instead, she said, 'What do you think of our house?'

'It's very . . .' Katherine, gazing around her, looked momentarily blank. Then she said, 'Well, it's a bit *Wuthering Heights*, isn't it?' Shivering, she groped in her pocket for cigarettes, lighting one as they walked back through the house.

Over supper, Stefan told Katherine about the vegetable garden, and about the hens and the geese.

Katherine scowled. 'Self-sufficiency . . . you're as bad as Felix.' Liv remembered walking with Felix Corcoran through a still, silent London. It seemed a long time ago. 'He's living in a commune,' Katherine explained. 'Some awful place in the middle of nowhere.'

Stefan refilled their glasses. 'Do you prefer the city, Katherine?'

'God, *yes*.' She looked around her. 'I mean, what do you *do* all day?'

'I have my work. I teach at the university most days. And I'm writing a paper.'

'I meant Liv.'

'Liv helps me, don't you, darling?'

'I write up Stefan's notes for him,' explained Liv.

'A major undertaking – my awful handwriting.'

'Yes, but,' again, Katherine scowled, '*people*. There's no *people*. Who do you talk to?'

'We have each other.' Stefan squeezed Liv's hand.

Katherine's lip curled. Liv said quickly, 'How's Stuart? And Toby?'

'Stuart's the same as ever. He's a pain in the neck, but he's good at his job. And as for Toby, he gets too steamed up about everything. Apart from that, he's fine.'

'And the magazine?'

'Oh, surviving. You know.'

'And your family? Your parents, your brothers?'

'Michael's still in Edinburgh, coming top in all his exams. Philip's weekly boarding at a special school, so Mum's not so tired. Simon's left Oxford. He's in France, the lucky thing. Dad got him a job with a wine exporter.'

Stefan's long fingers were drumming against the table. Liv, rising, kissed the top of his head. 'I'll make coffee and wash up. You sit down, darling.'

Stefan went into his study. Katherine stood in the kitchen doorway, smoking. Liv filled the kettle, and ground coffee. Katherine said suddenly, 'Writing up Stefan's notes ... digging his garden ... What do you do for *yourself*, Liv?'

'It's not like that. Stefan and I, we—'

'I know. What's yours is mine, and blah, blah, blah. But, still, you can't live all your lives in each other's pockets. I mean, he teaches at the university, doesn't he? What do you do then?'

'I cook and I read and I sew. I love going to jumble sales – if they're not too far away I cycle to them.'

'Hasn't Stefan taught you to drive?' Liv shook her head. 'Why not?'

She found mugs. 'We hadn't thought of it, I suppose.'

'It would give you freedom.'

'I don't need freedom,' said Liv crossly. 'I am free. I've never felt freer.'

'You mustn't allow your life,' said Katherine, stubbing out her cigarette, 'to revolve completely around Stefan.'

Liv lost her temper. 'Oh, for heaven's sake! You sound just like Mum!'

There was a silence. Then Katherine giggled. 'I'll soon be saying, "if you can't be good, be careful"!'

'Though in my case,' Liv patted her stomach, 'it's a bit late.' She, too, began to laugh. She went to stand beside Katherine, feeling for the first time the familiar affinity, and the falling away of barriers.

Then Katherine said, 'Do you think about her?'

'Rachel?' Though she did not need to ask. 'I try not to, but I do.'

'I have this dream,' said Katherine softly. 'I dream that I wake up and she's standing at the end of the bed, and she's trying to tell me something. But I can't hear what she's saying, and when I try to get up there's this weight on me, pushing me down. I try to scream, but no sound will come out. I feel as though I'm suffocating.'

They stood in silence for a few moments, side by side in the doorway, looking out across the darkened countryside. Then Katherine frowned. 'And Hector? Have you heard from Hector?'

'I tried writing to his house – to Bellingford – but there was no reply.'

'What about the baby?'

'She's still with the Wybornes. Mum says she's very sweet.'

'I haven't been home,' said Katherine. 'Not since . . . I must, of course, but I've been busy.'

Liv smiled. 'With anyone special?'

'I don't want someone special. Rachel had someone special, and look where it got her. Dead in childbirth at—' Katherine caught sight of Liv's face. 'Oh, Liv. *Livvy*. I'm so sorry. I'm such an idiot. My big mouth.'

'It's all right.' Turning her back on Katherine, Liv poured out the coffee.

'You'll be all right.' Awkwardly, Katherine hugged Liv. 'I know you'll be all right.'

Felix fitted easily into the rhythm of the community, rising early, working in the house or the garden till midday then dozing after lunch, and working again until dinner in the early evening. Every moment of the day was busy. At eleven o'clock at night, he'd go to his room, read a page or two of *The Glass Bead Game* or *The Magus*, then fall instantly asleep.

After a fortnight, he came to a decision. Late one evening, he found Nancy in the kitchen, her head bent over paperwork. 'Have you a minute?'

'Of course I have, Felix.' She sighed. 'To tell the truth, I'd welcome any distraction from all this.'

He glanced at the heaps of papers. 'What are they?'

'Tax forms. Inheritance tax. My father's affairs were very complicated. And I've always been hopeless with figures.'

'Can I help?'

'I couldn't ask you.'

'Of course you could.' He sat down beside her. 'I've known about profit and loss since babyhood. Weaned on it, along with Farley's rusks and rosehip syrup.'

The crease between Nancy's eyes momentarily disappeared. She pushed the papers towards him. 'I shall love you for ever, my dear Felix, if you can help me make sense of this lot. I should get an accountant, of course, but accountants cost money, and that's something I'm rather short of.'

She made tea while he worked. He said, after a while, 'You haven't much more than the house, you know. Your father's other assets – the stocks and shares – will have to be sold to pay the tax. If you intend to keep this place, that is.'

'Oh, I'm going to keep it. It's what I always wanted. And we don't need money, do we?'

He glanced at the depressing columns of figures, but he said only, 'I came to ask you something, Nancy.'

'Whether you can stay?'

'How did you know?'

'I had a feeling. And I'd love you to stay, Felix. I'll have to ask the others, of course. It's the community's decision, you know that. Only . . .'

'What?'

Nancy paused, and then she said, 'Why do you want to stay at Great Dransfield?'

'Because I like it here. Because I feel I've arrived somewhere at last. That I've found a place.'

'Or a person?'

He did not drop his gaze. 'Saffron, you mean?'

'You seem . . . fond of her.'

He said defensively, 'There's no harm in that, is there?'

'Of course not. And I don't mean to interfere.' Nancy seemed to be searching for words. She patted his hand. 'Just be careful, Felix dear. Falling in love requires a lot of effort, and in all the time I've known Saffron, I can't remember her ever putting a great deal of effort into anything. Pretty girls don't have to, you see.'

Felix's name was added to the rotas that Nancy pored over each week. He discovered that he wasn't much good at gardening – plants tended to shrivel at his touch – but he sawed logs and put up shelves, and scrambled hair-raisingly on the roof of the house, replacing tiles that had become dislodged in a storm. He cooked and cleaned and washed up when it was his turn, and minded the children. He silenced Zak by taking him on fast, bumpy pram rides, and offered to teach India and Justin arithmetic. He had noticed that they were almost illiterate. The lessons did not go well: India chewed her long, unkempt hair and complained of stomach-ache; Justin used the half-hour to practise the swear words taught to him by the hostile village children. When Felix spoke to Claire, she drawled, 'They'll learn when they're ready to learn, won't they? One shouldn't force-feed the poor little things.' Felix was relieved when the lessons fizzled out.

Nancy gratefully accepted his offer to take on the bookkeeping. It took him a while to disentangle Nancy's idiosyncratic accounting, much less time to see that Nancy was mistaken: they did need money. Felix brought up the subject at the next community meeting.

'We're running short of cash,' he explained. 'There'll be bills to pay, especially now that winter's coming. Coal and electricity, for instance. I was wondering whether we could discuss ways of raising money.'

'Surely,' said Claire scornfully, 'we should be looking at how to manage *without* cash. I thought that was what this place was about – getting away from the capitalist treadmill.'

'What do you want us to do, Claire?' asked Lawrence, yawning. 'Mine our own coal?'

123

'Couldn't we burn wood?' asked Nancy tentatively. 'There are several old trees in the copse, aren't there, Martin?'

'Too much ash,' he said. 'It would choke the boiler.'

'We don't need radiators. We should use open fires.'

'So *dangerous*.' Bryony sounded worried. 'I shouldn't like to leave Zak in a room with an open fire.'

'You should let him share your bed. Justin and India share mine. We keep each other warm.'

'But you know how poorly Zak sleeps,' Bryony looked close to tears, 'and I get so tired . . .'

Saffron's clear voice cut through. 'What were you thinking of, Felix?'

'I thought perhaps we could have a market stall.'

There was a silence. Six faces stared at him. Felix said quickly, 'We could sell things that we've made ourselves. Home-made jam and pickles . . . eggs and vegetables. It'd be a way of using up the gluts. And we could sell Bryony's batik and your weaving, Claire. I'm sure there'd be a market for that.' Surrounded by silence, his voice trailed away. 'If anyone's got a better idea . . . it was just a thought.'

'I'd hardly have come to live here if I wanted to work in a bloody shop.'

'Just becoming part of the rat-race again.'

'I think,' said Nancy firmly, 'that it's an excellent idea, Felix.'

He felt himself relax a little. 'Then I'll looked into it. Permits and things. Market-days are Saturdays and Tuesdays. If you like, I'll have the first shot at it. Then, if no one buys anything, I've only wasted my own time.'

'I'll help you,' said Saffron off-handedly.

Claire looked up. 'Good Lord. *Saffron*. Volunteering for work. That's not like you.'

Saffron smiled sweetly. 'We all have to do our bit, Claire.'

The market stall was a success. By midday on Saturday they had sold out.

'We deserve a reward,' said Saffron. There was a van selling drinks and snacks. 'A cup of tea,' she said. '*Tea-bag* tea, not that awful herbal stuff. And a Kit-Kat.'

Felix bought the tea. Saffron dipped her biscuit into her cup and looked at him consideringly. 'I didn't think you'd stay, you know.'

He was surprised. 'Why not?'

'Someone like you . . . You don't need a place like this.'

He let the 'someone like you' pass for a moment, and said, 'I like it here. Everything's pared down to the essentials. And I like the people.'

'All of us?' She looked mischievous.

'Well . . . Nancy's wonderful.'

'Of course she is. Nancy's a saint.'

'How did you two meet?'

'We worked in the same office.'

'*Oh.*' He was surprised. 'I thought – '

' – that we were born flower children? Of course not. Years ago, Nancy and I both worked for a firm of solicitors in Andover. Nancy was the boss's secretary, and I was a typist.'

The breeze caught her long, pale hair, whipping it around her face. She was wearing a mushroom-coloured velvet coat over an embroidered ochre dress. Felix struggled to imagine her sitting at a desk, tapping typewriter keys.

'We kept in touch after we left,' Saffron explained, 'and then, this summer, I was in a bit of a mess. I'd been unwell, and I wasn't up to working. Nancy suggested I live at Great Dransfield.' Saffron looked up at him through her lashes. 'You don't like *all* the others, do you, Felix? You can't possibly. Claire came here to get away from her husband, of course – or he ran away from her, poor devil.' She raised her narrow shoulders. 'I can never understand why plain women like Claire seem to go out of their way to make themselves even plainer. Not shaving their legs or plucking their eyebrows . . . never wearing any makeup.'

'Claire isn't plain.'

'*Felix.*'

'She has nice eyes. And lovely hair.'

The corners of her mouth curled. 'Do you fancy her, Felix? I hope not, for your sake. Imagine having to face dear little Justin and India over the breakfast cereal for the next dozen years. No wonder the old man did a bunk.'

'I didn't mean—'

Saffron stood up and dusted her hands together. 'Or perhaps you're more partial to Bryony.' She screwed up her face, and mimicked Bryony's colourless whine. 'My room is so cold ... and I get so *tired* ... and Zak has puked down the front of his Babygro *again*.'

Felix couldn't help laughing. 'I promise you I'm not in love with Bryony. Or Claire. And, anyway, Bryony has Lawrence.'

'At the moment,' said Saffron.

He had begun to load baskets and boxes into the back of Nancy's van. 'What do you mean?'

'Well, he won't stay with her, will he?'

'He's her husband. He loves her.'

'You're such a romantic, Felix. Lawrence is thoroughly sick of Bryony. If Lawrence possessed an ounce of initiative, he'd have found someone else long ago.'

He opened his mouth to argue, but she went on, 'The only people who believe in monogamy are women like Bryony, who want a man in order to breed. No one would be monogamous out of choice, would they?'

'If you loved someone?'

'It doesn't mean you have to *own* them.'

Felix threw the orange boxes and baskets on top of the trestle table. 'Of course not.'

'If we thought *that*, we'd end up like our parents – arguing like cat and dog and hating each other but staying together because of a wedding-ring.' Saffron's grey eyes sparked. 'So *hypocritical*.'

Felix said mildly, 'I was lucky, I suppose. My parents never argued.'

'Are they still together?'

He shook his head, and she said, 'Well, then.'

He explained, 'My mother died nearly three years ago.'

She put down her empty cup. 'I'm sorry, Felix. How awful. What happened?'

'She was driving along a country lane to collect my sister from a party. Just a couple of miles. Someone pulled out in front of her.' Momentarily the market-place, and Saffron, receded, and he was back in that stormy winter's night and Rose was screaming, 'It's *my* fault! She was coming to *me*! It's *my* fault!' He shuddered. Then he glanced across at Saffron. 'Is that why you're here? Escaping the family battleground?'

'Partly. And because it's nice at Great Dransfield. You don't have to get up at some God-forsaken time in the morning, and you don't have to struggle into a dreary office on a crowded bus. And *typing*. I hated it. Couldn't wait to get away.'

'Why didn't you do something else, then?'

'I left school at fifteen. CSEs in shorthand and typing. I'm not clever like you, Felix. My teachers told me I could be a typist or a hairdresser or a shop assistant, so I did a secretarial course. My first day at work I knew I hated it. Awful old men pinching my bottom, and bossy cows running the typing pool. No thank you.'

'You could be an actress ... or a model ...'

'Sweet of you, but to tell the truth I don't want to *be* anything. I just want to be me. Is that so dreadful?'

'It's not dreadful at all,' he said. 'Actually, it's quite perfect.'

She gave him a sideways glance. 'Do you mean that?' He nodded. 'Good,' Saffron said, and smiled to herself. 'Because I wasn't sure.'

Felix slept in one of the old vicarage's attic rooms. From its narrow, Gothic-arched window, he could see to the meadow and the orchard and, beyond, to the lake. In the evenings, a barn owl would fly from roof to branch, a grey ghost, puncturing the air with its unearthly shriek.

He had taken off his shirt and kicked off his shoes and moved

127

a pile of books from the bed to the floor when he heard a soft tapping on his bedroom door. Opening it, he saw Saffron.

He began to speak, but she silenced him, placing her index finger against his lips. He found himself reaching out and touching her silvery hair, letting it slide between his fingers like silk. When he kissed her, her pointed tongue darted between his teeth, and he drew her to him, pressing his mouth against her cool, clean skin. His palms traced the curves of her body, and he realized that beneath her dress she was naked. She reached back, undid a hook and eye, and the dress slithered to the floor. He groaned, seeing her, and she laid the palm of her hand against his face, and smiled. He knew that he was losing himself in her. He felt breathless, as though he were drowning.

Much later, when at last they lay quiet in the darkness, she said, 'I won't stay the night, you know. I never do. I prefer to sleep by myself.'

He said nothing, just tightened his arm round her, tucking his head into the curve of her neck as his eyelids became heavy.

'Lots of men snore,' she said. 'I can't sleep through snoring. Do you snore, Felix?'

'I don't know. I've never listened to myself.'

She giggled, and then she said, 'My husband used to snore.'

He was suddenly wide awake, staring into the darkness. 'Your husband? You were married?'

'*Am* married, unless he's fallen under a bus. You can always hope, can't you?'

'I didn't know.'

'Why should you? I don't go around with his name branded into my forehead – though he might have preferred it if I had. I haven't seen him in almost a year. He has no idea where I am, and I couldn't care less where he is.'

He found himself saying, 'How long were you married? Where did you meet him? What was his name?'

But she yawned, and did not reply, and wriggled out of his grasp. When he protested, she bent and touched his lips very

lightly with her own, and said, 'I told you, I never stay the night.'
She pulled her dress over her head, and left the room.

Katherine made sure she was always very busy. If she was busy,
if she was never alone, then she didn't have time to think. She
worked hard all day, and went out every evening, and didn't
return to Capricorn Street until, tired out by dancing and numbed
by Bacardi and Coke, she slept as soon as her head touched the
pillow. Those first few weeks after Rachel's funeral, she had lain
awake for hours each night, listening to the rattling of the pipes
and the creaking of the floorboards. Her thoughts had wearied
and frightened her.

She missed Felix. Opening his letter – 'such a wonderful place,
Katherine, absolute paradise, and Nancy is the kindest person you
can imagine' – she had, ridiculously, wanted to weep. She missed
their arguments, she missed the echo of his long, loping stride.
She knew that Toby, too, needed Felix.

Katherine was worried about Toby. Toby smoked the first
joint of the day with his morning coffee, and his last when he
went to bed in the early hours of the morning. He rarely left the
Chelsea house, shuffling between his bedroom on the second floor
and *Frodo's Finger*'s offices in the basement, emerging only
occasionally, blinking at the daylight, to buy aspirins or beer or
Rizla papers. Sometimes he didn't even come down to the office,
but remained in one of the upstairs rooms, watching television.
He had taken to wearing battered jeans and an embroidered silk
dressing-gown that had belonged to his father. The dressing-gown
was much too big for his slight, fragile frame. Katherine, shocked
one day by the hollows between his ribs, cooked him a plate of
bacon and eggs and toast, which he picked at. 'I owe people
money,' Toby explained, as he perched on the edge of his seat,
tearing up bits of crust and glancing furtively out of the window.
'I know they're watching me.'

Most of the antiques and pictures in Toby's house had gone,

sold to pay for food and cigarettes and for *Frodo's Finger*, or stolen by his less scrupulous acquaintances. There were cigarette burns in the Persian rugs and scorch marks on the wallpaper where people had knocked over candles. During the coldest part of the winter, the electricity was cut off, so Toby burned chairs and banisters to keep warm. There were always people staying at the house: they made Katherine uneasy, those somnolent shapes sprawled on the stairs, or wrapped up in old military overcoats on the sofa. The house had acquired a peculiar, idiosyncratic smell, a pungent mixture of unwashed bodies, stale food, smoke and joss sticks. Toby burned the joss sticks to hide the more incriminating odours. To Katherine, he confided his suspicion that some of the people who came to his house were undercover policemen. Katherine was privately certain that no undercover policeman could have achieved quite the depth of squalor that Toby's friends attained. They made her feel tidy.

Katherine broached the problem of Toby to Stuart. Stuart was unconcerned. 'Och, he's always been a worrier. Some folks are like that. Never happy unless they've something to belly-ache about.'

'Stuart,' said Katherine severely, 'Toby glues hairs across the office doorway. Like they do in spy films. He thinks people are trying to break in.'

Stuart snorted. 'Who'd bloody bother?'

'He doesn't eat. I cooked for him the other day – *me*. Cooked for a man!'

Stuart glanced up at her through his pale, feathery lashes. 'Make me a sandwich, would you, love? I'm starving.' Katherine threw a cushion at him, and went back to the typewriter.

She went home for Christmas. She had intended to stay with her family for the week, but after only two days found herself wanting to scream with boredom. Simon had remained in France, and Liv was in that freezing cottage with her handsome, moody husband, and Rachel was – well, she would not think about Rachel. Which left Mum and Dad and Michael, the dullest of her brothers. And Philip, of course, who was now twelve, but who was still given wooden bricks and cuddly toys on Christmas morning. Katherine's mother rushed around, cooking and cleaning from dawn, but the turkey was raw in the middle, and the custard lumpy.

On Boxing Day afternoon, Katherine cycled over to Fernhill Grange. At the gates, she paused, wanting to run away. But the parcel was clutched in her hand, and the memory of Rachel saying, 'You won't forget me, will you?' echoed too loudly in her ears. She walked up the drive and pressed the doorbell.

The housekeeper opened the door. Katherine said, 'I've come to see Alice. I've a present for her.' She was shown inside.

The changes to the Wybornes shocked her. Grief had sculpted the bones of Diana Wyborne's once plump face, and had shaded to purple puffiness Henry Wyborne's formerly handsome features. Katherine blurted out her errand, and was taken to the playroom. Seeing the baby, she cried, 'But she's so *big*!' In her imagination, Alice Seton had remained a tiny newborn.

'She's seven months old,' Diana reminded her.

Katherine went to the cot. Alice raised herself on her hands and knees, looking up. Her hair was fine and pale and silky, but her eyes were dark brown, like Rachel's.

'Is she . . .' Katherine faltered; she couldn't think what one asked about babies.

'She's very healthy. I took her to a paediatrician in Harley Street to make sure.' When Diana went to the cot, Alice's smile widened, showing two tiny, pearly teeth. 'She's a very good baby – she slept through the night when she was only a month old. Just like Rachel.' Diana lifted Alice out of the cot. 'You're a good girl, aren't you, poppet?' She kissed the baby's head. Katherine noticed how tired Diana looked, and how her arms trembled with the weight of the infant.

'Do you want to hold her, Katherine?'

'I can't stay,' said Katherine quickly. 'I have to go. I just wanted to give Alice her Christmas present.'

Outside again, she cycled very fast down the hill, back into the village. At the Fairbrothers' cottage, she paused. Suddenly, she longed to see Thea. Safe, calm, reliable Thea. Yet, sliding off her bicycle, glancing through the window, she saw that Thea was not alone, that that peculiar man she kept house for was standing in the kitchen, a sherry glass in his hand. Katherine was about to tap on the window, but something stopped her, something about the intimacy of the scene, and she walked quietly back down the path, and cycled home. The following day she packed her bags and returned to London.

It was Stefan's idea to make a surprise New Year visit to Thea, in Fernhill. Waking on the last day of December, he flung some clothes in a bag, bundled Liv into the car, and was heading down the M6 by ten o'clock. Heavy, sleety rain battered against the Citroën's tin roof, and Liv sat tightly in her seat, wedged in by presents for Thea: a basket of eggs, a paper bag full of Brussels sprouts, and a tattered first edition of *The Arthur Rackham Book of Fairytales*, discovered in a secondhand bookshop in Keswick.

They arrived at Fernhill in the early evening. Opening the door to them, Thea just looked at Liv, and the smile flowered through her face, curling the corners of her eyes and mouth. Then she hugged her, mindful of the bump.

'Such a long way ... come in and get warm ... Stefan, what a wonderful surprise ... Liv, you must be exhausted ...'

One of Thea's sprawling, no-particular-time-of-the-day parties was in full swing. Most of her pottery class were there, as well as Mrs Jessop from the newsagent and the neighbours on either side, and Mr Thorneycroft. Liv was surprised to see Mr Thorneycroft, who had never seemed to her a party sort of person; he still wore his tweeds and carried his walking stick, but had made a concession to the festivities by threading a sprig of holly through his lapel.

The party was fairly sedate at first, the potters discussing raku and slipware, and the neighbours spreading scandal and gossip. Then Stefan suggested charades, and somehow it wasn't sedate any more but, fed by Thea's mulled wine and Stefan's inventiveness, was punctuated by howls of laughter and shrieks of triumph. The party ended after midnight, 'Auld Lang Syne' echoing in their ears as the potters crammed into a taxi, and the neighbours lurched, hiccuping, out of the door.

Stefan and Liv slept curled up in Liv's single bed. When she woke, she was alone. She placed the flat of her hand on the bump, reassured by the baby's small, darting movements, and looked around. Her bedroom was just as she had left it: posters and paintings on the walls, every surface cluttered with tapestries, embroideries, patchwork, paper flowers and shell animals.

Thea brought her tea in bed. 'Stefan's in the garden,' she explained. 'One of the willows came down in a storm and he's cutting it up for firewood.'

After breakfast, she walked to the end of the garden. Stefan grinned briefly at her then went back to his task. She saw the glint of the axe as it arced through the air, and the splinters of wood that littered the ground. She watched for a while, but was shut out by the intensity of his concentration on the task. Indoors, she felt unsettled: all the evidence of her old hobbies and occupations surrounded her, reminding her of the girl she had once been, directionless, never quite sure what suited her.

She walked to the churchyard, and laid the treasures she had saved – the perfect fossil of an ammonite, a jay's sapphire blue feather, a piece of mistletoe – on Rachel's grave, but that, too, seemed empty, and lacking in resonance. No comforting ghost darted beneath the dank, dripping yews, no old confidences or half-heard laughter echoed against the ancient flint walls. There were only earth and stone and tree, and a landscape she had grown out of, a landscape that lacked both sea and hill. There were only whichever memories she could steel herself to confront. She recalled her first meeting with Rachel: Rachel spinning round and round, arms outspread. *If you do this, you might be able to see the sea*. Liv put out her arms and began to circle round, but was giddy immediately, and paused, her hands resting on her swollen belly, feeling the pounding of her heart and the baby's protesting movements.

As they drove north the following day, the intermittent sleet turned to snow. Snowflakes darted at the windscreen, and the yellow headlamps of the lorries on the motorway glowed balefully in the fading afternoon light. Caught in a long queue of traffic moving cautiously through the blizzard, they slowed to a crawl. A line of worry carved itself between Stefan's brows. They had been invited to a party that night at his professor's house in Lancaster.

Liv tried to reassure him. 'I'm sure Professor Samuels'll understand. It won't matter if we're late.'

'Of course it *matters*. I need that job.' Stefan had applied for a permanent post in the department.

'We could phone.'

He was crouched over the steering-wheel, peering through the small clear triangle left by the Citroën's inefficient windscreen wipers. He looked tired. The long drive to Fernhill, the late night at the party, the hard physical exercise of logging the fallen willow had taken their toll. A small muscle to the side of his mouth had begun to jerk uncontrollably.

They drove through Galgate at nine o'clock. They must go straight to Professor Samuels's house, said Stefan. There wasn't time to go home. But my hair, my clothes, thought Liv. Peering into the rear-view mirror, she pulled a comb through her hair and dabbed on lipstick.

In a three-storey Edwardian house in Lancaster, she moved through crowded rooms, touching a piping-hot radiator here, a heavy swag of brocade curtain there. She was wearing the dark green velvet smock Thea had given her for Christmas; underneath it, the two halves of her jeans were held together with a length of ribbon. Looking round, she saw that all the other women were wearing evening dresses or two-pieces, that their hair was permed or cut in a smooth page-boy, their faces carefully made up. Liv's legs ached, and she longed to sit down, but the sofa and chairs were occupied by a forbidding array of professors' wives. Stefan's voice, and his laughter, not far away, rose above the polite hum of conversation as he moved quickly from guest to guest.

An elegant young woman introduced herself. 'My name's Camilla Green. I didn't catch your name.'

'Olivia Galenski.'

'*Oh*. So you're our gorgeous Stefan's wife . . .' Sharp blue eyes stared curiously at Liv's belly. 'You were his student, weren't you? Very romantic, you and Stefan, though Samuels didn't approve, I hear.' Camilla Green smiled. 'An awful lot of us shed a tear when we heard Stefan'd got hitched. Embarrassing, isn't it, how so many females still hanker after that dark, tempestuous type?'

There was a howl of laughter from the far end of the room. Liv glanced round. Stefan was in the middle of a circle of people; she could hear the fast rise and fall of his voice. She saw that he had begun to build a card house. Cards fluttered between his fingers, forming triangle upon triangle. There was a ripple of applause, a roar of encouragement. Hearts, diamonds, clubs, spades flickered from the pack, balancing one on top of the other until Stefan leaped on to a chair to place cards on the summit. As he put the final card in position, the entire edifice shivered and crashed to the floor. The expression on his face altered, and he staggered slightly, almost losing his balance as he climbed down from the chair. A glass rolled from the table, shattering on the parquet floor. Someone muttered, 'A little too much of the Christmas spirit, perhaps,' as Liv pushed through the crowd to his side.

'Stefan,' she whispered, 'I think we should go.'

'It's too early.' He stared at his watch, blinking.

'I'm tired, darling.' Mrs Samuels, her mouth set in a disapproving line, had fetched a dustpan and brush and was sweeping up the broken glass.

Outside in the street, the cold bit into her. The snow had blown away to reveal a clear sky peppered with stars. They were driving out of the city when the car slewed over to the wrong side of the road. Liv screamed, and Stefan's eyelids jerked open. He swore, and grabbed the steering-wheel, jamming on the brake, halting the diagonal drift across the road. The Citroën's nose came to rest a few inches from a parked car.

Liv was shaking with fright. For a moment, Stefan's hands hovered over the controls almost as though he had forgotten what they were for. 'You idiot, Galenski,' he muttered to himself, as he forced the gears into reverse and swung the car round. 'You – utter – complete – idiot.'

Liv's heart was beating wildly. 'You're tired, darling, that's all. I ought to learn to drive, then we could share these long journeys. I must learn.'

'What are you saying, Liv?' He glanced angrily at her. 'That I can't manage?'

'Of course not! Only that it would be useful – for shopping—'

'Do you think I'd let you go tearing round the countryside on your own?' His voice was savage, and his fists were clenched. 'Don't be so bloody stupid.'

As they drove in silence back to the house, Liv stared out of the car window, blinking back the tears. Indoors, she was peeling off her gloves and scarf when Stefan came to her. 'Sorry. I'm so sorry, darling.'

When she turned to look at him, she saw the marks of exhaustion on his face: the dark hollows around his eyes, and the white skin.

'Lost my temper. Shouldn't take it out on you. Things on my mind.'

'What things?' she whispered.

His eyes darkened. 'My paper. I keep thinking maybe it's no good. Maybe it's all nonsense.'

'Stefan, how can you possibly believe that?'

'I can't seem to finish it.' He screwed up his eyes, rubbing his forehead with his fingertips. 'Maybe I'm not getting anywhere with it because it's not worth writing about. You see, I have to publish. I won't get a permanent position if I haven't published.' He looked despairing. 'So many others out there ... All wanting what I want.'

She put her arms around him. Abruptly, his mood seemed to alter. 'About the car,' he said. 'You know that I need the car to get to university, Liv. And when I'm at home I'll always drive you to the shops, you know that too, sweetheart.' When she started to speak, he interrupted, 'It would worry me if you learned to drive. What if you had an accident? I couldn't bear it. Perhaps after the baby. Yes, we'll think about it after the baby's born.'

Chapter Six

After the baby's born, Stefan had said. *We'll think about it after the baby's born.* It seemed to Liv that everything waited, poised on a balance, for the birth of her baby. At eight months pregnant, there seemed no part of her life that the unborn child did not affect. She could not climb out of the old-fashioned, steep-sided iron bath without Stefan's help, and the weight of the infant on her bladder forced her out of bed several times a night, shivering as she plodded downstairs and across the cold flags to the bathroom. Walking to the bus stop, she had to concentrate so as not to lose her balance on the icy, rutted track. She longed for mid-March, when the baby was due, longed for everything to be normal again.

January was punctuated by freezing weather, and by a series of domestic disasters. The seedlings in the vegetable garden were damaged by a heavy frost. The car broke down, and Stefan had to take the bus to work; late arriving at college, he discovered that Professor Samuels had begun to give his tutorial in his place. Then, one morning, Stefan went to refill the coal scuttle and found that the bunker was empty. He called Liv. 'Haven't Chapman's been?' Chapman's were the coal merchants. Their truck struggled up the track to Holm Edge once a month.

Liv peered into the bunker. Only a few nuggets of coal lurked in the corners. 'I can't remember . . . I don't think so.'

'You don't think so? Don't you *know*?'

They could not afford to take a newspaper, they had no television, and the radio's batteries needed replacing. Liv's days had begun to meld into each other, unidentified and indistinguishable.

'Dear God – no wonder I haven't finished the damned paper . . .' muttered Stefan. 'Impossible to work . . . frostbite when I hold the bloody pen . . .' He glanced at his watch. 'Hell – I'll be late again.' He left the house.

Liv walked the mile to the telephone box and called the coal merchants. Their last delivery hadn't been paid for; back at the house she found the unpaid bill among the clutter of notes and books on Stefan's desk. Searching in her purse and through the detritus at the bottom of her handbag, using the Christmas money that Thea had given her, she scraped up enough cash and caught the bus into Lancaster. The motherly lady in the accounts department at Chapman's promised that coal would be delivered that afternoon.

Four weeks till the baby was due. Liv hurried to get everything ready, knitting tiny cardigans and bootees, sewing nightgowns and a patchwork pram quilt. She saw an advertisement for a secondhand carry-cot in the post-office window, and bought it one afternoon, pushing it up the steep track to the cottage. The pamphlet the midwife had given her listed nappies and Babygros and plastic pants and feeding bottles and sterilizers. Liv herself was supposed to have three nightgowns for hospital, three maternity bras, and a dressing-gown. She wore Stefan's old T-shirts in bed, and her dressing-gown had been given to her by Thea for her fourteenth birthday; its sides no longer met around her vast middle. Since she had used her Christmas money to pay for coal, she had not a penny of her own. Liv showed the list to Stefan, and he frowned, but promised to go to the bank the next day. The twenty pounds that Stefan gave her paid for nappies, bottles and cot blankets. Liv bought two maternity bras, and a length of material from Lancaster market to make nightgowns for herself. The dressing-gown would have to do.

Two weeks to go. Liv thought she couldn't possibly grow any bigger or she would burst. Her navel poked out of the vast dome of her swollen womb, like a cherry on a cake. She no longer walked, she waddled. Peeling potatoes, hanging washing on the line, her back ached and she moved slowly.

Waking early one morning, Liv saw the frost flowers around the perimeter of the window-panes. There was a peculiar stillness to the air, as though the icy weather had permeated the house, gripping it with freezing fingers. She went downstairs. A few steps from the bottom, she stopped, rigid with shock, clutching the banister. The kitchen floor was an inch deep in water. Their rugs and furniture and books were awash. At the edge of the puddle, ice had begun to form.

She shook Stefan awake. Pulling on his clothes, he ran downstairs. Wading through the water, he stooped and picked up a book. As he turned the pages, the paper fragmented into a grey papier-mâché. His face blanched. He muttered, 'My books – my books,' and then, with a violent sweep of his arm, he hurled the damaged volume at the far wall, where it struck a shelf. A jar of holly berries, a bundle of pens and pencils and a ball of knitting wool, stuck like a sputnik with needles, tumbled to the floor.

'Stefan—' she said, but he shook her off roughly and walked out of the house, slamming the door behind him.

When she heard the rumble of the car engine, she ran to the window and looked out. The Citroën was heading down the track. She could hardly believe that he had gone. She thought, *What if the baby comes?* There was no telephone, and she had no transport. She imagined her labour starting: she would have to stagger down the treacherous track to the Littledale road and the nearest bus stop, her suitcase in hand. She found herself thinking of Rachel, Rachel who had asked for help but who had been given none. The silence and loneliness of Holm Edge terrified her. She took a deep breath, and ran her shaking hands through her hair, trying to calm herself. Stefan must have gone to fetch a plumber, she told herself. He'd come home soon.

She began to shiver, so she shut the door and went back into the kitchen. She found the burst pipe under the sink; crawling on all fours, her nightdress and dressing-gown became cold and wet, but she managed to turn off the stopcock. The stream of water trickled, then stopped. She dressed, and began to clear up the mess. Only the contents of the living room had been damaged; the water had not reached the books and papers in Stefan's study. Mopping the floor, she listened constantly for the sound of the car, returning up the track. She could not believe that he was not coming back. She could not believe that he had left her now, when she needed him most. She remembered, picking small, hard holly berries out of the matted rug, that it was unlucky to leave Christmas greenery up after Twelfth Night. She thought of that other desertion: the pink house by the sea, and the glass pebbles on the shore.

When she had finished the room, she glanced at the clock and saw that Stefan had been gone for four hours. She thought that she should eat, but the knot of tension in her diaphragm nauseated her. She recalled the fury in Stefan's eyes, and the force of his arm as he had thrown the book against the wall. In the bathroom, she caught sight of herself in the mirror, a lumbering, ungainly creature, not the slim girl Stefan had married. She went upstairs to the unfinished nursery, found a brush and began to paint.

At last she heard the car, heading up the track. She bit her lip and kept on painting; the task had acquired an urgency, and she felt compelled to finish it. She heard Stefan call her name, then his footsteps on the stairs.

He came into the room. 'Where have you been?' Her voice shook.

'Driving around. Just . . . driving around. I brought you these.' He was clutching a huge bunch of flowers. 'I'm sorry, Liv,' he whispered. 'So sorry. Forgive me. So stupid of me to lose my temper.'

'Leaving me alone . . . How could you?' She pushed past him, and sat down heavily on a chair. She was trembling with reaction, and her legs ached with tension.

He knelt in front of her. His eyes were anguished. 'I'll never lose my temper again, Liv,' he said softly. 'And I'll never leave you again. I'll always be here beside you. Always, I promise.'

He placed the bouquet of flowers on her lap. Closing her eyes, she pressed her face against the hothouse lilies, tightly budded roses and out-of-season carnations, but they had no scent.

Exhausted, she went to bed. Stefan made supper. Liv drank her tea, but picked at the food, then fell asleep and dreamed of waves that washed through the house, leaving in their wake a scattering of coloured pebbles, like jewels. Then Rachel poked her in the back, so hard it hurt, and said loudly, 'Wake up, Liv!' so she did.

It was quite dark, and only the dim light in the corridor illuminated the room. In the distance, she could hear the tap-tapping of Stefan's typewriter. She felt that something had changed, but she wasn't sure what it was. There it was again, that griping pain in her back. She must have pulled something, heaving all those books around. She tried to shuffle into a more comfortable position, but as she sat up, there was a rush of warm fluid between her legs. She thought for one awful moment she had wet herself, but then she realized that her waters had broken and that the pain in her back was not a pulled muscle but a contraction. She thought, But it's two weeks early and I haven't finished knitting the shawl. Then she found her voice and called for Stefan.

Though he tried to drive smoothly down the track to the road, the movement of the car jarred her, and she bit her lip to stop herself crying out. She was afraid that the baby would be born before they reached Lancaster, but when they arrived at the hospital and the midwife examined her, she said, 'Three centi-metres dilated, Mrs Galenski. Baby won't be here till tomorrow morning at the earliest.' Liv began to feel frightened. The pain was already awful, how could she possibly endure it for twelve hours more?

Afterwards, what she remembered most of all was her sense of shock. That anything could hurt so much, and that it had gone on for so long. The midwife at the birth preparation classes had talked of discomfort: this was agony. For a while Liv thought it must be her fault – she couldn't have practised the breathing exercises properly – and then they gave her pethidine, and she didn't think of anything much at all.

Freya was born at one o'clock the following afternoon. 'The head's coming,' the midwife said. 'Just one more push, dear.' Liv knew that if she pushed again her entire body would split in half like a banana unpeeling, but on the other hand, if she didn't push she'd stay like this for ever. So she pushed and cried out, and Stefan gripped her hand, and then the miracle happened, and there she was, in a last twist and squirm, her baby, emerging from her body. A thin, reedy cry, and the midwife said, 'You have a lovely daughter,' and she lay back on the pillows, drunk with pethidine and with the glorious relief that it was all over, too exhausted even to open her eyes.

After a few minutes, she felt the nurse place the baby in her arms. She looked down. Navy blue eyes, wide open, caught hers for a moment then drifted away again. A crimson, crumpled mouth pursed open and shut. A tiny star-shaped hand reached out, as though pursuing some errand of its own, and was then withdrawn. Looking down at her daughter for the first time, Liv thought that there was a puzzled, other-worldly air about her, as though she had travelled from a long way away, and now struggled to make sense of the new place in which she found herself.

Sometimes Katherine thought of just going away and fulfilling her childhood dream of travelling round the world. But she wondered what would happen to Toby if she was not there to keep an eye on him and, anyway, there was the magazine, in its death throes, certainly, but nevertheless her responsibility. Some of her friends, like Liv and Felix, were far away, and others, like Rachel and Toby, had become unreachable. The people she had replaced them with – the people she went to parties with, and spent her nights with – had an air of transience about them. She would meet them one day, and have no confidence that they would still be there the next.

In May, Katherine borrowed Toby's car, and drove north to visit Liv. She had bought a present for baby Freya, a bracelet of lapis-lazuli beads that she had found in a boutique on the King's Road. 'They're gorgeous,' Liv said, letting the string of limpid blue run through her fingers. 'She'd only suck them now, but she'll love them when she's older.' They spent an idyllic afternoon at Holm Edge, lolling on the grass in the warm spring sunshine, the baby asleep in her carry-cot. Puffy white clouds cast small shadows over the fell, and Katherine had a fantasy of herself pushing a pram, one of the louche, long-haired boys she spent her time with walking paternally beside her.

Then Stefan came home, and there seemed suddenly to be a tension in the air, the mood of the house altering with the tread of his feet across the grass, the click of his study door closing. Liv began to make supper, and the baby began to howl, and Katherine's fleeting vision of married and maternal bliss dissolved. She tried to help Liv with the food and the baby, but she had never been much of a cook, and Freya, in her arms rather than her mother's, just bawled louder. It all reminded Katherine too much of her own childhood, and she returned to London the next day.

The following week, she was drying her hair when there was a knock at the door. Opening it, Katherine shrieked when she saw Felix. 'Why didn't you tell me you were coming?'

'No phone, and I only decided yesterday.' He hugged her. 'Can I come in?'

'It's a bit of a mess.' Just the sight of his tall, rangy figure cheered her up. Kicking aside heaps of clothing, Katherine made a path through the room, and sat on the edge of the bed, brushing her hair, while Felix folded his long frame into a small basket chair.

'What are they?' Felix was carrying two parcels.

'I'm trying to sell some secondhand books. We need to raise money for the community – the books used to belong to Nancy's father, and no one reads them now. I thought collectors might be interested. They're military histories, mostly.' He handed Katherine the smaller parcel. 'And this is a present.'

'Not some awful hand-weaving, is it?' Katherine ripped open the wrapping-paper, and took out a box of home-made biscuits. They smelt heavenly.

'Nancy made them,' he said. 'I'd meant to give half to Toby but he wasn't in. Has he gone away?'

'He doesn't always answer the door. I have to do this special knock.'

'Oh.' Felix looked bewildered. 'Why?'

'He thinks he's being followed. And he thinks the phone's bugged.'

'Why on earth does Toby think his phone's bugged?'

'Because of the magazine. Our left-wing political affiliations. MI5, you see.'

Felix raised his eyebrows, and Katherine sighed.

'I know. And Stuart's gone back to Scotland. He's going to get married.'

'Married?'

Katherine smiled. 'The great revolutionary. But apparently there's always been a girl there, and with Toby the way he is and the magazine dying on its feet, he decided to go home.' She studied him. 'You look well, Felix.' He looked older, she thought, and he had filled out across the shoulders. 'Brown rice and sandals obviously suit you.'

'And you, Katherine? How are you?'

'Oh, I'm fine,' she said lightly. 'Terrific.'

Over sausage, egg and chips in a greasy spoon on the Brompton Road, Katherine asked Felix about the commune. 'Is it still a paradise? Are the people still angels?'

He stabbed the yolk of the egg with his knife. 'There's this girl,' he said.

'I thought there might be.' Katherine's voice was flippant, but she was aware of a dull feeling in the pit of her stomach, a mixture of disappointment and loneliness. Everyone was pairing off, she thought: Stuart and his Scottish bride, Liv and her dark, brooding Stefan, even Thea and Richard Thorneycroft. She didn't even know why she minded. Felix had never been any more than a friend. It had been foolish of her to assume that he, like herself, would remain unattached. But she said only, 'Tell me about her.'

He told her, at great length. She was called Saffron (*Saffron!* thought Katherine), and, of course, she was the most beautiful creature on earth. Eventually, the torrent of words trailed away. She thought that he looked miserable.

She touched his hand. 'What's wrong?'

'Saffron thinks that people shouldn't own each other. So do I, of course. Just because you've been to bed with someone, it doesn't mean that you've exclusive right to their company.'

'Unless that's what you both want.'

'But seeing her with other people – other men – I hate it. I didn't think I was like that.' His eyes had clouded.

'Like what?'

'Jealous. I didn't think I was the jealous type.'

'Is there a jealous type?'

He looked up at her. 'What do you mean?'

'If you love someone, isn't wanting to be with them a part of that?' She made a face. 'Though I'm not really the person to talk to, am I? I've never been out with anyone for longer than three months.' I've never *loved* anyone, she thought, but did not say.

'Surely it's possible,' he said wearily, 'to love someone without all those other things. Possessiveness and mistrust and anger, all that. That's what the community was supposed to be about – finding a different way to live. Sharing things, having a common aim, not being enslaved to money.'

She said gently, 'You always were an idealist, Felix.'

'When people say *idealist*, they usually mean *fool*.'

She squeezed his hand. 'I don't. I envy you, actually.'

'Nonsense.'

'Yes, I do. It must be nice to believe in something. More *cheerful*.' Katherine felt suddenly sad, thinking of her own family. 'My parents trust each other, but I'm not sure whether they *love* each other. My mother's always exhausted and cross, and my father's hardly ever home. He never thanks my mother for cooking his dinner or ironing his shirts. I suppose she stays with him because she's no good at anything else. She's just a housewife. And that's not a job, is it?'

Felix looked grim. He said, 'My parents loved each other. You just knew that they did. As soon as you walked in the front door. It made the house warm, somehow.'

Liv had thought that once the baby was born everything would get back to normal. By the time Freya was a month old, she had concluded that things would never get back to normal, that there wasn't a normal any more, and that the arrival of her daughter had altered her life more profoundly than she could have believed possible.

That such a tiny creature could take up so much of her time remained a source of continual astonishment to Liv. Freya demanded her attention constantly, day and night. It was hard to find time to cook the dinner or to do the washing, let alone read a book or write a letter. The health visitor told Liv not to spoil Freya, and to feed her four-hourly: 'Just put her pram at the bottom of the garden, dear, and then you won't hear her.' But Freya's cries tore at Liv's heart, and her breasts wept milk, so, racked by feelings of guilt at the spoilt monster she was creating, she fed Freya when she cried. Freya never ever managed four hours between feeds. Three and a half hours was her absolute best.

The nights were worst. Liv never became used to being torn out of deep sleep. She'd stumble into the nursery, sleep dragging at her. Sometimes she slept as she walked; once she staggered into the door jamb, hitting her head. In the nursery, she'd lift Freya out of the carry-cot, sink down into the chair, and Freya would seize her nipple, sucking madly. Sometimes Liv would doze, waking with a start, afraid that she had dropped her. But Freya always continued to suck, her eyes closed in bliss. After Freya had fed, she'd change her, burp her, put her back in the carry-cot, and tiptoe back to bed. Sometimes Freya slept, sometimes she didn't. Sometimes, afraid that her cries would disturb Stefan, Liv would carry her downstairs and put her in the pram, and rock her till she finally dropped off. She became accustomed to sitting alone in the cold, quiet darkness, her head propped up on one hand, the other gripping the pram handle.

And yet she could not have said that she was unhappy. Spring gave way to summer, and when Liv gave Freya her early-morning feed, the skies were alive with birdsong, and the first rays of sun ignited white fire along each blade of grass. When Stefan learned that his paper had been accepted for publication, they celebrated with goulash and a bottle of cheap red wine. He knew that Professor Samuels would ask him to stay on at the university, Stefan said. He just knew he would.

In the afternoons, Liv would feed Freya, then take her into the garden, look down at her daughter's small, serene face, and feel a perfect, unprecedented contentment. Hormones, Katherine would have said, dismissively. But Liv, who knew better, knew that she had found love.

She had learned to read Stefan's mood by the way he returned to the house after work. The speed of the car, heading up the track. The gate closing with a crash, or with a gentle click of the hinges. His footsteps on the grass, to the accompaniment of silence, or the cheerful humming of a tune.

That evening, the front door slammed, echoing through the house. Stefan was black-browed, angry-eyed. 'I won't be staying on at the university next year,' he said shortly. 'There's funding for only one research assistant, and they've chosen Camilla Green.' His fists were clenched, and his face was drained of colour. 'I was counting on it. I was so sure I'd get it. So bloody unfair.' Turning on his heel, he went to the window, and stood, his back to Liv, silhouetted by the late-afternoon sunlight. 'Whatever else has been difficult,' he said softly, 'I've always had *that*. I've always been the clever one. Exams, coming top of the class, winning prizes – all that was easy. Nothing else was easy, but *that* was. But now—'

and he swung round to face her. 'I didn't think I'd fail, Liv,' he said. He looked bewildered. 'I didn't think I could possibly fail.'

Later that night, when she woke for Freya's feed, Liv saw that she was alone in bed. After she had settled Freya, she tiptoed downstairs. The light was on in Stefan's study, and she could hear the sound of footsteps, and drawers slamming. Opening the study door, she saw that Stefan had up-ended his desk and filing-cabinet, so that the contents spilled over the floor, making a sea of white paper. His wild black handwriting scored every discarded page.

'*Stefan*,' she whispered. 'What are you *doing*?'

'What does it look like? Clearing up.'

'Your *work*—'

'A waste of bloody time, wasn't it?' He kicked savagely at the heaps of paper.

'That's not true! Your paper's going to be published and there'll be other jobs.'

Yet he continued to rip sheets from the notebooks. Mesmerized, she watched his strong, elegant hands tear the paper into fragments and crush it into balls. 'You could teach at a different university,' she pleaded. In the chaos of the room, her voice sounded hollow, echoing. 'Manchester or Leeds...' When she touched his hand, his muscles jerked and he moved away.

'The Citroën's on its last legs, you know that. It couldn't cope with such a long journey.'

'We could move house.'

'Move house?' He swung round to her. 'Never.'

'Why not?'

'Because this is my home. Why should I let them force me out of my home?'

She had begun automatically to pick up the balls of paper, to smooth them out and heap them up. 'But if you can't find work here—'

'I'm not leaving Holm Edge, Liv. Never.' He stared at her, blue eyes wide. 'And leave those bloody papers *alone*.'

'Stefan—'

'I said, leave them *alone*.' He grabbed the sheaf of papers from her hand, hurling them to the floor. Then he said softly, 'You don't know what you're talking about, Liv. You should learn to stop interfering in what you don't understand. Get out.' He seized her shoulders, twisting her round, pushing her towards the door. 'Why don't you just get out?'

She went back to bed, and fell eventually into an uneasy doze. In the morning, she found that Stefan had locked the door to his study. She knocked, but he did not reply. Her head ached, and she felt as though she had drifted into a nightmare. At mid-morning, she put a fractious Freya into her pram and walked out to her favourite place, a high point on the Littledale road. There was a narrow footpath leading upwards to a hilltop cluttered with boulders and clumps of gorse. The path was too narrow for the pram wheels, so she unclipped the carry-cot, hauled it up to the summit and sat down on a boulder, Freya asleep beside her.

As the rain cleared away, she could see down the sweep of the valley to Morecambe Bay and the sea. There was the remains of a bar of chocolate in her pocket, so she broke off pieces and ate them. It seemed to her that within the last year her life had almost run out of control. She had fallen in love, had left university, had married, and had given birth to a baby within the space of twelve months. She did not think she was the same person she had been a year ago. She felt as though she had been running, something nameless snapping at her heels.

She had to steel herself to head back to Holm Edge. Yet when Stefan came outdoors to greet her, she saw that he was smiling. She felt an overwhelming sense of relief: the edgy, angry stranger was gone, and her bright, loving Stefan was back again.

He took the carry-cot from her, parking it outside the front door. 'I've had a marvellous idea,' he said. 'I've been longing to tell you.' He had opened a bottle of home-made wine; he poured two glasses. 'I've decided you were right, darling. Of course I mustn't give up my work. So I'm going to write a book.' He passed Liv a glass. 'That'll show them, won't it? The paper wasn't nearly substantial enough to do justice to my ideas. And I'll be able to work at home – here, at Holm Edge – so we'll be together all the time.' He walked out into the garden. 'And that's not the only idea I've had. We must plant more crops – fruit as well as vegetables. And we must keep animals – a pig, perhaps, or goats. And I'll make a start renovating the barn.' He paused outside the tumbledown building. 'I can do that, can't I, now that I'll have more time?' When he turned to her, she could see the elation in his eyes. 'It'll be all right, Liv,' he said. 'I promise you, my darling, it'll all be all right.'

Felix knew that Saffron was drifting away from him. Once, their reunions had made her absences worthwhile; now, her off-handedness gouged into him, turning him, as the weeks passed, into someone he didn't much like. Turning him into someone who added up the days, who asked accusing questions, who looked suspiciously at each of her friends. One evening he found himself at her bedroom door, listening for – what? A man's voice, murmuring her name? That small, satisfied sigh, so familiar to him, that she made as she climaxed? He forced himself to walk away.

Sometimes he dreamed of her. He dreamed that he was shaking her, his hands gripping her upper arms, his fingertips pressing into her flesh. In his dream, the expression on her face remained unchanged, her grey eyes serene, undisturbed by his anger. Waking, he was revolted by the lingering intensity of his aggression.

One hot June day, he helped Martin repair the ceiling of one of the back bedrooms. In the late afternoon, Martin drove to Newbury to buy plaster. Perched on top of the stepladders, Felix put aside the trowel. His arms ached, and he was grey with plaster dust. The room was unbearably warm, though they had flung the windows wide open. He sat for a while, staring out at the lake. In places, the previous night's storm had caused it to flood so that only the tops of the reeds showed above the water-level: small, feathery candles that broke up the glassy surface. There was a movement at the far corner of the lake, and Felix saw Justin shinning up the tree to where a rope swing had been looped around the outstretched bough. Felix scanned the banks, but Justin appeared to be alone. It was Tuesday, market-day, Nancy and Claire's turn to run the stall. Justin was loosening the swing. The back of Felix's neck prickled as the boy hung precariously over the water. Then he seemed to lose his balance. For a moment Felix thought he would be able to right himself. Instead, his arms flailed, and he fell into the lake.

Justin can swim, thought Felix. Surely he can swim. The golden head disappeared below the surface of the lake, then bobbed up again. Arms beat the water wildly. Justin, thought Felix, as he scrambled rapidly down the ladder, couldn't add up, couldn't read, could hardly string a civil sentence together, so why should he be able to swim?

As he ran out of the house, the heat struck him. Shouting Justin's name, he tore down the terrace, across the lawn, through the orchard, kicking off his shoes as he ducked through the last of the trees. The banks of the lake were empty. He dived in.

The cold water knocked the breath out of him. Felix dived and dived again, searching desperately through the murk, grasping hanks of pondweed, and waterlogged branches that floated beneath the surface like sullen snakes. Something silky and tenuous drifted between his fingers. He gripped hard, and hauled Justin above the surface of the water by his long, golden hair. Then he half dragged, half carried the boy to the bank. The weed and reeds were almost impenetrable, and he kept slipping in the thick mud. Hearing voices, he called out for help. In his arms Justin was heavy, his motionless limbs trailing water.

Someone took the child from him. Seeing Claire, he knew that he would never forget the expression on her face. Nancy bent over Justin, and put her mouth to his. Felix staggered out of the water and sat on the bank, his head flung back, trying to force air into his lungs, his gaze fixed on the child. Breathe, damn you, breathe, he thought. The moment seemed to still, to freeze, waiting for the small movement of Justin's ribcage. When Felix heard the sound – a spluttering cough, then a cry – he pressed his fists against his eye-sockets. When eventually he was able to look again, he saw that Claire was cradling Justin in her arms, and that Nancy was wrapping her shawl around the boy's shaking shoulders. Aware of a sudden, awful anger at the nearness of disaster, Felix stumbled to his feet and walked back to the house. He could hear the two women following behind him. Justin was sobbing, and Claire's anguish echoed his own: 'What were you doing, Justin? You know you're not supposed to play on the swing on your own. Who was meant to be keeping an eye on you?'

Who was meant to be keeping an eye on you? Felix saw her, standing at the terrace's stone balustrade. Her long silvery hair was flowing over her shoulders, and she was wearing her indigo dress. Lawrence was beside her. Felix heard Nancy whisper, 'Saffron . . .' and then there was the sound of fast footsteps.

'It was you, wasn't it, you stupid cow?' Claire was running across the lawn.

Saffron focused on her. 'What are you talking about?'

'You were supposed to be looking after the children, weren't you?'

'I was busy.'

'You were *busy*!' The wooden soles of her clogs clacked as Claire ran up the stone steps. 'Do you know what you've done, you stupid bitch? Do you know?'

The sound of the flat of Claire's hand as she slapped Saffron's face was like a gunshot. The force of the blow made Saffron gasp and stagger backwards. There was a pink stripe across her chalk-white face. Claire shouted, 'Justin almost died because of you! He almost drowned!'

'Claire—'

'Shut up, Lawrence. You were supposed to be looking after him, you silly bitch, but you couldn't be bothered, could you?'

'Drowned?' Bryony had emerged from a downstairs room, Zak in her arms.

153

'He's all right. No thanks to her. If Felix hadn't seen him . . .'
Claire gripped Saffron's narrow shoulders, and began to shake
her. Felix remembered shaking her like that in his dream.

'Steady on, Claire!'

'Shut up, Lawrence!'

'Perhaps we should call an ambulance.'

'You only ever think of yourself.'

'If Justin did as he was told—'

'Should have taught him to swim.'

'Shut up, Lawrence!'

Felix pushed between Claire and Saffron, put his arm around
Saffron's shoulders, and steered her to the house. He took her into
the library and closed the door behind them. She was white and
trembling. He pushed her into a chair. He himself remained
standing, his wet clothes dripping on to the polished oak floor.

She said tremulously, 'Justin . . .?'

'Will be fine.' He tried to smile. 'The fright might even do
him good.' He paused. 'Were you supposed to be looking after
them?'

'Yes. I thought Justin was in the playroom with India. He was
when I looked earlier.'

'Didn't you see him leave the house?'

'No.' Her grey eyes were defiant. 'I was upstairs.'

He didn't want to ask, but he forced himself to. 'In your
room?'

'No.' She was sitting up very straight, but he noticed how
she had to clench her hands together to stop them trembling.
'Lawrence's room.'

'Oh,' he said. Just that. *Oh.* He sensed the ending of something. Of a dream, perhaps. He went to the window and looked
out. He could see the courtyard and the road. A green Mini
Cooper was drawing up against the kerb.

He said, 'Are you in love with Lawrence?'

'Of course not.'

'But you're sleeping with him?'

'I told you, Felix, I don't *sleep* with anyone.'

'But—'

'We screw, we fuck, we make love, whichever you choose.' Her voice was harsh.

He closed his eyes tightly, and heard himself say, 'I see.'

'Do you? I doubt if you do. I wish—' She broke off. Then she muttered, 'I wish it had been different. I really do. I wish I'd been different.'

When he opened his eyes, he saw that the green Mini Cooper had parked, and that Katherine was climbing out of it. He recognized her with the lack of surprise that was the product of emotional and physical exhaustion.

He paused only briefly as he left the room. 'Will you stay here?'

'I don't think I can after this.'

'And Lawrence?'

She shrugged. 'I don't know. Perhaps. He's not important.' Suddenly she reached out and took his hand. 'I'm sorry, Felix.' Her hand slipped from his. 'So sorry.'

Katherine said, 'I need you to come back to London with me, Felix.'

'Yes,' he said. She noticed that he was very wet. 'Why?'

'For Toby,' she explained. 'He's been busted.'

'*Hell.*'

'Will you come?'

'Of course.'

She looked at him again. 'Do you want anything? A towel? A change of clothes?'

He did not reply, but followed her out of the house, along the path to where Toby's car was parked at the front of the house. Driving away from Great Dransfield, Katherine said, 'You're rather wet.'

'I've been for a swim.' He wiped his dripping hair from his brow.

'Do you want to tell me about it?'

'Not now.' His eyes were hard, green stones. 'Not ever, perhaps.'

She told him about Toby. Toby had taken to leaving the Chelsea house only at night. In the early hours of the morning, he had gone out to buy cigarettes from a slot machine. A policeman had seen him, and had followed him home. The house had been searched.

'He was lucky, really. They only found the tiniest bit of dope. He's been dropping a lot of acid recently, so thank God there wasn't any in the house. But they arrested him and charged him all the same. He phoned me.' Katherine slowed for a junction. 'He's ill, Felix. He's completely freaked out. He thinks traffic lights are talking to him, and that the noises the pipes make are creatures from other planets trying to contact him.' She looked at Felix again. He really was awfully wet, she thought. As though he had had a bath with his clothes on. And his hair was a funny colour – a dark, murky grey, with bits of green stuff in it.

He was leaning forward, and squeezing water from the ends of his sleeves into the footwell. She saw him scowl. 'Poor old Toby. Has he got a lawyer?'

'Only the one the police gave him. I spoke to him this morning. I thought he was pretty hopeless.' Katherine fumbled on top of the dashboard for her cigarettes. 'Light one for me, will you?'

He lit two, one for each of them. Then he said, 'I'll phone my father, and ask him for the name of his lawyer. And then we'll think what to do next.'

In the early hours of the morning, Felix took Toby back to the Chelsea house. Katherine, making coffee downstairs in the wreckage of the kitchen, heard his footsteps coming down the stairs.

'He's fallen asleep, thank God.' Felix collapsed on the sofa. 'I've phoned his parents in Hong Kong. His mother's flying back as soon as she can.'

The house belonged to Toby's parents. Katherine imagined

what her own mother would say, seeing this kitchen. There wasn't a clean piece of crockery, and dog ends floated in the dirty brown water in the sink. The contents of the drawers had been tipped out on to the floor – the police, Katherine supposed – and there were scorch marks on the ceiling.

'Perhaps I'd better clear up.'

'I'll give you a hand tomorrow morning.'

'Don't you want to go home?'

Felix looked blank, as though he had forgotten where *home* was. But he shook his head. 'Not really. No.'

She thought, *And Saffron?* but did not say anything as she circled the kitchen, picking up dirty cups and plates and putting them beside the draining board.

'What are you doing?'

'I might as well make a start.'

'Don't be an idiot, Katherine. You look wiped out.'

She knew that she was exhausted, that she had been awake for almost twenty-four hours, but she said obstinately, 'I won't be able to sleep, I know I won't.'

He patted the sofa beside him. 'Come on.'

She sat down beside him. He said, 'You can't possibly think I have any evil intent. Today I've plastered a ceiling, I've been for a swim I didn't intend to have, and I've spent an evening talking to lawyers and policemen. Do you really think I've any energy left for *anything?*'

She managed to smile. 'The thing is,' he explained, 'that if I put my arm round you, we can sleep side by side on this sofa. And though there are beds in this house, I've seen the state they're in, and I can't say I fancy any of them.'

'Felix—'

'Hush, not a word.' He had pulled a rug over them. 'Go to sleep.'

Katherine lay still for a while, staring into the darkness, while the events of the day unreeled, like a speeded-up film, in her mind. The phone-call in the early hours of the morning. Visiting Toby at the police station, and driving to Berkshire to fetch Felix.

At last her muscles began to relax. Felix gave a little snore, and adjusted his position, so that his hand crept further round her waist. She did not push him away, but closed her eyes and, eventually, she slept.

Chapter Seven

Stefan took a part-time job in a crammer in Lancaster, teaching French to students who had failed their A levels. To begin with, he was optimistic. The students' accents were appalling and their demeanour offhand, but, Stefan explained to Liv, he would teach them to love French. He would inspire them. After a few months, his initial enthusiasm faltered. His students, their parents and the principal of the college had one common aim: to pass the exam. No one gave a thought to the beauty of the language, and a lesson spent studying anything other than dictates of the curriculum was, in all but Stefan's eyes, a lesson wasted. Stefan was rebuked by the principal. Complaints, he was told, had been received. If Mr Galenski did not concur with the ethos of the college, then Mr Galenski should reconsider his position. The principal reminded Stefan that, as a part-time teacher, he had no contract of employment. Stefan confined himself to irregular verbs and teaching translation by rote.

He began to research his book. Reference books, tattered secondhand tomes from distant Middle European countries that Liv would have struggled to place on a map, overflowed from the study shelves and were stacked in towers on the floor. Liv helped prepare the card index that would cross-reference mythologies by their place of origin, their subject matter and antiquity. The book, Stefan hoped, would make his name, and its success would show the university how mistaken they had been in choosing Camilla Green. Throughout the evenings and late into the night, he worked on it.

The teaching job paid for the basics – food, rent and electricity – but left little for anything else. Stefan's small savings paid for

Freya's clothes and for the secondhand cot that replaced the carry-cot she had grown out of. By day, when he was not teaching, Stefan worked on the house and in the garden. They must live off the land, he reminded Liv, so they planted potatoes and turnips, Brussels sprouts and cabbages. Stefan helped Ted Marwick, the farmer in the valley, repair a fence, and in return was given six pullets. The goslings, now grown to sizeable geese, prowled round the garden, hissing at the postman, charging straight-necked at his bicycle if he was foolhardy enough to open the gate.

Stefan began to renovate the barn. Perched precariously up ladders, he removed the remains of the old roof and made a bonfire of the damp, mouldy furniture inside. As the autumn turned to winter, Freya grew a fringe of fine black hair that circled her head like a monk's tonsure. She was long and thin, all arms and legs and restless energy, an utterly different creature from the plump, placid infants that Liv saw once a month at the clinic in Caton. At five and a half months she began to crawl, shuffling on to her hands and knees, rocking backwards and forwards and screaming with impatience when she could not reach whatever it was that had caught her eye.

Freya adored Stefan, and Stefan adored her. When Freya's frustration got too much for her and she became red-faced with fury, Stefan would scoop her up, wrap her in her coat and bonnet and carry her around the house and garden. The sight of the hens, pecking at the grass, would distract her. Her eyes would widen, and her mouth would open in a wide O of astonishment. She would smile her wide, gap-toothed smile, and reach out a hand to tug a lock of Stefan's hair, gurgling with laughter.

Liv began to plan. When Freya was a little older, she could leave her with Stefan for a few hours a week and take a part-time job in Caton or Lancaster. That would ease their financial worries and give Liv the company she had recently begun to miss. Visits from friends in the Cultural Studies Department had petered out completely after Stefan had left the university. 'I won't have them crow over me,' Stefan had said angrily, when Liv suggested he invite some of his former colleagues to supper. 'I won't have them *pity* me.' In the summer, two fellow students from Liv's university days had made the long trek out to Holm Edge, but, separated by marriage and motherhood as well as by geography, they seemed no longer to have much to say to each other, and the visit was not repeated.

She asked one of the women she met at the clinic to Holm Edge for coffee, but the afternoon was not a success. The other woman's pushchair stuck in the muddy track and Liv had to dig it out with a trowel, and the expression on her visitor's face when Liv showed her into the house both took Liv aback and made her want to giggle. For the first time she realized how someone else might see the whitewashed plaster, the stone floors, the ancient coal stove. She had almost forgotten the existence of electric cookers and telephones. She had almost forgotten that some people did not cover the holes in the sofa with a throw but instead bought new furniture, that they bought curtains instead of making them out of patchwork, and cushions instead of cobbling them together out of discarded jerseys that had gone too far for darning. It was how she and Thea had always lived. Never buy anything from a shop if you can make it yourself. Make do and mend. Like her marriage, Liv thought, which had to be patched up every now and then and made into something new.

Since *Frodo's Finger* had folded, Katherine had supported herself by temping. It was reasonably well paid: she earned more than she had working for Toby and Stuart, though the work was uninteresting and, moving to a different office each week, she made few friends.

Toby's parents had returned from Hong Kong in time for his court case to be heard. He had escaped a prison sentence, and his parents had paid his fine. He had then been spirited off to a luxurious clinic in the depths of the countryside. Katherine had visited him, and had found him altered: no longer hearing voices in the skirting-board, but in his striped pyjamas and royal-blue dressing-gown oddly subdued and reduced.

She knew that Felix had left the commune because he had sent her a postcard: 'Paradise most definitely lost. Am going away for a while.' She had telephoned Stuart to tell him about Toby, and he had made sympathetic noises and vague promises to visit, but she had known that he would not. The winter months passed in an endless and exhausting succession of parties, dinners and dates. Katherine told herself that this was what she had always wanted, an exciting metropolitan life to replace the stifling provincial boredom of home. Yet none of the boyfriends lasted, and she had little in common with the girls she met through her work. In her darker moments, she thought that she went out simply because she couldn't bear to be alone. If she was alone, her thoughts still sometimes drifted to Rachel, and the void that was the only legacy of her absence, and the way death erased you so speedily, so mercilessly, so absolutely.

The Australian couple on the top floor, Kerry and Jane Mossop, held parties at least once a week, to which Katherine was always invited. It was at one of the Mossops' parties that she met Graham. Kerry Mossop introduced them. 'Kathy,' he always called her Kathy, she had given up trying to persuade him to do otherwise, 'meet Graham Cotterell-Jones. He owns an art gallery.'

Graham was blond, neat and good-looking. Unlike most of the other male guests, who were in jeans, he wore a dark suit with a Nehru collar. Katherine talked to him, shouting over the record-player and the conversation of fifty people crammed into a small room. He told her about his gallery in Soho, filled up her glass and plied her with Gitanes. Then they danced, the palm of his hand caressing her bottom, his chest pressed against her breasts. Sometime in the course of the evening, she acknowledged that though she could have gone to bed with him she would not do so. There was something unsettling, slightly reptilian about him. Disentangling herself around one o'clock in the morning,

Katherine said brightly, 'Well, it's been lovely meeting you, Graham, but I must go. Work tomorrow.'

'*Go?*' he repeated.

'Yes. It's late. Work tomorrow—'

'You said that.' There was an expression of cold dislike in his eyes, which made her glad she had decided not to spend the night with him.

She found Kerry and Jane, and thanked them for the party, then wormed her way out of the room and went downstairs. Looking in the mirror in her bedsit, she saw that her cheeks had flushed and her makeup was smudged, giving her a rather lurid appearance. She splashed cold water over her face. She felt rather drunk, and her ears buzzed from the music and conversation.

There was a tap at the door, so she opened it. Graham was standing on the threshold. 'Yes?' she said.

'We've unfinished business, haven't we, Katherine?'

She felt frightened, and tried to shut the door, but he had jammed it with his foot. 'Bitch,' he said softly, then gave her a shove, the palm of his hand flat against her breasts, so that she fell backwards into the room.

She heard the door slam. She was crouched on the floor; he was looking down at her. He was smiling. 'You see,' he said, 'I don't like being given the brush-off, Katherine.'

Her mind went blank. She said, 'Get out. Just get out,' but the words did not come out as she had meant them to, and sounded uncertain and tremulous.

'I told you.' There was an expression of contempt in his eyes. 'Unfinished business.'

'What do you mean?' Her heart was pounding.

'I don't like teases, Katherine. And you're a tease, aren't you?' He hauled her to her feet as he spoke. When she cried out, he struck her, slapping her face over and over again until she fell back to the floor, stupefied by pain and humiliation.

Then he crouched beside her. 'You make a habit of this, do you, Katherine?' he whispered. His face was close to hers, and his eyes glittered. 'Leading men on, then keeping your legs closed. Turns you on, does it? Well, I'm not going to let you do that to me.' There was a tearing sound as he ripped open her blouse, and she knew, recognizing the pleasure in his pale eyes, that he had done this before, that he did not even think it was wrong.

She said, 'Please . . .' and then he slapped her again.

'Leading me on all evening, then giving me the cold shoulder. You're a bitch, aren't you? A first-class, frigid little bitch.'

Then he pushed her skirt up to her waist. She heard herself whimper as his fingers dug into the crevices of her body. 'Please don't . . . please don't . . .' His skin, warm and clammy, pressed against hers. She wanted to retch. She could hear herself sobbing. Her arms flailed desperately as she struggled to pull away from him. She heard him say sharply, 'Keep still, bitch,' and then, miraculously, her fingertips brushed against something smooth and cold: a bowl, discarded from her earlier rushed supper of tomato soup. Grabbing it, she flung it at him. It struck him on the side of the head, and as he momentarily relaxed his hold of her, she twisted sideways and stumbled to the door. Her muscles were nightmarishly weak and slow to respond, but somehow she managed to turn the handle and escape into the bathroom opposite, shooting the bolt just before he grabbed the door handle.

Then she sat on the bathroom floor, her knees pressed to her chest, her hands over her ears as he shouted at her and rattled the door. After a long time she heard footsteps going down the stairs. She did not dare leave the room; she did not think she would ever have the courage to leave the room. She made herself look at her watch. She would wait for twenty minutes, she told herself. She sat, shaking with reaction, her face and body sore and bruised, watching the hands of her watch go round. When twenty minutes had passed, she rose and opened the door a fraction, glancing quickly to left and right. She could see her hand trembling as it curled round the jamb. The door to her room was ajar. She tried to see into the shadows. The light was on, but darkness gathered around the furniture. She searched the room – inside the wardrobe, beneath the bed, in the cupboard under the sink – and then she locked the door, pushing the armchair against the handle.

Katherine tidied the room. All the dirty crockery went into the sink, and the remains of food into the bin. She hung her clothes in the wardrobe, and lined up her books on the shelf. Kneeling on the floor, she scrubbed the tomato soup from the lino, rubbing with the cloth, over and over again. She kept remembering how the red had stained his white skin. She only stopped scrubbing when she could not see for tears. Then she peeled off all her clothes, one by one, dropping them into the bin, ran hot water into the sink and washed every inch of her body as she wept.

When she had finished, she lay down on the bed. She was aware of self-loathing, and a crushing, terrible loneliness. She thought that she would not sleep – every creaking pipe was a footstep, every traffic noise his hot breath in her ear – but eventually she drifted off.

Katherine dreamed. Rachel was standing at the end of the bed. She was trying to tell her something, but Katherine could not hear what she was saying because there was a weight pressing down on her, heavy and smothering. Gasping for breath, she opened her eyes, and saw that the pale dawn sunlight was spilling through the window-panes.

She did not leave the house for three days. Not until her bruises and black eyes had faded. Driven out at last in search of food, she imagined his contemptuous eyes watching her. Every sudden movement or unexpected sound made her start. She phoned in sick to the temping agency, and screwed a bolt and chain to the inside of her door.

She thought of going home, wondering whether in her small, familiar bedroom, with its yellowing photographs of foreign cities and posters of *The Man from U.N.C.L.E.*, she might begin to feel safe again. She knew that no one would question her sudden return. Constants did not question, thought Katherine bitterly, Constants were expert in lack of curiosity. She had never been quite sure whether this was born of tact or of indifference, or whether the tenor of the household – her mother's perpetual angry exhaustion, and her father's preoccupation with his work – enforced such detachment. The Constant household had always been like a simmering saucepan: had an unexpected emotion or an unanticipated need been added to the witches' brew, then Heaven knew what might have boiled over. She was unsure whether this time she could hide what had happened to her; she was afraid that her desperation was written in her eyes.

Instead, she packed her duffel bag and took the train to Lancaster. Arriving at Liv's house, she half expected to feel once more that small flicker of envy – at domesticity, at married bliss – but did not, felt nothing much at all, in fact, other than a vague relief at not being in London.

Liv welcomed her with hugs, fed her vegetable soup and home-made scones, and stoked up the fire so that she would not feel cold. Katherine talked continuously, about anything and everything except the terrible thing that had happened to her. In the evening, Stefan retreated to his study, and Liv gave Freya her late feed. Katherine prowled round the room, glancing at books then putting them back on the shelves. She saw Liv watching her, and she said quickly, 'Stefan, a *teacher*. He hates it, doesn't he?'

Liv frowned. 'He did prefer the university, yes.'

'Will he keep on with it, do you think?'

'He has to,' said Liv bluntly. 'We haven't any other money.'

It took Katherine a moment to understand that Liv meant literally that: that Stefan's part-time teaching job was their only source of income. She said doubtfully, 'I suppose babies don't cost much, do they? I mean – they don't eat much, and their clothes and things are very small.'

Liv started to say something, then seemed to change her mind. Then she said, 'Hold her for me, while I get a clean Babygro,' and passed Freya to Katherine. Katherine held the baby awkwardly as Liv ran upstairs. When Freya burped, she thought,

God, my new Bus Stop top! but, glancing over her shoulder, saw that her blouse was still clean. Freya's head drooped against her shoulder, and her small, warm body relaxed. Katherine reached out a tentative finger to stroke Freya's soft cheek, and Freya smiled, an open-mouthed, milky, adoring smile, that in a single moment melted Katherine's heart. A tear trailed down her cheek, but she did not dare put up a hand to wipe it away for fear of dropping Freya. Then Liv came back downstairs, took the baby from her and said, 'Tell me.'

'Tell you what?' The words were snuffly and muffled.

Liv had put Freya on the rug and was changing her nappy and sleepsuit. 'Tell me what's upset you so much.'

Katherine thought of saying, 'Nothing's upset me', or, 'It doesn't matter', but couldn't get the words out and instead pressed the heels of her hands against her aching eyes. At last she said, 'Something awful. I can't . . .' Her voice trailed off.

Liv glanced up at her. 'To do with work?' Katherine shook her head.

'Your family, then. Simon . . . or Philip?' Another shake of the head.

'A boyfriend?' When Katherine did not reply, Liv said softly, 'Blood sisters, remember.'

Katherine recalled the bonfire, and Rachel's doll. As a small girl, she had always half envied, half despised Rachel for her vast collection of dolls, and there had been a particular satisfaction at watching smug Miss France go up in flames. She tried to smile. 'Does it still count, d'you think, when there's just two of us?'

'Of course it does. More, if anything.'

Liv had settled back in the armchair to give Freya the rest of her feed. Katherine heard herself say, 'It's just that I feel such a *fool* . . . and so *dirty* . . .' and then haltingly, it tumbled out: the party, and Graham who in no more than a few minutes had taken from her her dignity, her self-respect, and her confidence.

She didn't tell it all, of course. She didn't tell Liv that she had never enjoyed going to bed with a man: she was far too ashamed of that. When she had finished, she tried to laugh it off – 'He didn't really *do* anything, and he looked so funny with tomato soup all over his suit' – but she could tell that Liv wasn't remotely convinced. She was so used to being the strong one, the one who could look after herself, that it was hard to acknowledge the depth of her despair.

Liv looked at Katherine. 'Did you go to the police?'

'Of course not. What would be the point?'

'He assaulted you.'

'He'd say I led him on, wouldn't he? After all, I'm not exactly *virginal*, am I?'

'That makes no difference—'

'You know it does, Liv,' said Katherine fiercely. 'I wrote an article about rape cases for the magazine. Women have practically to be *nuns* to have any hope of winning in court.' She looked down at her hands. 'And, anyway, it's not that. I can bear that. It's the other things.'

Liv cradled the sleeping baby against her shoulder. 'What other things?'

Katherine gave a peculiar little laugh. 'I keep thinking it was my fault somehow. I know that's silly, but I can't seem to stop myself. He said that I was a – that I'd flaunted myself. And I keep thinking, Well, I was wearing a very short skirt, and I was rather drunk, and I do like it when men like me, and—'

'Katherine,' said Liv gently, and Katherine fell silent, pressing her lips together.

Then she said more calmly, 'I sometimes think it's as though I haven't quite got the hang of being a woman. I don't say quite the right things, or do the right things. It's as if there are rules I don't know about. I thought I'd worked everything out when I went to London. I'd got a job I liked, and friends, and nice clothes, and a place of my own. Everything I always wanted. But now it all seems to have gone wrong and, besides, what's the use of anything if I always feel afraid? If, when it comes to it, any man can make me do what he likes, just because he's stronger than me.'

'Not all men are like that,' Liv pointed out.

'But how do I *tell*, Liv?' Katherine thumped her palm with her fist. 'And I used to love my bedsit, but now I hate it. It frightens me. I keep thinking ... every night, I have to look under the bed and in the wardrobe. So silly, I know, but I can't sleep otherwise. Yet I don't like going outside, either. I don't feel safe. Nothing's right any more ...' Her face crumpled.

'You should go abroad,' said Liv, and Katherine's head jerked up. 'What?'

'Go abroad. Travel. It's what you always wanted to do.'

She thought of her going-round-the-world fund, untouched in the building society. Then she said, 'I can't.'

'Course you can.'

'You don't understand.' She felt angry with Liv for being so unsympathetic, so lacking in comprehension. 'If I can hardly get out of my front door, how can I possibly go abroad?'

'You'll manage.' Liv was stroking Freya's curled spine. 'You'll manage because you have to, Katherine. It's just a question of doing it. And you were always good at doing things.'

For the first time, she saw it as a possibility: just stepping on to a plane or a ferry, and leaving everything behind.

She heard Liv say, 'One of us has to travel. One of us has to see the world and do great things. And it's not going to be me, is it? And it wasn't Rachel. So it's rather up to you.' She stood up, Freya in her arms. 'And, besides, I need you to go. *Someone* needs to keep an eye out for my father, don't they?'

At Christmas Thea came to stay. As the first day of her visit drew to a close, it seemed to Liv that there was a distance between them. Thea was quiet, as though she was holding something back. Washing up that evening, Liv blurted out, 'What is it, Mum? What's wrong?'

Thea looked startled. 'Nothing's wrong.' She smiled. 'Everything's fine, Liv. Better than fine, actually.' She took a deep breath.

'The thing is that I have to talk to you about something important. I have to talk to you about Richard.'

Liv couldn't at first think who Richard was, and then she said, bewildered, 'Mr Thorneycroft?'

Thea looked flustered. 'I should have said something before, I know, only I wasn't sure what you'd think. And you've had so much to cope with. Marriage . . . and then Freya . . . that I didn't want . . . and telephone boxes are so difficult, and a letter would have seemed so *formal*.'

'Mum, what on earth are you talking about?'

Thea rubbed her forehead. 'Oh dear, I'm making rather a hash of this, aren't I? Liv, Richard and I are in love.'

The plate that Liv was washing slid back into the soapy water. *Richard and I are in love*. But, she wanted to say, you're *fifty*, Mum, and Mr Thorneycroft wears tweeds with leather patches on the elbows, and he limps, and . . .

'But you've known him for ages,' she said weakly, 'and I didn't think—'

'I've always *liked* Richard. And I've always *respected* him. He's had such a lot to bear – the war, and the death of his wife and child in the Blitz. He has endured all that. And I admire that, the capacity to endure.'

'Not like Dad, you mean?'

Thea put down the tea-towel. 'Richard isn't like your father, no, Liv.' She knotted her hands together. 'When I first went to work for him, I welcomed the fact that Richard was all the things that Fin was not. That he was taciturn whereas Fin could talk the hind legs off a donkey, that he was reticent whereas Fin was so open, so spontaneous. And for a very long time, Richard was just an employer. And then, I suppose, almost without my noticing it, he became a friend. He was very kind to me when poor Rachel died.' She sighed. 'I find that I value kindness and constancy and reliability more than I did in my youth. Unromantic, I know, but put it down to my great age.' Thea looked at Liv, and said gently, 'I loved your father for so long. But it became so exhausting, so diminishing. All that hope, all that disappointment. Every time he went away I thought I'd lost him for ever. Every time he came back, I thought, That's it, he'll never leave me again. But he always did, didn't he? And in the end, I just didn't care any more. I hadn't the capacity to care any more. I was almost relieved that it was over.'

'Are you going to get married?'

'We don't plan to. We thought—'

'Because Dad might come home, you know.'

There was a silence. Thea said gently, 'Darling, I really don't think that he will.'

'He sent me a postcard, remember.' Two and a half years ago. There had been nothing since. There was a dull ache inside her, as if from an unhealed wound.

'You know that I divorced Fin years ago.'

'But still—'

'And I believe, my dear, that if he had meant to come home, he would have done so by now.'

To my darling daughter Olivia . . . She had not thought that she still minded so much.

'I loved Fin so much,' added Thea slowly. 'I still do, I suppose, in a way. But we couldn't live with each other – I think I'd realized that even before he went away. And love, by itself, isn't always enough.'

It is, thought Liv. It has to be. She seized a dirty saucepan and began scrubbing it hard with a scouring-pad.

'You do grow tired of living on your own, you see. Fernhill has seemed very quiet since you left home, Liv.'

'There's Diana,' she said defiantly. 'And Katherine's mum.'

'If you scrub that pan much harder, you'll wear a hole in it.' Thea sighed again. 'You know how busy Barbara Constant always is. And Diana and I haven't had much to do with each other recently. I can't bear to see what she is doing to Rachel's daughter.'

Liv looked up, startled. 'To Alice?'

'Dressing her in Rachel's old clothes . . . giving her Rachel's toys to play with.' Thea sounded angry. 'She's already put the poor mite's name down for Lady Margaret's – and for ballet lessons and riding lessons, too, no doubt. And as for Henry – Henry does nothing to dissuade Diana of the illusion that Alice is just another Rachel. It breaks my heart to see it – for Alice's sake, and for Hector's. And for Diana's, too,' she added, her tone softening slightly. 'She doesn't look well. She's only fifty-three, but she looks ten years older.'

Liv looked out of the window. All day, she had hoped for snow for Freya's first Christmas, but the sky remained resolutely blue and unclouded. She said tentatively, 'If you and Mr Thorneycroft don't mean to marry . . .'

'We thought we might live together. That's what people do nowadays, isn't it?'

'*Mum!*'

'You're not shocked, are you, love?'

'Of course not.'

'And,' Thea took a deep breath, 'we're planning to rent a house in Crete.'

'*Crete!*' The saucepan slipped out of Liv's hands and hit the floor with a clang.

'Richard has always loved Crete, and the climate will be better for his health.' Thea smiled. 'It'll be a sort of very extended honeymoon, perhaps. Is one allowed a honeymoon, do you think, if one lives with someone?'

She managed to say, 'I don't see why not.'

'Then have we your blessing?'

'You don't need my blessing, Mum.'

'Nevertheless . . .'

Liv flung her arms around Thea, rubber gloves, scouring pad and all. There were tears in her eyes, but she blinked them back. 'Of course you do, Mum.'

It was dark the night Felix returned to Wyatts after six months' abroad, and his shoes crunched the frost as he walked across the grass. Light oozed beneath the dining room's crimson velvet curtains, and he heard, muted by the glass, the low hum of conversation. The side door was open, so he went indoors. When he walked into the dining room, there was a sudden silence.

Then Rose shrieked, 'Felix!' and jumped out of her chair, and Mia smiled her wide, curving smile, and his father said, 'Shut the door, old boy, and get yourself warm.' Rose clung to Felix's arm, her small hands gripping his frozen ones. He hugged her, holding her to him, and she pressed her face against the folds of his coat.

Over dinner, he had time to observe them all. Rose had cut her hair – with garden shears, by the look of it. It stuck out in short brown tufts around her peaky little face, giving her the look, he thought, of a Victorian street urchin. The candlelight that his stepmother always insisted on in the dining room lit Mia's long, red-brown hair, and her unchanging, classic beauty, but emphasized also the hollows around Bernard Corcoran's eyes, and the furrows that ran from his nose to his chin.

They asked him about Europe, and Felix told them about washing up in the café in Amsterdam, and picking grapes in southern France, and just wandering around the streets of Florence, and breathing in the city's beauty and antiquity.

He had slept overnight on a bench in the Boboli Gardens. 'But it began to get cold after a while,' he explained, 'and I was down to my last thousand-lire note. Then I was lucky – I got talking to someone in a bar one night, and ended up teaching English to a contessa's three fat little daughters.' He grinned. 'Well, *trying* to teach them. They spent most of the lessons eating sweets and gazing at me with their mouths open. They hardly said a word, and they all had big, brown eyes. It was like educating a herd of heifers.'

'What were their names?' asked Rose.

'Marietta, Constanza and Fiametta,' said Felix.

Rose repeated them under her breath. 'Such beautiful names. If Bridie has daughters, I'll call them Marietta, Constanza and Fiametta.'

'Who's Bridie?'

'My guinea-pig. They were selling them at a fête, Felix. It was terrible – six guinea-pigs in a cardboard box. They could hardly *move*. I only had enough money for two. It's awful when I think of the others ... what might have happened to them ...'

'How are the dogs?' asked Felix, changing the subject quickly. 'How are Bryn and Maeve? And the horses?' he added, noticing too late his father's warning eye.

'Beauty died just before Christmas.' Beauty was Rose's pony. Tears spilled from her eyes, trailing down her cheeks.

'She must have been quite old,' said Felix comfortingly.

'Seventy-seven in horse years.' Rose wiped her nose on her sleeve.

Distraction was provided by Mia bringing in the pudding. Mia followed recipe books only approximately, substituting absent ingredients for whatever came to hand. Paprika for cinnamon, treacle for honey. Ill-matched tastes fizzled on the tongue and burned the throat, then bubbled uncomfortably in the stomach for hours afterwards.

'It was supposed to be lemon and ginger pudding,' Mia explained, as she dolloped great wodges of mottled sponge on to plates, 'but I hadn't any lemons, only oranges, and the ginger had fallen down behind the fridge, so I had to use coffee. And there's Tia Maria instead of Grand Marnier.'

'Lovely,' said Bernard, heartily.

'Are there eggs in it?' asked Rose suspiciously.

'Half a dozen.'

'I don't eat eggs.'

'Rose has become a vegetarian.'

'A vegan, Daddy. I don't eat eggs, cheese or milk. Or murdered animals, of course.'

'You eat chocolate, don't you?' asked Felix. 'I brought some back from Switzerland.' Rose's eyes brightened. 'It's in my ruck-sack, in the hall.'

She darted out of the room. Mia wandered off to feed the cats, leaving Felix and his father together. Felix asked after the business. Bernard Corcoran frowned. 'We've had a tricky six months, to tell the truth. But I hope we're over the worst.' He offered cigarettes to

Felix, and lit one himself. 'We seem to have become unfashionable all of a sudden. All these new places – London shops full of chrome and corduroy – are taking our business.'

Corcoran's specialized in hand-printed historic wallpapers. Throughout the century of their existence, Corcoran's had acquired a huge stock of old pattern-blocks: elegant Regency stripes, floral chintzes and delicate chinoiseries.

'Apparently, we've the wrong *image*.' Bernard scowled. 'That's what one of those City boys told me. Consultant chappie. Someone recommended him. Dreadful little Flash Harry – wore *jewellery*, for Heaven's sake. Anyway, he more or less told us we were dinosaurs, stuck in the past. Fetch the Scotch, would you, Felix old chap? Could do with a drop, and I'm sure you could, after your journey.'

Felix poured out two measures. He heard his father add, 'Told us to invest in new designs. *Cheaper* designs.' Bernard's distaste was palpable. 'For all those tin-pot little houses they're putting up nowadays, I suppose, and selling at extortionate prices.' Bernard sighed. 'Had to borrow some cash – investment costs, you understand.'

Felix looked at his father. 'But you hate borrowing. You've always said—'

'Neither a borrower nor a lender be. I know. No choice. Beggars can't be choosers, and though we've assets, we haven't much in the way of liquid funds.' Bernard poured himself more Scotch, and made a visible effort to smile. 'Anyway, this is dull stuff. It's good to see you back, Felix.'

'It's good to be back.' And it was: the intensity of his pleasure in coming home took him by surprise.

'It's a pity you couldn't manage Christmas. Just the three of us here, rattling around like peas in a pod.'

'I couldn't get away for Christmas, Dad. I'd promised to stay till the New Year.' Not quite true: he had been glad of the opportunity to remain in Italy. Christmas, more than any other season, showed up absences and changes.

'Will you go back to that hippie place?'

'Great Dransfield? No. I haven't made any plans yet. I'll probably go to London for a few days ... see some old friends ... try and sort out what to do next ...'

'You know there's always a place for you here. And at the factory, of course. Could do with the help, to tell the truth.'

Later that evening, he wandered around the house, reacquainting himself with all his favourite familiar haunts. The attics, with their porthole windows set in curved dormers. The landing, with its large and beautiful art-nouveau stained-glass window that looked out over the front garden. The pergola that bridged the space between house and garden. The house was harmonious without being finicky; the wallpaper was Corcoran's, of course, and the furniture and fittings, much of them especially designed for Wyatts, embodied the William Morris dictum of being both beautiful and useful.

He dumped his rucksack in his room, and went to find Rose. She was curled up on the window-seat in her bedroom, eating chocolate.

'Is there room for me?'

'Course there is.' She folded up her legs, and he sat beside her. She settled her head into the crook of his shoulder, and said, 'Not coming home for Christmas, Felix! So *mean*! Leaving me with awful Mia!'

'Sorry.' He gave her a hug. 'I brought you this.' He handed her a parcel.

She opened it. 'It's beautiful!' It was a silk scarf, handpainted in shades of blue and green and gold. 'I shall wear it all the time.' She wrapped the scarf around her shoulders, and he thought that its magnificence dwarfed her, emphasizing her fragility and defencelessness.

He asked tentatively, 'How's school?'

'Hateful. I want to leave. I can do if I want to, can't I? I'm almost seventeen – that's grown-up, isn't it?'

She looked, and behaved, younger than her age, he thought. He held out his hand and she placed a piece of chocolate on it. 'If you leave school,' he asked, 'what will you do?'

'Daddy wants me to go to secretarial college in Norwich.'

'What about you, Rosy? What do you want?'

She mumbled, 'I don't know.'

'Do you want to stay here?'

'I would do if *she* wasn't here.'

Her continued hostility to Mia depressed him. He said, 'Mia's Dad's wife. It might be easier if you tried to like her.'

'*Mummy*'s Dad's wife.' Her lower lip stuck out. 'And she's always hanging round Dad ... never lets me have him to myself ... and her cooking's awful.'

He smiled. 'True.' He tried again. 'Whatever career you want, Rosy, it'll be easier if you stay on another year or so at school. If you wanted to work with animals, for instance.'

Reluctantly, she glanced at him. 'Do you think so?'

'Certainly. Tell you what, stick it out a bit longer and I'll give you a weekend in London. We'll go anywhere you want – Harrods, the theatre – anywhere.'

Her sad little face was transformed. 'Really?'

'Promise,' he said. 'Cross my heart and hope to die.'

The following week, he met Nancy in a café in Soho. When they had ordered coffee, Nancy asked Felix about Italy, and he told her about the contessa's three plump daughters.

Nancy laughed. 'Less of a challenge than India and Justin, I imagine.'

He smiled. He knew that, of the original community, only Claire and her children remained at Great Dransfield.

'How are they?'

'They go to the local school now. They've settled in well.'

He made himself ask, 'And Saffron? Is she still with Lawrence?'

'No.' Nancy touched Felix's hand. 'Saffron never cared two pins about Lawrence, you know.'

'I was never sure, to tell the truth, whether she cared two pins for anyone. Including me.'

Nancy, frowning, said, 'When I first met Susan—'

He glanced at her sharply. She said, 'Saffron's real name is Susan. You did know that, didn't you, Felix?'

'She never told me much. Only that she'd failed her eleven-plus, and that she left school at fifteen. And that she was married.'

'She married one of the partners at the solicitors' office where we worked. She was eighteen, and he was forty-one.' Nancy looked thoughtful. 'I've always mistrusted men who marry much younger women. It smacks of a need to control, don't you think? And after she lost the baby—'

'*Baby?*' He stared at her.

'Didn't she tell you? She had a late miscarriage. She was very ill. Anyway, that was at about the time my father died, and I had the idea of setting up the community. And the rest you know.' Nancy sighed. 'Saffron never loved her husband. I suppose she married him for all the usual things . . . for security, perhaps.'

'Or money,' said Felix.

Nancy's cool brown eyes met his. 'She is not *venal*,' she said softly, and he remembered Saffron in her frayed indigo gown, Saffron in her Oxfam furs.

'No,' he admitted. 'She isn't.'

'She never loved Ronald, but she longed for that baby, and she was devastated when she lost it. That was what I wanted to say to you, Felix, that loss takes people in different ways. Some try to fill the void, and others become wary of involvement.'

He thought that perhaps he himself was rather like Saffron, and that in the years since his mother's death he had avoided responsibility. He found himself reviewing uncomfortably the half-dozen jobs he had had since leaving university, the many different places where he had lived, the succession of dead-end relationships. All his belongings fitted into a rucksack. He had felt proud of his lack of possessions; now he found himself questioning his motives.

Taking his leave of Nancy later, he wondered what dream had prompted him to join the community. Perhaps he had tried to recapture what he had lost: the safe, close family that had fragmented for ever on the distant stormy December night on which his mother had died. Walking through Piccadilly, he felt free, as though a weight he had carried had slipped from his shoulders. *Saffron's real name is Susan.* In replacing the exotic with the mundane, he had begun to exorcize some of her feyness and mystery, and to see a more realistic – and forgivable – flawed humanity. Felix stood at the edge of Piccadilly Circus, loving the roar of the traffic, and the familiar cold, dusty London air. He thought that tomorrow he would look for a place to live, and a job. He knew that he wouldn't go back to Wyatts: he had forged his own path too long to do that and, besides, one could never go back. But he could become a better brother, a better son. He set off through the crowds to the tube station.

Postcards from Katherine, in America, arrived at Holm Edge throughout the winter months. Postcards of red and ochre deserts, and of white-capped mountains, and an arching golden bridge. Liv put them on the mantelpiece, where the blue skies contrasted with the grey winter clouds outside. They were a link to an outside world that was becoming increasingly remote.

Stefan threw himself into his plans for the vegetable garden and the barn, but his energies were dissipated in a rainswept spring. Digging the garden, the rain would beat against his back and on his uncovered head, the soil turning to mud as water trickled down the hillside. When the tarpaulin with which he had temporarily roofed the barn caved in, weighed down with water after a heavy storm, soaking the newly plastered walls, he shut himself in his study, emerging only fleetingly for meals. He looked unwell, white-faced, exhausted and edgy. There was a brittleness about him that made his temper snap at the smallest thing: a burnt supper dish, or a toy left underfoot on the stairs. Liv chose her words carefully when she spoke to him; when she pleaded with him to rest, he turned on her angrily.

One night towards the end of March, they were woken by the clamour of the geese. Stefan pulled on his coat and dashed outside in time to see a fox, red-brown and scarlet-mouthed, slide out of the garden gate. The hen-coop was a charnel-house of headless corpses, strewn around the bloodied straw. In the torchlight, Stefan's face was pale.

'The door – how did it get in the bloody door?'

She saw the accusation in his eyes. 'I put the latch on the door, Stefan, I'm sure I did.'

'Can't I trust you to do *anything*?' Pushing past her, he seized a pick and shovel and began to hack a hole in the sodden ground to bury the dead birds.

He didn't speak to her for the next two days. At mealtimes, he sat in silence, his fingertips drumming against the table-top. Liv cooked him his favourite food, made sure Freya did not disturb him while he was working, darned the holes in his jerseys, and made cups of tea and homemade cake. She'd show him how much she loved him, she thought, and then he'd love her again. She'd do everything right, and then he'd never be angry with her again.

When Stefan left the house on Monday morning to drive to Lancaster, every muscle in Liv's body ached with the aftermath of tension. The house's low ceilings and small windows seemed to press in on her; she could not bear another day at Holm Edge. She would take Freya to Lancaster, she decided. She would buy her a pair of shoes.

Stefan usually tucked the housekeeping money behind the clock on the mantelpiece, but when she looked, Liv found nothing but the row of postcards, with their blue skies and shimmering landscapes. Scraping together the contents of her purse and pockets, she bundled Freya up into her pushchair and left the house. The rain began again as she waited at the bus stop, fine cold needles that clung to her eyelashes and trickled down her nose. The bus was late, and Freya, always bored whenever motion ceased, grizzled. Liv picked her up, sheltering her beneath the folds of her own duffel coat. Freya pulled away, straining to be allowed down to the ground, but just as her face reddened with frustration, the bus came round the corner, and she was transformed by delight.

The shoe-shop was busy with half a dozen children being measured for new shoes. Freya sat on Liv's lap for a few moments, then slithered down and began to explore, walking from chair to chair. More mothers and children squeezed into the small shop. In the time it took Liv to collapse the pushchair and push her bags beneath her seat so that the newcomers could sit down, Freya had scrambled to a display of shoes, had reached up to a particularly enticing pair and slipped, her stockinged soles slithery on the polished wooden floor. Shoes, price tags and Freya tumbled to the ground.

Freya howled, the shop assistant tutted. There was a pink bruise the size of a penny on Freya's forehead, and when the assistant tried to measure her feet, she writhed irritably and began to cry. The assistant went away for what seemed like hours, reappearing with several pairs of shoes just as Freya had calmed down a little. She began to whimper again as the assistant buckled on a tiny red pair, curling her toes and throwing her head back. When Liv asked the assistant the price of the shoes, her heart began to hammer. She glanced in her purse. She had seven pounds two shillings and eightpence, and the shoes cost nine pounds ten. She had not imagined a pair of baby shoes could cost almost ten pounds. She felt in her pockets and peered in the bottom of her bag, looking for loose change, but there was nothing.

'Shall I wrap these up for you, madam?'

Her face felt hot. 'How much are those canvas shoes?' There was a display of gingham sandals.

'We don't recommend those as a baby's walking shoe, madam. Everyday wear might damage the child's feet.' The assistant looked disdainfully at Liv. 'Are you taking these, madam?'

Liv shook her head. 'Not today. I'll think about it.'

She grabbed her bags, Freya and the pushchair, and walked quickly out of the shop. Outside, the rain cooled her face. Tears of humiliation ached behind her eyes. She was half-way down Market Street when she heard a voice call her name.

'Olivia? It is Olivia Galenski, isn't it?' She spun round. 'You probably don't remember me. I'm Camilla Green. We met at Professor Samuels's party.' Sharp blue eyes moved from Liv to Freya then back to Liv again. 'And this must be . . .?'

'Freya. This is Freya.'

'What a poppet. Isn't she *gorgeous*?' Camilla Green touched Freya's wet cheek. Her curious eyes returned to Liv. 'I thought you'd moved away. No one in the department's seen Stefan for ages.'

'We're still living at Holm Edge.'

'I never thought Stefan would stay there. So isolated. The worst place in the world for someone like him.'

Ice-cold rain was running down the back of Liv's neck and beneath her duffel coat. If she did not hurry away now, she would miss the next bus. But she had to know. 'What do you mean, "someone like him"?'

Camilla Green tucked a strand of hair beneath her velvet hat. 'Stefan needs an audience, doesn't he? As a mirror, almost. It's as if without other people he'd begin to wonder whether he really existed.' She laughed. 'Those little girls who used to crowd round him at the end of his seminars . . . his maenads, we used to call them. At first we thought that he was bedding them, but he wasn't, was he? He just needed them to reassure him that he was there.'

Liv made herself say, 'Stefan's fine. We're very happy at Holm Edge. I have to go.' Then she headed quickly down the street.

She missed the bus; in a café, she bought tea for herself and a biscuit for Freya. As the rain battered against the window, she had to suppress a wave of fury. That awful assistant in the shoe-shop . . . not having enough money to pay for the shoes . . . Camilla Green. She remembered Katherine saying blithely, 'I suppose babies don't cost much, do they?' She thought of all the things she hadn't told Katherine: the weeks they ate only lentils and chips, the long hauls from shop to shop to find the cheapest loaf of bread, the least expensive packet of tea. It did not matter that she bought her own clothes from jumble sales, but it mattered terribly that she could not afford a pair of shoes for Freya.

And the loneliness. That mattered, too. For the first time she admitted to herself the depth of her loneliness. Isolation had crept up on her, the product of poverty and geography and Stefan's pride. She did not mind being alone: an only child, she was used to that. But she was not used to loneliness. First there had been Fin and Thea, then there had been Rachel and Katherine. Now, Fin had gone away and Rachel was dead, Katherine was in America and Thea was in Crete. Liv knew that if she confided in Thea, then she would be on the first plane back to England. She would not do so, of course. She would not disrupt the happiness that shone out of Thea's letters. It was hard to acknowledge even to herself that Stefan's love was not, as she had once believed, all that she needed.

As she opened the gate, she saw Stefan silhouetted at the kitchen window. When she waved to him, he did not respond. She went into the house.

'Where have you been?' His voice was hard and cold.

'Lancaster. I've just been to Lancaster.'

'Who were you with?'

Her misery and exhaustion boiled over. 'The only people I've spoken to today have been the bus driver and a shop-assistant and Camilla Green. Oh, and the lady who serves in the tea shop.'

'Camilla Green?' he repeated sharply. 'Why were you talking to Camilla Green?'

'We met by chance in the street. We spoke for about five minutes, if that. But really, Stefan, it's my business, isn't it? I'll go where I want, and I'll speak to whom I choose.'

He said, 'Then you won't have any housekeeping money next week, either, will you?' and she went cold inside, her anger replaced by shock.

She whispered, 'I thought you'd *forgotten*.'

183

'I don't *forget*,' he said. He smiled. 'I never *forget* things.'

She remembered the hens, and Stefan's certainty that she was to blame. 'You wanted to punish me ...'

'I wanted to help you to remember not to be so careless. To teach you a lesson, Liv.'

He left the house. She heard the fading rumble as the Citroën headed down the track. She remained where she was, her arms wrapped around herself. Freya was asleep in the pushchair, and the silence of the house seemed to surround her. The only sound was the fast pitter-pattering of her own heart. After a while, she peeled off her wet coat and hung it on the peg, and put her gloves and scarf to dry by the stove. She moved round the house very slowly, almost as if she was unwell, tidying away a dirty plate here, a handful of toys there. Picking up a pile of Stefan's books from the table, she went into his study.

Stefan had pinned huge sheets of paper to the walls. A complex spider's web of spokes and lines, drawn in coloured felt-tips, sprawled over the paper. The diagrams plotted the outline of his book. When she examined them closely, Liv saw that the coloured spokes linked one topic to another, tracking the development of myths and their spread from country to country. She felt as though she was trapped inside a garish cobweb.

She glanced at Stefan's desk, hoping to see finished chapters, but there were only a few dozen pages of typescript, scored with angry crossings-out. Looking around once more, it seemed to her that the coloured lines wound about the room like a tangled mass of ropes, knotted inextricably together.

Chapter Eight

Katherine had been abroad for seven months when an offer of the sort of job she had always dreamed of brought her back to England in July 1971. She had met Netta Parker, *Glitz*'s editor-in-chief, in San Francisco. Netta was about to leave the USA for London, to start up an English edition of the magazine. *Glitz* had been selling successfully in America for more than two years. It was, Netta had explained to Katherine over a great many whisky sours, a women's magazine with balls. Sassy fashion spreads, challenging interviews and plenty of outspoken articles about sex. And not a whiff, of course, of recipes or motherhood. By the end of the evening, Netta had commissioned Katherine to write a monthly column about her American travels. Netta had been pleased with the work Katherine had sent, and had promised Katherine a job when she returned to London.

Katherine went home for a hurried weekend, where she made a fuss of Philip, and lectured her mother about feminism while helping her with the cooking and housework. She phoned Toby, who was now employed in his parents' interior-design business, and Felix, who was working for a housing co-operative in Hoxton, and spent a noisy evening at the pub with both of them.

Katherine started work the week after she returned to England. *Glitz*'s offices were large and open-plan. Her desk was one of twenty in a room of ringing phones and clacking typewriters. She found a first-floor flat in Islington (a separate kitchen, bedroom and living room – no more dirty dishes on the bedspread). She no longer minded being alone; the isolation she had experienced when abroad, cut off from all that was familiar, had forced her to learn to cope again.

In the crumbling beauty of European cities, in the bright vastness of America, Katherine had promised herself a new start. Never again would she allow herself to be vulnerable. She learned to make herself physically safe – to avoid walking at night in poorly lit streets, to lock car doors from the inside when she was driving, to check the security of the rooms in which she slept. She resolved to earn a good salary, because a well-paid job would mean that she could find a decent flat instead of a bedsit with a shoddy lock, and that she could afford to run a car. As for love, she had learned that was not for her. It was ironic, she sometimes thought, that she worked for a magazine whose every page extolled the necessity of an active sex life: she, who had readopted virginity for the last year.

At the beginning of September, her editor dumped a handful of photographs on Katherine's desk.

'Job for you, Katherine. Netta's idea – a piece on successful men. Businessmen, actors, sportsmen, anything *hunky*. A short interview and a picture, you know the sort of thing. Sally was going to do it, but she's got chicken-pox, for Heaven's sake.'

There were half a dozen portraits. Katherine leafed through them.

'Sally picked them out. Gorgeous, aren't they? You'll have to get a move on – we need the article by the end of the week. Must dash.'

Alone again, Katherine looked more closely at one of the photographs. Cropped light brown hair, grey eyes like chips of granite, a slightly cleft chin.

When she turned the picture over to read the name pencilled overleaf, she was suddenly seventeen years old again, wearing her Biba dress and plum-coloured boots at Rachel's wedding. *Dear me, Katherine*, a dry, amused voice said, *I should like to put you on ice for a few years* . . .

Katherine arranged to meet Jordan Aymes at a pub near St James's Park. It had taken her some time to track him down –

Parliament was in recess – and his secretary had been doubtful that he would co-operate. 'Which magazine? *Glitz*? Mr Aymes has a very busy schedule, I'm afraid.'

Yet an appointment had been made, and now Katherine waited at a table in the saloon bar. She wore a pale blue seersucker suit, and had recently had her hair cut in a short, feathery crop. She knew that, though she might recall him, he would not remember her, that for him she had been a pleasant but fleeting distraction, which had helped while away a dull, formal occasion. Waiting, sipping tonic water, she remembered her seventeen-year-old self, and how flattered she had been that such an obviously sophisticated man should single her out. Liv, she thought with amusement, would have fantasized about Jordan Aymes for months afterwards, imagining herself in love with him, inventing chance meetings and secret assignations. But she herself had never been a dreamer; her feet had always touched the ground.

She saw him silhouetted in the pub doorway: a little over medium height, broad-shouldered and classic-profiled. He seemed unchanged since they had last met. When he turned and saw her, she rose and held out her hand. 'Mr Aymes, it's very good of you to agree to see me.'

'Miss Constant, the pleasure is all mine. Can I get you a drink?'

'Tonic water, please.' She watched him go to the bar. When she attempted to write, her hand trembled. Spider's writing, she thought, remembering a hot summerhouse and musty cobwebs.

He returned to the table with the drinks. She said, 'If I could just begin by recapping a few facts . . .'

'Anything you wish, Miss Constant.'

'You were born in nineteen thirty-five.'

'In Reading, yes.'

'No brothers or sisters?'

'I was the late and unexpected only child of hardworking, hard-up and unimaginative parents.'

'Did you mind?' She looked up at him. 'Being an only child, I mean.'

'I don't know. Should I?'

She thought of Rachel, and how, as a child, she had envied her privacy and uniqueness. She shrugged. 'Perhaps. Some people mind, I believe.'

'I don't think I did.' The corners of his mouth curled, and his eyes rested on her. 'I'm afraid I've always liked being the centre of attention.'

She looked down at her notes. 'You went to prep school, and then to grammar school. Were you happy at school?'

'Very. I had a good brain, and I was good at sport, too, which helped, I suppose.'

'A couple of years' military service . . .'

'Again, perfectly congenial.'

'Then Oxford, and then the City.'

'You are making me sound nauseatingly predictable and dull, Miss Constant.'

She looked up at him. 'Your life hasn't been *dull* at all, Mr Aymes. Charmed, perhaps.'

'Would you prefer stories of abandonment and deprivation?'

'If you have them.'

'Sorry.' He smiled, and sat back in his seat. 'I've known only the most ordinary tragedies. Parents who were in middle age when I was born, and didn't live to see me succeed. The experience, common to so many of us who come up through the ranks, of never quite fitting into the milieu in which one finds oneself. That sort of thing.'

'No thwarted ambitions?'

'Oh, I have ambitions, but I think it's a bit too soon to consider them thwarted. And I'm sure those incomprehensible squiggles in front of you detail my career most meticulously, Miss Constant.'

She read aloud, 'You won the by-election for Litchampton East in nineteen sixty-six, when you were thirty-one. When the Heath government came to power in nineteen seventy you were appointed a parliamentary private secretary in the Department of Trade and Industry. You married Patricia de Vaux in nineteen sixty-two, you've no children, and you live in Hertfordshire.' She looked up at him. 'So you have everything you want, Mr Aymes.'

'Oh,' he said softly, looking at her, 'I wouldn't say *that*.'

'Well then ... the future ... Would you like to become Prime Minister?' She knew that she was gabbling.

'Now, that would be telling, wouldn't it?'

She saw the laughter in his eyes, and wondered whether he was laughing at her. She heard him say, '*Glitz* ... Isn't that the magazine which made its name by persuading several ill-advised gentlemen to pose wearing little but a ship's tiller, or a strategically placed rosebush?'

'Not a *rosebush*,' murmured Katherine. She forced herself to meet his gaze. 'The thorns ...'

He laughed out loud. 'Any more questions, Miss Constant? Don't your readers like to know their interviewees' tastes? Their favourite cars? I drive an E-Type. Favourite holiday destination? My wife enjoys Portofino, but if I'm honest I have to say that I prefer Scotland. Favourite food? Well, most definitely not quails' eggs ...'

Her head jerked up. She stared at him. 'Mr Aymes—'

'Miss Constant. Or perhaps, since we are old acquaintances, I may call you Katherine.'

She remembered the chill slither of half a dozen quails' eggs down her throat; she had eaten them because his measuring gaze had defied her not to. She said furiously, 'You remembered me! You remembered me all along!'

'Of course I did. I never forget a face. Especially a face like yours.'

He *was* laughing at her, she thought. 'Why didn't you tell me?'

'Because I wasn't sure whether *you* remembered *me*.'

'That's different. Of course I remembered you.' *You*'re memorable, she wanted to say. *I*'m not. Feeling very foolish, she bundled her pad and pens back into her bag.

He said gently, 'I didn't mean to offend you, Katherine. Please stay. Let me buy you another drink.'

'It's all right,' she said stiffly. 'I've got all I need. Thank you for sparing me your valuable time, Mr Aymes.' She walked out of the pub.

Two days later, a letter marked 'Private and Confidential' was delivered to Katherine's desk. When she glanced at the signature, she took a deep breath and lit a cigarette.

> Dear Miss Constant, since to apologize in writing is a
> coward's way out, I hope that you will be generous
> enough to allow me to make amends in person. I have
> booked a table at the Terrazza in Romilly Street
> tomorrow night, at eight o'clock. I would consider it a
> great kindness on your part if you were to meet me there.

The letter was signed *Jordan Aymes*.

When Katherine recalled the meeting in the pub, her embarrassment lingered. But now it was her own behaviour that embarrassed her: her anger, in retrospect, seemed unreasonable. Jordan Aymes had explained that he was unsure whether she remembered him. To have assumed otherwise would have shown an unbearable arrogance on his part.

She dressed carefully in a black midi-dress and black patent-leather shoes. In the restaurant, Jordan Aymes was waiting at a corner table. He stood up as she crossed the room to him.

'Miss Constant.'

'Katherine,' she said. 'Please call me Katherine. And there's really no need for all this. *I've* come to apologize, actually – I had no right to be annoyed, especially since you were so kind as to agree to do the interview.'

'But now that you're here,' he said, 'you will dine with me, won't you, Katherine?' To do otherwise would have seemed churlish, so she sat down.

The food was delicious, and Jordan Aymes's conversation was light-hearted, amusing and entertaining. The waiter was pouring out coffee when Jordan said, 'You went through my curriculum vitae with a fine-tooth comb the other day, Katherine. So now it's your turn. I'll see what I can remember. You are the only daughter of a country GP and his wife. You have three brothers – one older, one younger, and a twin.' He offered her the plate of chocolate mints. 'How are all the brothers?'

'Michael's a junior doctor at Addenbrookes Hospital in Cambridge. Simon's working for an antique dealer's in Edinburgh. As for Philip, he's just the same.'

He looked up at her enquiringly. 'Philip was brain-damaged when he was a few months old,' she said flatly. 'Measles. So he doesn't *get on*, like most people do.' She fell silent. She couldn't think why she had told Jordan Aymes, whom she hardly knew, about Philip.

'I'm sorry,' he said. 'That must be very hard on your family.'

She glared at him. 'He's not a *burden*, you know. He's a lot easier to like than most people, in fact.'

He touched her hand. 'I didn't mean to imply—'

She made an effort. 'Sorry. I'm sorry.' She smiled. 'We do seem to apologize to each other a lot, don't we? And of course looking after Philip has been difficult, especially for Mum. It's just that people make assumptions which annoy me and—' She looked away.

'You are protective towards your brother. That's admirable, Katherine.' His cool grey eyes narrowed. 'Anyway, I've been working it out. You were almost eighteen in nineteen sixty-eight, which means that you were born in nineteen fifty. So now you're twenty-one.'

'It was my birthday last month.'

'If only I'd known. Congratulations. You've no ring on your finger, so I assume you haven't married ... What else do I know about you? That you like champagne and quails' eggs, of course. That you're a journalist. And that we have a mutual acquaintance in Henry Wyborne.' He frowned. 'It was three years ago, wasn't it? That poor girl's wedding.'

She thought of Rachel, in her powder-blue going-away suit.

I'm Mrs Seton, and I feel as though I should be going back to school next month.

'Such a pretty girl,' said Jordan softly. 'Poor old Wyborne hasn't been the same since. I never took to the fellow, to be honest, but since then – well, sometimes I find myself feeling sorry for him.'

'I haven't seen Mr Wyborne for ages. And I haven't seen Hector since the funeral. I wonder what he's doing – where on earth he's gone. Whether he ever got over it.' Katherine grimaced. 'That's the thing about awful things happening, isn't it? You'd think it would just be this dreadful gap – the person gone – but there's more than that, isn't there? It's like ... like a crack in glass.'

'A knock-on effect, you mean?' Jordan looked thoughtful. 'Henry Wyborne's star was in the ascendant in the party just before his daughter died. He was tipped for a ministerial position. But since then his heart just hasn't been in it. He's just going through the motions.' He shrugged. 'Which gives people like me the opportunity, I suppose.'

Katherine thought of the chaos of her life after Rachel: her lack of direction, and her frantic search to fill every hour of the day. She said slowly, 'I suppose, after she died, I rather lost my way.'

'And have you found it again?'

Once more, his gaze disconcerted her. 'I hope so,' she said softly. 'I believe so.'

Often it seemed to Liv that the land itself was turning against them. The vegetable garden, which was still only a fraction of the size of the vast *potager* that Stefan had planned, seemed to be plagued permanently by disease and infestation. Worms writhed inside the tiny, blackened fruits of the apple and plum trees, and the leaves of the cabbages and lettuces were turned to lacework by an army of slugs and snails. In the spring, wind and rain lashed the plants, battering the half-formed seedlings into a sea of mud. In the summer, it did not rain for four consecutive weeks, so they had to haul endless cans of water from the house to the garden. Nothing ever seemed to grow to the size it was supposed to; they lived off wizened miniatures.

She understood now that Stefan blamed her for their setbacks because he could not bear to blame himself, or their situation. There were many setbacks that year. Each one – the soot that clogged the flue setting alight to the chimney, the twin-tub's hose splitting and spraying water over the floor, the geese disappearing for weeks to be discovered nesting on a clutch of infertile eggs – brought with it disapproval and blame. When Liv tried to reason with Stefan he became angry, or withdrew, absenting himself from the house or shutting himself in his study until his mood changed and he presented her with an inappropriate and expensive peace-offering – a bunch of shop-bought flowers, a canary in a cage, or a string of Victorian beads from an antique shop in Lancaster.

As the months passed, they gradually yet inexorably slipped into poverty. Liv struggled to make do and mend, but a great deal of what they possessed had gone beyond repair. The sheets were already sides-to-middled, and she was darning darns and patching patches. She did not mind that her own clothes were threadbare, though she found herself gazing longingly in shop windows in Lancaster, but she did mind that Freya's were. Once, when she ran out of housekeeping money and there was nothing in the vegetable garden, she and Freya ate chips for a week. Often Liv found herself scraping up Freya's leftovers. Stewed apple and custard, rice and plums, mince and potatoes, she ate them whether they were tepid or cold, standing in the kitchen at the end of another long day, aching with weariness, too tired to cook for herself.

In July, she helped Stefan revise the indexing system for his book. With the new system in place, he explained, he'd be able to start writing at last. Working into the night, Liv remembered her first visit to Holm Edge, their easy, unforced closeness, Stefan's charm and cheerfulness. They finished the indexes at dawn, went to bed and made love. Lying in his arms, she believed they had made a new beginning.

But throughout the next few weeks there remained on Stefan's desk a chaos of papers, pocked with Tippex, laced with cut and pasted paragraphs. The spider's web of diagrams on the walls of the study grew, crawling across the ceiling. Stefan's elation faded, and was replaced by edginess. Because it was August, he had no teaching work. When the bills arrived in the morning post, he snatched them up and disappeared into his study.

They were letting things slip, he announced one morning. They had failed to become self-sufficient, which meant that they remained at the mercy of others. They would pick nettles for soup, and would bottle berries and fruits to tide them through the winter months. Old iron preserving pans, discarded in the barn, were cleaned and scoured. A dark green sludge of leaves bubbled unappetizingly on the stove. They bottled onions, carrots, cauliflowers and beetroot; lined up on shelves in the barn, the jars reminded Liv of the nauseating pickled things in the biology lab at Lady Margaret's. She only had to look at them and she felt ill. She had even stopped finishing up the remains of Freya's supper; confronted by a bowl of junket into which Freya had spat several pieces of sausage, she had to run to the bathroom to be sick.

At the southern perimeter of Holm Edge's garden grew a wild tangle of blackberry bushes. They would harvest the lot, declared Stefan one hot, late-August afternoon, and make jam and jelly. Full of vitamin C, so good for Freya. They dragged baskets, stepladders and secateurs down to the bottom of the garden. The brambles were thick, and barbed with long thorns. Though it was easy enough to pick the first few berries, the best seemed always to be just out of reach. The sun beat down on Liv's head, and when she sat down to rest, Stefan cried, 'Oh, for Heaven's sake, Liv, you've only just started!' There was that dangerous edge to his voice, that early-warning indication of storms to come.

She forced herself to work on. Freya pricked herself on a bramble and began to cry. A frond tore Liv's skirt, so that a ragged strip hung from the hem. Their fingers were stained black with juice, and wasps buzzed around the fruit in the baskets. Some of the berries were pulpy, others unripe. Stefan was climbing the stepladders to reach the ones on top of the bush. 'There must be pounds and pounds here,' he said. 'You're missing those ones by your feet, Liv – you should be more careful. You pick them, Freya. Silly Mummy, missing lovely berries like that. Once we've got this lot in, we can have a go at the hazelnuts. I've found a recipe for hazelnut spread – lots of vitamin D. If we can get in enough food to last us through the winter, I'll be able to give up that bloody crammer ...'

That night, Liv lay awake, staring at the darkness. She saw them all so clearly: herself, in her torn dress, picking because she dared not stop; Freya, with stained hands and face and scratches on her arms and legs. And Stefan, perched on the stepladder, exhorting them to greater efforts. They had not finished until the sun had gone down. Freya had slept, curled in a ball on the grass, her thumb in her mouth. Liv had been too tired to bathe her, too tired to eat, too tired to do anything other than lie down, her muscles shaking, trying to shut away all the frightening thoughts.

I'll be able to give up that bloody crammer ... enough food to get us through the winter ... the hazelnuts next ... lots of vitamin D ...

The note of irrationality in Stefan's voice echoed in the darkness, and Liv shuddered. I am afraid of him, she thought. It was the first time she had admitted it to herself. She stared out at the stars and thought, I am afraid of Stefan.

One weekend Katherine drove north to visit Liv. Heading up the track, parking outside Holm Edge, she looked at the house and thought it had a sad, neglected air: there were slates missing from the roof, and the grass was uncut. Stefan was standing on the front doorstep. Katherine waved, but as he crossed the garden to her there was no welcome in his eyes, and she found herself saying uncertainly, 'It's me, Stefan. Katherine.'

'Liv didn't tell me you were coming.'

'I drove up on the spur of the moment. I hope you don't mind.'

There was a preposterous and disturbing interval when it seemed as though he might just say, 'Well, yes, actually I do,' and send her away. But then he unlatched the gate. 'You'd better go in.'

Opening the front door, she called out Liv's name, and heard footsteps running down the stairs.

'*Katherine.*'

'Livvy.' Katherine gave her a quick hug, but Liv was stiff and unresponsive. 'You are pleased to see me, aren't you, Liv?'

'Of course I am.' Yet Liv looked strained. 'I just wasn't expecting . . .'

Trying to make a joke of it, Katherine said, 'You're as bad as Stefan. I thought he was going to make me drive back to London.'

Liv went quickly to the window and looked out. 'Was he cross?'

'Why on earth should he be?'

Liv smiled, but the smile was taut and unconvincing. 'So nice to see you, Katherine. I'll make some tea.'

While Liv made the tea, Katherine talked about America and looked around the room. Since her last visit the previous year, it had taken on a dreariness that shocked her. There were springs coming through the sofa's upholstery, and there were scorch marks on the rug, presumably where coals had fallen from the stove. Books – tattered, broken-backed, secondhand volumes – were stacked against the walls, their musty odour pervading the house. It took Katherine a moment to pinpoint what was so odd about the room. Then she realized that the Galenskis had none of the clutter that most people have: there were no newspapers or magazines or cigarette packets or bars of chocolate. There was no television or record-player. It was, Katherine thought with a shiver, both monastic and miserable. Katherine found herself remembering the Fairbrothers' cottage in Fernhill, which had been crammed with Thea's colourful pots and Liv's decorations and posters and paintings. The cottage had been a treasure-cave, its long, thin garden secret and enchanting. Liv and Thea had always been poor, they had always been eccentric, but they had never been squalid, never dreary. Katherine knew in her heart that Liv would never have *chosen* to live like this.

She watched Liv pour out the tea and noticed for the first time her thinness, and the hollows round her eyes and beneath her cheekbones. She wore no makeup – Katherine recalled the hours she, Rachel and Liv had spent experimenting with eye-liner and lipstick – and her long Indian dress had a patch on the hem.

Katherine asked, 'Where's Freya?'

Liv put a cup of tea in front of her. 'Having her nap. She's teething . . . her back molars . . .' She looked out of the window again. 'I'll take Stefan a cup of tea.' She went outside.

The tea was some odd herbal stuff with leaves floating in it. Katherine drank it unenthusiastically.

Liv came back into the house. She was still carrying the cup. 'He didn't want it.'

That same taut smile. Katherine noticed that Liv's hand trembled as she put the cup down on the table. 'You must get Stefan to help you with the baby at night, Liv. You're looking unwell.'

Liv said, 'I'm not unwell, I'm pregnant,' and Katherine stared at her.

'*Pregnant!*'

'Yes.'

'But Freya's only—'

'She's eighteen months.' Liv's voice was level.

'And this house – you're obviously hard up – you haven't even a *phone*.' Katherine heard herself blundering tactlessly on, but could not stop herself. 'How can you *think* of having another baby?'

'I *am* having another baby, and that's all there is to it. It wasn't *planned*, you know. These things aren't always *planned*.'

There was a brittleness in Liv's voice that made Katherine attempt to swallow her shock and say more gently, 'But the *Pill*, Liv. Why didn't you go on the Pill?'

'I did try. It made me sick every morning. Though I might as well have persevered because now I'm sick every morning anyway.' Liv gave an unamused laugh. 'So we thought we'd use the sheath, but we forgot once, and . . .' She shrugged. 'I do seem to get pregnant awfully easily. When you think that some women take years and years.'

'You're going to keep it, then?'

Liv's brows contracted. 'You don't think for a minute that I'd do anything else, do you?' She sounded angry again.

'I just thought—'

'I *want* this baby.'

There was a silence. Katherine made an effort. 'Of course. I didn't mean to upset you. It's just that—' She broke off. It's just that you don't look well enough to manage one baby, let alone two. It's just that your way of life seems to be becoming positively *medieval*. It's just that you are losing your self, your youth, your talents beneath this devouring burden of domesticity.

Liv was looking out of the window again. Katherine heard her say more calmly, 'Freya's the best thing that ever happened to me, you have to understand that. Absolutely the best thing.' Her hands were knotted together. 'I suppose I sometimes wonder whether I'll be able to love this baby as much as I love Freya. I can't imagine ever loving anyone as much as I love Freya.'

'But love isn't the only thing—'

'It's the only *important* thing.' Liv sounded fierce.

But what about *you*, Liv? Katherine wanted to say. Instead she asked, 'What does Thea think about it?'

Liv looked away. 'I haven't told her yet.'

'Why not?'

'I haven't had time to write. She's living in Crete now, did you know that?'

'*Crete.*' Katherine felt rather flummoxed. It was as though she had been away *years*, she thought. No one seemed to be quite where she had left them.

'And Stefan?' she asked. 'What does he think about the baby?'

'Oh, he's delighted, of course.' Yet Liv's voice was toneless.

She began to tidy away plates, to wash up cutlery. She glanced out of the window again. 'Is that your car, Katherine?'

'I bought it a few days ago.' Katherine looked at Liv. 'Have you learned to drive yet?'

'No.'

'You should ask Stefan to teach you.'

'He won't.' Liv seemed about to add something else, but then stopped.

'"Won't"?' repeated Katherine.

A light laugh. 'It's not supposed to be a good thing for a husband to teach his wife to drive, is it?'

'Then have lessons.'

'I can't afford it.'

'Stefan teaches, doesn't he? That'd pay for it.'

'He's not keen.'

'Then don't tell him,' said Katherine, exasperated. 'He doesn't have to know, does he? Have lessons when he's at work. It would make such a difference to you, Liv. I know, because when I learned to drive—'

She fell silent, looking at Liv. Liv's face was pale, and she was biting her lip. Katherine said slowly, 'You do have money of your own, don't you?', and Liv shook her head.

'But you have a joint account . . .?'

Liv said nothing. Katherine found herself looking at Liv's unmade-up face, her worn clothing, and the bleak room, with new eyes.

She said slowly, 'You haven't any money of your own, and I suppose you haven't a cheque book for Stefan's bank account. Surely you've *something* . . .' She frowned, thinking. 'Family allowance . . .?'

'You don't get that with a first child.'

'So you let him treat you as a *servant*.'

'It's not like that.'

'Isn't it? Look at you – look at this place, stuck in the middle of nowhere—'

'I like it here.' Liv's eyes were very dark, set in a bone-white face. 'And things have been difficult for a while, I admit, but they'll get better, I'm sure of it.'

'Has Stefan got a full-time job yet?'

'No. But he's writing a book.'

'Has he a publisher – or a contract?'

Again, that shake of the head. Katherine said harshly, 'It takes ages to find a publisher, and ages for a book to be published, and ages to earn any money from it, if you ever do. Particularly academic books. He can't possibly be counting on *that*.' Yet, looking around the room again, with its teetering towers of books, Katherine knew that the whole household revolved around Stefan's work, and Stefan himself.

'And we're trying to become self-sufficient,' added Liv defensively. 'Growing our own vegetables.'

'I suppose that's Stefan's idea as well? I suppose he'll have you grinding your own wheat next, making your own flour.'

'Well, actually, we—' Liv broke off.

Katherine recalled her brief glimpse of Stefan earlier that afternoon, and her unsettling suspicion that he might send her back to London without seeing Liv. And her own realization that he was capable of doing such a thing.

And Liv had looked out of the window and said, 'Was he cross?' Katherine's anger lessened at last, replaced by anxiety. 'Liv, is everything all right between you and Stefan?'

'Course it is.'

Part of her would have liked to pretend that she believed Liv, but she made herself go on. 'I mean, he doesn't hurt you, anything awful like that, does he?'

'He's never hit me.' Liv's eyes evaded Katherine's.

'But he refuses to teach you to drive ... and he doesn't let you have your own bank account ... and you've never once in all the time you've been married visited me in London.'

'Katherine, shut up.' Liv's voice was dangerously quiet.

' – and your clothes look like they've come out of a jumble sale – and there doesn't seem to be any food in the house—'

'Katherine, I said, shut *up*.' Liv's fists were clenched. When she swung round, Katherine could see the fury in her eyes. 'You go away for months on end, you turn up without a by-your-leave ... How dare you criticize the way I live? What part do you have in my life now, if any? What do *you* know of marriage, or of children?'

There was a silence. Then Katherine whispered, 'Liv, come home with me now. Just get Freya and your things and come back to London with me now.'

The door opened. Stefan was standing on the step. Katherine heard Liv say quickly, 'Katherine was just going, Stefan. She's just leaving.'

Driving down the M6, Katherine kept remembering the expression on Liv's face when Stefan had come back into the house. She had to make a deliberate effort to concentrate on the road, to check her mirror, to remember to signal.

Returning to London late that night, she did not go home but dropped in first to an off-licence, then headed for Felix's flat in Hoxton.

'I know it's late,' she explained to him, 'but I've a bottle of wine, and you never go to bed early.'

'I'm papering the front room,' he said, and kissed her cheek. Felix rented the ground floor of what had once been a rather splendid eighteenth-century house. He showed Katherine into a large, bay-windowed room. It was empty except for a pair of stepladders, a naked lightbulb, a bucket of paste and a great many rolls of wallpaper. One of the walls was covered in dark red paper, decorated with large gold fleur-de-lis.

'My father let me have the paper,' Felix explained. 'Damaged stock. Rather baronial, isn't it?'

Katherine ran her fingers over the fleur-de-lis. 'The expression "decaying grandeur" does spring to mind.'

'It does, doesn't it? The paper's holding the walls together.

Literally. It was either paper it or have the whole room replastered. And I couldn't afford that.' He unwrapped the bottle of red wine. 'I'll find a corkscrew and something to drink out of.'

They drank the wine sitting on floor-cushions in the half-decorated room, because it was, Felix explained, the nicest room in the house. He lit candles, put on a Joni Mitchell record, and found a packet of Rich Tea biscuits, which Katherine devoured ravenously. He told Katherine about his job, which involved organizing the renovation of old houses, Victorian terraces mostly, and Katherine told Felix about her latest assignment for *Glitz*. Then she said, 'I drove to Lancaster and back today.'

'Hell of a distance.' He looked at her. 'Why?'

'To see Liv.'

'Liv ... Lovely smile ... about five foot two ... eyes the colour of Marmite ...'

'That's right.'

'Friend of your other friend who died.'

'Yes. Anyway, she's married, and has immured herself in domesticity. It's insane – she has one baby already, and now there's another on the way.'

'Perhaps,' said Felix mildly, 'she likes children.'

'But the *waste*, Felix! Liv was studying for a degree when she met Stefan – and she gave it up, just like that! And she was always so good at sewing and making things, and making a place look nice – all the things I'm so *bad* at ... And now she's living in this awful *hovel* in the middle of nowhere, with no central-heating or telephone. Just because *he* insists—'

'"He?"'

'Stefan.' Katherine scowled. 'Liv's husband.'

'Trainspotter? Bloated plutocrat? Wall-eyed? Or just plain boring?'

She smiled, and refilled their wine-glasses. 'None of those. Stefan's terribly handsome and terribly cultured, and not boring at all.'

'So what's the problem?'

Katherine shivered. 'I can't bear him.'

He lit cigarettes for both of them. 'Tell me.'

'If he's not the centre of attention, he sulks.'

'Lots of men are like that. Attribute of our sex.'

'*You*'re not like that, Felix. And he prowls about like – like . . .' she searched for the right simile '. . . like *Heathcliff.*'

'The dark, brooding type?'

'Yes. He's unpredictable – it's like being with a firework that hasn't gone off, you can't relax. And he's not remotely interested in *me*. There's no reason why he should be, of course, but you'd think that he'd *try*, for Liv's sake. When I first met him, he seemed very charming, but now, when I look back, I can see that was because he wanted me to give him *my* attention. And I suppose I didn't fall under the spell, so since then he hasn't bothered even to try and impress me. And today – ' she shivered ' – he was awful.'

'Unfriendly?'

'Worse than that. People always pretend, don't they, Felix? They always *try*, even if they're feeling awful. Even when Toby was freaking out, he'd still try and make you think he was all right. It didn't work, of course, but at least he made an effort. But Stefan,' Katherine bit her lip, 'he dislikes me, I know he does. And he didn't bother to hide it.' She ate another biscuit, staring out at the darkness. There were no curtains at the windows, and she could see the crescent moon, lying on its back in an inky sky. 'Liv has no money of her own,' she said slowly. 'None at all. She can't go out to work because of Freya, and Stefan's bank account is in his name only. As far as I can see, he doles out money to her when he feels like it.'

'Some people don't mind that.' Felix's profile was outlined by the pale candlelight. 'I know it seems old-fashioned – repressive, even – but they don't necessarily see it like that.'

'Liv is totally dependent on Stefan. She's trapped, and I think he wants her to be trapped. I'm not sure that she even has enough to eat. And I don't believe that she has anyone to turn to. They don't seem to have any friends. Liv's mother's living abroad just now, and she hasn't seen her father for decades. He's probably dead, in fact. Rachel is dead, too, of course, and I – well, I haven't exactly been a frequent visitor. And after today I probably won't be welcome again.' She rubbed her furrowed brow, recalling the brief, unpleasant scene at the end of her visit. Stefan had come into the room, and had taken her elbow to show her out of the house – had actually taken her elbow; Katherine had shaken him off, and Liv had just looked away. Had not protested. Had not asserted her right to have an old friend visit her. Had just turned aside, her long hair sweeping across her haunted, frightened eyes.

'I told her she should leave.' Katherine crumbled the remains of her biscuit into a small, dusty heap. 'I said she should come home with me.'

'What did she say?'

'Nothing. Stefan came in. I'm not sure whether he heard me.'

'If she has a child . . .' said Felix slowly. 'It's not so easy to cut and run – to start again – when you have a child.'

'And I asked her whether he hurt her, and she said that he'd never hit her. That's not an answer, is it? There are other ways of hurting someone, aren't there?'

His silence was his agreement. After a while she went on, 'The worst of it is that there's nothing I can do to help. Liv made it clear that she'd rather I hadn't visited, and that the best thing I could do was to leave them alone. And she was right, of course. What do I know about marriage or babies?' Katherine gave a rueful smile. 'The thing is, I was hoping Liv could give *me* some advice. Only it became rather obvious that my problems were nothing to hers.'

He rolled on to one elbow, grinning, looking up at her. 'What problems can you possibly have, Katherine? You've a glittering career in journalism, a flat with plaster on the walls . . .'

'A long time ago,' she said, 'I met this man . . .'

'*Oh*,' he said. 'About time *your* heart was pierced. Poor old Toby and Stuart used to *pine* after you.'

'Nonsense. And my heart isn't pierced.'

He looked sceptical. 'What's the problem, then?'

'Well, for one thing, he's married.' The previous day, she had received a note from Jordan Aymes. The note had told her that his wife was away on holiday, and that he had been given an unexpected gift of two theatre tickets. Would Katherine accompany him to a performance of *Waiting for Godot*? He did not especially care for contemporary theatre, so her company might ameliorate what promised to be a bleak evening. The letter remained on her dressing-table, unanswered.

'I don't mind *that*, of course – you know I'm not the marrying sort. It's just that I'm not sure why he's bothering with *me*. I'm not sure what he wants.'

Felix was lying on his back, his hands cushioning his head. He snorted.

Katherine rose and went to the window, and looked down at the hands of her watch. It was a quarter to two in the morning. She felt suddenly desperately weary, all the complications of the long day exhausting her, and she said, 'I've drunk far too much to drive. I couldn't crash here, could I, Felix?'

Sometimes Liv felt as though she was slipping down into a deep, dark well. Just now, her fingers were still managing to grip the stone rim, but she had to struggle not to tumble into the blackness. Any pretence she had managed to maintain to herself that her marriage was good, if a little stormy, and that their way of life was sustainable, if unconventional, Katherine had destroyed. Katherine had taken hold of the self-deceptions with which she had comforted herself, had held them up one by one to the light, and had shown them clearly for what they were. They would never become self-sufficient because the thin covering of soil around Holm Edge was incapable of growing healthy crops, and because they themselves lacked both knowledge and skill. The house itself was falling into dereliction. Stefan's book was no nearer completion than it had been a year ago. And Stefan's obsessiveness and irrationality were not a consequence of their temporary problems, but deeply rooted aspects of his character.

The trouble was that recognition of her situation did not bring with it solutions. Every avenue of escape was blocked – by Stefan, or by Freya, or by Fate. Her suggestion that she look for part-time work in Caton had been met with outrage on Stefan's part, and a furious prohibition. She could not defy him because she needed him to look after Freya. She had thought of taking in sewing at home but her pregnancy had put paid to that. Whereas with Freya she had felt well throughout her pregnancy, with this second child she seemed to feel ill almost from the moment of its conception. The exhaustion she felt was out of all proportion to the size of the tiny foetus that nestled in her womb. The nausea, which was supposed to last for a few hours in the morning, could and did strike at any time of day. Freya, watching her leaning over the lavatory bowl, patted her head and said soothingly, 'Poor Mummy. Poor Mummy.'

She was consumed by fury and by shame that Katherine had seen her at her worst. Katherine could not have arrived at a more inopportune moment. Stefan had been touchy and ill-tempered for days, his mood sparked by her disclosure to him of her unplanned pregnancy. He had only voiced to her what they both knew: that they could not afford another child. That he blamed her for what they both had created, she endured at first with weary resignation. But on the morning of Katherine's visit they had quarrelled bitterly: Liv pointing out to Stefan that his withholding of the housekeeping money affected Freya as well as herself, Stefan claiming that it was she, Liv, who was to blame because she made him lose his temper.

That evening, though, after Katherine had gone, his hostility had dissolved in self-recrimination and abasement. He had begged her forgiveness; she was too good for him, he said, and he dreaded that he might lose her. Taking her hands in his, his face pale and drawn, he had promised never to be angry with her again. They had embraced and kissed, and for a moment she had lost herself in the reassuring strength and warmth of his body. Yet she had known that this reconciliation was only part of a cycle that had become all too familiar. Stefan's wild enthusiasms seemed always doomed to failure. Failure brought with it first rage and depression, then exhaustion and self-loathing. Liv had come to fear the elation as greatly as the anger.

It seemed to her that all their problems had been born at Holm Edge, and that all their difficulties were magnified by it. She did not, as she had told Katherine, love Holm Edge. Once she had loved it, but now her love had turned to loathing. Sometimes she felt as though the walls of the house were closing in on her, imprisoning her. She had not thought till then that it was possible to hate stone and slate. She remembered Camilla Green's words. *Holm Edge is the worst place in the world for Stefan.* Stefan's temper was sparked off by the capriciousness of Holm Edge itself: by the gales that blew tiles from the roof, the fox that mauled the hens and the stove that refused to light. Her own exhaustion was exacerbated by the distance of the house from the shops and post office and clinic – from all the normal, everyday things that most people took for granted. Often she did not see anyone other than Freya and Stefan for days at a time. She wondered whether she might forget how to talk to other people: sometimes it seemed to her that in the shops, at the clinic, they looked at her oddly, as if her features, her stance, betrayed the eccentricity and isolation of her life.

Yet she knew that Stefan would never willingly leave Holm Edge. Voices echoed. Katherine's: *Come home with me, Liv. Come back with me to London.* And Thea's: *Sometimes love isn't enough.* For the first time, she found herself wondering whether, if Stefan refused to leave Holm Edge, she might one day have to leave without him.

Chapter Nine

Katherine and Jordan Aymes became lovers in December 1971. They had been friends for several months – or had said to each other that they were friends, though a part of Katherine had always known this to be if not a deception then a postponement. They saw each other intermittently, the frequency of their meetings dictated by the demands of their careers and, of course, by Jordan's marriage. Between these encounters, when there was nothing else to occupy her mind, Katherine thought about him, his strong, Roman features, cool grey eyes, and sudden smile.

Jordan had a small flat in St James's Park, where he stayed whenever the House was in session. Shortly before Christmas, he invited Katherine there for supper. They ate Brie and French bread and prawns, glistening in their coral-coloured shells, and drank a bottle of Frascati. Fortnum and Mason, Jordan explained as they ate: he never cooked, he was a hopeless cook.

She smiled. 'And I suppose you send your shirts to the laundry, and you have a woman who comes in and cleans?'

'I'm afraid I do. And you?' He looked at her. 'I can't imagine you the domestic sort, Katherine.'

'I used to be terribly untidy. It was almost a principle with me. Recently, though, I've discovered that I like to be organized. Life's more pleasant if you don't spend the mornings discovering that there's nothing to eat and you haven't a pair of tights without ladders.'

He rose and went into an adjacent room, returning with a package. 'Merry Christmas.' He placed the package in front of her.

'*Jordan.*'

'Go on. Open it. We'll pretend it's Christmas morning.'

A tawny-brown silk shirt gleamed within a nest of gold tissue paper. She gasped. 'Jordan, it's beautiful!'

'I chose it because it's the same colour as your eyes.'

'You shouldn't have—' She stopped as lips touched the back of her neck.

'I suppose I shouldn't do this, either?'

She became quite still. After a few moments, he came to stand beside her. 'Katherine?'

'Such a beautiful present...' Her voice trailed away. Her heart was pounding.

'But...?' he enquired. 'There is most definitely a "but" at the end of that sentence, my dear.'

She did not reply, so he said, 'Let me complete it for you, then. But you don't find me attractive, perhaps.'

She whispered, 'It's not *that*.'

'Then you're quite understandably rejecting the advances of a married man.'

It was the easy way out. But she found that with him, she must be honest. She shook her head.

He frowned. 'Is there someone else?'

She rose and went to the window, looking down towards St James's Park. He said, 'If you'd rather I dropped the subject...' Though he tried to conceal it, she could hear the hurt in his voice.

She turned back to him. 'You asked me whether there was anyone else. Well, there isn't now, but there has been in the past.'

'Someone special, perhaps?'

'Oh,' she said lightly, 'there was Jamie – he was the first – the back of a car, I'm afraid. Very unoriginal. And then I moved to London, and there was Mark – he was a poet – and John – he was the manager of a pop group – and Julian – he did nothing much at all, he just had terribly rich parents. And then there was Sacha – he printed *Frodo's Finger*, and he seemed to think I was a perk of the job – and Gian. I interviewed Gian, something about student protests at the University of Milan, I think. And then there was Howard – he was a trainee vicar, very shy but rather sweet – and, oh dear, rather a lot of others, but I can't remember their names.' She fell silent, and then she said, 'And lastly, eventually, there was Graham, but I try never to think about him. And since Graham, there hasn't been anyone else. For more than a year now.'

'Not for want of offers, I assume.'

'No.' She smiled. 'I must be the only woman who ever went to America to find herself, and ended up doing just that – found herself, I mean, and no one else.' Then she clenched her fists and said softly, 'The thing is that I just don't seem to be any good at it.'

'I don't understand.'

She twisted her hands together. 'I don't enjoy it. Sex, I mean. I've never enjoyed it.' There, it was out. She had hoped to feel a weight rolling from her shoulders, but instead she just felt empty and miserable. She forced herself to go on. 'I'm frigid, you see, Jordan.'

'Who told you that?'

She glanced at him sharply. 'Does it matter?'

'It's the sort of thing some men say to girls to justify their own lack of skill in bed.'

'I'd love to believe that, but it seems a bit coincidental that I should get all the duffers.'

'If you had one or two bad experiences – and the back of a car might not be a great place to start – then you might, consciously or otherwise, fear sex, rather than look forward to it. A great deal of pleasure is in the mind, my beautiful Katherine. I know that's not the philosophy of your magazine, which seems to dwell rather on the physical, but what's going on in one's head can count for rather a lot.'

'I did keep trying, though, didn't I?' She smiled. 'You can't say that I didn't try.'

'Then how about just one more attempt?'

He was very close to her. She could smell the expensive cologne that he wore.

'For instance,' he said softly, 'could you enjoy this?'

His lips touched her inner wrist, and she shivered. 'Jordan, I don't know—'

'Or this?' Now, his mouth caressed the palm of her hand.

She swallowed. 'A little, I think.'

'And this?' His lips traced the hollow of her elbow, the arch of her shoulder.

'Perhaps,' she whispered. 'If I practised.'

'How about this?' He drew her to him, and she closed her eyes as their lips touched. She had never before lost herself in a kiss — there had always been a part of her that stood outside, watching, cautious, assessing — but now, for the first time, she surrendered herself to the delight of it.

'What do you think, Katherine Constant? Better than quails' eggs?' His palms skimmed the contours of her body, and he bent his head, pressing his mouth against the curve of her neck.

'I'm not sure . . .' she murmured.

'I'll keep trying, then.' One-handedly, he drew the curtains across the window, enclosing them in the ivory elegance of the room. His fingers threaded through her short hair, and he pressed the fine strands against his face. 'Like silk,' he murmured. 'Like the best Italian washed silk.' Then, reaching down, he began to unbutton her blouse. When she trembled, he whispered, 'Hush, my lovely Katherine. Whatever you want and nothing more, I promise.'

Then he led her into the bedroom. There he stroked her and caressed her until the miracle happened, and she found herself wanting him, opening herself up to him, welcoming him. And when he eased himself into her, she cried out with delight at the pleasure of it.

She didn't know which she enjoyed most: the first time they made love, or the second, or the third. At last, her head cradled on his shoulder, seized by a glorious lassitude and hardly able to move a limb, Katherine lay still, too blissfully exhausted even to reach out to pull the sheet over her naked body.

It occurred to her that she had taken her first lover assuming that pleasure would be easy, that she had taken her second and third believing that soon she must enjoy it, and had continued after that because she couldn't bear that anyone might guess her shameful failing. And then Rachel had died, and there had been the sudden, shocking understanding that life did not go on for ever, and her need to experience everything there was in whatever time she had. The fear she had felt, and her self-destructive need for company. And then, of course, Graham had voiced all the self-loathing she had ever felt, and had unwittingly forced her to take a look at herself, to begin to start again.

Jordan's lips touched the top of her head. 'What are you thinking about?'

'America,' she said. 'I was thinking about America.'

'Did you like it?'

'I loved it.' She was smiling in the darkness. 'Everything seemed so *new*, and on such a different scale. I spent a week in the Rocky Mountains. They seemed to sparkle, somehow. And the birds and the butterflies and the flowers ... they were all so big and beautiful and colourful. You could imagine that the Garden of Eden was like that.'

They lay in silence for a while, and then she said, 'I should go ...'

'Must you?'

She sat up. 'I have to be in the office early tomorrow morning.' She smiled. 'And I really can't go to work wearing this.'

She stepped into her sleeveless black crêpe dress. When his fingers brushed against her skin as he zipped up the back, she shivered. 'When ...?' she began, and bit her lip.

He was pulling on a navy blue silk dressing-gown. 'I go back to Hertfordshire tomorrow. The House is in recess, you see. That's why I gave you your Christmas present tonight.'

She understood what he was telling her. She said lightly, 'Of course. Give me a ring sometime.'

'Katherine—'

'When you have time. Though I'm going to be terribly busy as well.'

'Katherine.' He had come to stand in front of her. *'Don't.'*

She closed her eyes tightly, and sat down on the bed. She had not thought she would mind so much.

He sat down beside her. 'Why are you angry with me?'

'I'm not angry.' The words were blurred and muffled. She tried to smile. '"Whatever you want and no more,"' she repeated. 'That's what you said, wasn't it, Jordan?'

He glanced at her sharply. 'What are you saying? That you think this is unimportant to me? That it's a – a one-night stand?'

The tears in her eyes smudged the strong lines of his features. 'Well, isn't it?'

'Dear God.' She could hear the anger in his voice. She wiped her eyes with the back of her hand as he said quietly, 'No. No, it's not like that at all.'

'You're married, Jordan.' She remembered the entry in *Who's Who*. Jordan Christopher Aymes m. Patricia Mary de Vaux.

He sighed. 'Yes.'

'I expect you've had other affairs.'

'Yes,' he said evenly. 'I've had other affairs.' She looked round for her shoes.

'But they were never like this,' he said, and she paused, one shoe on and one shoe off. He crossed the room to her, taking her hands in his. 'Dear Katherine,' he said, 'had you been just another affair, then I would not have waited four months. I would have invited you here after a fortnight's courtship, we would have met occasionally, and then we would have parted. But with you it's different. *You* are different. I knew that the first time I saw you, at Rachel Wyborne's wedding.'

'*Oh*,' she whispered.

He went into the adjacent room and poured out two brandies. He placed a glass in Katherine's hands.

'I have to be honest with you. I'll never leave Tricia. She's always been loyal to me, and I owe her a great deal.'

Tricia, thought Katherine. She imagined her overweight and horsy, with a tweed skirt and twinset and pearls.

'You do understand, don't you?'

'Of course.' She thought of Rachel's short-lived marriage, and Liv, trapped with Stefan. 'I'm not interested in marriage, Jordan. I never have been. I value my freedom too much.'

'If we're to see each other,' he touched her hand, 'and I should like very much to be able to see you, Katherine, then we'd have to be discreet. Flagrant indiscretions wouldn't do a lot for my career. And, besides, as I've explained, I don't want to hurt Tricia. Would you hate that?'

'Not at all.'

'Good,' he said. 'I'm glad you said that. Because if you hadn't, I'd have found it damnably difficult to be festive over the next few weeks. Damnably difficult.'

Liv's second daughter was born at the beginning of April. They called her Georgette Thea, after Stefan's mother and Liv's own. Because she was tiny, less than five and a half pounds, and because her birth had been difficult, she was taken to the special-care unit. Liv and Georgie remained in hospital for a week. Afterwards, Liv saw that week as a turning-point, just as Katherine's visit had also been a turning-point. It gave her time to think, and time to see things clearly. For the first time in two years she was able to slough off her responsibilities and let others care for her in a place that was warm and clean and civilized. The food, which the other mothers complained about, seemed to Liv delicious. She wasn't required to eat awful bottled vegetables, or to make something edible from scrag end of lamb or belly of pork and, best of all, someone else cooked her meals for her. When her stitches became less painful, she took to shuffling along to the day-room in her dressing-gown, and flicking through magazines, or just sitting in an armchair, enjoying the peace. Georgie was an easy baby, waking at four-hourly intervals, sleeping between feeds. Liv felt none of the nervousness and diffidence she had experienced with

Freya. There was a delight in getting to know this tiny, dark stranger. Love was easy, and untinged by anxiety.

Stefan visited each day, bringing Freya with him. His difference from the other husbands was noticeable. Once, she would have rhapsodized about it, believing it romantic, but now it disturbed her. Once she would have thought his tattered cords and flamboyant emerald scarf original and unconventional; now she saw the multiplicity of patches that pitted the olive-green material, and the grubby, fraying inch at the ends of the scarf, and was disquieted. The other husbands sat quietly, talking in muted tones to their wives and children; Stefan, if he felt like it, would burst into song, or attempt to include the families around the adjacent beds in the conversation. Sometimes Stefan was the first to come into the ward when the nurse opened the doors for visiting hour; on other days he turned up only at the very end of the hour. On one occasion he did not arrive at the hospital until five minutes after visiting time had ended. Liv heard him arguing, shouting at the nurse as she escorted him back down the corridor. When he had gone, she pulled the curtains around her bed and wept.

Returning to Holm Edge after her week's absence, it was as though she saw the house, too, through colder, clearer eyes. The bare floors and peeling paint, the chill dampness, the dilapidated furniture and worn rugs, black mould on the walls. The litter of flour and sugar that scattered the kitchen like volcanic ash. The way that Stefan's books and notes flowed lava-like out of his study into the living room, towering against the walls, pooling in boxes on the floor.

Feeding Georgie one evening, she thought how much the years had changed her. Looking back, the girl she had once been now exasperated her: her lack of realism, and her blind trust that, in spite of all the omens, everything would work out for the best. Warning bells had rung, but she had not heeded them. At nineteen, waiting for her hero, she had glimpsed Stefan and had thought she had heard the sound of a white charger's hoofs drumming against the ground. Stefan had fulfilled a romantic ideal – tall, dark and handsome, with that seductively foreign inflection to his voice, he had strode into her life as if from the pages of a romantic novel. She had seen in him all that she had longed for, and had fallen in love with his spontaneity and charisma, with his exotic, dislocated past, and with his disregard for convention. And with his need of her. But the passing of time had taught her that impetuosity could turn to irrationality. It had taught her that Stefan's unhappy childhood had left him with a deep insecurity and a fractured sense of self-worth. And it had taught her that need could devour and destroy.

Thea had believed that her marriage to Stefan had been a reaction to Rachel's death, a new love to replace the lost friendship. Now, Liv acknowledged the truth in that, but acknowledged, too, that her hasty marriage had filled the gap left by another, older abandonment. Like Fin, Stefan had been well travelled, charming and cultured. Just as she had always believed that her father would come home, so had she also believed that love, and only love, mattered. She knew now that, though a part of her would always love Stefan, he was nevertheless a flawed and deeply troubled man. Knew also that her chief duty was to her children, who needed her protection. That night, she burnt Fin's postcard in the stove, kneeling on the flags, watching the blue seas and green palm-fronds blacken and curl. The end of a dream, she thought; the end of dreaming.

Gradually, she was withdrawing from him, subtly, almost imperceptibly at first. She began to save money, odd coins, five and ten pences, squirrelled away from the housekeeping money. She put aside half of the family allowance she now claimed for Georgie. She did not yet know what the money was for, or why she did not spend it on the many things they needed instead of hiding it in a sock at the back of her drawer. She only knew that the knowledge of it comforted her.

The health visitor, coming to the house when Georgie was six weeks old, said tactfully as she left, 'I'll just give you this leaflet, dear, it might come in handy.' The leaflet described how to claim supplementary benefit. Liv threw it in the bin because she knew that nothing would induce Stefan to claim state help to feed his family. These days, she tried to let nothing disrupt the precarious quiet of the household. Not because, as she had once believed, that by being good, by becoming the perfect wife, she could earn Stefan's uncritical love and approval, but because she sensed that she needed an interval in which to gather her strength, to recover fully from childbirth, to see the way forward. At night, Stefan worked on his book, coming later and later to bed. The tapping of the typewriter keys was like a death knell.

The barn became infested by rats, so Stefan borrowed a shotgun from Mr Marwick. He made Liv and Freya stand behind him as he leaned out of the window, aiming the gun at the rats that darted from the barn to steal food from the geese's bowl. Gunfire shattered the silence, and the lawn was blotted with small, bloodied corpses. Stefan kept the gun in the barn, high up, out of Freya's reach. Yet sleek grey rats still chewed at the dry crusts in the bowl, and the cardboard boxes put out for the dustmen were pinked by a filigree of toothmarks. Once, a box of Stefan's papers, left by the front door, was ripped to black and white confetti.

Stefan brooded about the rats, dreamed about the rats. A movement behind him, and he'd twist and turn and reach for the shotgun. He'd wait in the barn, perched on top of the stepladders, his eyes glittering, listening for movement, watching for the flick of a naked tail. 'I thought I saw one,' he'd say. 'There was something in the grass – look, Liv, can't you see?'

Waking one night, she saw him standing by the window. He was holding the shotgun. He smiled fleetingly. 'I heard something.'

'Come back to bed, Stefan.' Liv's mouth was dry.

'Sometimes I think I hear them in the attic.'

'It's probably just the wind . . . or a loose slate.'

When Georgie began to whimper, Stefan started. 'If they get into the carry-cot—'

'Stefan, they're not going to get into the carry-cot. There's nothing in this room except you and me and Georgie.' She picked Georgie up. 'Put down the gun, darling, and come back to bed.'

Stefan opened the window. Cold air rushed into the room, and the crack of gunfire ripped through the fabric of the night. Georgie stiffened in Liv's arms, and there were footsteps in the corridor. Freya opened the door. 'Mummy, I don't *like* it. Make it stop.'

'Go back to your room, sweetheart.' Liv was trembling with reaction. 'Daddy's finished now.' She got out of bed. 'It's gone, Stefan. You can put the gun away.'

Exhausted, he leaned against the sill. Through her fear, she felt a wave of pity and pain. 'Come back to bed, love.'

'No point. Can't sleep.'

'I'll make you a hot water bottle, and something to drink.'

There were dark shadows around his eyes, and his chin was rough with stubble. 'I told you, Liv, I can't sleep. I haven't slept for ages.'

'How long?' She touched his gaunt face.

'Days . . . weeks . . . I can't remember.'

'You should go to the doctor. He'd give you something to help you.'

'It's the book, you see. I can't do it. I see it when I close my eyes. It branches off in all directions and I can't get hold of it.'

She thought of the spider's web of coloured lines that sprawled across the walls of his study. 'Perhaps you should have a rest from the book. A proper rest.'

'I have to get it right. Two years, Liv. I've been working on it for more than two years, and I've still only finished half a dozen chapters! And when I read them . . .' Stefan paused, his fists clenched '. . . when I read them, they seem specious . . . empty . . . a collection of clichés.'

She felt as though any hope that she could save this bruised, tattered marriage rested on her choosing the right words. 'You could do something else,' she said carefully. 'You don't have to write the book.'

He blinked. 'Give it up, d'you mean?'

When she nodded, he laughed. 'Don't be ridiculous, Liv – I can't possibly give it up.'

'Stefan, it's making you ill.'

He made a dismissive gesture. 'I'm tired, that's all. If I could just get some sleep—'

'Stefan, you're *ill*. Don't you see?'

For a moment she thought he was going to lash out at her, but then the taut energy dissipated, and he sat down on the bed, his head in his hands. 'If I don't finish the book,' he said slowly, 'then everything I've tried to do has been futile. What have I achieved? A garden that doesn't grow anything . . . a house that's infested by vermin.' He looked up at her. 'Sometimes I think this place is cursed. Do you think so, Liv? Because of the holly trees?'

'Stefan—'

'Everything turns against us, doesn't it?' He frowned. 'I often think of him, you know.'

She pulled the blanket around herself, but it failed to warm her. The cold seemed to come from inside her. 'Who, Stefan?'

'The tenant who lived here before us. You remember. Shot himself. I wonder whether he felt like this.' Stefan pressed his fingertips against his forehead. Then he said, 'When I do sleep, I dream. I dream that I wake up and the house is empty. I walk from room to room, and no one's there.' He looked up at her and whispered, 'I'll never let you go, Liv. You do understand that, don't you? I'll never let you go.' His eyes were dark blue and opaque, like sea-smoothed pebbles.

The limitations of her affair with Jordan Aymes suited Katherine. *Glitz* had been a runaway success, and Katherine was quickly promoted to assistant features editor. She worked long hours, and was often busy seven days a week. She travelled a great deal, flying to Edinburgh to interview a rock band, or driving to Cornwall to talk to a coven of white witches. She loved her work, and was never bored. She loved the rhythm of the magazine from its conception when they trawled for new ideas and made mock-ups of cover and centrefold, through to the gathering together of articles and regular items, to its eventual appearance on the news-stands.

Her irregular meetings with Jordan were a delicious treat, a private and pleasurable secret. She did not mind the secrecy that their situation imposed on them, or that sometimes they had only a half-hour snatched at lunchtime, a half-hour in which they made love without preliminaries and fell away from each other exhausted and breathless. For a late starter, she thought ruefully, she seemed to be doing a lot of catching up. Away from him, she felt hungry for him, and longed to feel his arms around her and his body against hers. It was as though something inside her had been unleashed, and could no longer be held back. She tried to work out why it was that Jordan Aymes had been able to ignite that spark in her where none of her previous lovers had been able to induce so much as a glimmer. It could not only be that he was better in bed (though he was), or that he was patient and took his time (though he did). It was as though, she thought, Jordan possessed the secret of some mystery ingredient, some magic X-factor that she was unable to identify.

He gave her a key to his flat. She was nervous at first about using it, but he reassured her. 'Tricia only comes to London when she has to, for functions and parties,' he explained. 'She prefers the country. So I have plenty of warning.' Waiting for him in the flat, Katherine fed herself from the jars and packets in the tiny kitchen, and had a long luxurious bath before wrapping herself in Jordan's dressing-gown. Then she lit the gas fire and curled up in front of the television. Scenes of bombings in Northern Ireland, and miners picketing coal depots unfolded before her. Enclosed in the cream and white luxury of the flat she felt safe and warm, as if she lived in a different world from the troubles portrayed on the television screen. Hearing his key turn in the lock, her heart would pound, and she would feel the tension in the pit of her stomach. Often, they did not speak. Touch took the place of words, and kisses were their only punctuation. Sometimes they did not pause long enough to reach the bedroom, but made love where they were, with the thick pile of the carpet beneath her back, and the warmth of the fire on her naked limbs. Only afterwards, when they had satiated themselves and were curled up, limbs entwined, muscles relaxed, all passion spent, did they begin to talk.

It was on one of those occasions that they came close to quarrelling. Jordan had been late at the House; they had not paused long enough to switch off the television, so when eventually their bodies separated and Katherine closed her eyes, full of drowsy delight, there was still the subdued mutter of the late night news. *Another rise in commodity prices . . . pickets at a factory in Leeds . . .*

Jordan glanced up. 'Dear God, it makes you despair.' He stood up, flicked the switch, and there was silence.

'What does?'

'*That.*' Scowling, he gestured to the television. 'The *greed . . .*'

'Do you think they're greedy?'

'Well, it's hardly the time to ask for a pay-rise, is it? Inflation's going through the roof.'

Katherine picked up his shirt, discarded on the floor beside her, and wrapped it round her shoulders. 'I shouldn't think they think of things like that. I expect they're just thinking how their pay affects them.'

'Exactly. Greedy, short-sighted and selfish.' He pulled on his trousers, and went into the kitchen.

'What I meant,' she explained, 'was how much food they can buy, for instance, or whether they can go on holiday. That's not selfish, it's just practical.'

'It is selfish when it holds the whole country to ransom.' Jordan opened a packet of peanuts; it split, and nuts cannoned to the floor. '*Damn.*' He passed the remains of the packet to Katherine. 'The working classes have a higher standard of living than they've ever had. Why can't they be grateful for that? All the Government's asking for is a bit of restraint.'

She shrugged. 'It won't work. People always want what other people have got. *I* always have.'

His irritation lessened, and he glanced at her affectionately. 'I forgot your left-wing tendencies. Your years spent working for that scurrilous rag.'

'I don't know that I'm particularly left-wing, Jordan. I just know that I've spent ages and ages wishing I had things – the biggest bedroom like Michael, or lovely dresses like Rachel – and I know *I* wouldn't settle for less, so why should anyone else?' She looked around. The spilt peanuts still lay scattered on the floor – for his cleaning lady to sweep up, she supposed. The entire flat spoke of confidence and wealth. 'And you're just the same, Jordan,' she said, 'you know you are. You may have been born in a semi in Reading, but you certainly didn't want to *stay* in one.'

He was pouring out two measures of Scotch, his back to her. 'True. But I've done it all through my own efforts. It hasn't been given to me on a plate.'

She thought, But you were born clever, talented and good-looking. And you're a man, and success has always been easier for men. And you made an advantageous marriage. Yet she pushed that thought to the back of her mind: not thinking about Tricia meant that she remained a shadowy, insignificant figure. Instead Katherine said, 'What *you*'re good at has always been valued. What *they*'re good at has always been undervalued. Who's to say which is worth more, or whose is the more difficult job – the Member of Parliament's, or the miner's?'

'You can't seriously be suggesting that manual labour should be dignified with the same status as the professions?' Jordan handed Katherine a glass. 'That's ridiculous. What next? Perhaps we should all earn the same – High Court judge, heart surgeon, cleaning lady and dustman. Then none of us would have any incentive to better ourselves.'

There was a silence. Then he groaned and sat down beside her. 'Sorry. Sorry, darling.' He took her hand in his, and she saw how tired he looked.

'A bad day?'

'Your friend Henry Wyborne droning on for hours about nothing very important didn't exactly help.'

'Henry Wyborne isn't my friend,' she said mildly. She looked at him. 'Why don't you like him?'

He drank his Scotch. 'Because he's pompous and self-important. And humourless. And he's manipulative. All politicians are manipulative, of course, to a greater or lesser degree, but Henry Wyborne takes it to an art form.'

Katherine remembered the bright-eyed baby in the cot, and the grief that had marked the Wybornes' faces.

'Such a head start in the Party,' mused Jordan. 'Hero of Dunkirk, all that. I've always rather envied that generation. Good and evil – choosing sides – was so much more straightforward in nineteen forty, don't you think?'

'I've never really thought much about it. The war's always seemed such a long time ago.'

'Wyborne drinks, you know. Since his daughter died. Everyone knows, but no one mentions it, of course.'

Katherine's smile faded. 'I did mean to talk to Rachel's father after she died. To ask him whether he knew what she wanted to speak to us about. But I couldn't. He looked so . . . so *haunted*.'

She explained about Rachel's phone-calls to Liv and herself the day before she had died. 'It still bothers me,' she said. 'I've always thought – oh,' and she sighed, 'if only I'd gone back to my bedsit that day. If only I hadn't stayed out overnight. It wasn't as though the man I was with meant anything to me. I can't even remember his name. I know Liv feels the same. It was one of those awful things. Wanting to turn the clock back.'

She fell silent. Several times over the past few months she had thought of driving up to Lancashire, dragging Liv and the children out of that awful house and bringing her back to London. She hadn't, of course, because you couldn't make someone take that sort of decision: it had to come from them. So she had confined herself to writing and to sending generous presents for Freya's birthday, and to welcome the new baby. She had had no replies to her letters – she wondered sometimes whether Stefan destroyed them; she believed him capable of that – and only a polite note of thanks for the presents. Once or twice she had considered writing to Thea, but had not done so. It would have seemed a betrayal. Yet she remained troubled, haunted by the thought that once again she might offer too little, too late.

In June, after his pupils had taken their exams, Stefan's teaching hours were reduced once more. In previous years he had made up the shortfall in income by taking on private pupils; this year he did not do so. He had decided to convert the barn to a separate dwelling so that, he explained to Liv, they could take in paying guests. Bed and breakfast, and an evening meal as well, perhaps. He set to work once more, whitewashing walls. He hauled furniture from the house to the barn – 'To get the feel of it,' he told Liv. The living room was empty now except for the towers of books and a few cushions.

The shotgun remained in the barn. Liv felt as though she was waiting for a storm to break. The warm summer weather intensified her feeling of dread. Taking Georgie to the doctor for a check-up, she asked her tentatively whether not being able to sleep might make a person ill. The doctor looked at her sharply. 'Are you talking about yourself, Mrs Galenski?'

'My husband.'

'Prolonged insomnia can lead to mental problems. Or it can be a consequence of mental problems, of course.'

'What sort of problems?' Her mouth was dry.

'Irritability ... lack of concentration ... mood swings ... in extreme cases, psychosis.'

'Would sleeping pills help?'

'They might do. But if your husband's having trouble sleeping, then I'd suggest he makes an appointment to see me.'

She knew that Stefan would never do that. 'I thought – ' she cleared her throat ' – I thought that perhaps you could give me something to take home to him.'

'I'm afraid I can't do that, Mrs Galenski. I'd need to see the patient first.'

Her heart sank. She heard the doctor say, 'I could call at the house, though, if you're concerned.'

She pictured it. The doctor's car struggling up the rutted path to Holm Edge. Showing this kind, perceptive woman into rooms that contained no furniture other than cushions and books. Introducing her to Stefan. On a good day, he would charm and deceive and refuse any offer of help. On a bad day . . . She had to suppress a shiver. She imagined Stefan fetching the shotgun from the barn, and throwing the doctor off the premises.

She made herself smile. 'There's no need for that. It's not important.'

On the bus home, she clutched Georgie to her, seeing the trap she had almost fallen into. Social workers took children away from houses that were unsuitable for them, from fathers who were a danger to them, from mothers who could not protect them. At all costs, she must not let that happen.

Once more, she tried to plan. If she were to leave Stefan . . . *if.* What had once seemed preposterous and inconceivable had become a possibility. Yet the practical difficulties of such an undertaking were overwhelming. She had saved almost twenty pounds, but how long would that feed Georgie and Freya and herself? How long would it house them? She would have to get a job, but what job could she do? She would be prepared to try anything – waitressing, cleaning, bar-work, anything at all – but there remained the problem of the children. How much would she have to pay someone to look after Freya and Georgie while she was working? Once she had paid for babysitting, how much money would be left over to feed, clothe, and house them all?

And if she left Holm Edge, where could she go? Whatever the drawbacks of living at Holm Edge, they had at least a roof over their heads. She could not return to Fernhill – the cottage was now let to another tenant and, besides, Stefan would follow her there. She had not seen Katherine since the previous year, and when they had last met they had quarrelled. Her pride rebelled at the thought of inflicting the three of them on Katherine, who didn't even like children. But there was no one else.

The actual business of leaving also presented daunting problems. Taking the two children on public transport was in itself a major undertaking. Georgie was not yet old enough for the pushchair, which meant that she had to be taken everywhere in the carry-cot. To get on to the bus, Liv had to dismantle the carry-cot from its wheels and, taking several journeys, carry the heavy wheels up the steps and put them in the luggage rack, settle Freya in a seat, then put the carry-cot and Georgie between them. Bags of shopping meant another trip in and out of the bus. She imagined trying to get on to a bus or train with Georgie, Freya, the carry-cot and the luggage they would need to take with them if they were to leave Holm Edge. It took her half an hour to get both children ready for the shortest outing. She imagined having to do that, and having to pack children's clothes and bottles and nappies, all the time wondering whether Stefan – the length of whose outings was always unpredictable – were to return to the house. Worst of all, she imagined what he might do if he were to discover her trying to leave. *I'll never let you go, Liv.*

She must wait, she thought, wait for the right time. Make do and mend a bit longer. Wait until Georgie was old enough for the pushchair, or until she had saved more money . . .

The following day, she was hanging out washing on the line when she heard noises from inside the house. She put down the pegs and peered upstairs. The clattering and banging continued. Upstairs, she saw that the bedroom door was open. When she looked inside her heart stood still. Stefan was searching through the chest of drawers. Books, clothes and shoes were scattered in heaps on the bedroom floor. He had opened the top drawer, and was flinging jumpers and T-shirts aside. She felt sick with fright. She said, 'Stefan,' and he turned and looked at her.

'Barentov . . . *Eastern European Myths* . . . I can't find it anywhere.' He slammed the empty drawer shut.

'It's not in here.' She could hear the panic in her voice. 'It's downstairs, I'm sure of it.'

'Someone's taken it. Freya, perhaps. She put my shoes in the laundry basket the other day.' He opened the second drawer, where she kept her savings, and she dug her nails into the palms of her hands and prayed.

Gloves and tights scattered across the room. There was a thud as a pair of socks struck the floorboards. Then a whirring noise as the coins escaped from their imprisonment and rolled in whorls and spirals around the room.

Stefan paused. Liv saw him frown as he stooped to pick up a coin. She said quickly, 'It's my birthday money.'

'Thea sent you ten pounds. There's twice that here.' He was cradling the coin in the palm of his hand.

When he crossed the room to her, she saw that his eyes had hardened. 'Where did you get this from, Liv? Did someone give it to you?'

'I saved it. Honestly, I saved it. It's for the children – for Christmas—'

'*Liar.*' She had no chance to duck the blow. As the flat of his hand struck her face hard, her legs buckled beneath her.

'*Liar.*' He hauled her upright. 'What's it for?' His fingers dug into her flesh as he shook her violently. 'What were you planning to do with it?'

'Nothing.' The side of her face throbbed, and she tasted blood. Her mind was blank with shock. She heard herself gabble, 'I told you, it was for the children—'

'Then why were you hiding it from me?' His expression altered, and she saw in his gaze both fury and unreason. 'You were going to leave me, weren't you, Liv?' He must have seen the truth in her eyes because he seized a hank of her hair, dragging her across the room. 'Are you too stupid to understand?' he hissed. 'I meant what I said. You'll not walk out on me, Liv. Never.'

Then he flung her from him. The back of her head ricocheted against the wall, and she slid to the ground. Crouching, her knees to her chin, she folded her arms protectively around herself. She heard Stefan leave the room. Then a scraping sound as the key turned in the lock. She ran to the door, yet though she shook the handle and shouted his name, his footsteps faded as he ran down the stairs.

From the garden, there was the rumble of the car engine. Looking out of the window, Liv could see the carry-cot beneath the holly tree, and Georgie asleep inside it, and the Citroën careering at speed down the track. Clutching the sill, she struggled to take in her situation. She was locked in the bedroom, and Stefan had gone. The children were alone. She endured a moment of complete panic as all the things that might happen occurred to her. Freya might take it into her head to lift Georgie out of the carry-cot, and drop her. Or she might go into the barn and climb the ladder and take the shotgun from the shelf ...

Somehow she got hold of herself. She wiped the blood from her mouth with her sleeve, and forced herself to think. She could hear Freya, playing on the stairs, so she went back to the door, knelt down and peered into the lock. No key; Stefan must have taken it with him. But all the keys in the house fitted all the locks. She called to Freya.

Small footsteps pattered along the corridor. 'Mummy?' The door-handle rattled as Freya tried to open it.

'Mummy? Let me in, Mummy.' Tears quivered at the edge of Freya's voice.

Liv took a deep breath. 'Darling, there's no need to be frightened, but Mummy can't open the door. I want you to be a very clever girl and go and get the key from Daddy's study door and bring it upstairs.'

'Mummy, I want to come in.'

'You can come in if you go and get the key, Freya. Then we'll open the door. Can you do that?'

'Yes, Mummy.'

'And be careful on the stairs, love.'

There was a moment's silence, and then the sound of footsteps down the corridor. It seemed an age before Freya came back. Liv heard her fit the key in the lock, but the key did not turn. The lock was too stiff for a child's small hands.

'Try to slide the key under the door, Freya.'

More scrabbling noises. 'It doesn't fit, Mummy.'

She could have screamed with frustration and fear. She took a deep breath. 'Go downstairs and out into the garden, darling. Take the key with you.'

Freya disappeared down the corridor once more. Liv opened the window. The garden – and freedom – seemed so tantalizingly close. Liv up-ended the contents of her sewing basket on to the floor and tied a length of wool to the handle of the basket. Looking down, she could see Freya standing on the grass, so she lowered the basket out of the window and told Freya to put the key in the basket. Then she hauled it back up to the room.

Unlocking the door, she paused only long enough to gather up the money from the floor. Then she ran downstairs and out into the garden. Georgie – dear, good little Georgie – was still asleep. Liv grabbed what clothes and nappies she could find and flung them into a carrier-bag. Then she swept all her old letters, postcards and address books into her Greek bag, and filled another bag with bottles, dummies and Freya's favourite books and toys. As she packed, she listened for the sound of a car, heading back up the track. She knew now that there would never be a right time, and that she could no longer make do and mend. She flung the carrier-bags on to the carry-cot tray, and her Greek bag over her shoulder. Then she took Freya's hand.

She looked back just once at the house. The sunlight glittered through the branches of the holly tree, marking patterns on the grass. She remembered the first time she had seen Holm Edge, and how Stefan had risen and smiled as he had walked across the lawn to greet her. And she remembered a map drawn on the back of her hand, and how the blue-violet lines had echoed the tracks of her veins. She was following a different map now; she quickened her footsteps, hastening to be away.

Felix met Rose at Liverpool Street station. She hooked her hand around his arm, snuggling up to him as they made for the tube.

They walked along the King's Road, where Rose exclaimed at the shops and Felix bought her supper (spaghetti Bolognese followed by ice-cream) in a trattoria. He asked after his father ('I hardly ever see him, Felix. He's always at work') and Mia ('She was wearing Mummy's wellington boots the other day. I saw her. *Mummy's*') and the animals ('Fiametta is pregnant, so I suppose either Marietta or Constanza must be a boy'). Then he explained to her that they were to spend the evening at Katherine's flat because he had promised to put up a curtain rail for her. Rose looked suspicious. 'Who's Katherine?'

'A very good friend of mine. You'll like her. Come on.'

In Katherine's flat, Rose sat curled up in an armchair reading magazines while Felix was busy with the stepladders and the drill. At about eight o'clock, the doorbell rang.

He called into the entryphone, 'Who is it?'

There was a silence in which he realized he could hear a baby crying. Then a voice said, 'It's Liv. I was looking for Katherine.'

He was going to say, 'She's not home yet,' and get back to the curtain rail, but then he thought *Liv*. Liv of the jealous husband and the two small children and the tumbledown house in Lancashire. What was Liv doing in London?

He said, 'Hang on, I'm just coming down,' and left the room. Running down the stairs, he could hear the crying before he saw their silhouettes framed by the window in the front door.

He opened the door. She was holding one child – a little girl – in her arms, and there was another smaller infant in a pram. Both were howling. She said tremulously, 'They've been awfully good, but they've had enough. I didn't think that Katherine ...' Her voice became wobblier as she spoke.

'Katherine will be home soon,' said Felix. 'I'll help you with the baby.' He unhooked the carry-cot body from the wheels and carried them both upstairs. The baby bawled at him, purple-faced. He heard Liv following behind him. He didn't need to ask questions – or to see the angry red bruise down the side of Liv's face, obvious as soon as she was in the brighter light of the living room – to know that something dreadful had happened. He concentrated on practical help. He telephoned Katherine's office, but there was no reply, and then he made tea and sandwiches while Liv fed the baby. Rose helped the little girl – Freya – out of her coat and hat, and cuddled the baby after she had been fed. Felix knew, glancing at Liv, that she had reached a state of exhaustion where she was hardly able to speak, let alone explain what had happened to her. When he looked at her damaged face, he was aware of a deep, dark anger; when he looked at Rose, cradling the baby, he saw to his astonishment that all the resentment, all the unhappiness, had vanished from her features, and that she was looking down at the sleeping infant with an expression of utter serenity.

Katherine came home at ten. By that time, Georgie was asleep in her carry-cot, and Freya had curled up in Katherine's bed. Liv started when Katherine's key turned in the lock. She said, 'Katherine, I hope you don't mind—' and then she burst into tears.

Katherine hugged her. 'Of course I don't mind, you idiot. I don't mind a bit.' Felix noticed that there were tears in Katherine's eyes, too.

Chapter Ten

Liv stayed only three days with Katherine. Her initial relief at having reached sanctuary was quickly followed by fear: fear that Stefan might trace her, fear of the retribution that would follow. Stefan might guess that she had gone to Katherine; although she did not think he knew Katherine's address, and though Katherine's phone number was ex-directory and she had scooped up every letter, postcard and address book before leaving Holm Edge and thrown them into her bag, she was nevertheless haunted by the possibility that he would find her.

It was Felix who came up with the solution. The flat – the ground floor of a Victorian house – was in Beckett Street, a quarter of a mile from where Felix lived. It was a short-term let, due for renovation in six months' time. 'It'll give you a breathing space,' he said, and, looking around it, she knew that it would. The rooms were cold and echoing, and the bathroom floor was curiously uneven, where damp had come up through the foundations. There was a kitchen and a living room, and a small, dusty garden full of leggy roses and mildewed lilacs. An old espaliered pear tree grew against the back wall of the house; its branches tapped the kitchen window-panes with small, lichened fingers. A little of Liv's anxiety and exhaustion began to fall away, and she felt within her a small kernel of hope. However cramped the flat was, and however shabby, it would be *hers*.

The previous tenants had left a few pieces of furniture: an old electric cooker and a scratched yellow Formica table in the kitchen, and in the large, light front room a lumpy double bed. The first night, Liv, Freya and Georgie slept curled up together in the bed. Katherine had lent blankets and cups and plates, and donated several carrier-bags of food. The following day, Felix appeared with lengths of wood and a saw, and made a bed for Freya. Liv steadied the slats while he screwed them in place; when he hit his thumb with the hammer, she waited, tense with dread, for his mood to alter, for the inevitable criticism and raised voice, but he only winced and said, 'Oops, butter-fingers,' and went back to work. She watched him warily, wondering whether his calmness was a pretence. It was a long time before she let herself relax again.

The sounds of Holm Edge – the birdsong, and the soughing of the grass in the wind – were replaced by the rumble of traffic, and her neighbours' sharp, public quarrels. The city brought with it a different sort of isolation: lowered gazes in the tube, and a jumble of unknown languages in the street. She was not fast enough, hard enough, quick-witted enough for urban life. Cars hooted at her when she crossed the road; drunks staggering home from the pub jostled her. She could not fix in her head a map of the city. There were streets with metal gates and large, barking dogs, streets of no shops and blank, glassy-eyed offices, streets where at night cars slowed, lowering their passenger windows to speak to the girls who lingered on the pavement. She took wrong turnings, headed up blind alleys. Going to bed at night, closing her eyes, the city continued to assault her, a flicker of disconnected images.

She would have liked to hide away in the flat, secure within her own four walls, but Freya and Georgie tied her to the outside world. Felix and his sister, Rose, visited one sunny afternoon. In the garden, Rose played hide and seek with Freya, while Felix lay on the grass, his eyes closed, his arms cushioning his head. 'Will you get a job, Liv?' he asked. 'Or will you sign on?'

The mere thought of becoming entangled in the social-security system alarmed her. 'I'd like to get a job,' she said, 'but there's the children. What would I do with them?'

'Find a babysitter to look after them.' He sat up and yelled, 'Rose!' and Rose scampered over to join them.

'Rose, you'll look after Freya and Georgie while Liv goes to work, won't you?'

'Course.' Rose went back to the game of hide and seek.

'Felix, you and Rose have done so much for me already, I couldn't possibly.'

'Why on earth not? You'd be doing me a favour. Rose refuses to go home. She's eighteen now, you see – she's left school. She wants to stay in London with me.' Felix sighed. 'She looks after me. Cooks enormous meals and stands over me while I eat them. It's awful, Liv. She *irons my clothes*.' He was wearing a T-shirt whose slogan had faded to illegibility, and faded denims. There were crease marks in the denim. 'I have to find her something to do. If she babysat Freya and Georgie then at least she'd be out of the house.' He lay down again and closed his eyes, as though the matter was settled.

On Monday, Liv scoured the local papers for a job. A café a few streets away was looking for someone to help with general duties. Sheila, the proprietor, had short grey hair and huge stripy earrings, chain-smoked and called Liv 'duck'. Sheila offered her the job; Liv started work the next day. She worked a mixture of lunch-times and evenings so that she was never away from the children for too long at a time.

The work was tiring, but she loved it. Working meant that she was part of the world again. Though she earned only fifteen pounds a week, the rent on the flat was low and, besides, she was used to living on a small income. When, at the end of the week, she opened her pay packet and counted out the notes, she felt a thrill of pride. Earning her own wages, supporting herself and her children single-handed, enabled her to hold her head high once more. Walking home, her fifteen pounds safely in her bag, she felt free. Never ever again, she promised herself, would she be dependent on a man.

She bought a cot for Georgie from a charity shop, and made loose covers for a junk-shop armchair. She found a chest of drawers on a skip, which she sanded and painted. She disguised the front room's bare, peeling walls with a mural of a jungle, with monkeys swinging from tree to tree and Rousseau-esque tigers peering through the grass. There was both reassurance and pleasure in making the flat her own, and in rediscovering the skills that enabled them to live comfortably in it. Slowly and painstakingly, she was regaining the confidence that her marriage had taken from her.

At six months, Georgie adapted easily to the changes in her young life; Freya, at two and a half, found it harder. Bright, restless and demanding, she reverted to the habits of babyhood. Though she had been dry at night for three months, she now often wet the bed, and her temper tantrums could be heard half-way down the street. She missed Stefan, and she missed Holm Edge. Often she would perch on the window-sill, looking out at the pavement. When Liv asked her what she was looking for, she would mumble, her thumb in her mouth, 'Daddy.'

On Monday afternoons, they all went to a mother-and-toddler group at the church hall. Liv drank cups of watery Nescafé, and talked to the other mothers about the minutiae of small children's lives, the sleeping and eating problems, the little triumphs and landmarks, the sort of things which, if she mentioned them to Katherine, produced a look of glazed boredom. One day, one of the other mothers asked her where she had lived before she had moved to London. 'Lancashire,' she explained, and she described Holm Edge.

'You must miss it,' the other woman said sympathetically. 'Are you happy in London?' She smiled and said, yes, of course she was happy, but, walking home, she acknowledged that happiness, for her, was now parcelled up in little pieces: Georgie's wide smile when she greeted her each morning, Freya's hand in hers as they walked along the pavement.

She was too bruised by the past and too apprehensive of the future for full-time happiness. There were times when she seemed to be missing a layer or two of skin, when everything that touched her left its mark. Times when Freya's crying woke her in the middle of the night, and Liv herself lay wakeful for hours after she had comforted her, staring into the darkness, her worries crowding in on her. Some nights she wept, quietly so as not to disturb the children. Her mood swooped and swung between relief and regret. When, each morning, the sounds of the traffic and the clacking of feet along pavements woke her, she still felt, even before she opened her eyes, a rush of gratitude that she was in London and not at Holm Edge. The iron lump, which had formed permanently beneath her ribs during the last months of her marriage, began at last to melt and to disperse. She no longer started at the sound of a footfall on the path. She had almost learned not to flinch when, glancing out of the window, she caught sight of a dark-haired man.

Liv made a painting smock for Freya from a length of cotton bought at the market. One of the mothers at toddler group saw it and asked her to make her daughter a similar smock: within a fortnight she had made and sold half a dozen.

She, Felix and Katherine had fallen into an easy friendship. Evenings and weekends were spent at each other's houses, eating spaghetti, listening to records, mulling over the events of the day. Liv cooked suppers, which they ate off market-stall plates, and washed down with cheap red wine. Sitting at the yellow Formica table in Liv's kitchen, they talked for hours. Arguments rose and fell, their voices muted only by their awareness of the sleeping children in the adjacent room. The clock's hands circled, and in the early hours of the morning, gaps yawned in the conversation and ideas seemed to slip out of reach. Sentences trailed and slowed, fragmented by fatigue, until Katherine rose and stumbled to the front door, or Felix fumbled for his jacket.

Sometimes Katherine left early, muttering excuses. One night, as the front door closed behind her, Felix yawned and said lazily, 'Rose thinks she's got a secret lover.'

When Liv looked at him, he shrugged. 'Katherine's not the going-to-bed-early type, is she?'

Liv pictured Katherine that evening: her dress of tawny brown velvet, her carefully made-up face. 'Have you noticed, Felix,' she said, 'that she always wears her nicest clothes on the nights she goes off early?'

Felix grinned. 'You don't think it's for us, then?' He offered her more wine.

Liv shook her head. 'No thanks. I have to wash up – I'll drop everything.'

'It'll bounce.' He refilled her glass anyway. Liv felt pleasantly fuzzy, as though the wine had knocked all the hard edges from this new life that she was only just getting used to.

She washed and he dried, and they drank the rest of the wine. Their conversation slipped and slid into nonsenses, unrestrained by Katherine's cool, acerbic wit. For some reason she could never afterwards remember, Felix insisted on teaching her his school song, which was jingoistic and in Latin, and she laughed so much that she dropped a glass, which shattered on the floor. He said mournfully, 'It didn't bounce, did it?' and she found herself leaning against the sink, giggling helplessly, her fingers pressed against her mouth as he swept up the shards of glass.

She realized, watching him, that she had grown used to him, that she no longer feared that he might change and turn into that familiar stranger, the one with contempt in his eyes. She realized also that it had been years, literally years, since she had laughed like that. Not since university, not since Rachel had made up that other threesome.

She had never, ever laughed so much with Stefan. How odd, she thought, that it should be friendship, rather than love, which had allowed her to laugh.

One Wednesday, Katherine realized that she was in love with Jordan Aymes. It was her lunch-break, and she was completing the *Glitz* quiz: '*How To Tell If You're Truly, Madly, Deeply*'. Ticking off the little boxes, she giggled with the other girls, but when she totted up the result, her heart began to hammer. *Phew, you've fallen for him hook, line and sinker!* She tore out the page, threw it into her waste-paper basket and went back to her typewriter. It was complete nonsense, of course. She couldn't possibly be in love with Jordan Aymes, could she? Love couldn't possibly be the secret ingredient, the mysterious X-factor, could it?

The following day she went to see Liv. Her unease remained with her: she prowled restlessly round Liv's kitchen, fiddling with a baby's rattle and a tube of Smarties, gazing empty-eyed at a child's picture-book. She heard Liv say, 'What's up?'

'Nothing's up.'

Liv said flippantly, 'Rose thinks you've got a secret lover.' Katherine flicked ash on to the garden steps. 'Katherine . . .?'

She remembered the first time she had met him. The Wybornes' house: *Quails' eggs in aspic. Supposed to be a treat, I know . . .* She said suddenly, 'Actually, I think I might be in love with someone. But I can't be, can I, Liv? I don't believe in love, do I?' She did not wait for a reply but, crushing the stub of her cigarette beneath her heel, muttered, 'I thought I just liked him. And fancied him, of course.' She could hear her disbelief, disbelief that she, Katherine Constant, should have tumbled into such a well-worn abyss. She tried to smile, but felt more like weeping. 'I can't stop thinking about him . . . I dream about him . . . If I was fourteen I'd be writing his name on my pencil case, I daresay. *Hell*,' she muttered. 'I could do with a drink.'

'There's only tea, I'm afraid.' Katherine recognized sympathy in Liv's eyes; she turned away.

'If you've found someone, then that's wonderful, isn't it?'

Swinging back, Katherine stared at Liv blankly. 'But there's sex, and there's friendship, isn't there? All the rest of it – hearts and roses and all that rubbish – they're just a trap to get women behind the kitchen sink, aren't they?'

'You can't say *love* doesn't exist. You can't deny *feelings* – caring about someone more than you care about yourself, even. It doesn't mean you have to *marry* them, but—'

'Well, it certainly won't in my case. He's married already.' Katherine lit another cigarette. 'You mustn't tell anyone,' she said, more calmly. 'I promised Jordan I'd keep it secret. Only I had to . . . and I didn't think . . .' She was unsure whether she felt better for having shared her secret with Liv or worse. Better for having shared some of her uncertainties, or worse for having confessed her vulnerability. She said brusquely, 'He's an MP, so he has to be terribly respectable. And his wife's the loyal-housewife type, and he's much too nice to hurt her feelings.'

'How long have you known him?'

'A year. Longer if you go back to the first time we met. He was a guest at Rachel's wedding.'

'Do you *mind* that he's married?'

'Course not.' She did not pause to wonder whether she spoke the truth. Some thoughts were best glanced at, accepted, then shut away. 'I sometimes think I prefer it. You know I've never wanted *that* – losing my independence – children, domestic slavery—' Katherine broke off. The small kitchen was littered with toys and tiny garments. There was a closed expression in Liv's eyes. 'Sorry,' she said softly. 'My big mouth again . . .'

Liv began to pick up the toys, to drop them into a cardboard box. 'Tell me about him. Is he handsome?'

Katherine had a passport-sized photograph that she kept in her purse. She showed it to Liv. She supposed that some women might find Jordan's air of distance off-putting, but she, who had lain beside him and had seen her desire for him mirrored in his eyes, found him faultless. She added, 'He knows Rachel's father, of course. He can't bear him, actually. Says he's manipulative.'

'Well, he is, isn't he? Remember how he lied to Hector and told him that Rachel had decided to leave him to go to Paris? Just because he didn't want them to get married. I suppose he thought it was for the best,' she said slowly, remembering. 'I suppose he thought he was protecting Rachel.'

Liv stood at the doorway, looking out into the inky night, Freya's rag doll cradled in her hands.

Rose took her position as Freya's and Georgie's babysitter with great seriousness, reading Dr Spock in her spare time. Bernard Corcoran had accepted his daughter's leaving home with good grace, and sent her a small allowance each month. The change in

Rose, during her months in London, was marked. Gone was the sulky truculence, as well as the childishness. She no longer lay in bed till midday, or expected others to fetch and carry for her. She even managed the occasional telephone conversation with Mia. She spent much of her time minding Liv's children, and some of the remainder working at a nearby dog rescue centre. Rose's intense attachment to Freya and Georgie had initially surprised Felix, but then he had at last understood that her capacity for devotion, which had for a long time wearied him, had only required an appropriate direction.

It had occurred fleetingly to Felix that some might find his friendship with Liv and Katherine unconvincing, or disreputable, or evasive. He was twenty-five: he was supposed to be sowing his wild oats, or looking for a partner and for permanence. He brushed those thoughts aside. One Sunday, he borrowed the van they used for the house renovations and drove the six of them – Rose, Katherine, Liv and the children – to Bushey Park. The late autumn weather was bright and blowy, and the fallen leaves whirled in little vortices along the grass.

The sun, falling slowly through the sky, cast lengthening shadows. Georgie slept in her pram while Liv took Freya to find a ladies' lavatory.

Rose watched them go. 'You should marry Liv, Felix,' she said. 'Then I'd be Freya and Georgie's aunt.'

'Liv's married already, Rose,' Katherine pointed out.

'I know, but it'll be so awful if she goes back to her horrible husband. I'd miss them *so much*.'

'Don't be daft, Rose. Liv's not going to go back to Stefan.'

'There's no need to be cross, Felix. Women do sometimes go back to their husbands, even when they're horrible.'

'They've been living apart for almost five months.'

'She might change her mind.'

Felix could hear the fear in Rose's voice. He jammed his hands into his jacket pockets and walked away from her, kicking up heaps of dead leaves. Rose's words echoed. He had known, of course, that Liv was afraid that Stefan might trace her to London, but as the weeks and months had passed, he had fallen into the habit of assuming the danger was over. Rose's words unsettled him. Wives – even battered wives – did sometimes return to their husbands. He saw suddenly how he had let himself grow used to her. How he had let his life mesh into hers.

On the way home, the children slept in the back of the van. Felix dropped Katherine at her flat, and Rose at the dogs' home. They had paused at a traffic light, when Felix asked Liv, 'Have you decided what you'll do when we renovate your flat? You'll have to move out of it, you see.'

'I hadn't thought about it. I never think more than a day or two ahead.'

'Why not?'

'Because it worries me, I suppose.'

The bright colours illuminated her profile and the dark halo of her hair. 'I'm sure you'll be able to find somewhere else,' he said reassuringly. 'I could look out for you, if you like.'

'It's not that.' Liv bit her lip. 'It's Stefan. I don't think more than a day or two ahead because if I do then I have to think what to do about Stefan.'

'There's nothing to do, is there? You left him, and sooner or later you'll get a divorce, I suppose, and then . . .'

'It's not that simple, Felix. Things never are that simple with Stefan.' She glanced out of the window. 'I just can't believe I'm safe yet, you see.'

'Of course you're safe.'

'Am I?' She turned to look at him.

'Have you heard from him?' Liv shook her head. 'Well, then. He's probably accepted the situation.'

Another silence. It had begun to drizzle. Car headlights were reflected on the silky black tarmac. Liv said slowly, 'Sometimes he used to time my visits to the shops. If I took longer than the allotted time then I'd have to explain where I'd been. Five minutes at the baker's, ten minutes in the supermarket, that sort of thing. Once, when I couldn't account for every moment – I was twelve minutes out, I think – he emptied my purse into the bramble patch. So that I couldn't go out again, you see.' The expression in her eyes as she turned to him was cool and appraising. 'Do you really think that a man like that will just *accept the situation*, Felix?'

The rain had thickened; he turned on the wipers. Some of his contentment, which he had acquired almost without noticing, dissolved. He made himself ask, 'So you still think he's looking for you?'

'I'm certain of it.' She blinked. 'When I've had a good day, then I say to myself that there's nine million people in London, and that he can't possibly find just three. But on other days I remember that Stefan is clever and determined and obsessive enough to search day and night until he finds us.' Her gaze was fixed on the rhythmic sweep of the wipers. 'I don't think he knows where Katherine lives – he'd have found us by now if he had. And Mum certainly wouldn't tell him where I am, and no one else knows. So I should feel safe, shouldn't I? There's no reason why I shouldn't feel safe, is there?'

He said, with a confidence he no longer felt, 'No reason at all.' Rain battered against the screen; behind them, Freya whimpered in her sleep.

Katherine decided to give a dinner party. She invited Liv, Felix and Rose, Netta Parker from work, and Netta's boyfriend, Gavin, and the couple in the upstairs flat, Martin and Beth. Planning the menu, her thoughts drifted, as they so often did, to Jordan. She had not, of course, told him that she loved him. She knew that such a confession would alter the tenor of their relationship. Fleetingly, she allowed herself to imagine inviting Jordan to her dinner-party, introducing him to her friends. She pushed the thought away, knowing that she was treading on dangerous ground, and forced herself to concentrate instead on the unfamiliar business of cookery. Rather furtively, Katherine bought a copy of *Woman's Own*, which promised instructions for a simple dinner party for eight. The shopping took up three lunch hours, and the preparation, which Katherine began as soon as she arrived home from work on Friday, took far longer than she had anticipated. When, at half past seven, the doorbell rang, she shrieked and ran downstairs, her hands covered in flour.

She opened the door. 'You're early,' she began to say. 'I haven't even started the—' She stopped. '*Simon*,' she whispered.

Simon was standing on the doorstep. He was carrying a holdall. 'Aren't you going to ask me in, Kitty?'

She showed her twin up to the flat. In the kitchen, Simon stared at the debris – the chicken carcasses and vegetable peelings and the grey, sticky mess that was supposed to be pastry – and said, 'What on earth are you doing?'

'I'm having a dinner party. Only it's all taking much longer than I thought it would, and I'm not sure I'm doing it right.' She looked at him. 'Why are you in London, Simon? You're supposed to be in Edinburgh.'

'I'd had enough. Bloody cold place, and my landlady was John Knox's sister.' He mimicked a refined Edinburgh accent. 'No ladies in the bedroom, Mr Constant. I run a decent house.'

Simon was smiling; superficially, he appeared to be his familiar, indolent self, but Katherine, who knew him so well, detected an edginess about him.

'So you handed in your notice?'

'Not *exactly*.'

'What, then?'

He said carelessly, 'Actually, the old bastard gave me the sack.' He looked at her. 'Could I have a drink, Kitty, while you're giving me the third degree? At least then it wouldn't remind me quite so much of home.'

She poured him a glass of wine. 'Tell me what happened.'

He drank the first glass quickly, and by the time he had finished the second she had learned enough to be able to fill in the gaps. The antique shop hadn't paid well, so Simon, who had always appreciated the better things in life, had begun to help himself to a few extras. Pens and paper-clips at first, then small change from the petty-cash box, and then – the incident that had provoked his sacking – a couple of items from the shop.

'Hideous little Minton statuettes,' said Simon. He sounded aggrieved. 'They'd been in the back of a cupboard for years. I didn't think Gerald would miss them.' Gerald was the owner of the antique shop. 'But he absolutely freaked out.' He shrugged. 'The shop hasn't been doing too well. I think he was just looking for an excuse to get rid of me, to tell the truth.'

Katherine thought, You wouldn't know the truth if it bit you. She felt cold inside. She said, 'Simon, it was *stealing*,' and he looked up at her, his blue eyes wide.

'Nonsense. Don't be so sanctimonious, Kitty. Everyone does it. The perks of the job. How else are you supposed to get by?'

She couldn't think of a reply. 'Have you told Mum and Dad?'

'I gave them the edited version, of course.' Simon filled his glass again, and she wondered, looking at him, whether he was right, whether she was just being holier-than-thou, but realized that she could not imagine any of her close friends – Jordan, Liv, Felix – doing what Simon had done.

He gave her his sudden, charming smile. 'I wondered whether I could sleep on your sofa, Kitty. Just for a few days, until I sort something out.'

'Of course.' The doorbell rang once more and Katherine shrieked again, and dashed downstairs. She let in Liv and the children.

'I haven't started to peel the potatoes yet,' she said, as they followed her upstairs, 'or begun to make the crème brulée.'

Liv's eyes widened when she saw the kitchen. 'Do rice instead of potatoes, you don't have to peel it. And don't bother with crème brulée – fruit salad and apple pie will be plenty.' She looked up. 'Oh, hello, Simon. I didn't know you were here.' She went into Katherine's bedroom to settle the children.

When they were alone again, Simon said, 'That was *Liv* . . .?'

'She's living in London now. Didn't I tell you? She left her husband.'

Simon blinked. 'She's changed,' he said, and she saw him glance at the door, as though, if he looked long enough, he could see through the solid wood to the woman inside.

Felix and Rose arrived late to dinner. One of the dogs at the rescue centre had had to be put down, so Rose had been distraught and had needed a great deal of comforting and coaxing; then the van had punctured, turning a corner, and Felix had only just been able to prevent it ploughing into a plate-glass shop window, and had then spent an uncomfortable quarter of an hour in the rain, changing the tyre.

He made his apologies. Katherine, who looked hot and flustered, offered him a towel to dry his hair. 'You're awfully wet, Felix. Perhaps Simon has a spare shirt.'

Simon looked at him and said, 'I've only an overnight bag,' and Felix, who knew a snub when it was offered, smiled at Katherine.

'It doesn't matter. I'll dry out.'

The dinner was one of those occasions that never quite sparked and soared. The rice was sticky and the *coq au vin* was stringy and overcooked: Felix, who was always ravenous, ate with enthusiasm, but Simon, sawing theatrically, said, 'Not in the first *flush* of youth, d'you think, Kitty?' Felix thought that the guests were all pleasant and interesting (with the exception of Katherine's loathsome twin), but did not somehow fit together.

Rose told them about the dog. 'She had such a lovely character . . . she'd been so badly treated, and yet she was so sweet . . .'

'What sort of a dog was she?' asked Netta sympathetically.

'Oh . . . a bit of collie and a bit of Labrador, and a bit of red setter . . .' Rose's face crumpled.

'Not exactly *pedigree*, then,' murmured Simon.

Tears were dripping from the end of Rose's nose to her plate. Standing up, pushing back her chair, she ran out of the room.

'I'll make sure she's all right.' Liv left the table.

'Poor little mite,' said Netta. 'And she hasn't eaten a thing.'

'I could keep her dinner warm in the oven,' said Katherine, 'but the salad...' She looked dubiously at the rice and salad on Rose's plate. 'I forgot she was a vegetarian.'

Felix helped himself to more wine. 'Vegan.'

Simon snorted.

Netta eyed him. 'You don't approve?'

'People go in for these dietary fads to draw attention to themselves, don't they?'

'Plenty of people don't eat meat,' said Felix truculently. 'You surely aren't suggesting that entire nations are vegetarian just to draw attention to themselves, are you, Simon?'

'I'm not talking about the starving millions in India. They do it because they haven't any choice. If you could afford to eat meat there, it would probably be crawling with something, wouldn't it?'

Liv came back to the table. 'She's feeling much better. She'll be back in a minute – she's just washing her face.'

'We were talking about vegetarianism,' said Felix smoothly. 'Simon believes all vegetarians are attention-seeking.'

'That wasn't *quite* what I said. Of course I admire genuine principles. I just think that some of these fads – well, it's all about trying to prove you're better than everyone else, isn't it?' Simon sat back in his chair. 'I bet most of these so-called vegans eat junk-food on the sly. A burger from the Wimpy when no one's looking ... a bar of Dairy Milk when they can get away with it ...'

Katherine said, 'You're just judging everyone by your own standards.'

'Oh, come on, Kitty, don't be naïve. I'm being less hypocritical than most, that's all. I admit to doing the things that all of us do.'

'Lots of people stick to their principles.'

'Who? I bet you can't name me one.'

'Nancy Barnes,' said Felix. 'I lived with her for a while, in a commune in Hampshire. She was trying to live the life she believed in. It wasn't easy, but she tried.'

'And was it a success, this experiment in self-sufficiency?'

Talking to Simon, he realized that he hadn't thought about Saffron for weeks – months, perhaps. That she had slipped into the past, a sweet, sharp episode that seemed now quite separate from the rest of his life.

'Not really,' he admitted. 'There were – difficulties. Personality clashes, I suppose.'

Simon shrugged, as though that proved his point. Katherine said quickly, 'I'll get the pudding.'

Felix grabbed some plates. It was either help Katherine clear away, or hit Simon Constant, which might make him feel better but wouldn't improve the evening.

In the kitchen, Katherine said, 'Sorry.'

'What about?'

'Simon. And the food.'

'The food's lovely.'

'No, it isn't. It's awful. And look at these.' She stared hopelessly at the apple tarts, which were the colour of concrete, with blackened edges. 'I think I left them in the oven too long.'

Felix was looking through the open door. Simon was leaning towards Liv, talking to her. His arm curled proprietorially around the back of her chair, and he punctuated his phrases with a touch of his fingertips to her shoulder.

'*Felix.*' He spun round. Katherine was following the direction of his gaze.

'I said, can you fish the bits of banana out of the fruit salad? They've gone brown. They look like slugs.'

A few days later, Liv called at Katherine's flat after work one evening. The door was ajar, so she pushed it open. Simon was lounging on the sofa. She greeted him.

'Is Katherine home yet?' He shook his head. 'If you could tell her I called,' she said. 'And give her these,' she was carrying a bunch of chrysanthemums, 'to say thank you for Saturday.'

'You don't have to dash off, Liv.' Simon unfolded himself from the sofa, and went into the kitchen. 'There might be a glass of wine.' He opened the fridge.

'I can't. I have to get back to Freya and Georgie, you see.'

'Oh. What are you doing later this evening?'

Reading bedtime stories and catching up on the ironing, she thought.

'Only we could go to a film.'

'No babysitter.'

'Tomorrow night, then. That girl – the droopy-looking one, Thingy's sister – works for you, doesn't she?'

His description of Rose irritated her. She said, 'Rose helps me out, yes.'

'Well, then. We could go to the pictures, then get something to eat. Or there's a club in Wardour Street . . .' He looked at her. 'You must get sick of all that domesticity, Liv.'

He was asking her out. For a date. It had been so long since that had happened, that she had almost failed to recognize it. She had forgotten that men asked women out for dates, just as she had forgotten how to refuse gracefully dates one did not want.

'Simon, I really can't.'

He looked sulky. 'Why not?'

'Because . . . Because I'm married.'

'But you've left him.'

'Still . . .'

'Just a *date* . . .'

'It's too soon. I'm not ready to be involved with anyone else. And the children take all my time and energy.'

Going home, making supper and putting the children to bed, she forgot her conversation with Simon Constant. Yet later, when the girls were sleeping and the house was quiet, and she was getting ready for bed, she caught sight of her reflection in the bathroom mirror. She seemed to have altered since she had glanced at herself in a similar fashion that morning. It was as though she could see herself clearly again: dark eyes, pale skin, the unruly cloud of dark hair. She put up a hand to her face, touching it as though it had become unfamiliar.

Over the last few years, she had put herself into a different category, no longer classing herself with young women such as Katherine or Rose. She had been Stefan's wife, Freya and Georgie's mother. Yet she was beginning to exist once more as a separate human being, slowly rediscovering herself, peeling aside the layers to find the half-forgotten Liv hidden beneath.

A month after his arrival in London, Simon was still sleeping on Katherine's sofa. She was never quite sure how he spent his days: if she enquired, then he pointed to the heap of newspapers on the floor and to the small pile of washing-up by the sink. He claimed to be looking for a job (thus the newspapers), but though there were always prospects of jobs, he was invariably lounging on the sofa when she left for work in the morning, and on the sofa still when she came home at night.

She had not realized how much sharing her flat with another person would irritate her. Though she never noticed her own clutter, someone else's – even her twin's – got increasingly on her nerves. Worse, Simon's presence emphasized the limitations of her relationship with Jordan. She had thought of telling Simon about Jordan, but had quickly discarded the idea. Katherine knew her brother's faults as well as she knew her own. Discretion was not Simon's strongest suit: he would share secrets for amusement, or to provoke, or as a weapon. The long evening telephone calls that she and Jordan had formerly enjoyed were curtailed because the telephone was in the living room, where Simon slept. Katherine took to slipping out at night and calling Jordan's office from the phone-box on the corner. Later, she would always associate the stale, metallic smell of the public telephone box with the intensity of first love.

She and Jordan had discovered a handful of places they thought of as their own. A curry house in the Fulham Road, a smoky pub in an unfashionable part of London, and a small park – not much more than a pond and a handful of horse chestnuts – that no one else seemed to know about. Twice in the summer, they had spent an entire day together, driving at speed in Jordan's E-Type through leafy country lanes, stopping at a village pub for a ploughman's and a pint. There was a delicious sense of irresponsibility in those outings: as though, Jordan said, they were on their half-term holidays.

Yet since the end of August, she had seen him less frequently. Pressure of work, he told her, and, reading the newspapers, with their depressing litany of strikes and bombs and hijackings, she could only sympathize. Once, she had found the unpredictability of their assignations exciting; lately, it had begun to grate. He always contacted her, never the other way around. Once she had not minded; now she saw that there was a dependency in the arrangement that sat ill-at-ease with her supposed liberation.

That she loved him she continued to keep to herself, treasuring her secret. They spoke of liking, and of adoration and desire, but never of love. If, sometimes, when a week or a fortnight had gone by without her seeing him, and she found herself questioning his feelings for her, then she let that question remain unanswered, telling herself that it was unimportant. He sought her company, he laughed at her jokes, and he pleased her in bed – what more could she want? If he had been unattached, then would she have married him? She thought not: marriage to Jordan Aymes would have made her into that creature of mild ridicule, the Tory MP's wife. Imagining herself in pleated skirts and Pringle twinsets, Katherine smiled. When she tried to picture herself at constituency functions – politely applauding his speeches, and chatting to the Party faithful – her imagination faltered. She knew that their political differences were many, and that had she been paraded as his partner, she would have been unable to stop herself voicing them. Their present arrangement was perfect, she told herself. Jordan was interesting, intelligent and attractive – what did she care that in some matters their beliefs were far apart? In bed they were one, their bodies melding together, indivisible.

Most of the time, she believed that she was first with him. When his grey eyes clouded with desire, and when he said, after a few days' absence, 'I just needed to hear your voice,' she knew that she was first. She wondered why she needed to be first. Because she was the third of four children, she supposed; because she was a daughter in a family of sons; because she was a twin, so had never been the only one, the special one.

Felix phoned his father every Saturday evening. They talked about the cricket or the rugby, according to season, and the uselessness of the government, and about the business. One Saturday in early December, though, Bernard Corcoran's replies were monosyllabic, verging on the incoherent. Gaps yawned between phrases, and eventually Bernard, with a brusque farewell, put the phone down. Waking early the following morning, Felix decided to drive to Wyatts.

He reached the house by ten. Mia was in the kitchen, opening tins of dog food. She looked up when he came into the room. 'Felix, what a surprise.'

He kissed her cheek. 'How are you, Mia?'

'I'm very well. Coffee?'

'Please.' He watched her pour him a mug. 'Where's Dad?'

'At the office.'

He stirred sugar into his coffee. His father never went into the office on Sunday. Never.

'Do you want something to eat, darling?' Mia looked vaguely around the kitchen. 'A sandwich?'

Bryn and Maeve were chewing noisily, and there was a scattering of dog biscuits across the kitchen floor. 'No, I'm fine, thanks,' said Felix. 'Dad was a bit distant on the phone yesterday. Is he ill? Or is he worried about something?'

Mia swept back a long strand of tawny hair. 'I wouldn't know. He doesn't *confide*. At least, he doesn't confide in *me*.' She lit a cigarette. 'Bernard was in a Japanese prison camp in the war, wasn't he? He's never spoken about it to me, you know. Never,

ever. I only found out by accident – one of his golfing cronies mentioned it.' She blew out a thin stream of smoke. 'And I have asked him whether anything's wrong,' she said softly, 'but he tells me not to worry. As though I were a *child*.'

He could not recall ever before having heard Mia sound angry. 'I'm sure he doesn't mean ...' he began. 'He'd tell you if ...' His voice trailed away.

'Would he?' She stooped to fondle Maeve's long, brindled head.

Felix stood up. 'I'll try and catch him at the factory.'

'You'll stay for a few days, won't you?'

He saw suddenly how lonely it must be for Mia, marooned in the middle of the countryside with an uncommunicative husband and a vast, echoing house that still bore the imprint of her predecessor.

'Course I will.' He was due some time off work.

He drove to Norwich. Corcoran's factory was a huge Victorian edifice, built on the outskirts of the city and surrounded by rows of terraced houses. The building's red-brick walls were punctuated by tall, arched windows, giving it a cathedral-like grandeur. As a small boy, learning 'Kubla Khan' at prep school, Felix had always imagined the pleasure dome to be much like Corcoran's: vast, light-filled rooms, filled with the gentle churning of the conveyor-belts and the smells of dye and paper.

He made his way to the office. Through the half-open door, Felix glimpsed the heaps of papers and ledger-books on the desk. Then he saw his father. He was sitting motionless, his back to the door, but there was something about the hunch of his shoulders and the way his head fell against his supporting hand that made Felix's stomach turn. But when he said his father's name, Bernard Corcoran rose and smiled. 'Felix. How unexpected. What brings you here, old son? Not that it isn't marvellous to see you.'

'I was worried about you, Dad.'

Bernard turned back to the desk. 'Worried?'

'On the phone ... you sounded a bit ... preoccupied.' Felix

indicated the heaps of paper. 'Can I give you a hand with any of this?'

'No need for that.' Bernard stood up. 'I've a much better idea. Lunch. That nice little pub . . .'

They went to the Rose and Crown a few streets away. After they had placed their orders at the bar, Bernard bought whiskies for both of them and they found a table in the corner.

Felix tried again. 'You don't usually go to the office on a Sunday, Dad. Is anything up?'

Bernard made a face. 'Bit of a contretemps with the dear old Revenue, that's all. Thought I'd better check some figures. Nice and peaceful on a Sunday.' He put down his empty glass. 'Another one?'

'No thanks, I've got the van.' He frowned. 'Have things picked up at all? The business, I mean.'

'Oh, we're ticking along.' As Bernard rose to go to the bar, he stumbled slightly, almost knocking over the table.

Felix put out a supporting hand. 'Dad—'

'I'm all *right*, I said.' Bernard's voice was sharp. There was a silence. Felix's hand slid from his father's shoulder. Then Bernard said, 'I'm sorry. Shouldn't take it out on you.' He sat down. Eventually he said, 'We've cash-flow problems, you see. Some of our bigger customers take an age to pay their invoices. They know they can get away with it – what can we do, after all? They know we need them. I've had to borrow to cover the shortfall, and with interest rates as high as they are . . .' The words trailed away. Felix did not know which worried him more: the unhealthy purplish tinge to his father's face, or the hopelessness in his voice.

'You've had to take out another loan?' he prompted.

Bernard nodded. As he started to speak, the waitress arrived, interrupting their conversation. When they were alone once more, Felix said carefully, 'Are you afraid you won't be able to meet the repayments, Dad?'

Bernard was showering salt on to his steak and kidney pudding. His eyes did not meet Felix's. 'Oh, no, nothing like that.

It's just taking a bit longer to get us shipshape again than I thought it would. You know I hate to borrow.'

'So there's no ...' it was hard even to contemplate the possibility '... no *threat* to Corcoran's?'

'Threat?' Bernard smiled. His eyes, blue to Felix's green, were wide and untroubled. 'Of course not. How could you think such a thing? Of course not.'

Walking home from the mother-and-toddler group on Monday afternoon, Freya held up her painting. 'It's a green dragon, Mummy.'

'It's lovely, darling. Shall we put it up on the wall when we get home?'

'On the cupboard. Not Georgie's drawing.' Freya glanced with derision at her sister's wax-crayon scribble.

'We'll put Georgie's drawing beside her cot,' said Liv tactfully.

They were nearing the house. Suddenly Freya stopped still on the pavement, and began to laugh.

'Freya? Come on, love, hurry up, it's tea-time.'

Then she looked across to the house, to where Freya was pointing, and she, too, became motionless.

'Daddy,' said Freya, and clapped her hands for joy.

Chapter Eleven

Stefan crossed the road to her. Freya ran to him and he scooped her up in his arms.

Liv wrapped her own arms around herself in an attempt to still her shaking limbs. The muscles of her face seemed stiff. She whispered, 'How did you find us?'

He smiled. She thought that he had altered, that he was thinner, his features hollowed and gaunt. 'I was lucky,' he said. 'I was travelling by train, and someone had left a magazine on the seat beside me. I flicked through it, and saw your friend Katherine's name. 'Katherine Constant, assistant features editor.' So I knew where she worked, you see.'

Her mind seemed to be working very slowly, yet she realized how it must have happened. 'So you followed her home?'

'She came here a couple of nights ago. I saw you open the door to her.' He hugged Freya. 'My goddess . . . my beautiful little girl.'

'I painted a picture, Daddy.'

'Did you, sweetheart? Show me.'

Liv gave the painting to Stefan. The flimsy piece of paper fluttered in her grasp, in time with her trembling hand. She imagined Stefan waiting outside *Glitz*'s Fleet Street offices till Katherine left the building, and following her to her flat. Stefan trailing Katherine to Beckett Street. And watching. And waiting.

Freya had slipped out of Stefan's arms, and was leading him to the house. Liv followed them. At the front door, he hesitated. 'If I could come in. Just for a moment.'

The dry, cold December weather seemed to seep through her

clothing, chilling her skin. She heard him say softly, 'I know I have no right . . . I expect – nothing.'

She unlocked the door, and he followed her into the house. Her cold hands were clumsy as she struggled to unclip Georgie's harness, so he stooped beside her and threaded the straps through the D-rings, lifting Georgie out of the pushchair. She saw how he cradled his baby daughter against his shoulder, and the blissful closing of his eyes.

She put the kettle on. That was what one did when one wanted to feel normal. Freya chattered, filling in the gaps.

Stefan took from his coat pocket a doll with golden hair and fairy's wings. 'Here, Freya. This is a present for you, my love. Take her outside and show her the garden. Mummy and I have to talk.'

Freya ran out into the garden. Georgie's eyelids had begun to close. Liv tucked her into her cot. Alone for a few moments in the front room, she pressed the tips of her fingers against the pulsing bones of her skull.

When she went back to the kitchen, he said, 'I don't know where to begin.'

She made tea. Strong, no sugar; his preferences were unnervingly familiar. She heard him say, 'I don't know how you could forgive me, Liv, because I can't forgive myself. When I remember what I did, I hate myself.'

The crack, like gunfire, as his hand had struck her face. He had seized her by her hair and pulled her across the room, as though he were reeling in a fish.

'You hurt me.'

He bowed his head. 'If I could alter the past, I would do so, Liv. But I can't. All I can do is to beg your forgiveness, and to promise that it'll never happen again.'

Did he expect her to smile, to let him take her in his arms, to pack up children and belongings and the new life she had made for herself, and follow him back to Holm Edge? She ran the tip of her fingernail along the grooved edge of the work surface, marking a thin line across the pale wood. 'It won't happen again,' she said, 'because I won't let it happen again. That's why I left you, Stefan, so that I wouldn't have to be afraid that things like that might happen. I've changed, you see.'

She saw him glance round the shabby room, and then his gaze drifted to Freya, playing in the garden.

'I've changed too, Liv. That's what I wanted to tell you.'

She clutched her cold fingers around the mug, trying to warm them. Her lids felt heavy, as though she, like Georgie, might drift into sleep.

'Don't you want to know how I've changed, Liv?'

'If you want to tell me.'

'I've got a job.'

In her memory, Stefan's schemes collided, piled up one upon the other like logs rushing through a narrow gorge. The book, the *potager*, the guest-house . . .

As if he read her mind, he said, 'This time it's different. It's a real job. I start in three weeks. An export company in Manchester. They needed someone with languages. Full-time. I'll have to wear a suit and tie.' He grinned.

She wondered what he wanted. Approval? Congratulations? *Stefan, that's wonderful, I'll just get the children and then we can go home* . . .

'I'm pleased for you, Stefan. I hope it'll work out.'

'I've been thinking about everything, you see, Liv. I've had a lot of time to think, these past few months. We were never lucky, were we? You can't say that we were *lucky*.' He frowned. 'The fox . . . the rats . . . the storms. They made it all so hard, didn't they? And we weren't ready for the children, were we? Of course, as soon as you have them, you love them more than anything in the world, but I often think that it might have been different if we'd had time to get used to each other, time to understand each other. And if I'd got the permanent job at the university, that would have helped, wouldn't it? It would have made all the difference if we'd had a bit of luck, don't you think?'

'Stefan,' she said. She felt unbearably tired. 'Why have you come here?'

'To see you,' he said simply.

Momentarily, she closed her eyes. 'You must understand that I've made a new life for myself.'

There was a silence. Then he said, 'I wouldn't have expected otherwise, Liv.'

'I have a home ... a job ... friends ...'

'Katherine,' he said.

'Yes. Katherine's been very good to me. I couldn't have managed without her.'

He had gone to stand in the doorway. She studied his face, searching for evidence of jealousy or anger, but his features were shadowed by the branches of the pear tree.

'I'm not asking for anything, Liv. Well – just one thing. To be allowed to see the children. I've missed them, you see. Especially Freya.'

It seemed only fair to say, 'She's missed you too, Stefan.'

'I wasn't a bad father, was I?' She shook her head.

'You'll let me see them, then?' he said. 'Just these few weeks I'm in London?' She nodded.

When he had gone, she stood in the kitchen, the palms of her hands pressed together, looking out at the garden. The small square of lawn and shrub now seemed filled with shadows. Gusts of wind made the fingernails of the pear tree scrape and tap at the window-panes, as though someone begged to be let in.

She began to prepare supper. She had to remind herself what to do: the action of the knife, peeling the potatoes, the turn of the tap as she filled the basin with water. Her hands felt numb, and she found herself imagining pressing the tip of the knife against her palm, and watching the ball of blood gather on her pale skin. Just to feel the pain. Just to feel something. Just to jolt, to shock her jumbled thoughts to coherence. *Blood sisters.*

But she was alone now and, besides, she had long ago lost faith in the ordered world of her childhood. Stefan supplied a darker magic, a world in which nothing was quite as it seemed, in which she was unable to trust her own instincts. Walls sprang up before her, mazes twisted and turned. How easy, she thought, to believe that he had changed; how much less painful, and much less humiliating, to accept his penitence.

Yet she thought of how the hours of her life had gone by, while he had been standing across the road in the shadows, watching, waiting. And when, once more, the branch tapped the window, she started and turned, her heart beating wildly, staring into the darkness.

Rose was in the kitchen, eating Maltesers and reading *Honey* when Felix returned to London.

'Aren't you babysitting for Liv?' He opened the fridge, which was empty except for a half-pint of milk and a curling slice of ham.

'She didn't need me.' Rose sounded miserable. 'Her husband's looking after Freya and Georgie.'

Felix swung round. 'Her *husband*? Are you sure?'

'He's going to look after them tomorrow lunch-time as well, so I won't see them then either.'

He put the milk bottle down. He didn't feel hungry any more. He glanced at his sister. 'Did you see him? What was he like?'

She made a face. 'Like Vinegar Tom.' Rose had once had a cat called Vinegar Tom. 'D'you remember, Felix? You wouldn't think he was there, and then you'd turn round and he'd be under the sofa, watching you. And he was nice as anything when it suited him, but if you annoyed him, he'd lash out.' And she made a sudden movement, like a cat unsheathing its claws.

Katherine showed Felix into her bedroom. There were heaps of discarded dresses on the bed, and one of her eyelids glittered with pale green frosted eyeshadow, while the other was unpainted.

'Simon's out,' Katherine explained. She looked at Felix. 'You're *glowering*, Felix.' She sat down at her dressing-table and picked up her eyeshadow brush.

'Did you know that Liv's husband's here? In London?' Felix sounded angry. 'I just couldn't believe it when Rose told me ... And she's letting him look after the children—'

'They're his children, too.'

He stared at her. 'You think it's all right, then? He beats her up, locks her in a room, then thinks he can just turn up and play Happy Families?'

'Of course I don't think it's all right. And stop *pacing*, Felix. You're making me go cross-eyed.'

'Do you know how long he's planning to be in London?'

'A few weeks, Liv said.'

'And then?'

'He's got a job in Manchester, apparently.'

'So he's no intention of staying? He's not here to – well, he's not trying to persuade her to go back to him?'

'Stefan told Liv that he only wants to see the children.' Though, Katherine thought, Stefan is duplicitous, cunning and clever. That he had followed her home from work, that she had walked along darkened streets, unaware of him, disturbed her. How long had he hidden in the shadows, watching her?

She put down her mascara brush, and turned to him. 'Coffee? Or a beer?'

'No thanks. I think I'll see if I can catch Liv at work.'

Katherine studied her reflection in the mirror and scowled. 'How is it that something you thought looked great only a week ago can suddenly look just *awful*?' She was wearing a long dress of black filmy stuff, with embroidery around the collar and cuffs.

He paused at the door. 'You look wonderful. You always do.'

'Flatterer.' But she rose and kissed his cheek. 'I'll have to change.' She began to pull the dress over her head. 'Off you go. I'm going out in ten minutes, and I'm nowhere near ready.'

She exchanged the black dress for a silver panne velvet skirt and turquoise crocheted top. She was brushing her hair when she heard Simon return to the flat.

'What's up with Whatsisname? He nearly ran into me, tearing down the stairs.'

'Felix? Nothing's up.' Yet the conversation with Felix had unsettled her. Threading an earring through her lobe, she added absentmindedly, 'He was asking me about Stefan. He was awfully cross. I didn't think—' Glancing up, she saw the expression in her brother's eyes, and broke off.

'What?' said Simon. 'You didn't think what?'

'Nothing. He was in a mood, that's all.'

The phone rang. Simon picked it up. 'Kitty?' He passed her the receiver.

It was Jordan. 'I can't make it, love. Something's come up.'

Simon was watching her. She rearranged her features, and said smoothly, 'Work?'

'I'm at home,' said Jordan. 'I'm calling from a box – told Tricia I was nipping out for cigarettes. Have to dash, darling...'

She put the phone down. She wanted to tear off the skirt and top, to destroy the perfection of her makeup with a smear of tissue, but instead she turned to Simon and said, 'My date can't make it. What shall we do? A film ... or a restaurant?'

Felix arrived at the café where Liv worked just as her shift finished. The quickest route back to Beckett Street took them through the park. It was sharply cold, and a ragged mist floated between the clumps of shrubs and trees. Ornate Victorian streetlights gleamed beside winding paths.

They walked in silence for a while, and then he said, 'Rose told me your husband's turned up. And that you're seeing him – you're letting him look after the children.'

'Of course. They're Stefan's children too.' She turned to look at him. 'There'll always be that tie, won't there? I can't just pretend my marriage never happened.' Her skin was pinched with cold, her lips bluish, and in the darkness her eyes were hard and black, like obsidian. 'I can't even regret marrying him, can I?' Her voice was bitter. 'If I hadn't married Stefan, then I'd never have had Freya and Georgie.'

He made himself ask her, 'Will you go back to him?'

'Of course not,' she said, and he felt a rush of relief. She swung round, staring at him. 'How could you think I would do that? How could you?'

'As you pointed out, Stefan's your husband. He's the father of your children.'

'That doesn't mean I'd live with him again.'

'He isn't staying at your house, then?'

'Of course not.'

'Only I thought—'

'That he'd crook his finger, and I'd come running?'

He did not reply, but took her hand in his, tucking it through his arm as they walked through a tunnel of grimy rhododendrons. After a while, he said, 'When Rose told me about Stefan, I wondered whether—' He paused at the junction of four pathways, looking down at her. The mist beaded her hair and eyelashes with tiny translucent pearls. 'Sometimes,' he said, 'seeing someone can make you feel differently about them. You can remember what you saw in them in the first place.'

She was scuffing the ground with the toe of her boot. Then she looked up at him. 'I was afraid, when I saw Stefan.' Her voice was bleak. 'That was all, Felix. I was afraid.'

'You see,' he said, 'I'd miss you if you went away.'

'I'm not going away,' she said fiercely.

'Liv,' he said, very softly, and his hands rested lightly on the hollow of her waist. And when, eventually, inevitably, he kissed her, she did not pull away, or say any of the expected things about the inappropriateness of the time, the place, the circumstances. Instead, she threaded her fingers through his hair, drawing him to her, her mouth as urgent, her breath as ragged as his own.

Footsteps in the darkness: she moved away from him. A

middle-aged woman, walking her dog, passed them. 'Liv—' he said, but she put up a hand to silence him.

'Don't say anything. Please. Don't – say – anything.' She jammed her hands in her pockets and began to walk. He thought he saw in her eyes a defiant, almost martial light.

And after he had taken his leave of her, wheels clicked and whirred as pieces fell into place. He knew how foolish he had been, smugly congratulating himself on his easy, platonic friendship with Liv and Katherine. He knew why he had kissed her, he knew why he no longer thought about Saffron, and he knew why, throughout Katherine's dinner party, he had resented Simon Constant's flirting with her. And why, most of all, he had feared Stefan's homecoming. He was in love with Liv Galenski, had been in love with her for weeks, for months, perhaps. It occurred to him that this sort of love, this stealthy, unexpected sort of love, was something that would cling to him like ivy, and would not, perhaps, ever let him go.

The tenor of Liv's days seemed to have altered. When she looked back at the five months of her separation from Stefan, they seemed to be dissolving, collapsing, taking on an air of unreality, almost as though they had never happened. The look on Rose Corcoran's face when, once more, Liv had to tell her that she was not needed, saddened her. With Stefan, the girls did different things. They went for outings – a journey on the top of a double-decker bus, or a visit to Harrods to see the puppies. They flew kites in the park, or Stefan dressed Freya in her wellingtons and let her splash in puddles. A whole hour, jumping in and out of puddles, Stefan holding her hand, his jeans and her mackintosh soaked, her eyes blank with ecstasy and exhaustion.

Stefan's arrival had disrupted her life, destroying established routines. She saw little of Katherine, less of Felix. Felix called at the house only once while Stefan was in London. They were in the kitchen; Stefan was showing Freya how to make paper angels.

Scraps of paper littered the floor. Liv introduced the two men. They shook hands, and there was a brief, strained, flurry of conversation. The scissors dug into the paper: snip, snip, snip. It seemed to her that they circled each other like dogs, and she shivered as she remembered the touch of Felix's lips, as chill and fleeting as the mist.

Stefan was in the kitchen when Liv came home from work. He looked up. 'You're late.'

She glanced at the clock. 'Just ten minutes. We were busy.'

'We need to talk.' He ran his hands through his hair. 'I thought we should discuss the future, Liv.'

Her stomach twisted. 'The future?'

'I think we should try again.' When she began to speak, he put out his hand, silencing her. 'No, hear me out, please.' Mechanically, she unwound her scarf and undid the toggles of her duffel coat. 'It's not just us, is it? Whatever we feel about each other, there are the children to consider, aren't there?'

Her heart was pounding, but she forced herself to speak calmly. 'You know that Freya and Georgie's well-being is the most important thing in the world to me.'

'To me also.'

Her mouth was dry. 'Stefan, I left you so that I could give the girls a better life.'

'Better? This? Two rooms and a garden the size of a postage stamp?'

'There's the park.' She knew she sounded defensive.

'You'll never be able to let them out of your sight. Have you thought about that? Not with that busy road on your front doorstep.' Stefan focused on the warped window-frame and on the places where plaster had fallen from the ceiling. 'Holm Edge may not have been luxurious, but at least it was solid. This place doesn't look as though it'll last out another year.'

'They're going to renovate it.' Yet she saw traps yawning.

'Where will you and the girls live while they're doing the work?'

'We'll find somewhere.' But there was a victorious light in his eye. She whispered, 'I don't know.'

He smiled. 'Be honest with yourself, Liv. You may prefer the city, but Holm Edge was better for Freya and Georgie, wasn't it?'

'I'll work hard—'

'An absent father, and a mother who's always out at work. Is that what you want for our children?'

'I'll find us somewhere else. Felix said he'd help us.'

'Felix?' His fingers were drumming against the table-top.

'He works for a housing co-operative ... He said he'll be able to find us a place.'

She knew that she was talking too fast, and that her nervousness was evident. She thought of the park: that sudden and incongruous access of joy and desire.

Stefan's hand rested on her shoulder. To convey comfort, she wondered, or ownership? 'I don't mean to upset you, Liv,' he said. 'That's the last thing I want. All I wanted to say was that I still love you. And that I've always loved you, and I always will.'

She pulled away from him. '*Love!* Locking me in a room – hurting me – do you call that *love*, Stefan?'

'I told you that I've changed. You have to believe that I've changed.' The words were soft and hypnotic, like a mantra. 'I told you that nothing like that will ever happen again. How can I make you believe me? How can I make you give me a second chance?'

She thought, I gave you a second chance. A third chance, a fourth chance, a tenth and twentieth chance.

'After all, we both made mistakes, didn't we, Liv? If you hadn't been quite so taken up with the children ... if you'd had more time for me. If I hadn't sometimes felt that I existed on the periphery of your life ...'

A small smile curled the corners of his mouth. His voice coaxed and persuaded. She wondered whether he spoke the truth;

whether, absorbed by Freya and Georgie's needs, she had neglected her husband's.

'But we can learn from our mistakes, can't we? It was good once, wasn't it, Liv? Don't you remember the first time you came to Holm Edge, how perfect it was? Don't you remember the things we did together – the places we went to? We made them ours, didn't we? We didn't need anyone else. It can be like that again, I know it can. It can be good again.'

He had come to stand behind her. She trembled as his arms encircled her. Protecting her? Or trapping her? His voice, low and soft, whispered in her ear, 'I've a question for you. What's the most important thing you can give to a child?'

'Love, of course.' Her voice shook.

'And the love of two parents is better than one, wouldn't you agree?'

She became quite still. She remembered a small girl, walking along a beach. How Thea's and Fin's paths had diverged, and how that divergence had torn her apart. And her unfounded, pathetic belief that love would win out, and that her father would come home to her, a belief that had persisted through the years of her childhood.

'Whatever you think of me, Liv, however little you care for me, isn't this the time to put Freya and Georgie first? Isn't it rather ... rather *selfish* not to do so?' Each syllable seemed to tear her limb from limb. 'Aren't they worth it?' She could feel the warmth of his body against hers; his lips brushed against the tip of her ear. 'Aren't they worth just one more try?'

Often, when he was at work, when he was with friends, snippets of his conversation with his father would drift into Felix's mind. *Cash-flow problems, you see ... I've had to borrow to cover the shortfall ...* Often, he'd recall the expression in his father's eyes, and the almost unprecedented anger in his voice when he had stumbled over the chair. Though he tried to reassure himself, repeating to himself his father's denials, there remained, coiling and uncoiling in his stomach, a worm of unease.

He went home for a few days, but the weekend was not a success. When Bernard was not in company, he was breezy and dismissive of Felix's enquiries about the business. And, besides, away from London, Felix's uncertainties about Liv increased. At Wyatts, he had too much time to think. Too much time to see clearly just how possible it was that Liv should go back to Lancashire with her husband.

He had needed to see Stefan Galenski for himself. Stefan hadn't been as Felix had imagined him. He had pictured Liv's husband brutal and crude, the thick-fisted, low-browed wife-beater. The reality had jolted him. Good looks, intelligence, and a charm that Felix sensed he could snuff out like a candle-flame. As they spoke, Stefan's hand had curled round his little daughter's shoulder in a gesture that said, as clearly as if he had uttered the word, *mine*.

He seemed to lurch perpetually between one set of fears and another. His father; Liv. The days passed. Then, one evening, when he was about to leave for home, Mia telephoned the housing co-operative's office. 'Felix,' she said. 'I think you should come home.'

'What's happened?' His voice was sharp.

'Just come home. Please.'

He drove to Wyatts. Nervousness made him drive fast, overtaking whenever he reached a straight stretch of road. Head-lights loomed out of the darkness, and the branches of the tall trees reached out to him, as if to pull him from the road.

At Wyatts, Mia was in the drawing room. The curtains were open, and Felix could see through the picture windows the sweep of the lawn, silvered by the moon. The dogs were curled up on the sofa beside her, and there was a bottle of Scotch on the table. 'Bernard's gone to bed,' she said. 'I told him to take a sleeping pill. Get yourself a glass.'

'No, thanks,' he began to say. 'I don't want—'

'Oh, you will, Felix, believe me.' Her voice was quiet and steely. He fetched a glass.

He said, 'It's the business, isn't it?' and she glanced at him quickly.

'You knew?'

'I . . . put things together.'

She laughed bitterly. 'That's more than I managed. But, then, I don't suppose Bernard married me for my brains.'

'Mia—' The door opened and his father came into the room.

'I heard the car.' Bernard looked at Mia. 'My job, don't you think, to tell my son what I've done?'

There was a brief, taut silence, then Mia rose from the sofa and left the room, the dogs following her.

When the door had closed, Felix said, 'Tell me what, Dad?'

His father was standing with his back to him, looking out of the french windows. 'I should have told you months ago, but I couldn't face it. Hadn't the guts.' He turned to face Felix. 'Hadn't the guts,' he repeated, 'to tell my only son that I've lost everything.'

'Corcoran's . . .?'

'Is bankrupt.'

The words were like a hammer-blow. Felix's heart seemed to plummet down, rib after rib. He heard his father add, 'Things haven't been too good for years. You know that I had to borrow to keep going. The bank and . . .' The words trailed away. 'Made some bad decisions. Borrowed money off a chap I thought I could trust. I went to school with his father. Thought that meant something. But there you are – different world now, isn't it?'

There was a horrible coldness in the pit of Felix's stomach, and a premonition that just now his life teetered unsteadily on a fulcrum. He remembered that on the night his mother had died he had been upstairs. He had looked out of the landing window and had caught sight of the police car heading down the drive to the house. He remembered that he had not run down to the door, but had waited, wanting to extend the moment of not knowing. He had the same impulse now.

'We've lost the lot.' Bernard took an unsteady breath. 'Everything. The whole caboodle. You see, when I needed to invest money in the factory, I put up the house as collateral.'

I put up the house as collateral, thought Felix. His mind seemed to be working very slowly. 'Wyatts?' he whispered.

Bernard nodded. He looked frightened.

'We've lost the house?' Even to his own ears, his voice sounded odd.

'Yes.'

He wanted to say, *That's not possible, Dad*. He whispered, 'But it's *ours*.'

'Not any more.'

'But if you asked, surely they'd give you more time. If you explained, we could get the business back on its feet.'

'Our creditors don't want the business back on its feet.' Bernard's hand shook as he poured himself a Scotch. 'They don't give a damn about the business. They'll get the receivers in, close the place down. Then they'll sell off the land to developers. They'll make a fortune.' His mouth stretched in a travesty of a smile. 'It's called asset-stripping, apparently.'

He turned to Felix. 'Whatever this means to you and me, think how much worse it'll be for the men. Some of them are in their fifties and sixties – they won't get another job, will they? Some of the craftsmen, the printers and the dyers, have been working for me for forty years.' Bernard's skin was greyish, and his eyes were empty and dazed.

'I always hoped that you'd work for Corcoran's one day, Felix. It should have been yours. Always thought you were short-changed anyway, losing your mother like that. I've let you down, haven't I?' said Bernard quietly. 'Let everyone down.'

There was an article in *Glitz* entitled 'The Mistress'. The photograph beside it showed a woman wearing a black négligé and ostrich-feather slippers. Her hair swept across her face, hiding her eyes, giving her a duplicitous air. Duplicitous or blindfolded, Katherine was unsure. She struggled to give due precedence to the events of the day: the strikes, the terrorist atrocities, the constant chatter of imminent doom. She couldn't quite convince herself that her own need of Jordan wasn't somehow the more urgent. She needed to feel the tips of his fingers running the length of her spine. She needed him to listen to the small incidents of her day. She needed him to tell her that she was beautiful. She told herself that their separation was a temporary phase. But it was almost Christmas, and she had to bite back her anger, imagining Jordan trapped with his dumpy, cardiganed wife in Hertfordshire, escaping to make occasional calls from an unreliable public phone-box.

She received a note at work. Jordan asked her to meet him at his flat. *Just an hour or so, I'm afraid. Sixish. I miss you, darling.* In the ladies' cloakroom at work, she retouched her makeup carefully before leaving early. At the St James's Park flat, she made herself a gin and tonic, and waited for him. She felt unexpectedly nervous. She did not, as she sometimes liked to do, undress and bathe and go to bed. Instead, she prowled around the flat, her fingertips running along the marble surfaces of the bathroom, her high-heeled shoes sinking into the thick pile of the carpet.

She never knew what made her look out of the window. She could not imagine – all the possibilities were awful – what would have happened if she hadn't. But, moving aside a curtain, she looked down to the street, and saw Jordan climbing out of a taxi. A woman followed him. Her dark hair was cut in a smooth pageboy bob, and her full-length, fur-collared coat emphasized her height and elegance. The coat was unbuttoned. Jordan gave her his hand, helping her out of the car. The taxi sped off. The woman turned aside, and Katherine saw her in profile. The curtain fell away from her suddenly nerveless hands.

A moment's shocked, unbearable understanding, and then she threw the remainder of the gin down the sink and wiped the smear of lipstick from the rim of the glass. She grabbed her handbag and gloves, plumped up the cushions, and switched off the lights. Then she walked out into the corridor.

She heard his voice, echoing in the stairwell. 'God, Tricia, not the *Dawsons*. Anyone but the *Dawsons*.' She had to pass them as she walked downstairs. She did not look at him, but flicked her gaze to the woman who clung to his arm. Automatically, she registered Jordan's wife's long, delicately drawn face, and her expensive, beautifully cut clothes.

In the tube, she stared into the window, and saw Tricia Aymes' features imposed on the darkened glass. She put up her collar, folding her arms around her, hugging herself. She was shivering, as though she was ill. The chill of the cold December day seemed to reach inside her, and the intensity of her humiliation was a physical pain.

She went back to her flat. She had forgotten Simon, but when she unlocked the door, she saw him lying full-length on the sofa. He was watching a game show in which the audience shrieked as the contestants attempted to perform some Sisyphean task. Katherine stared at the screen with blank incomprehension. Then her gaze drifted to the coffee cups and plates and magazines and novels that littered the floor.

When the telephone rang, she jumped. Simon picked up the receiver; she had to dig her nails into the palms of her hand to stop herself screaming at him. He passed the receiver to her. 'Katherine,' said Jordan, and she slammed it down.

'Wrong number.' She stared at Simon. He had gone back to the sofa – *her* sofa. There was a packet of cigarettes and an ashtray balanced on one of the arms, and the remains of his supper on the other.

He sniggered, watching the flickering screen. 'Morons...' he muttered.

All her anger and misery gathered and focused. She said, 'Aren't you *ever* going to get a job?'

'God, not you as well, Kitty. I had a letter from the parents this morning—'

'And don't call me Kitty. I hate it. It makes me sound ... trivial.'

'My, my,' he said. 'Touchy.'

Something snapped inside her. 'Or perhaps you mean to bum

off me till the end of the fucking *decade*. Hasn't it occurred to you that I might like to have my flat to myself? That I might not want my layabout brother here whenever I bring my friends home?'

'Shut up, Kitty.'

But there was some relief in venting on Simon her anger and misery. 'You've been here for six weeks, and you haven't given me a penny. You've eaten my food, drunk my wine, hogged the bathroom for hour after hour. If you had an ounce of self-respect – or an ounce of honesty – you'd work in a grotty café, like Liv, rather than scrounge off me. Felix would have got you work ages ago, you know that, don't you, Simon? But you didn't want to get your hands dirty, did you?'

All the colour had drained out of his face. 'I said, shut *up*.'

'Just go away!' she hissed. 'Just go away and leave me alone!' Then she ran out of the door, slamming it behind her. The sound echoed as she fled down the stairs.

Before he left Wyatts, Felix walked around the house. He had been born there; so, seven years later, had Rose. He had always expected to come back: that Wyatts would one day belong to him had been as much a part of him as having green eyes, or being good at maths. He walked from room to room, bidding them, he supposed, a sort of farewell. When he looked out of the window, he saw that a mist had settled on the countryside, and that the box hedges and rose arbours were shrouded in grey, as though they were in mourning.

He drove back to London. There was Rose, after all. She wasn't at his flat, though, so he set off towards Beckett Street.

Liv was shutting the front door behind her as he reached her house. 'Rose has taken the children to the park,' she explained to him, as she headed to the shops. She was walking fast through the crowded street. Her eyes evaded his. Then she said suddenly, 'Stefan has asked me to go back to him.'

He stared at her, but her gaze was fixed on the road ahead. 'And you said . . .?'

'That I'd think about it.'

The cold weather bit into him, and he dug his hands into the pockets of his army greatcoat. For the second time in twenty-four hours, there was the odd sensation of his heart falling like a stone beneath his ribs. He said furiously, 'You're seriously considering going back to Stefan?'

'I don't know—' She turned aside, her gloved hands fluttering in the cold air. 'I have to think.'

'What is there to think about?' Anger rose in his throat like bile. 'He hit you, Liv. Have you forgotten that?'

'There are the children. You're forgetting the children.'

'Dear God . . .' He swung round to her. 'How can it be good for Freya and Georgie to live with a man like that?'

'Stefan says he's changed. He swears he's changed.'

He gripped her arm, staying her. 'And you believe him?'

'I don't know.' Shaking him off, she went into the small supermarket.

He followed her. 'People like that don't change,' he said.

Her dark gaze jerked towards him. 'You're an expert, are you, Felix?' she said sharply. 'On marriage – and on children?'

On commitment, she might have added, voicing the shame that had haunted him through the past twenty-four hours. Corcoran's, Wyatts, his father: over the past few years he had evaded them all, telling himself he was being true to his ideals while escaping involvement and responsibility.

'I have to think about what Stefan said.' She seized a basket from the pile. 'He's the girls' father. Freya adores him. I can't just pretend that doesn't count, can I?'

He wanted to take her by the shoulders, to shake her, to make her listen. The shop was busy with people returning home from work. Besuited men jostled them; women with small children in tow wove between them, separating them. Liv seemed to be taking items from the shelves at random: a tin of shoe polish, a

Rowntree's jelly, a packet of Lux soap flakes. He heard her say more quietly, 'When Stefan talks to me, I can't seem to see things clearly. Was it my fault as well? Was it my fault our marriage fell apart? I've always thought Stefan was to blame, but perhaps I was wrong. If I'd behaved differently, would it have been all right?'

He said wearily, 'Liv, you know that's nonsense.'

'Is it? How can I be sure? And how can I be sure that my needs are more important than my children's?'

He had hardly slept the previous night. He felt suddenly exhausted, defeated by the speed and ferocity of events. He wanted to sleep, or to get achingly, blindingly drunk. Just so as not to think any more. But he made one last attempt. 'And me?' he said. 'Where do I fit into all this?'

She stared at him blankly, the handles of the basket clutched between her fingers. He said softly, 'Oh, I see. Point taken.' Then he turned on his heel and walked out of the shop.

Stefan called at Katherine's flat. Simon answered the door. He was wearing a coat, and there was a scarf slung round his neck. There was a holdall beside him, with shirts and socks and novels spewing through the open zip.

'I was looking for my wife. For Liv,' Stefan explained. 'I thought she might be here.'

'Liv? Haven't seen her.' A small curl of the lip, white fingers running through silky dark hair. A lowering of long-lashed lids. 'I expect she's with Whatsisname,' said Simon suddenly. 'Thingy. Felix.' Focusing on Stefan, Simon added innocently, 'They're as thick as thieves, you know.'

And where do I fit into all this? Walking through the park to the café, Liv folded and unfolded Felix's words in her mind, recalling the expression on his face as he had said them. When she reached the place where the four paths joined, she closed her eyes, remembering the touch of his lips on hers. Her decision, that had until then seemed so hard to make, suddenly became clear.

She would not go back to Stefan because she no longer loved him. Stefan was part of an old life, which she had grown out of. *She* had changed, because she had learned that fear and love could not co-exist, and that nothing, not even the children, justified such a lack of love. However much Stefan himself had altered, she could not forget the reasons why she had left him. The bad memories lingered, ingrained and ineradicable, so that whenever she was with him she chose her words carefully, tiptoeing around old sensibilities and familiar fears. She had almost come to believe her fears acceptable, a normal part of living with a man. It had been Felix – at first a friend, but one day, perhaps, something more than that – who had shown that to be untrue.

She would talk to Stefan tomorrow, she thought. She felt just then a wave of pity for him: for Stefan, who loved his children; for Stefan, who hated to be alone. At the café, she greeted Sheila, put on her apron, and set to work. She was kneeling on the floor behind the counter, tidying out one of the cupboards, when she heard the chime of the doorbell announce another customer. She looked up.

'Stefan.' He came to the counter. Glancing over her shoulder, Liv saw that Sheila was making up the weekly accounts in the small back room. 'I'm working,' she said quickly. 'It's not a good time for me—'

'You're not exactly busy, are you?'

The only customers were a cloth-capped old man, who was taking an age over a cup of tea, and two leather-jacketed teenage boys, wolfing down crisps and Coke.

'Surely you can make time to talk about our daughters' future? Surely you can't believe this,' and Stefan glanced contemptuously around the café, 'is more important than Freya and Georgie's well-being?' His eyes focused on her, narrowed, calculating. 'Or are you just prevaricating, Liv? Paying me back. Making me wait – showing me who's boss.'

She began to say, 'Oh, don't be ridiculous, Stefan—' but bit the words back. She mustn't let this conversation deteriorate into insults, into a struggle for power. She must be restrained, practical and adult.

'All right. If that's what you want, we'll talk now.' She glanced at him. 'Would you like anything? A drink – anything?'

'Nothing.'

She came out from behind the counter. 'Let's sit down, shall we? More civilized.'

They sat at a corner table. Stefan smiled. 'You asked me whether I wanted something, Liv. There's only one thing that I want, and that's to hear you tell me that you're coming home with me.' He was unwrapping sugar cubes, and placing them in a neat tower in the centre of the table.

Liv took a deep breath. 'Stefan, I'm sorry, but I can't tell you that.'

He didn't seem to hear her. He placed another sugar cube on top of the tower. 'We could pack up tonight, catch the train tomorrow. I've checked the timetable. There's a Carlisle train at half past ten.'

'Stefan, I'm not coming back to you.' Her fists were clenched, and her mouth was dry. She was on home ground, she reminded herself; she had no reason to be frightened. 'I've thought and thought about it, but I can't come back to you.'

A succession of emotions darted across his face: shock, bewilderment, pain. She wondered whether every step he had taken, every word he had uttered during his stay in London had been meant to secure her return, that he had intended from the beginning that she should come back to him.

'Why not?' he whispered. 'You *have* to.'

'Stefan.' She touched his clenched fingers, and felt the sinews, hard and taut. 'Please try to understand. We were very young when we married, weren't we? Well, I was very young. Only nineteen. That's not much more than a girl, is it? And I was silly and romantic, and I didn't know what love and marriage entailed. And perhaps you were right the other day when you said that we hadn't had much luck. Perhaps if things had been easier, perhaps if the children hadn't come so quickly, then maybe it would have been different. But I tried and tried to be the sort of wife you wanted, Stefan, and I just couldn't do it. And in the end, I think ... I *know* ... that I haven't the heart to try any more. I'm so sorry, but I just haven't.'

As she spoke, his expression altered, as though a curtain had been lifted, or a veil ripped aside. She recalled, dispersed through their conversation the previous day, like spores of mould among grains of wheat, the small reminders of why she had learned to fear him. His greeting to her when she had come home from work. *You're late.* The drumbeat of his fingertips on the table-top.

'You can see the children, of course,' she said quickly. 'I'll arrange it properly, with a solicitor, so that when we're divorced you can have right of access—'

'Divorce? Never.'

'It'll be better that way. A clean break. Better for both of us.'

'Never.' That familiar warning edge to his voice. 'You're my wife, Liv. Till death do us part, remember? You promised. You're mine. You'll always be mine.'

In the silence, her temples throbbed, and she felt unbearably tired. 'I looked for you earlier,' he said suddenly. 'Where were you?'

For a moment she could not recall, but then she remembered the supermarket, and a basket full of shopping she had not needed. And Felix: *Where do I fit into all this?*

'I went for a walk.'

'On your own?'

She nodded. He said, 'Liar,' and she flinched. In the back room, Sheila looked up from her accounts.

'You were with Felix Corcoran, weren't you?'

She struggled to quell the flutter of panic. 'I told you, Stefan. Felix and I—'

'Go on. Say it. "Felix and I are just friends."' His falsetto mocked her.

'It's true.'

'But I don't believe you, Liv. After all, you've lied to me before, haven't you? Promising me you'd never leave me, when all the time you were saving up money to go away.'

'I'm telling you the truth. Felix and I—'

'Is he your lover?'

Such venom in that single word. The black-jacketed boys glanced up, sniggering. Sheila called out from the back room, 'Is everything all right, Liv?'

'My husband's just going.' Her voice trembled.

Stefan rose from the table. The tower of sugar cubes swayed and tumbled to the floor. The small drum-roll echoed the pitter-patter of Liv's heart. She clenched her fists. 'The reason I won't come back to you is because I no longer love you, Stefan. You have to try to accept that.'

A sudden, sharp sweep of Stefan's arm, and a stack of cups and saucers plummeted from the counter with a crash. Liv jumped back as fragments of crockery scattered across the floor. Out of the corner of her eye, Liv saw Sheila pick up the telephone.

'I'm not going anywhere without you, Liv.'

'Stefan, please leave. Please.' The whir of the telephone dial; Sheila's voice, low and urgent.

'You've forgotten what I told you, haven't you?' His eyes glittered. 'I told you that I'd never let you go. Did you think I didn't mean that? Do you think I've changed my mind?'

A basket of cutlery next, hurled to the ground. A glint of metal as knives, forks and spoons skated across the linoleum. One of the boys swore.

Sheila came out of the back room. 'That's enough, Mr Galenski.'

'Shut up.' Stefan turned back to Liv. 'You haven't listened to a word I said, have you?' His face was contorted with fury. 'I'll do anything to make you come back to me. Anything at all.'

'Mr Galenski—'

'I said, shut up.'

'I've called the police. They're on their way.'

'Stefan, you don't understand—'

'No, *you* don't understand, Liv.' The words were cold and clear. 'What you don't understand is that I'll do whatever it takes to get you back. Because you're mine. Because you belong to me.'

And in a swift, sudden movement, he pinioned Sheila with his right arm, and with his free hand seized a handful of her hair, jerking her head back. 'Whatever it takes,' he said. He was smiling.

'Stefan, *please*—'

'If you promise me you'll come home with me, then I won't hurt her.'

Tears trailed down her cheeks. She was mesmerized by the shock in Sheila's eyes.

'Promise me,' Stefan said again, as the sound of the blood pumping through her head almost masked the distant wail of the police siren.

Chapter Twelve

After her quarrel with Simon, Katherine walked aimlessly for a while. She called at Liv's flat, but Rose, who was babysitting, explained to her that Liv was at work. Katherine couldn't face going home yet, so she headed for Felix's house.

He opened the door to her.

'Are you busy?'

'Very.' He held up a glass of Scotch. 'Want one?' She followed him indoors.

She looked around the room. She had always liked Felix's house: the bare floors and high echoing ceilings and crumbling architraves, the pomposity and irony of those gold fleurs-de-lis.

She heard him say, 'Are you cold?'

'A little.' She was clutching her coat round her. She knew that the chill came from inside her.

'I could light a fire.' There was a blurred expression in his eyes; she realized that he was very drunk.

'Do you mind if I help myself?' She indicated the bottle.

'Feel free.' He crumpled paper and laid kindling.

She sat down on one of the floor cushions, pressing the tips of her fingers against her forehead, trying not to weep. The fire hissed and spat.

She heard him say, 'Katherine?' and she gasped, 'I've been so *stupid*!'

'Well, that makes two of us. Though I doubt if your stupidity's on quite the same level as mine.'

She scrubbed her eyes with the back of her hand. 'What do you mean?'

He ticked them off on his fingers. 'The family business has

gone bust. We've lost the home we've lived in for the last seventy-five years. The woman I thought I loved doesn't love me at all.' He swallowed the remainder of his whisky.

She looked up at him. 'Liv?' He nodded.

She thought, *Liv*, who has a husband, however imperfect; who has two children. There had been a time when Felix had been *her* best friend. When she had not had to share him. Her drink seemed bitter, as though one could taste jealousy.

He gave an unamused smile. 'See. Bet you can't compete with that.'

She thought of Jordan. 'I've been having an affair with a married man,' she said abruptly. 'For more than a year now. But it's finished. It's over.' Baldly, she sketched in for Felix how she had waited at the flat, and how she had looked out of the window and, for the first time, had seen Tricia Aymes.

'I thought she'd be plain,' she said. She couldn't keep her bewilderment from her voice. 'I just . . . assumed. Sensible tweeds and a big bottom. But she wasn't like that at all. And if it had been just that, perhaps I could have borne it, but—' She remembered how Tricia Aymes had turned, and how she had seen the curve of her belly silhouetted against the misty light.

'She was pregnant,' she whispered. She sipped her whisky, trying to deaden the pain. She found herself remembering how it had felt to hold Liv's children in her arms. She knew that she would never bear Jordan's baby, and that she would never hold his child. That was what being a mistress was. *Glitz* was wrong, it wasn't black négligés and satin sheets. It was belonging to only a part of someone's life. It was being second best.

'I thought I didn't mind sharing him with someone else,' she said slowly, 'but I do, Felix, I do.'

She had never, she thought bitterly, known what it was not to share. She had never known undivided love. From the moment of her birth, her parents' attention had been focused on Simon, on the bright, beautiful boy. Whatever she had achieved, she had done so by herself. She had become accustomed to lack of recognition, and to the absence of praise. She had believed she did not mind, but now she became aware of a terrible, burning anger.

Why should she not be first with someone? Why should she, too, not expect – demand – love?

Felix had gone to stand by the window. She went to him. His eyes were slightly unfocused. He said, 'It's all the memories, isn't it?', and she, understanding, said, 'All the times I've waited for Jordan ... all the times he's phoned at the last minute and said he couldn't make it because of work. I expect he was with *her*!'

He drew her to him as she wept. But a small part of her remained separate, coldly aware that if she clung to him then he would comfort her, drawing from whatever she offered some comfort for himself. She heard him say, 'I'd always taken it for granted, I suppose. I'd never thought what it would be like not to have Wyatts. But I'm going to find out, aren't I?'

'Hush,' she said softly. 'Hush.' Her fingers caressed the back of his neck. She knew that she needed the obliteration of the present that sex could supply. And she knew how badly she needed someone to want her.

She looked up at him. 'Dear Felix,' she murmured, 'we've been friends for ages, haven't we?'

'Years and years.'

She let the back of her hand slide slowly down the contours of his face. Her body pressed against his. She could feel bones and sinews and the fast beating of his heart.

'So much easier being friends with someone ... Love's such a waste of time, isn't it?' And when she raised her face to him, he kissed her, as she had known that he would.

At the police station, the sergeant said, 'We're calling in a psychiatrist ... we thought it best. Has he ever shown suicidal tendencies, Mrs Galenski?' Liv shook her head, and signed the paper he placed in front of her. Later, out in the street, she clutched her arms around her, trying to keep warm. The cold, cloudless night gave the London streets a perfect clarity: she saw the ice crystals that glittered on the pavements, and the Christmas trees in the windows, pyramids of sparkling coloured lights. A gritting lorry moved slowly down the road, and a black cat walked across an empty square.

At first the roads were unfamiliar, intensifying her sense of isolation and loneliness, but then she saw that she had reached the corner of the street where Felix lived. She began to walk faster, to try to run, but, clumsy with exhaustion and shock, found herself slipping on the glazed surface of the pavement.

She saw them, Katherine and Felix, silhouetted against the wide uncurtained window. Sometimes, these past few weeks, she had believed he loved her. Now, as she clutched the collar of her coat to her throat, she watched them embrace, and knew the extent of her mistake. She took a step back into the darkness, understanding that she was an interloper, seeing clearly that she had misinterpreted everything, had misunderstood everything. Then she walked away through the night, back to her children.

He must have fallen asleep, but the sound of the front door closing woke him. Katherine, too, slept beside him: he noted with a sense of slight astonishment her naked, freckled skin. Then he pulled on his shirt and jeans and went to find Rose.

She was sitting at the kitchen table. Her hands were over her face, and she was weeping. He touched her narrow shoulders. 'Has someone told you? Did you phone home?'

The lattice of fingers slid down, and she looked at him, red-eyed, blank.

'Did you talk to Dad?' His mind was jumbled by alcohol and sex; he couldn't think straight. He put the kettle on, and searched for the Nescafé.

'Dad . . .?' she repeated.

He took a deep breath. 'Has Dad or Mia told you about the house, Rose?'

'What house?'

'Our house. Wyatts, of course.'

She wiped her nose on her sleeve. 'I don't know what you're talking about, Felix.'

So he told her. About the business going bankrupt, and about losing the house. When he had finished, she said only, 'Poor Daddy.'

His confusion doubled. 'Don't you *mind*? I thought—'

'Not about *houses*. You know I don't mind about things like *houses*.'

He sat down opposite her, and drank some black coffee to clear his head. 'If you weren't crying about the house, then what were you crying about?'

'About Freya and Georgie.' Her face crumpled.

Suddenly understanding, he said, 'Because they're going away?' She nodded.

He struggled to summon comfort from a comfortless situation. 'Perhaps you'll be able to visit them in Lancashire.'

'*Lancashire?* They're not going to *Lancashire*.'

He blinked. 'But Stefan—'

'Liv's not going back to *Stefan*. Stefan's at the police station.'

There was a packet of cigarettes on the table; Katherine's, he assumed: he hadn't smoked for months. But he lit one now, and said carefully, 'Tell me, Rose.'

'Liv told Stefan she wasn't going back to him.'

Something inside him seemed to crumble. 'I thought—'

'Liv told him that she wasn't going back to him because she didn't love him any more.'

He whispered, '*Oh*,' and sat still for a while, as the tip of the cigarette burnt down to his fingers. Liv wasn't going back to Stefan. Liv didn't love Stefan. For a moment, hope flared, and then, just as quickly, it died.

Rose was still talking. 'So he lost his temper and he smashed up the café, and they called the police.'

'Dear God.' He stared at her. 'Did he hurt her?'

'Not Liv. He hurt Sheila. Sheila had to go to hospital.'

He pressed his fingertips against his forehead. 'But you said that she's going away—'

'With Freya and Georgie. Yes.' Rose looked despairing. 'I told her I'd go with her, to help her look after them, but she said that wouldn't be a good idea. And anyway, *Daddy* . . .'

'Where to? Where's she going?'

'I don't know. She didn't say.'

There was a sound from behind him. He looked round. *Katherine*. Katherine, to whom he had made love that evening. He had forgotten Katherine.

He caught up with her as she left the house. Beneath the street-lamp, her face was bone white, and her eyes were dark and expressionless. At first, she did not speak, but then he grabbed her elbow, turning her towards him. 'Katherine—'

'It's all right, Felix. You don't have to explain anything. And you don't have to declare undying love, or ask me to marry you, anything silly like that. Tonight was just a horrible mistake, wasn't it?' Her high heels clicked on the icy pavement. 'Only, if you wouldn't run off to Liv *tonight*. Not just an *hour* after we—' He saw the tears that glittered in her eyes. 'I do have my pride, you see,' she whispered. 'I do have my pride.'

She walked away from him. He glanced at his watch. It was past eleven o'clock. Katherine's perfume lingered on his skin. He went back to the house.

Liv dreamed of the pink cottage by the sea. Surf lay like lace on the moraine of coloured glass that littered the shore, and in her dream she felt safe and secure.

Waking early, she knew where to go. She moved silently around the rooms, emptying drawers, taking books and toys from shelves, and packing them into bags. When the girls woke, she fed them and dressed them in their warmest clothes. Freya asked her where they were going.

'We're going on holiday, my love. We're going to the seaside.' She looked around the rooms that had been their home for six months, and said a mental farewell. She had never really fitted into the city, she thought.

As she closed the front door, she saw Felix. He crossed the road to them. She held out the keys to him. 'I was going to put these through your letter-box.'

'Rose told me what happened.'

'It made things clear,' she said. 'Now I know he'll never change.'

'So you're going away?'

'Well, I can't stay here, can I?'

'Without saying goodbye?'

She did not reply, but swung one bag over her shoulder, and strung the other across the handles of the pushchair.

He said, 'And Katherine?' and in her mind's eye she saw them, framed in the window, Felix and Katherine, embracing. She turned away from him, heading down the street.

He cried out angrily, 'I thought we were *friends*.'

'We were.' The exhausts of the passing cars made clouds in the icy air. 'But I have to move on, Felix. I have to learn to manage on my own, don't I? This was only . . .' she searched for the right word ' . . . an interlude.'

They had almost reached the tube station. Commuters dashed into the ticket office. She heard him ask, 'But where will you go?' and she smiled at last, and said, 'I'm going home.'

On the train, Freya stared wide-eyed out of the window, and Liv hugged Georgie to her as the city gave way to the red-brick uniformity of suburbia. Images interrupted the rows of neat semi-detached houses: the fury in Stefan's eyes when the policemen came into the café; the crack of bone as he flung Sheila against the wall. The stillness and passion on Felix's face as he kissed Katherine; the ecstasy in Katherine's thrown-back head and closed eyes. Liv shut her own eyes, trying to erase the images, but they persisted, as if burnt like light on to her lenses.

At midday, she bought cheese rolls and Penguins from the buffet for herself and Freya, and fed Georgie a jar of Heinz babyfood. Now the train was heading through open countryside, where ploughed furrows gleamed silver where the frost lingered. On the summits of gentle, undulating hills, crows circled around clumps of leafless trees. It seemed to Liv that there was a brightness about the sky, an opalescence she remembered from her childhood, which announced that they would soon see the sea. She remembered how, a long time ago, she and Rachel had spun round, their arms outstretched, so that they might see the sea. *Our dark-eyed girls*, Diana had said. Now, staring at the horizon, waiting for that small miracle, she hugged her own little girls to her. It occurred to her that, in spite of the terrible events of the last twenty-four hours, there was a certainty about her journey. It was as though, for the first time in years, she was heading in the right direction. Then the sun showed through the clouds, and the horizon seemed to glimmer, like a string of pearls. 'Look, Freya,' she whispered. 'The sea.'

They booked into a guest-house that night. Rooms were cheap in the off-season. Soon she would find somewhere to rent, somewhere quiet, somewhere where he would never find them.

The next day, they took the bus to the coastal village where she had once lived with Fin and Thea. She walked around for a while, trying to get her bearings, searching for the pink house by the sea. At the post office, she bought sweets for Freya, and a stamp so that she could write to Thea. The postmistress was grey-haired and comfortable-looking. 'I used to live here,' Liv explained, 'when I was a child. More than twelve years ago. There was a pink cottage on the sea front.'

'Foursquare, like a child's drawing?'

She remembered crayoning it herself: four windows, a door and a chimney, and bright flowers that had almost reached the roof.

'Sounds to me as though you mean the old coastguard's cottage. It had pink pebbledash, and it was on the sea front. I'm afraid it's gone, love.'

'Gone?'

'Washed away. A storm, a couple of years ago . . . It happens, this part of the coast. Whole villages wear away, fall into the sea. They won't let them build so close to the coast now.'

She felt dazed, unable to absorb this further blow. She heard the postmistress say, 'Are you all right, dear?' and she struggled to pull herself together.

'I'm fine. Fine.'

Later, they went to the beach. She had come full circle, Liv thought. Here, a long time ago, walking along the shingle, she had watched her parents' paths diverge. Now, she was on her own. She had left her mother, her husband, her friends. All those once-protective circles had gone. She thought of the house below the waves, and imagined the fish swimming through its unglazed windows, and the shells and weed encrusting its roof and walls.

She carried one daughter, and observed the other's halting progress along the beach. Stooping to pick up a pebble here, a shell there; suddenly stopping to watch, entranced, the endless rise and fall of the waves. Their dependency terrified her, yet they also gave meaning to her life, gave it shape and purpose. She alone was responsible for their future happiness and well-being. My dark-eyed girls, she thought, as she looked out to sea.

In the New Year, Jordan came to see her. 'Tricia arrived in London unexpectedly,' he began. 'She never comes to London unless she has to, hates the place. I didn't know . . .' Katherine twisted her hands together as she gazed out of the window and watched snowflakes fall from a leaden sky.

He told her about his marriage. Tricia came from a wealthy, well-connected family. Marrying her had enabled him to pursue his chosen career, had allowed him the possibility of success. A marriage of convenience, he seemed to be saying.

Katherine found her voice at last. 'She was *pregnant*, Jordan,' she said. 'She was *pregnant*!'

He bowed his head. When he looked up again, she saw that

some of the layers – of self-deception, and of pride – had peeled away. They had been trying for a baby for ten years, he explained. Tricia loved children, longed for children. He himself had long ago given up hope. Then the miracle had happened. He said, 'I couldn't find the words to tell you, Katherine. I'm so sorry.' He had come to stand behind her. His arms encircled her waist. 'Just as I couldn't find the words to tell you that I love you.'

She closed her eyes. His mouth pressed against the hollow of her neck, and his hands, as he stroked her, reignited the old familiar fire. Behind her closed lids she saw only a memory of the falling snow. That memory – themselves, enclosed in the room, and the cold white world outside – persisted throughout the ensuing months.

She went back to him because she was unable to do otherwise. There was a level of loneliness that was simply unendurable. Yet the balance between them had changed: she had become his equal. She no longer believed him perfect. She knew his flaws: the sense of inviolability that power and success can bestow, and the greedy desire to have the best of everything, no matter the cost. Faults, she knew, some of which she herself shared. It was just that she had insight, and he didn't.

Time passed. She made up her quarrel with Simon. He was a part of her – a part she did not always care for, but could not deny. At the end of February 1974, the Conservative government fell. Jordan held on to his seat, just. Though she continued to love him, and believed that she would always love him, she was aware of that raw place inside her, the place that his deception had touched. She made sure that she had a life apart from him, visiting her family regularly, one weekend each month, spending evenings with friends. She left the magazine, and took a new job in a women's publishing house. She needed a change, a challenge. She joined a consciousness-raising group, and went on Reclaim the Night marches and campaigned for a shelter for battered wives in Islington. She moved to a bigger flat, bought a new car and drove to Scotland that summer. She'd intended only to visit Edinburgh, to sample the civilized delights of the festival but, driving to Loch Lomond one day, found herself unexpectedly charmed. So she headed north, spending the days by herself, venturing up midge-ridden mountains and exchanging her platform shoes for a pair of hiking-boots, her French Connection jacket for a kagoule.

Towards the end of the year, she was travelling by tube to Piccadilly Circus when the train halted at Russell Square, and the doors of the carriage remained closed. One of the male passengers tried unsuccessfully to push them open, and people glanced out of the windows, and tapped their feet impatiently on the floor. Five minutes passed before there was an announcement from the station Tannoy. 'Ladies and gentlemen, we apologize for the unavoidable delay, which is due to an incident at Russell Square tube station'. An *incident*, thought Katherine. Out of the corner of her eye, she caught sight of a fireman coming down the steps to the platform. Trapped in the carriage, she heard a woman behind her mutter, 'A bomb. They're searching for a bomb,' and she pressed her hands together, staring at the floor, as the fear that she had first experienced after Rachel's death, the fear of chaos and nothingness, rose once more to the surface. All the headlines she had ever read of IRA atrocities came to the forefront of her mind: Guildford, Birmingham, the Tower of London. She could almost feel the impact of the explosion, see the shattered glass and broken bodies, hear the screams.

Ten minutes, twelve minutes. A young girl in the corner of the compartment began to cry, a thin, high wail that set Katherine's teeth on edge. She felt as though she was suspended in a sort of limbo, between the core of the earth and its surface, between life and death. Fifteen minutes. No one spoke. Her palm itched to slap the crying girl. Then the train started up at last, shuffling slowly out of the station. At Holborn, Katherine hurled herself out of the carriage, running up stairs and escalators until the mouth of the station disgorged her on to the pavement.

She did not stop running until she cannoned headlong into someone. Her face was smothered by a cashmere scarf, a woollen coat. She gasped, and tried to cry out. Then she looked up.

'*Hector*,' she said.

He had a place not far away, in Bloomsbury. He took her briefcase from her and steered her away from the crowds, through a maze of streets and squares, into a block of flats, and up several flights of stairs.

A Jack Russell terrier began to bark as Hector unlocked his front door. 'Pack it in, Charlie,' he said. He made coffee, sloshing a shot of brandy into each mug. Sitting on a chesterfield so old the dark brown leather had cracked and split, Katherine cradled the mug in her hands and let the tension drain out of her. She looked around. The room in which she sat was untidy and dimly lit; there were a great many books and dark, heavy pieces of furniture. The sideboard and bookshelves were covered in framed photographs. There were a few snapshots of a little girl – Alice, Katherine assumed – but almost all the photographs were of Rachel. Rachel at Bellingford, Rachel in a sports car, Rachel windswept and pink-cheeked on a hillside, Rachel radiant and serene in her wedding-dress.

It was five years since Rachel had died. Katherine thought of Rachel and Hector's wedding and, not quite a year later, the funeral. So long ago. She said, 'I didn't know you were living in London, Hector.'

'Almost four years now.' He sat down opposite her.

'I did try to write to you,' she explained, 'but you'd gone away.'

'I went back to Bellingford after the funeral, but I didn't stay long.'

'Why not?'

He smiled. 'I remember Rachel once asked me whether the house was haunted. I told her it wasn't. But after she had died, there were ghosts everywhere.'

'Ghosts?'

'Everything reminded me of her. All the things that had belonged to her, all the places we had been. I just had to look at her sunglasses, for instance, or her watch. So strange, how inanimate objects can have such power . . .'

His voice trailed away. She saw him glance at the banks of photographs. The intensity of his continuing grief appalled her.

'I went away,' he added. 'Went abroad for a year. To somewhere new, to get away from the memories. But that's worse, isn't it?' His smile was self-mocking. 'Not even to have the memories. To be left with nothing.'

'So you came back. And Bellingford . . .?'

'I've closed it up. I can't sell it because it's held in trust.'

'Are you still working for the bank?'

'Chucked it in. I own a secondhand bookshop in Bayswater. Chap I was at school with suggested I came in as a partner. Then he decided he'd had enough, so I bought him out.'

'It sounds fun – I've always loved secondhand bookshops.'

'It's a living.'

Something about his tone silenced her. After a while she said tentatively, 'And Alice? How is Alice?'

'She's very well.'

'She's still living with the Wybornes?'

He nodded. She thought at first that he wasn't going to say any more, that she must once again search desperately for a change of subject, but then he said, 'Diana's been ill. Cancer. Did you know?'

Katherine was shocked into silence. She remembered the last time she had seen Diana Wyborne: how she had aged, and how her arms had trembled, lifting her infant granddaughter out of the cot. 'How awful,' she said at last. 'Is she . . .? Will she recover?'

'I don't know. You don't think the Wybornes confide in *me*, do you?'

His bitterness shocked her. She realized then that the rifts of the past remained unhealed. Her thoughts drifted to Liv, and then to Felix. Other partings, other betrayals.

As if he had read her mind, he said, 'Your friend – the dark-haired girl – Rachel was very fond of her . . .'

'I haven't seen Liv for a couple of years. She's living on the east coast, I believe. We've rather lost touch.'

Three little sentences that summed up the ending of a friendship that had lasted almost fifteen years. Katherine rose and went to the window. 'We just drifted apart, I suppose,' she said. She threaded her fingers together, looking out. It was almost dark and, below her, the cars moved slowly down the street, travelling in procession for a while, then turning away from each other, to left, to right, the gleam of their headlights becoming fainter and fainter until they were out of sight.

PART THREE

Briar Rose

1975–1978

Chapter Thirteen

Diana Wyborne died in April 1975. A fortnight before her death, Henry Wyborne took Hector, who was at Fernhill Grange to visit his daughter, aside.

Hector was invited into the drawing room, and offered a whisky. The two men sat in silence, drinking. There was a stillness about the evening, as though the house itself was aware of the dying woman upstairs.

Henry said, 'After Diana's gone, you must take the child.'

Hector, who was longing to escape the house as soon as decently possible, stared at his father-in-law. 'Alice?' he said, dazed. '*Me?*'

'You are her father.'

'Yes, but . . .' Unusually, Hector wished he hadn't had a drink. 'I assumed – I thought . . .' He took off his glasses, and polished the lenses with a handkerchief. 'My flat . . . It isn't big enough. There's only the one bedroom.' He knew he sounded feeble, pathetic.

Henry said calmly, 'Then you'll have to look for somewhere bigger, won't you?' He refilled his own glass, and topped up Hector's. He added, 'It'd be miserable for the poor little thing here, with Diana gone. The nanny's well enough in her way, but nannies come and go, you know that. And I'm away a lot of the time. And besides,' he looked up at Hector, 'Alice should never have come here. She should have gone to you after Rachel died. I always thought it was wrong, what happened.'

Hector felt winded. He began, 'But Diana said . . .'

'A part of Diana died with Rachel.' Henry had gone to stand by the window. 'It was the same with each of us, wasn't it? And she was so determined the child should live with us. She thought it'd fill the gap, I suppose, and I knew I hadn't the right to deny her. But it was wrong, nevertheless.'

'But Alice is fond of you,' said Hector. 'And she hardly knows me.'

'Then you must remedy that, mustn't you?' Henry Wyborne's tone was hard and unsympathetic. Then his expression softened slightly. 'I shall miss her, of course. But I'm almost fifty-five, remember. When Alice is eighteen, I'll be nearly seventy. Almost an old man. She deserves better than that.' He looked down, and whispered, 'Those damnable doctors won't tell me how long my poor Diana's got. Days or weeks, they say, though how she can go on living for weeks like *that* . . .'

Hector had to look away. It seemed indecent to witness the depth of pain in Henry Wyborne's eyes.

When Henry spoke again, his tone was defiant. 'I'm not saying I regret what we did. Alice was a consolation to Diana and, by God, she deserved whatever consolation she could find. But it wouldn't be right for me to keep the child now.' He swallowed the contents of his glass. 'I'd prefer you to let Alice stay here until – until it's over. Just in case Diana asks to see her.'

Hector managed to mutter something suitable. Henry unstoppered the whisky decanter. 'You can always send her to boarding-school, you know,' he said, 'if you're not sure whether you can manage. Some of these places will take 'em young . . . Infants with fathers in the services, that sort of thing. And she's always been a biddable little creature, hasn't she?'

Hector took his leave shortly afterwards. Walking to his car, he noticed in the air the sharp tang he always associated with the beginning of spring. On such a night, seven years ago, he had stopped to offer a lift to Liv. Shortly afterwards, Liv had introduced him to Rachel. Hector closed his eyes, trying to recall his first sight of Rachel. She had worn a silvery sheath of a dress, and her chestnut hair had been caught back in some sort of band. But the image was shifting and evanescent, and he acknowledged bitterly that the original memory was fading, and that what substituted for memory was little more than a check-list, a wearily repeated narrative.

He lit a cigarette. The extraordinary conversation with Henry Wyborne echoed. *After Diana's gone, you must take the child.* He found himself recalling that other conversation, after Rachel's funeral. Diana's choice of phrase had been cold and cruel and efficient. 'You must be realistic, Hector. You are single man now, who has to earn a living. What do you know about looking after a child? What kind of life can you offer her? An infant – a girl, especially – needs a woman to care for her.' Every word had been a knife-point, digging into a spirit already wounded beyond repair. He had not argued, had not fought for the child. He had meekly accepted Diana's estimation of him. He had given away his daughter because he himself had felt for Alice an inkling of the same emotion that Diana had felt for him. It was Alice who had taken Rachel from him. And in a world filled with unbearable reminders of the woman he had loved and lost, the child had been one reminder too many.

He had gone away to escape the memories. Yet, as he had explained to Katherine, he had soon discovered that without the memories he was left with nothing at all. Returning to Britain, he had renewed his brief acquaintance with his child. Since then, he had visited Alice dutifully once a month. Every visit had been made an ordeal by Diana's almost palpable dislike of him, and by his own awkwardness with his daughter. The afternoons spent at Fernhill Grange beneath his mother-in-law's judgemental eye had shown him that Diana had been correct: he knew nothing about caring for a child. Now five years old, Alice remained a distant stranger. He sensed that to her, also, his visits were a duty rather than a pleasure.

Visiting Alice, his primary emotion was one of guilt. Guilt that he did not love her; guilt that she did not love him. Guilt at his profound betrayal of Rachel in failing to care for their child. Guilt sometimes seemed to be the only deeply felt emotion of which he was now capable. Hector found himself recalling the expression in Henry Wyborne's eyes that evening, when he had said, *I always thought it was wrong, what happened*. How unexpected, Hector thought, as he started up the car, to learn after so long that Henry, too, felt guilty.

Three weeks later, he showed Alice her bedroom at the Bloomsbury flat. He had cleared out the little room he used as a study, substituting a bed and a chest of drawers for his desk and bookcase.

'Do you like your new room, Alice?'

'Yes, Daddy.'

Hector thought there was a despairing edge to the whispered words. The room, which was north-facing, still looked dark, and the musty odour of the books seemed to linger. But he said heartily, 'That's good. Shall we put your things away?' He unclasped her case, and began to unload all the small dresses and cardigans and nightgowns that the nanny had packed for her into the chest of drawers. He heard her indrawn breath; when he turned to look at her, he saw that there was an expression of horror in her eyes.

'What is it, Alice?'

'You're putting the socks in with skirts, Daddy. Socks go with knickers and tights, and skirts go with dresses and trousers.'

'Oh.' He tried to rearrange things. She came to stand beside him, patting her clothes into neat shapes, tucking a sleeve in here, a lace away there. He had a sudden sharp vision of Rachel at Bellingford, unpacking her trousseau into an ancient chest of drawers that had smelt of camphor.

'We'll finish this later, shall we?' he said, and glanced at his watch. It was half past four. He did not know the pattern of her day. His own Sunday afternoons (pub for lunch, then a half-hearted attempt at household chores, then, at four-ish, the first drink of the evening) were plainly unsuitable for a child.

He said tentatively, 'Is it tea-time, do you think?'

They went into the kitchen. He had got some food in. He asked, 'Bread and honey and cake all right?' and she nodded.

When he had given her her tea, he collapsed thankfully on the sofa with the *Observer*. He was half-way through the colour supplement when he looked up and saw that she wasn't eating.

'What's up, Alice?'

'There are *crusts*!'

He found a knife and cut them off. 'And there's *currants*!' she said, pointing at the Chelsea bun he had bought.

'Don't you like currants?'

She shook her head. Her eyes were wide and alarmed. 'Granny gives me a straw with my milk,' she whispered, 'so it doesn't go up my nose.'

He managed to coax her to eat two of the sandwiches, but the bun remained uneaten, the milk undrunk. Over the next few days he seemed to commit an endless series of transgressions. Her bathwater was always too hot or too cold, the towels were not fluffy enough, he put the wrong amount of toothpaste on her toothbrush, he expected her to wear the blue cardigan with the pink dress and vice versa.

'Whatever I do is always wrong,' he complained to Katherine, when she visited one evening. 'I don't make her toast into fingers like Granny did, and I don't remember to jump her down the last two stairs like Grandfather did. I can't do a thing right.'

'It'll get better,' said Katherine vaguely.

'Do you think so?' Hector wasn't convinced.

'You'll learn each other's ways.'

'And it's so *wearing*. I've got used to there being just me and Charlie.'

He caught an unguarded expression on her face, and realized how he must sound: a self-pitying, set-in-his-ways bachelor. He often wondered why she continued to visit him: she was sorry for him, he supposed.

'Anyway,' he said, 'we're going to look at a school on Friday. A boarding-school called St Johanna's. Henry suggested it.'

'Isn't she rather young?'

'I explained things to the headmistress. They take five-year-olds in special circumstances. And Alice is six in June.'

'I suppose it must be difficult,' said Katherine, attempting sympathy. 'Work, I mean.'

'Kevin's holding the fort.' Kevin was Hector's assistant at the bookshop. 'I haven't been in all week.' Not that he missed the shop: work, like every other part of his life, was a stopgap, to be neither loved nor hated, but endured as a way of getting through the days.

The next day was a series of disasters. First he overcooked Alice's breakfast egg, and then, attempting to wash her fine, silky light brown hair in expectation of their visit to the school the following day, he got shampoo in her eye. She didn't cry or scream – she never cried or screamed – there was just, as he bathed her eye in cold water, that look of hopelessness. Then he had to go into the shop – there had been a muddle with the accounts, and the tax inspectors were threatening a visit. On the Underground, he found himself enraged that some of his fellow passengers seemed to take so little account of a small child, brushing past her on the escalator, pushing ahead through the carriage doors to grab a seat. Alice seemed to like the bookshop, though, and sat happily in a corner for an hour, absorbed in a Kate Greenaway picture book while he and Kevin went through the figures.

Then, taking her for lunch, things deteriorated again. They went to a nearby Italian restaurant, where she stared at her spaghetti Bolognese in disgust. 'Everything's mixed together!' she hissed. Hector's depression deepened; he longed for a glass of wine. The kind Italian waiters offered Alice delicacies: an olive, a macaroon, a bowl of minestrone. She refused all of them, and did not eat a morsel. He was vividly reminded of Rachel at her most imperious.

In the afternoon, to cheer her up, he suggested an outing to the park. She went, but did not enjoy it, he sensed, limiting herself to a few dutiful and cautious tours of slide and swing. Then they did a little shopping, she close beside him, nose in the air, disapproving of the crowds. He burned the fish fingers he made for her tea, so she picked at them, as he had known she would. As soon as she was safely in bed, he poured himself a large drink, collapsed in a chair, and tried to ignore his pounding headache.

The next day, they drove to St Johanna's. The school was in Surrey, not far from the leafy and expensive enclaves of Virginia Water. The headmistress, Miss Framlingham, welcomed them. They were shown round. Hector inspected little beds in little dormitories, each bearing a row of teddies and dolls, and was shown a splendidly equipped gym and vast hockey fields. After the park the previous day, he found it hard to imagine Alice shinning up the ropes in the gym or striding confidently across the field. In the dining room, watching hordes of little girls at their midday break, he could not help noticing that the crusts were not cut off the bread, and that they had no straws through which to drink their milk. Filling in forms in Miss Framlingham's office, he was aware of an unease, yet he brushed it aside.

Outside, as they drove away, he said encouragingly, 'You liked it, didn't you, Alice?' She nodded.

'It'll be fun, won't it? All those other girls to play with.'

'Yes, Daddy.'

He caught sight of her expression in the rear-view mirror. The flutter of fear in her eyes, the way her teeth pressed against her lip. He found himself remembering, years ago, his own first day at boarding-school. 'Best days of your life,' his father had said, with a heartiness that he himself had just now equalled. Yet he had loathed it from the first day of term, and had continued to loathe it until the day, ten years later, that he had left.

It occurred to him then that he had got it all wrong. For the first time he saw himself in her. Alice might look like Rachel – a similarity that haunted him – but her diffidence, her lack of physical confidence, her need for order and routine all came from him. He remembered how she had held the Kate Greenaway book close to her face, and how she had stumbled in the park, and it occurred to him that her great dark eyes – the mirror of Rachel's – might even be myopic, like his own.

He pulled into a lay-by. He said gently, 'You don't want to go to that school, do you?' and she stared at him, and shook her head.

Then he said, 'You miss Granny, don't you, sweetheart?' and a tear trickled down her cheek.

He scooped her on to his lap, and held her as she cried. He didn't know how he was going to manage, but he was at least going to make a better fist of trying. After a while, he wiped her face with his handkerchief, settled her in her seat in the back of the car, and drove home.

Since they had left London, Liv, Freya and Georgie had crawled their slow way up the East Anglian coast, from Suffolk to Norfolk, living in a succession of bedsits and furnished flats. All were uniformly dreary and draughty, and crammed with the sort of furniture no one else wanted: fold-down sofas with upholstery worn shiny by decades of use, flimsy chests that overturned when you tried to tug open their eternally jamming drawers, and shared bathrooms with peeling tiles and green stains on the enamel where the taps dripped.

They endured a winter in a caravan parked among dunes on the blowy east coast, where their food and clothes were always gritty with sand. They briefly shared a squat in Great Yarmouth, a vast, once-splendid Victorian house, where Liv's fear of involvement with the police or social services soon persuaded her to move on. They stayed only a couple of weeks in the holiday let where the landlord, coming into the kitchen almost daily to read the meter, patted Liv's bottom and brushed against her breasts.

She supported the three of them by working in shops and cafés, pubs and farms. Childcare was an endless and insoluble problem. She worked out complicated rotas with other mothers, minding their children in turn so that she could spend the mornings behind a supermarket till. She picked strawberries while Freya and Georgie played in a corner of the field. She cleaned offices, the girls in tow as she vacuumed and dusted. She addressed envelopes at home, and sold clothes and jewellery through party plans. She worked in a fish-and-chip shop when the children were in bed, nipping back every hour or so to make sure they were still sleeping.

None of the jobs lasted. The shop job fell through when the girls contracted German measles. Unreliable, the manager of the supermarket said – 'We can't always be covering for you, Mrs Galenski, whenever you've a domestic problem.' She had to give up the cleaning job when one of the supervisors complained to her employer about the girls. The farm jobs were seasonal, and, in the end, she couldn't stomach earning a pittance selling tacky jewellery and ill-made clothing to women not much better off than herself. And the chip shop lasted only a few evenings because she was unable to bear the guilt and anxiety of leaving Freya and Georgie unattended.

Yet all the jobs were preferable to the periods of unemployment between them. Sometimes it took only a day or two for Liv to find another job; once she was out of work for almost a month. A month of searching for work in the employment exchange, in the columns of the local newspaper, and in shop windows. As the days mounted up, she lay awake at night, cold and frightened, afraid of the future. She imagined Freya and Georgie going hungry; she imagined them catching pneumonia because she couldn't afford the fifty pences for the meter. She imagined that they would lose the roof over their heads because she could not pay the rent, and that her children would be taken away from her.

Somehow, she always survived. Thea sent money whenever Liv was staying in one place long enough to receive mail: without that she could not have managed. The winter passed, and it was summer again, and with the summer came temporary seasonal jobs. In July 1974, they moved into Samphire Cottage. Liv was working at a lavender farm when she mentioned to the farm's owner, Mrs Maynard, that she was looking for somewhere to live. Daphne Maynard had taken to Freya. She reminded her, she said, of her own daughter when she was little. She answered Freya's incessant questions with patience and thought, and did not mind when Freya trailed her from field to kitchen to office.

Mrs Maynard told Liv about Samphire Cottage. The small red-brick house stood a few hundred yards from the Norfolk coastal road, beside the gateway of a lane that branched out towards the salt marshes. There was a clump of willows, and a square of garden bordered by ditches, which, in the summer, were bright with marsh marigolds and purple loosestrife. The cottage was two-up, two-down, with a wooden lean-to added to the back, which in the mornings caught the sun. On fine days you could see the distant line of shingle sea-wall, which was all that kept the North Sea from the marshes. On other days the wind howled, and coast and sea were curtained in grey.

The house was heated by an Aga in the kitchen and by an open fire in the living room. Showing Liv around the cottage, Mrs Maynard apologized for the lack of radiators: they had meant to have central-heating installed, but there was no gas in the village and, since the Arab-Israeli war and the subsequent oil embargo, the price of oil had soared. Then she said doubtfully, 'Won't it be rather lonely for you?' and Liv shook her head and smiled, and told her that Samphire Cottage was just what she wanted.

Freya and Georgie slept in the back bedroom, Liv in the front. The downstairs rooms were decorated with the girls' paintings, and the lean-to housed Liv's sewing-machine. She had bought the old Singer sewing-machine in a jumble sale for a pound, carrying it home in Georgie's pushchair. She put up an advertisement in the post-office window: 'General sewing – cushions, curtains and children's clothes made to order.' The commissions didn't exactly flood in, but after a while her reputation seemed to spread by word of mouth, and she had enough work to fill the evenings. She enjoyed her sewing, rediscovering old skills and learning new ones. She made patchwork, she embroidered and appliquéed, and experimented with printing fabrics. Sometimes, when things were a little easier, she took the bus to Norwich and visited the craft shops and libraries, looking for new ideas. The red tiled floor of the lean-to was always scattered with offcuts of material and strands of cotton, like brightly coloured autumn leaves.

Outside, dragonflies darted above the reeds, and brownish-green frogs crouched in the ditches. The cottage was hidden from the road, protected by the trees. Liv wanted to stay there for ever. In the spring term of 1975, Freya began at the village school, a couple of miles away, and Georgie started playgroup. For the first time in years, Liv had a few child-free hours each morning. She took in more sewing, and saved up and bought a secondhand bicycle, with a seat for Freya on the back, and a little perch behind the handlebars for Georgie. She made patchwork cot quilts, and sold them to mothers at the school gates. She minded other people's children after school. She took morning cleaning jobs and, at the beginning of the summer term, a part-time job in a pub in the village. She managed, just.

Her days were a knife-edge of carefully judged routine. In the morning, she would take Freya to school and Georgie to play-group, then she would clean a wealthy commuter's house for a couple of hours. Then she would cycle to the pub, to help with the cooking and in the bar. Another mother collected Georgie from playgroup and gave her lunch. When Liv left the pub at half past two, she'd pick up Georgie, do the shopping or go home and catch up on the housework, then cycle to the school to wait for Freya. Then she'd give the girls their tea, play with them, and read them stories. After bath and bed, she'd get out her sewing-machine. She made all Freya and Georgie's clothes, and most of her own. Other mothers saw and admired the original designs, and asked her to make clothes for their own children. She made sure that Freya and Georgie were always well clothed and well fed, and she tried always to be there for them when they needed her.

Freya, at five, was tall and slight, with black silky hair that Liv cut into a bob with her sewing scissors. She buzzed with restless energy, like a taut bowstring. She talked to anyone and everyone, at length, questioning them, trying to make sense of the world. Her openness with strangers sometimes alarmed Liv. It was as though she was searching for something, hungry for something. Georgie, at three, was Freya's small, sunny, good-tempered opposite. Looking at her mercurial elder daughter, thinking about the changes and losses she had suffered, Liv was aware of an enduring sense of guilt.

Over the past year and a half, Katherine had sometimes wondered why she continued to visit Hector. It was not that he was good company; rather, he was often morose and self-absorbed. An hour would pass, and she would struggle to get more than a few sentences out of him. Her suggestions for outings – to the cinema, or for a walk in Regent's Park – were often met with a shrug of the shoulders, or an expression of indifference. She would find herself wanting to shake him or to shout at him, or flounce exasperated out of his flat, which sometimes, pushed beyond endurance, she did. Yet she always went back. Hector was her penance, she sometimes thought, a reminder of a past she might have preferred to forget. Two and a half years ago, her misery over Jordan and her envy of Liv had led her to seduce Felix. Two friendships had ended that night. There had been a mutual, unspoken conclusion between herself and Felix that a boundary had been overstepped. He had moved away, changed job; she had not seen him since. Nor had she heard from Liv since she had left London. Katherine was aware of a lingering hurt. Once, Liv had needed her; now she did not. She told herself that Liv had kept her whereabouts secret because she was afraid that Stefan might trace her again. Yet there remained at the back of her mind the uncomfortable thought that Liv somehow *knew*. And that she minded.

Katherine had come to the conclusion that she persisted with Hector because by doing so she could repay the debt she owed to at least one of her friends. Reacquainting herself with Hector after meeting him on the day of the bomb scare, the emotional emptiness of his life had troubled her. The loneliness that she herself had once endured had been nothing compared to Hector's partly self-imposed isolation. He had no friends, and no family apart from a maiden aunt in Henley-on-Thames to whom he paid duty visits at Christmas and on birthdays. Katherine could imagine only too well how he must have repelled all overtures of friendship in the weeks and months and years that had followed Rachel's death. Friendship could only endure so much rejection, so much silence and self-absorption. He had his job, in which he took only as much interest as was necessary to keep the second-hand bookshop going. He had no hobbies unless becoming acquainted with the bottom of a whisky bottle could be counted a hobby. He didn't even seem to care greatly for the dog. Hector tolerated Charlie because Charlie had once belonged to Rachel, taking him for duty walks around Hyde Park, enduring his bad habits – a tendency to chew the leather arms of the sofa, and a fondness for chocolate drops – with a patience that stemmed from an utter lack of interest.

Yet there had been another reason why Katherine continued to visit Hector. Because, on that awful day at Christmas 1972, she had understood what it was to lose someone you loved. She had not forgotten the intensity of the pain she had suffered, looking out of the window of Jordan's flat, and seeing him with his wife. She had understood then how vulnerable love made you, how the loss of it could erase all optimism, and how it could tear away at your defences, leaving you naked and exposed. She sensed that since Rachel's death, Hector had existed in a world which lacked rules or meaning, a world in which happiness could turn to grief in the span of a single heartbeat.

Though Hector rarely mentioned Rachel, her memory dominated the small flat. She was there in the ranks of photographs, and in the pictures and ornaments that Katherine remembered from her bedroom at Fernhill Grange. Hector dusted the photographs and ornaments each day. It was the only housework he ever did, Katherine had sometimes thought: the remainder of the flat suffocated beneath a blanket of dust.

But since Diana Wyborne's death, a change had begun. Alice

had now been living with Hector for three months, attending a small day school a few streets away from the Bloomsbury flat. Slowly the rooms of the flat were losing some of their mustiness. Brightly coloured toys scattered the faded Turkish rugs; childish paintings of houses and horses and boats bouncing on improbably turquoise seas concealed some of the darkly bound books. Now that he accompanied Hector and Alice on their daily walks to the park, even Charlie had lost some of his rolls of fat. It was as though, Katherine thought, a curtain was by degrees being pulled aside, letting light through a previously opaque window.

In the summer, Philip fell ill. He had a fit, from which he did not recover consciousness for several hours. Katherine, visiting him in hospital, thought that though he smiled at her and said her name, and curled his hand in hers, something had been rubbed out: yet another little piece of the original Philip had been taken away. In the hospital bed, pale in a white gown, his body seemed to diminish, to sink back into the tightly tucked bedclothes, his bright red hair the single splash of colour.

Returning to London, the telephone rang as she unlocked the door to her flat. It was Jordan. 'I've a couple of hours,' he said. 'I'm at the flat.'

She felt tired: the long drive, the anxiety about Philip. She twisted the flex of the telephone around her finger. 'Couldn't you come here, Jordan?'

'You know that's not a good idea, darling. It just takes one nosy journalist and my face is all over the front page of the *Sun*.'

'Still . . .'

'"Kinky Katherine in MP's Secret Love Nest". I'm only thinking of you, darling.'

She went to the flat. Jordan had bought oysters, which he fed to her one by one, washed down with champagne. In the final oyster shell there nestled a pair of pearl earrings.

'They're lovely, Jordan.' Kneeling over him, she held aside her curtains of strawberry-blonde hair as she kissed him.

'They're to soften the blow, I'm afraid.'

Katherine straightened, eyes narrowed, looking down at him.

'Tricia's insisting we go away for the whole of August,' said Jordan. 'Tuscany. I can't say no, I'm afraid, darling. She hasn't been all that well since Edward was born. She needs a break.'

She thought, I don't want to know, I just don't want to know. But she said lightly, 'Tuscany . . . lucky you. I'm terribly envious.'

'Katherine . . .' He touched her taut shoulders. 'I shall think of you all day, every day.' His voice pleaded with her, his mouth caressed her. 'And when I get back, we'll have a weekend together, I promise you.'

'We've never had a weekend. Only afternoons, days, and nights. Do you know, Jordan, that we've never spent more than eight consecutive hours together? I've worked it out.'

'Maybe that's why it's so good . . . maybe that's why it's so special . . .' His fingers had strayed down to her belly, coaxing her, stroking her, reigniting the fire between her legs. Momentarily, she wondered how it was that she could feel so angry with him at the same time as wanting him so much. Then she swung herself on top of him, straddling him, taking him inside her, her movements slow at first, taunting him, teasing him, making him wait, until she saw that he, too, suffered.

Afterwards, she soaked herself in the bath with the gold taps. Jordan brought her a glass of champagne.

Katherine shook her head. 'No thanks.'

He ran his fingertip across her breasts. 'There's still half a bottle left.'

'You finish it. I'd rather have coffee, Jordan.'

'How sedate.' His voice was mocking. 'That's not like my wild little Katherine.'

'I have to drive.' She heard him go into the kitchen. After a few moments, he called out, 'Tricia's bought a new Thing. I don't know how it works.'

She had noticed this with him: a complete cluelessness about anything domestic. Once she had found it endearing; now she felt irritated.

'What sort of Thing?'

'You plug it in,' he said vaguely.

311

'Fill the jug with water, and put the coffee in the top,' she said. She sank beneath the scented water again, so that strands of her hair floated on the surface like pale, reddish seaweed.

He came into the bathroom. 'I can't find the grinder. Where on earth is it?'

Suppressing a sigh, she climbed out of the bath, and wrapped herself in a towel. In the kitchen, the grinder was where it always was, behind the pepper mill. She was searching through the cupboard for coffee beans, when Jordan came to stand behind her, threading his hands beneath the folds of the towel. His palms were warm against her wet skin. His mouth nuzzled her tangled hair, and caressed the lobes from which his earrings swung.

'We've twenty minutes,' he whispered. 'You don't really want that coffee, do you?'

She let him kiss her for a while, but for the first time she could remember, her body failed to respond. She was tired, she thought. Or it was the wrong time of the month. After a while, she made the excuse of having work to do, dressed herself, gathered up her belongings and went home.

At autumn half-term, Liv and the children caught the bus to Norwich. Liv bought dressmaking material and offcuts for patchwork, and then they walked the half-mile from the city centre to a craft shop. Though the day had begun fine, rain had set in by the time they left the shop. Liv put up her umbrella as they walked past a building site; Georgie gazed open-mouthed at the trucks and JCBs. The site was adjacent to a disused factory. 'For Sale' signs hung aslant from the high iron railings that surrounded the factory, and some of the windows in the huge, red-brick Victorian edifice were broken. There was a shabby, gloomy air about the place. Raindrops bounced in vast puddles on pitted tarmac, and part of the building had been fire-damaged, black smoke-stains gouting from charred windows.

Further along the pavement, a man was standing at the front gates. Tall, dark-haired and broad-shouldered, he was wearing dark blue jeans and a well-cut black-leather jacket. There was something familiar about him; Liv looked harder, straining to see. Freya had run ahead and was talking to him.

'I've got a red mackintosh at home, but we forgot to bring it. We're going to have milkshakes in a café. We live in a house called Samphire Cottage. Samphire's a plant, did you know that? My name's Freya Galenski, what's yours?'

And at that, the man standing at the gates stared at Freya. Liv's heart began to beat wildly. His voice carried down the street to her. 'Your name's Freya. And your sister's called Georgie.'

She heard herself whisper: *'Felix'*.

'And your mother's name,' he said, 'is Liv.'

Freya looked up at Felix. 'Are you my daddy?'

'No. No, sweetheart.'

Liv scooped Georgie up in her arms. She was shaking. As she neared him, she saw how Felix had altered. How the cropped hair seemed to emphasize the bones and planes of his face, to age him, to harden him.

'How unexpected to see you, Liv,' he said. Not *marvellous*, she thought, not *wonderful*. Just *unexpected*. Such a bland, unrevealing word. 'What on earth are you doing here?'

'Shopping.' She was out of breath. 'And you, Felix?'

He glanced at the disused factory. 'Just contemplating a spot of breaking and entering.' He blinked. 'How are you?'

'We're fine, fine. So amazing, to run into you like this.' Yet she recalled that the Corcorans owned a splendid house somewhere in Norfolk. Not so surprising, then, that they should meet.

'It's been a while.'

'Two and a half years.' The words seemed to echo against the high walls of the factory. The events that had prompted her leaving of London flickered through her mind: Stefan, Katherine . . .

'Freya's at school now,' she heard herself say, 'and Georgie goes to playgroup.'

'Rose misses them,' he said.

'I had to leave London.' She knew she sounded defensive.

313

'You know I had to leave London.' Georgie slithered out of her arms, back into the puddles.

'Because of Stefan?'

'Yes.' And because of you, she thought.

A silence. If they had still meant anything to each other, she thought, she would have minded that they struggled to find anything to say.

'Are you still living in London, Felix?'

'I've a place in Fulham. What about you?'

She told him the name of the village. He glanced at his watch. She said quickly, 'I have to go – I promised the girls lunch in town.'

Freya was climbing up the wrought-iron gates. 'I'll give you a lift,' he said.

'There's no need.' She picked up her bags. 'Freya, get down.'

But he was unlocking the door of the dark blue Renault that was parked by the pavement. 'The rain . . .' he said.

Freya's wet sandals lost their grip on the wrought-iron, and she slipped to the ground, landing awkwardly. She began to howl.

'I did *say*, Freya—' One-handed, Liv tried to help Freya up, but Georgie had wrapped her arms around her knees.

'There's blood!' yelled Freya. 'Go *'way*, Georgie!'

'Here.' Felix took Liv's shopping bags, and swung them into the boot of the car. Freya slapped Georgie; both children roared. Liv felt a wash of exhaustion: the long walk with heavy bags and two children in tow. The exhaustion was mixed with anger, that Felix should see them at their worst. She almost said, 'They're not always like this,' but managed to bite the words back.

As she shooed the children into the car, he said, 'What's this? Rose madder . . . and ultramarine . . .' The square of lino and the bottles of dye were protruding from the top of one of the carriers. He closed the boot. 'What do you make?'

'Curtains . . . cushions . . . children's clothes, mostly.' She climbed into the front passenger seat.

Driving through rainswept streets, the windscreen wipers swooped to and fro, and the sound of the engine struggled to fill the recurrent silences. She thought, I wish you hadn't offered me a lift if you are going to be so morose, if you are going to make me feel awkward. It seemed to her that there was a clipped, angry restlessness about him that went with the smart clothes, the short hair, the chill in his eyes.

She broke the silence. 'Are you still working for the housing co-operative?'

'I'm with an investment company in the City.'

She thought, *Oh*, suddenly understanding the alterations in him. 'Do you like it?'

'It's all right. I needed to learn how money makes money.'

They had reached the city centre. She brushed back her wet fringe from her face. 'You never used to bother about money.'

'Didn't I?' He smiled humourlessly. 'How naïve of me.'

The streets and shops drifted by, a smudge of grey and brown. Felix pulled into a side-street, and handed Liv her bags from the boot. 'Well, it was nice to have seen you all again,' he said, as though she was a vague acquaintance. Which was what she had become, she supposed.

She heard herself blurt out, 'You've changed, Felix.'

'Have I?' She could not read his expression. 'Yes, I suppose I have.'

Standing on the pavement with the girls, she watched his car drive out of sight. She recalled, *I needed to learn how money makes money*, and thought, Well, you didn't take long to revert to type, did you, Felix Corcoran? And then she took a deep breath and said, 'Well, then, who's ready for a milkshake?' and the children shrieked with delight.

Felix drove on through Norwich, to the house where Mia and his father now lived. Going to look at the old Corcoran's factory for the first time in years, he had not noticed Liv until the child Freya had told him her name. Then it was as though time had twisted back three years, returning him to those heady, intense days in London. The shock of seeing her had been mixed with his anger at witnessing what neglect and the passing of time had done to a once thriving business, and with his careful consideration of doors, windows, locks. Memories and emotions had collided: pleasure in seeing her, an unresolved resentment at her sudden leaving of him, and a naggingly uncomfortable recollection of the day he had begun by learning that he was to lose his home, and ended by making love to Katherine.

He had been made aware that time had moved on, and that the parameters of both his life and hers had altered so profoundly that the past had become both distant and irrelevant. Hardest of all to come to terms with was the knowledge that he still found her beautiful.

Coldness and disapproval had emanated from her as they had driven into the city centre. *You've changed*, she had said, making it clear that the change had not been for the better. He knew that he had been taciturn and difficult. The smoke-damaged factory, the prospect of lunch with his father had both weighed heavily on him.

Since they had left Wyatts, Bernard and Mia had lived in a small villa on the southern fringe of Norwich. Felix parked outside the house. Mia was at work, so Bernard cooked eggs and bacon that Felix did not particularly want to eat, and poured him a Scotch he would rather have not drunk. The bacon was burnt, and the yolks of the eggs were broken. His father's clumsy attempts at cooking always made Felix feel depressed, but he feigned enthusiasm, finishing everything on the plate.

Felix studied his father as they talked. Bernard had lost weight since the heart-attack he had suffered in the early months of 1973. That had been a time that, even now, Felix could hardly bear to remember. It had been thought for a while that Bernard would not recover: he recalled a bleak ten minutes with an overworked junior doctor, who had explained to them the severity of Bernard's condition. He remembered feeling numb, unable to absorb the reality of this further disaster.

But Bernard had pulled through, confounding the doctors' expectations. During his slow recovery, the dreary mechanisms of bankruptcy had ground on, destroying the familiar fabric of their lives. The factory had closed down, and Wyatts had been put up for sale. Mia had found a house for Bernard and herself, and had taken a secretarial job working for a firm of actuaries. Rose, for whom material objects held so little emotional pull, had sorted out Wyatts' contents. Some of the best pieces of furniture had been put up for auction, to raise much-needed cash; a few were kept, crushed into the much-smaller Norwich house.

Felix knew that his father would never work again, that his health had been ruined by the heart-attack, and his spirit broken by the bankruptcy. Bernard accepted no division of responsibility for what had happened, and viewed his own role with humiliation and shame. There were personal as well as company debts. At the time that Corcoran's had been losing money heavily, Bernard had taken out a loan in his own name to cover the shortfall in household income. Felix had visited the bank, hoping for a sympathetic understanding of his father's situation. He had received no sympathy, no understanding. When he pointed out that his father has been a good customer of the bank for more than forty years, and that until these last few years he had never owed a penny, his pleas fell on deaf ears. A schedule was drawn up of loan repayments. Two-thirds of Mia's salary must be paid to the bank each month to cover the loan. Bernard and Mia must subsist on what was left over.

That had been the last time he had pleaded with anyone. Shock and anger had hardened then to a cold determination. Through an old schoolfriend, he found a job in a City bank. He needed, as he had told Liv, to learn how money made money. With the small legacy he had inherited from his mother, he had been able to make a down-payment on a terraced house in Fulham. He did not intend to work for the bank for long; it was just a stepping-stone. He sent money to Mia each month, to help her with household bills.

For the past two years, Rose had been living at Great Dransfield with Nancy. It was an arrangement that worked well, suiting both women. The dogs, the peacocks, Mia's horse and the guinea-pigs lived at Great Dransfield too, remnants of a different life. It was because of Rose that Felix had gone to Corcoran's old factory that morning. Since it had closed down, he had avoided the factory, equally depressed and angered by the housing estate that was springing up adjacent to it, and by the fire the previous year that had damaged part of the Victorian building. But visiting Rose at Great Dransfield, he had asked her what she missed most about Wyatts. 'My wallpaper,' she had said, unexpectedly. 'Don't you remember, Felix? In my bedroom. It was called "Briar Rose".' She had smiled. 'I was the only girl at school to have a wallpaper named after her.'

Before he left his father that evening, Felix took from the outhouse a pair of wire-cutters, a hammer, a wrench and a torch. He put them in the boot of the car, and drove carefully, sticking to the speed limit. The thought of being stopped and searched by the police was not pleasant. Parking a few streets away from the factory, he took the bag of tools out of the boot. It was midnight, and a covering of clouds masked both moon and stars. He had noticed that morning that the side gate was secured only by a single loop of chain. The wire-cutters bit easily through it, and then he was in the courtyard behind the factory. Once, this square of asphalt would have been crowded with lorries and vans, waiting to be loaded. Now it was empty except for curls of litter in the corners, and a few empty bottles and matted blankets in a doorway where a down-and-out had once slept. Felix walked around the building, searching for a point of entrance. Many of the windows were high up, out of his reach, and all the doors were padlocked. But in the part of the factory damaged by the fire, he discovered a ground-floor window with a broken pane. Then it was just a matter of climbing on to an old dustbin, wrapping his leather jacket around his hand and punching through the remaining shards of glass, flicking the catch, and he was inside.

The building reeked of soot and damp. Away from the exterior windows, Felix switched on his torch. The pale light illuminated the dereliction: the charred, blackened rafters, the

318

mouldering rolls of paper, and the wide puddles beneath the gaping holes high overhead in the roof. He focused on the task in hand. The fire had destroyed only a part of the factory. The pattern blocks, from which the wallpapers had been printed, had always been stored in a cellar beneath the main printing room. Felix walked along cold, silent corridors, heading for the cellar steps. Mentally, he prepared himself for disappointment. If the conflagration had reached the cellar, then the blocks, made of deal and fruitwood, would have been destroyed. Similarly, someone might have guessed the potential value of the blocks and stored them elsewhere.

He swung the torch around the cellar. There was only the faintest tang of smoke, and the wooden shelving appeared unscorched. He walked around, reading the labels on the shelves. 'Summer Trellis' . . . 'Japanese Garden' . . . 'Harlequin'. Corcoran's wallpaper might no longer exist, but the original designs remained, almost three thousand of them, locked in those carved squares of wood. Felix found the shelf he was looking for, and pulled it out. 'Briar Rose' – he recalled it, pink and gold on the walls of Rose's bedroom. The design had been specially commissioned at her birth. He wrapped the blocks in a cloth, and placed them in his bag.

He was half-way up the stairs when he paused, the torch gripped in his gloved hand. He thought of the rows of identical houses already rising from what had once been Corcoran's land. He knew that it was only a matter of time before the council admitted that a buyer would never be found for the factory, and the derelict building was declared unsafe. Then planning permission would be granted, the factory would be razed to the ground, and a hundred years' history would be recalled only in the name of yet another undistinguished but profitable housing estate.

Yet, for now, history lingered, clutched in his hands. Felix walked back down the stairs, circling the room, opening shelves, helping himself to what he wanted.

As he set off for London, the first pale light of dawn gleamed on the skyline. The pattern blocks filled up the boot and the back seat of the Renault. Twenty miles or so out of Norwich, in open country, he pulled over to the side of the road and sat staring out of the windscreen as the engine idled. Remnants of the last twenty-four hours' events flickered through his mind. A pattern of pink and gold roses. A bottle of rose-madder dye. Liv's dark eyes, and the child's. There was a tightness beneath his ribs, as though he had been running for miles and miles. How odd, he thought, so abruptly to supplant one obsession with another. During the past two and a half years, his sole *raison d'être*, the single motivating force that had driven him day and night, had been his determination to reclaim Wyatts. He had vowed to himself that somehow, some time, the house would belong to them again. Everything he had done had been with that one aim in mind. He had let nothing distract him. He had put aside his former ideals, believing them outworn and self-indulgent. He saw Rose only infrequently, his old friends hardly ever. His relationships with women were little more than one-night stands. He worked long hours, and made careful investments. The anger that had seized him when he had learned that Wyatts had been taken from them, the pity that he had felt for his father, and his shame at his own role in their ruin had not been diminished by the years. He dreamed of the house. He schemed for the house.

And yet today he had hardly thought about it. He blinked, uncurling his hands from the steering-wheel, watching the first rays of sunlight wash along the ploughed furrows in the fields. Liv's image had taken the place of Wyatts; Liv's voice had erased the rustle of the beech trees that lined Wyatts' driveway, and the drip of the fountain in the garden. Felix pressed his clenched fists against his forehead, as if by doing so he could rub her away, yet she persisted, something bright amid the darkness, and after a while he put the car into gear and drove on.

November gales had blown the leaves from the trees, blocking the gutters at Samphire Cottage. Rainwater cascaded over the front porch, treating the unwary to a sudden cold shower. Liv was teetering on the kitchen stool in the drizzle, trying to dislodge the pulp of dead leaves from the gutter with a stick, when she heard a car draw up on the grassy track that led to the house. She glanced over her shoulder, expecting to see Daphne Maynard's Land Rover. Instead, she recognized Felix Corcoran's dark blue Renault. The stool wobbled precariously, Liv dropped the stick, and had to grab at the bargeboard to keep her balance.

A car door slammed shut, then there were footsteps on the gravel and the sound of the gate opening and closing. She heard Felix call up, 'Liv? Are you all right?'

'The stool's slipped . . . I think it's sort of fallen into a hole.'

'Here.' Before she knew what he was doing, he had put his hands around her waist, and lifted her down. Much as she herself hauled Freya about when she was up to something she shouldn't be.

Felix glanced up at the porch. 'What on earth were you trying to do?'

Trying to do. The cheek of it. 'I was clearing the gutter,' she said irritably. 'It's blocked.'

'Haven't you any stepladders?'

'If I had,' and she gave the stool a vicious shove, 'I'd have used them, wouldn't I?'

'I'll do it for you.'

'There's no need . . .' she began, but he had already climbed on to the stool, which mysteriously refused to wobble for him, and had cleared the blockage with one efficient prod of the stick. 'There,' he said, jumping down.

She thought, If you say, *nothing to it*, I shall hit you. But instead he grinned. 'Messy business, gutters.' She looked down at herself. Her jumper was soaking and spattered with pieces of blackened leaf.

She muttered, 'You'd better come in,' and opened the front door. In the kitchen, she flung off her grubby jumper. Her T-shirt was reasonably dry. She saw that Felix had gone into the lean-to, and was looking at the lengths of cloth that hung from wires suspended from the ceiling.

'Did you make these, Liv?' When she nodded, he smiled. 'Of course, you were buying dye, weren't you? They're lovely. Really lovely.'

She was slightly mollified. 'The lino print's a bit lumpy, I'm afraid.' She had spent evening after evening carving shapes into the piece of lino, laying colour on colour. Tiny squares, each infilled with a stylized design of a flower gathered from the north Norfolk coast – sea lavender, samphire, horned poppy – made up the pattern.

'I wasn't sure whether this was the right place,' he said. 'I mean, there could be hundreds of Samphire Cottages, couldn't there? Anyway, I'm sorry for turning up like this, Liv. I'd have phoned, but you didn't seem to be in the book.'

'We haven't a phone.'

'I brought you this.' He handed her a carrier-bag. She peered inside. There were books, a tiny pair of socks, and a sheaf of paintings. Children's paintings. *It's a green dragon, Mummy*, Freya had said, and then she had looked across the road and seen Stefan.

'I was looking through a cupboard, and I came across them,' he said. 'I'd put them by, years ago. You left in rather a hurry, and I had to clear out the Beckett Street house before they renovated it. I didn't like to throw them away, in case . . .'

The remainder of his sentence hung in the air. *In case you came back.* 'Anyway,' he added, 'most of it doesn't look very important, so throw it out if you don't want it. Don't know why I hung on to it. Though there's a couple of things . . .'

'Freya's bracelet.' Liv took a small silver and lapis-lazuli bracelet from the bottom of the bag. Katherine had given the bracelet to Freya just after she was born. She remembered Katherine visiting Holm Edge, treading delicately in her high heels across the muddy ground.

She offered Felix a cup of tea. He thanked her, and said, 'This is a nice place. Rather out of the way, though.'

'*I* like it. I don't think I ever really fitted into London.'

'There were good times,' he said, looking at her, 'weren't there?'

She remembered the evenings she and Katherine and Felix had spent together. Washing up with him, he had taught her the words of his school song. She still remembered them.

'When I look back at it,' she said slowly, 'it seems such a short time. Almost six months, but I can't remember that much about it. It doesn't seem quite real. There was Stefan on one side, and this life on the other side, and London seems to have got squashed between them.'

'Do you see Stefan any more?'

'No. He was in prison for a while, after what happened in the café. They charged him with grievous bodily harm. He broke Sheila's arm.' Her voice was flat. 'And then, after he came out of prison, he had a breakdown, and ended up in hospital. And after that he went back to Canada. I've heard nothing since. Stefan has a Canadian passport, you see. His father was Canadian.'

She had tried, over the past few years, not to think about Stefan. Not to imagine him caged in prison, or ill in hospital. Most of all, she had tried to forget that he had said, *I'll do anything to get you back, Liv, anything at all.*

'That's good, isn't it?' said Felix. 'That he's gone abroad?'

'Of course.' Yet when I wake in the middle of the night, she thought, every creak of the old house is a footfall, and every whisper of the wind through the reeds is a curtain being moved aside, or a door opening.

'And you, Liv? What do you do with yourself now? Apart from making those beautiful fabrics?'

'Oh,' she said, 'I clean houses, and I work in a pub. And there's my sewing, of course.'

He had put down his mug, and was walking restlessly around the room. 'It must be a struggle,' he said. 'With two children to support.'

'We manage. We keep going.'

'A pub . . .' he repeated. He glanced at her. 'Isn't it rather . . . well, rather *boring*?'

'It's OK. I don't mind.'

'Rather a waste of your talents.'

'Felix . . .'

'I mean, an intelligent and creative woman like you—'

'I *like* it!' she hissed. 'I told you, it's fine! The pub's fine, and the house is fine, and we're all fine!'

His lip curled. 'A perfect life.'

'Yes. Perfect. I have everything I want.'

There was a silence. Then he said, 'There's smut on the end of your nose. Shall I . . .?' and he licked his finger, and with a small, deft movement swept away the fragment of leaf.

She said softly, sarcastically, 'I suppose you've taken a different direction, haven't you?'

He looked wary. 'The bank? It pays well.'

'Money's not the only thing.'

'Isn't it?' His mouth twisted. 'Damned useful, though.'

His tone annoyed her. 'I can't believe how much you've changed,' she said suddenly.

He was leaning against the sink, his hands in his pockets, his gaze focused on her. 'We've all changed, haven't we, Liv?'

She disregarded his implication. 'When I first met you, I rather admired you. You'd come from a privileged background, but you'd managed to shake all that off. You hadn't let it dictate the course of your life. But that didn't last long, did it?'

'What do you mean?' Suddenly, his voice was low, dangerous.

'That you've gone back to your roots, haven't you, Felix? Getting and spending.'

Again, that crooked, humourless smile. 'Piling up treasures on earth.'

'Yes.' And it seemed to her just then that those gold-green, familiar eyes looked upon her house, her self, her life with a disdainful, contemptuous gaze. 'Despise me if you want to,' she said coldly, 'look down on the work that I do – but at least I'm *honest*, at least I don't exploit anyone, at least what I've got I've earned through my own hard work.'

His eyes had narrowed into dark, angry slits. 'Meaning that I haven't?'

She shrugged. 'I suppose it was inevitable,' she said lightly. 'A house to inherit – the family business just waiting for you – so *easy*, isn't it, Felix?'

She saw him pale visibly. Then he said, 'I'd better go. I didn't mean to take up your time. I just came to give you back your things.'

As he reached the door, she said, digging in the knife, 'Oh, by the way, how's Katherine?'

'Katherine?' When he glanced back at her, she saw that his expression was blank, empty. 'No idea. I haven't seen her for years.'

She felt deflated suddenly, the anger draining out of her. She watched him leave the house, and go to his car. He did not look back.

A few days later, Liv met Daphne Maynard in the village shop. Daphne drove to Norwich once a week to visit her sister. She offered to go to the craft shop for Liv, to buy another piece of lino.

She couldn't remember the name of the street. 'There was a Victorian church,' Liv said, thinking hard, 'rather big and ugly – and a disused factory. It had been fire-damaged.'

'The old Corcoran's place, you mean?'

'Corcoran's?'

'Made wallpaper. Closed down a while ago. Old family firm. Been in Norwich a hundred years or so. Terrible shame.'

'They sold it?'

'Went bankrupt, I believe. A few years past. It was in the local paper – the job losses.'

The family business just waiting for you, she had said, and she had seen the colour drain from his face. Walking home, she felt ashamed of herself. Felix had driven all the way from London to

Samphire Cottage to return her belongings, and what had she done? She had thrown the past back in his face, a past that, she had begun to realize, she neither knew about nor understood. And why? Because he had voiced what she knew to be true: that she eked out a living doing monotonous, unfulfilling jobs that neither satisfied nor challenged her, which provided only the bare necessities of life. And of course she wanted more than that, for Freya and Georgie particularly. Of course she wanted her daughters' horizons to be wider than her own had been, so that when it came to it they made wiser choices.

Was that, she thought bitterly, what the years with Stefan had made of her? Someone who hid herself away in a cottage in the marshland, who took routine jobs, and who allowed no one except her children to come close to her?

She had assumed that everyone else's life had gone on just the same, while her own had changed and changed. You have grown hard, Liv Galenski, she thought, as she wheeled the pushchair fast along the narrow road. You have grown hard and bitter, and you have cut yourself off from the world.

She wondered whether she would ever see him again. She wondered why it still mattered to her that she might not see him again. She needed to apologize, she told herself. She needed to explain to him that she had not known. She was almost sure there was no other reason. Almost sure that beneath the layers of anger and self-protectiveness there did not still burn a small flame of longing, of desire.

Chapter Fourteen

Katherine helped Alice decorate the Setons' Christmas tree. After Alice had gone to bed, Katherine and Hector ate their supper, balancing plates on their knees, sitting in front of the open fire. Hector explained, 'I know it's a bit early for the tree, but I had to get it because Alice was so upset. We were shopping in Dickins and Jones, you see, and Alice wanted to go to the lavatory. I couldn't go into the ladies', of course, so she had to manage by herself. And she took ages and ages, and I was beginning to get worried, so I had to ask one of the shop assistants to go and find her.'

'What happened?'

Hector sighed. 'She'd locked the door of the cubicle because she was afraid of people coming in, and she couldn't open it. The bolt was too stiff. She was in tears. She only cheered up when I said she could choose the Christmas tree.' Hector filled Katherine's wine-glass. 'I can remember much the same thing happening to me, when I was about seven. I'd just gone to boarding-school, and it was all utterly confusing – lots of rules that didn't seem to make any sense – and I locked myself in the lavatory in the games block. I thought I'd be there for ever.' He smiled. 'Alice has all my worst attributes, I sometimes think. Now, Rachel, in the same circumstances, would have just called for help. But Alice didn't. Too embarrassed, you see.'

'Rachel was never embarrassed,' said Katherine, remembering. 'She always did exactly what she wanted – not that she ever seemed to want much. Not like me.' She smiled. 'I was terribly envious of her, you know.'

'Were you? Why?'

'Oh, because she had a pony. And she had ballet lessons. I had ballet lessons for a term. I was hopeless, of course – two left feet. And Rachel had proper pink satin ballet shoes, when everyone else had red leather, and she had a tutu when everyone else wore awful blue tunics with matching knickers.'

Hector smiled. 'I am struggling to imagine you in a blue tunic with matching knickers, Katherine.'

'Don't, please.' She shuddered. 'And, of course, Rachel's home was always so neat and tidy. And there were home-made cakes. And table napkins. And guest towels. And no one ever shouted. It must have been my conventional streak coming out, I suppose, longing for all that. Beneath this raffish exterior there's a bourgeois housewife.' Katherine scrabbled in her bag for her cigarettes. 'When I was little, I used to think that the Wybornes were just pretending. That when Liv and I left the house, they'd start yelling at each other, the same as my family did.' She offered her cigarettes to Hector.

'No thanks, I'm trying to give them up. Because of Alice.' He added thoughtfully, 'It wasn't *yelling* with my family, it was the silences. There was just me and my father, you see.'

'Oh, we were yellers. The Constants are expert yellers.' Katherine lit her cigarette. 'No one had enough time for each other, I suppose. My father was always working, and Mum was always answering the phone for him and doing the cooking and cleaning and looking after Philip. So we had to yell to get any attention.' Her eyes narrowed. 'I think that's what I envied most. Rachel was so obviously the apple of her parents' eye. Their whole life seemed to revolve around her. No one has ever felt like that about me.'

There was a silence. She thought, Shut up, shut up, you tactless fool. But Hector only said, 'Alice adores you, you know.'

She looked sceptical. 'It's true,' he said, 'you know it is. Look.' Hector took from the sideboard a drawing of a stick woman with mad orange curls and enormous platform-soled boots. 'The spitting image, I thought.'

'Idiot.' Katherine grimaced as she pulled at one of her spiralling sandy locks. 'I knew the perm was a mistake.'

Hector stood up. 'Coffee? And there's some grapes.' He filled the kettle and turned on the gas. Then he said, 'I suppose that's partly why I've always felt so guilty. Destroying something that was so perfect. Ruining the Wybornes' lives as well as Rachel's and my own.'

She looked up sharply. 'Hector, it wasn't your fault. You can't possibly believe that it was your fault.'

There was a clattering of mugs and teaspoons, and she wondered whether he would change the subject. But as he placed the coffee and fruit bowl on the hearth, he said, 'But it was, you see. I insisted on marrying Rachel, even though she was only eighteen, even though her parents wanted her to wait. And I got her pregnant. No, Katherine,' he shook his head, silencing her, 'I was a lot older than Rachel, and a great deal more experienced. It was my responsibility to take care of things like that. And,' his face was grim, 'I was away at a time when I should have been there, looking after her. I wasn't there with her when she needed me. I always think, if she hadn't driven all the way back to Bellingford by herself, perhaps it would never have happened. The doctors said that it was nothing to do with that, but—'

'Back to Bellingford?' said Katherine. 'What do you mean, Hector? I thought Rachel was *at* Bellingford.'

'No. She was staying with her parents. I was working in London, you see.'

Katherine felt confused. 'But she phoned me from Bellingford the day before she died.'

He made an impatient gesture. 'That's what I mean. I was supposed to be catching the train up to the Wybornes' house on Friday, when I'd finished in London, and driving Rachel back to Northumberland on the Saturday.' He rubbed his hand across his forehead. 'I should have told the bank I couldn't do it. Alice was due in three weeks. I should have put my foot down.'

Katherine lit another cigarette. 'So you took Rachel to Fernhill Grange?'

'At the beginning of the week, yes. She wanted to collect some of her old baby things. Then I went on to London. I left Rachel the car – I thought she might need it, and I've always loathed driving in London. Anyway, when I got back to Fernhill Grange on the Friday, Henry told me that she'd already gone home. Taken the car and driven back to Bellingford on her own. I couldn't get a train till the next morning. And when I got there in the early afternoon, she was already in labour.' His face seemed to fall in on itself. 'Pains coming every three minutes, but she hadn't wanted to go to the hospital by herself. Alice was born a few hours after we got to the hospital. Very quick for a first baby, they said. And I've always thought – I've always thought that was why it happened. That the journey brought on the early labour. That she suffered the embolism because it all happened so quickly.' Hector took one of Katherine's cigarettes from the box. She saw how his hands shook as he lit it.

'Rachel was my miracle,' he said quietly. 'She was the best thing that ever happened to me. I never knew why she loved me – couldn't see it at all. I'm awkward, clumsy, and I find it hard to say what I mean. I couldn't see why someone like her should love someone like me.'

There was a long silence. Tears stung the corners of Katherine's eyes. But there was something she had to know.

'Hector,' she said. '*Why* did Rachel go back to Bellingford early?'

He looked up. 'I've no idea. No idea at all.'

After he left Liv's cottage, Felix, filled with a black anger, had at first intended never to go back. Whatever they had once felt for each other – and now, looking back, their friendship seemed slight – was over, done with. She had made plain to him how much she despised his way of life. She had also made it clear that he was not welcome at the cottage. He had been a fool to think that he could pick up where they had left off. He would put her out of his mind, he told himself.

He tried hard at first, working overtime at the bank, filling the evenings with long hours spent in pubs and wine bars. But she would not let him go. Any empty moment, and he'd find himself envisaging her face, remembering her voice. Recalling the softness of her skin beneath his fingertip when he had swept the fragment of leaf from her nose, and the narrowness of her waist as he had helped her down from the stool. As the weeks passed, it occurred to him that he, after all, had been the first to offer criticism. That he had ignited the quarrel. *Isn't it rather boring?* he had said, when she had told him about her job at the pub. The arrogance of it. The arrogance of reappearing uninvited in her life, and presuming to judge her.

In a pub in Leicester Square, he ran into Toby Walsh. Toby hailed him as an old friend, and suggested they lunch together. Felix went one midday to the shop in the King's Road at which Toby worked. His parents owned it, Toby explained, as he showed Felix round, but he had managed it for the last few years. It was crammed with soft furnishings and old farmhouse tables and dressers. 'Well, not *precisely* old,' Toby said airily. The dressers and tables were made in a disused railway shed in Swindon. Toby himself sourced the old pine – vast bedsteads, he explained, that sort of thing, far too big for modern houses – and had them transformed into decorative dressers and tables and corner cupboards.

'And the textiles?' asked Felix, eyeing the murkily coloured, hand-printed fabrics that festooned the walls. They reminded him of something, but he could not immediately place the memory.

'Oh, they come from all over the place,' said Toby. 'I get them made up into cushion covers, tablecloths, aprons.' He grinned. 'So that fashionable Chelsea housewives can indulge their rural fantasies while remaining safely in the city.'

It was not until he was going home that evening that Felix managed to pinpoint the fleeting memory. Crammed between other commuters in a crowded carriage, he saw, clearly in his mind's eye, a length of fabric swaying in the breeze from an open window. Greys and purplish-pinks and ochre yellows. Poppy and sea lavender, and the pale, fleshy stems of samphire.

*

He took a day off work, and drove back to north Norfolk. Some time during the last week, winter had got a grip, and the sky was lost in a landscape greyed and blurred with fog. The fog had frozen overnight, so that the road was glazed black and treacherous.

He timed his visit carefully. Liv worked in a pub at lunch-time, and had to pick up the children after school. Twoish, he thought. A reasonable time of day.

In the end, he reached the turning to Samphire Cottage just as Liv was climbing off her bicycle to open the gate. He saw her turn and stare at the car. He waited for her. Give her the choice, he thought. If she turned her back on him and went into the house regardless, he'd know he hadn't a chance.

But she parked the bike against the gate, and crossed the grass to him. She was muffled up in woollen hat and scarf. 'Felix,' she said.

'I'm sorry.' He got out of the car. 'Once again. Turning up unannounced.'

'It doesn't matter.' She was holding her bag in her gloved hands. He saw how she twisted the straps between her fingers as she spoke. Then she said, 'Do you want to come in?'

'I wondered how long you had,' he said, 'before picking the girls up from school.'

She glanced at her watch. 'They're playing with friends today, so I don't have to get them till five.'

'You see, I thought you might like to come for a drive.'

'A drive?'

'I wanted to show you something.'

She had twisted the leather straps into a knot. But then, between the folds of wool around her face, a sudden bright smile, and she said, 'That would be lovely, Felix,' and his heart lifted.

Driving out of the village, he said, 'About the other week ... what I said to you ... so damnably arrogant. I wanted to apologize.'

'It's me who should be apologizing.'

'No. The nerve of it, barging in and telling you how to run your life—'

'I didn't know that your father's business had folded.' Her voice interrupted him, and he fell silent. 'I didn't know, Felix. When I found out, I felt awful. So tactless of me.'

He drove in silence for a while, and then he said, 'Why should you know?'

'No reason. But I could have asked, couldn't I?'

The corners of his mouth twisted. 'I suppose we could quarrel again . . . over which of us has the most cause to apologize.'

She touched his hand. 'Quits,' she said.

He smiled. 'You have a forgiving nature, Liv.'

'Tell me what happened,' she said.

'The factory?' He slowed, careful where black ice lingered on the surface of the tarmac. 'My father couldn't make the payments on a loan. So Corcoran's went bust.'

'How awful. How awful for your father.'

'It nearly killed him.' He told her about his father's heart attack. 'It's OK,' he said quickly, seeing her expression. 'He pulled through. They didn't think he would, at first, but he showed them all.' He flicked on the windscreen wipers to clear away the mist that blurred the frozen landscape. 'Dad and Mia are living in Norwich now,' he explained. 'Mia's got a secretarial job.'

They had driven inland, through the lush, rolling countryside of Norfolk. Like a thin covering of glass, ice encased the bushes in the hedgerows. Around the streams, the reeds had frozen, and were fringed with sharp white fragments of frost.

'Not far now.' He smiled to himself. 'Almost there.'

They headed down the familiar curving sweep of narrow road, where the silvery grey trunks of the beech trees stood like sentries by the gate. Felix parked the car. Opening the passenger door for Liv, he said, 'Just a bit of a walk.'

They headed down the drive. When she glimpsed the roof of the house, its red muted by the fog, she said, 'Who lives here? Are they friends of yours?'

Felix shook his head. 'No one's here just now. The family

who own the house use it as a weekend cottage.' He could not keep the acid from his voice. He dug his hands into his pockets and, walking fast, said, 'You don't get to know a house, living like that, do you? You don't get to *love* a house.'

Their breath made white clouds in the cold air. She was silent for a moment, her footsteps echoing his, and then she said, 'It's yours, isn't it? It's your house.'

'*Was* our house.' He paused as they reached the front court-yard, looking up at doors, windows, gables. 'Dad put it up as collateral. So we lost Wyatts, as well.'

He heard her say, 'I'm so sorry, Felix,' and he said quickly, 'I'm not asking for sympathy. That wasn't why I brought you here. It's just that I wanted to talk to you about something, and I thought I could explain it better if you saw Wyatts.'

He led her round the side of the house. Frost greyed the box hedges, carving them into monoliths of granite. The fountain in the centre of the ornamental pond was frozen. He thought that if he looked hard enough he might see the golden shimmer of a carp, stilled in the ice, waiting for the thaw.

'It's beautiful,' she whispered. He saw her gaze drift from the rose garden to the meadow to the fringe of woodland that marked the garden's boundary.

'Let me show you round the house,' he said.

'*Felix* . . .'

He heard the nervousness in her voice, but he had already found the window latch that, if you twisted it a particular way, gave access to the lobby at the back of the gable.

'Felix,' she whispered again.

He opened the window. 'It's all right,' he said. 'We won't leave so much as a footprint. We won't take more than a breath of air.' He swung himself through the open window.

'You seem rather good at this,' she said. He thought that she was laughing. 'Do you make a habit of it?'

Reaching out to help her, he recalled Corcoran's and the pattern blocks. 'I suppose I have, recently.'

She scrambled inside. He led her through rooms and passageways. He told her about his grandfather, Silas Corcoran, who had built the house, and about Edward Lutyens who had designed it. He showed her the room in which he and Rose had been born, the room to which they had taken his mother home after her death.

At the front of the house was a tall, arched window. The jewelled colours of the stained glass gleamed in the panels, forming into figures, flowers, and a distant, fanciful castle.

Liv smiled. 'Snow White and Rose Red.'

'Well done.'

'It's Freya's favourite story, but it always makes her cry.' She ran her fingers slowly across the glass. He saw how the colours reflected on to her pale skin: gold, azure and blood-red. She said, 'What was it you wanted to talk to me about?'

He told her about his visit to Toby's shop. And how he had gone back there a week later, and described to Toby the textiles he had seen hanging up in the lean-to in Samphire Cottage.

'He says you'll need to use a silkscreen. That would avoid the lumpiness of the lino cut. He'd take things on a sale-or-return basis at first, so there'd be no risk.'

'Felix, what are you saying?'

'That I help you sell some of your prints.'

Her eyes widened. 'Through Toby's shop?'

'Yes. Why not?'

She listed all the reasons why not. Because it wouldn't work. Because people in Chelsea wouldn't want to buy her clumsy, amateurish designs. Because there must be lots and lots of people who were more skilled than she.

'Let me try,' he said. 'Why not? What's there to lose?'

'Nothing, I suppose. Only ... *why*? If it works, it'll be marvellous for *me*, but ...'

'What's in it for me?' He looked out through the window, down to the avenue of beech trees, and thought of the answers he might have given her. 'Because it'll give me a pretext for seeing you,' he might have said, or, 'Because I love you.'

335

But instead he said, 'Because something may come of it. I've a hunch that it might work. For both of us, I mean. You see, my father's only sixty-one. That's not *old*. With luck, he should have another ten or twenty years. That'll be long enough.'

'Long enough for what?'

His lashes lowered, blurring the coloured panels into a mist of garish colours. 'Long enough to make money,' he said. 'Long enough to get *this* back.' He pressed his palm against the stained-glass window, as if by doing so, he could draw back all the memories encased inside.

Katherine spent Christmas with her family. Her eldest brother, Michael, had brought his fiancée, Sarah, who was also a doctor. Simon was accompanied by his girlfriend, Coralie. She was small and curly-haired and big-eyed; squeezing into the crowded kitchen, she lisped, 'Room for a little 'un?' and Katherine had to bite back a sarcastic remark.

Katherine was sneaking a quick pre-lunch cigarette in her bedroom when Simon knocked at the door.

He collapsed on the bed beside her. 'It still feels furtive, doesn't it, smoking in the parental house?'

Katherine grinned. 'I used to spray Aqua Manda all over my room to disguise the smell.'

'If you give me one of your fags, Kitty,' said Simon, 'I'll tell you a secret.'

She tossed the packet to him. He said, 'Sarah's pregnant. Turn-up for the books, eh?'

'Are you sure?'

'Mmm. She was puking in the car on the way up.' Simon tapped ash into the wastepaper basket. 'Rather Michael than me, anyway. She's a bit broad in the beam, isn't she?'

'At least Sarah's grown-up,' said Katherine, rather sharply.

Simon grinned. 'Coco's eighteen.'

'*Coco*. Honestly, Simon.'

'And she's terribly obliging. Doesn't seem to have heard of women's lib.'

'Honestly, Simon,' she said again.

After lunch, Katherine drove to a phone-box a mile away. She and Jordan had a routine at Christmas: solitary outings after the Queen's speech, then a phone-call in the privacy of a public telephone kiosk.

Katherine dialled the number of the phone-box where Jordan would be waiting. Though it rang and rang, there was no reply. Eventually someone rapped on the window, and she went back to her car. When the phone was free again, she tried once more, but with no success. She imagined Jordan impatient, eager to leave the house, prevented in making his escape by the demands of his relatives. Or Tricia, perhaps, insisting on walking the dog with him. *I'll just get my coat, darling . . .*

Of course, there were other possibilities. Sitting in the car, staring out of the windscreen, Katherine wondered whether he had simply forgotten. Caught up with his wife and his child, Jordan's obligation to his mistress had simply slipped his mind. Or, worse, he had remembered, and had looked out of the window, had seen the rain, and had decided to put off the task until the weather had improved. Katherine wondered whether, the next time he saw her, Jordan would give her another present. She wondered whether the silk shirts, the earrings were consolation prizes, to assuage his guilt.

She started up the car, driving aimlessly in no particular direction. Rain trailed down the windscreen. She wondered what Jordan would say if she were to tell him she wanted a child. Once, she might have believed that he would understand, sympathize. Now, she imagined how his voice would chill, and how the grey of his eyes would turn to ice.

And if she quietly, silently, stopped taking the Pill, what then? If she were to give birth to their child, would he love and welcome it? She knew that he would not. A child was an ineradicable proof of infidelity. It could not be hidden away, could not convincingly be denied.

She realized that she had reached Fernhill. She parked the car by the side of the road. The direction of her thoughts shocked her. You're just feeling maudlin, she told herself. You don't really want a baby. You're only thinking like that because of Sarah, and because you've become fond of Alice. Babies cost a huge amount of money. They ruin your career, they clutter up your flat, and take away your looks, your prospects, and your independence. Just think of Liv. Just think of Rachel. And, besides, it's Jordan you love, not some imaginary baby.

Katherine got out of the car, and walked through the village. It was years since she had been to Fernhill. The changes took her by surprise. There was a neo-Georgian housing estate wedged between the school and the village hall, and the field with the dew-pond was now a building site. The local shop had closed down, and outside the terraced cottage in which Liv and Thea had once lived there were carriage lamps and a carport.

She reached Fernhill Grange. She knew that Hector had invited Henry Wyborne to spend Christmas with him and Alice, and that Henry had refused. She supposed that he was spending Christmas with friends. Staring through the gates, looking up the driveway, Katherine saw that it was empty of cars. On impulse she opened the gate. She felt both daring and lawless, invading the manicured privacy.

And yet, looking around her, she saw that Fernhill Grange wasn't perfect any more. There was a discarded Coke bottle by the side of the drive; it seemed almost blasphemous, so she picked it up. Dried brown flowerheads lingered on the roses, and the lawn needed cutting. Katherine remembered how, visiting the house as a child, she had both envied and despised the Wybornes. Now she looked through different eyes, and saw only a place of mourning, lonely and desolate.

Looking up to the house, she glimpsed a flicker of movement

behind a window. Then the door opened. Henry Wyborne said, 'How can I help you, Miss Constant?'

Her heart was pounding, and she found herself holding up the Coke bottle and saying, 'This was on the lawn.'

He took it from her, dropping it into the dustbin beside the garage. 'They come into the grounds sometimes, when they think I'm away. Youths ... yobs from the village ... I telephone the police, but they're useless, of course.' Henry made as if to return indoors. Then he glanced back at Katherine. 'Would you like a drink? After all, it is Christmas Day, isn't it?'

Surprised, she followed him into the house. Inside, she failed to disguise her sudden indrawing of breath. Dirty cups and plates littered the occasional tables and hearth. Old newspapers shrouded the armchairs and sofas.

Henry Wyborne said, 'Not exactly *Good Housekeeping*, is it? Mrs Whatshername from the village doesn't come any more. Better wages in the supermarket.'

Staring at the chaos, Katherine blurted out, 'But couldn't you—' and then she remembered Jordan's ineptitude with any household task, any domestic appliance.

But Henry Wyborne was regarding her with a beady, contemptuous eye. 'Turn my hand to a spot of vacuuming? I don't think so, Katherine – you don't mind if I call you Katherine, do you? After all, I remember you in a school uniform, with your hair in pigtails. And I may not be entirely in favour with our new leader, but I don't think I need descend to being a Mrs Mop quite yet.'

There was an unstoppered bottle of Scotch on the sideboard in the drawing-room; Henry Wyborne poured out two measures. He handed Katherine a glass, and motioned her to sit down. After a few polite, uninterested enquiries about her health and career, he said, 'Hector mentioned you, I believe.'

'I see Hector and Alice quite often now. Alice is doing awfully well at school.' She felt oddly nervous. She was longing to leave.

'Hector will insist on writing me long screeds about the child. A misplaced sense of duty, I suppose.'

She stared at him. 'But – *Alice*. She's your only grandchild, Rachel's daughter.'

'You seem expert at stating the obvious, Katherine.'

Yet she ploughed on, ignoring the sarcasm. It had occurred to her that there was something she could do, some advantage to be salvaged from the embarrassment of this encounter.

'Hector still feels guilty about Rachel,' she said.

Henry Wyborne's back was to her as he refilled his glass. He gave a small shrug. She could have been talking, Katherine thought, about the weather, or the price of potatoes. She began to feel angry. 'Didn't you know?'

'Hector's state of mind is no concern of mine. He must consult a psychiatrist, if he wishes to relieve it.' A fleeting smile. 'Or take to the bottle, like me.'

'There's something you could do.'

'Do you think so?'

There was a dangerous edge to his voice, but Katherine ploughed on. 'Something you could do for Hector.'

'But do I wish to, Katherine? Do I care?'

She swallowed. 'He is your son-in-law. He is Alice's father.'

'I've made it clear to Hector that I have no further claim on the child. I have discharged my debt, I believe.'

'You see, Hector thinks that it was his fault Rachel died.' Katherine's knuckles were white as they gripped her glass. 'But I've wondered whether there were things he didn't know about. Whether there was some sort of quarrel, for instance.'

A family quarrel was the obvious explanation for Rachel's sudden return to Bellingford. An argument with her parents and, distraught, she had left Fernhill. When Rachel had arrived home, she had phoned her friends, needing their comfort and advice.

'Hector told me,' she explained, 'that Rachel had driven back to Bellingford on her own. I presumed there'd been some sort of family argument.'

'You presume too much, Miss Constant.' There was a warning in the words, but she disregarded it.

'Only I think it might help Hector if he knew.'

Henry Wyborne's face had paled and his eyes had hardened. Katherine heard herself talking fast and loud to fill in the treacherous silence. 'Then he might stop thinking it was all his fault. If he properly understood what had happened. Of course, it was no one's fault, really, but you always feel dreadful, don't you?, if someone asks for help and you don't give it to them for one reason or another, and then when something awful happens, you . . .' Faced with the anger in his eyes, she whispered, 'I'm right, aren't I?'

Henry Wyborne glanced at his watch. 'I don't wish to hurry you, Miss Constant, but I have an engagement.'

His shadow fell over her. He was a tall and powerfully built man, and she was surprised to feel a frisson of fear. But for Hector, and for Rachel, she persevered. She forced herself to meet his eyes. 'I can't think why you won't admit it. All families quarrel. It's normal to quarrel.'

'I said, I don't wish to rush you, but . . .'

In his eyes, she saw rage, dislike, and something else – she was not sure what. Guilt? Grief?

'You don't have to hide it, you know. Every family falls out from time to time.'

'You shouldn't judge others by your own standards.'

'There's nothing to be ashamed of.'

'Get out.' Henry Wyborne's voice was very soft, very controlled. 'Get out.'

Katherine rose from her seat. Her legs were shaking. As she walked out of the house and down the drive, she found herself questioning whether the high wrought-iron railings and the long, curving driveway were to keep the rest of the world out or to fence the Wyborne family in.

Alice had settled in well at her new school. She wore a uniform of a royal blue jersey and a plaid pleated skirt, and a royal blue hat and coat. Hector took her to school each morning then went straight on to the bookshop. At four o'clock in the afternoon, he collected Alice and took her back with him to the shop, where she would sit in his office, reading a book or crayoning, until he closed at half past five.

In the course of the ten months she had lived with him, Hector had grown used to her likes and dislikes. He always remembered to cut off her crusts and give her a straw with her drinks; he had learned to let her choose her own clothes for the day, and to be patient with her small routines. At a parents' evening, Alice's form teacher suggested he make a scrapbook. 'You could put in pictures of Alice's mother and grandmother, Mr Seton,' Mrs Tavistock suggested. 'And photographs of the houses she has lived in and places she has been on holiday. It would be an acknowledgement of what she has lost, and it may help her feel more secure.' Hector was initially doubtful, and said so. Mrs Tavistock said, 'Perhaps you should ask Alice's opinion, Mr Seton.'

Hector asked; they made the scrapbook. There were photographs of Henry and Diana Wyborne, and of Rachel. Rachel at school, Rachel in her wedding-dress, and a photograph of a very pregnant Rachel, taken during the last week of her life: he crushed back the memories, and gave Alice a quick, rather tangled explanation of babies and mummies' tummies. A picture of Fernhill Grange went into the scrapbook too, and Hector dug out from the back of a drawer a blurred black and white of Bellingford. Alice stared at it, and said, 'But it's a castle, Daddy!' Hector blinked, remembering Rachel saying just the same thing on her first sight of Bellingford.

In a stack of letters held together with an elastic band, he found a photograph of Rachel, Katherine and Liv. He showed it to Katherine.

She shrieked. 'Rachel's wedding! Oh, *God*. I look so *fat*!'

'No, you don't. You look very fetching. I like the boots.'

'You can't possibly put that in Alice's scrapbook.'

'Yes, we can, can't we, Alice?' Hector handed the photograph to Alice, who stuck it on to a page.

He conceded that the scrapbook had been a good idea: it

seemed to give Alice something solid to refer to, a substance to events she had not followed, could not understand. He wondered whether he would take her one day to Bellingford. He shrank away from the idea, recalling the day he had left it, a couple of months after Rachel's death. He imagined how the felting of dust and cobwebs must make only a thin covering for his memories.

In February, there was a spell of cold weather, when frost lingered throughout the day. Waiting outside school to collect Alice, Hector had to turn up the collar of his coat, and blow against his chilled fingers.

Alice was late coming out of school and, after a trail of little Samanthas and Lucys and Emmas had left the building, Hector began to look at his watch, to peer around corners, to check the street, anxious that he had missed her. Then he saw her, burdened with her satchel and shoe-bag and some enormous and cumbersome piece of art.

He kissed her cheek. 'What on earth is that, sweetheart?'

Egg boxes, loo-roll tubes and pieces of macaroni had been painted and glued to a large sheet of sugar paper. 'It's a monster, Daddy.' Alice pointed with a small, gloved finger. 'Those are the eyes and that's the mouth.'

'It's fearsome,' he said. 'Most fearsome.'

She glanced up at him. 'Can we walk through the park?'

Sometimes, as a treat, when they had time, they took a detour through Regent's Park.

'I'm a bit late, Alice.'

'*Please*, Daddy.'

'Oh, all right, if you like.'

She clapped her hands with glee. In the park, he walked quickly, carrying Alice's satchel and shoe-bag. Alice insisted on carrying the monster herself. Hector glanced now and then at his watch. One of his regular customers was due to call at five, to inspect a book of Audubon prints he had recently acquired.

Alice had trailed behind; he heard her call out to him, and he swung round, waiting for her to catch up.

'Hurry up, love!'

He was never sure exactly what happened – the icy path, her clumpy school shoes, the wretched picture – but she slipped and fell backwards. He heard the crack as her head struck the path. He expected screams, sobs. But there was silence. She just lay there, motionless on the path, a small heap of royal blue and plaid.

He began to run. Reaching her, he saw that her eyes were closed. His shaking fingers could not immediately find her pulse. All he could think was, Dear God, not again. Dear God, not again.

He found a pulse at last, beating regularly at the side of her jaw. He wanted to weep. He felt sick. He scooped her up in his arms. He had a vague idea that you were not supposed to move an injured person, but he could not bear to leave her lying on the cold asphalt. Hugging her to him, he ran to the exit from the park. His legs were infuriatingly weak, slowing his pace. Out in the street, he flagged down a taxi, and told the driver to take him to the nearest hospital. In the cab, he felt the lump at the back of her head. When he took his hand away from Alice's matted hair, his fingertips were scarlet. He could see himself shaking.

He thought of all the worst things. That she should die. That she should suffer brain damage, like Katherine's brother. Though he hadn't prayed since Rachel's death, he prayed now. He thought that if this accident were to have some terrible, permanent effect on her, then it would be a punishment to him for not having understood sooner just how much he loved her. For having taken so long to understand how lucky he had been to be given a second chance.

But then she stirred, and whispered, 'Daddy?'

'Alice.' She had opened her eyes. 'Alice, are you all right?'

'My head hurts.'

'You banged it, darling. The doctor'll make it better.'

They had reached the hospital. Hector paid the cabbie, and carried Alice into the casualty department. Then he had to wait for half an hour as Alice sat, subdued and shivering on his lap, cradled against him.

'Mild concussion,' the doctor said, 'and she's a bit shocked.' Then he put a couple of stitches in the cut on the back of Alice's head. Alice cried, and buried her forehead into Hector's chest, as if to hide from the pain.

That evening, he stayed by her bedside until she slept, and then he went into the living room and poured himself a Scotch. He thought of how he had cut himself off from everyone after Rachel's death, and how it had been Alice who had taught him to feel again. To love again. He knew that, after so many years in the desert, to love again was almost unbearable. It frightened him. He knew only too well that with love came the possibility of loss, making him, once more, in thrall to chance. He sat, listening to the sounds of the traffic, his fingers gripped against the cold, hard glass, feeling the protective layers fall away, feeling as though he had been flayed.

Chapter Fifteen

Liv ordered books from the mobile library, and read up about silkscreen printing. Felix arrived one weekend, his car packed with rolls of cloth and slats of wood, and built a silkscreen on the kitchen table. After he had gone, she wrestled with the cumbersome and temperamental contraption. By the end of the weekend, she had printed a length of material. The colours were smooth and even and clear. Over the next few weeks, she made cushion covers and tablecloths, mats and aprons. A cheque arrived in the post from Toby. Cashing it, holding the banknotes in her hand, she felt a glow of pride.

The winter deepened. Outdoors, waves lashed against the pebbled beach, and the wind made the willows bend and moan. Indoors, yellow poppies flourished against a lichen-green background, and the spiky flowers of sea holly bloomed like pewter stars. Between herself and Felix she thought that there existed a sort of truce: a mutual, unvoiced agreement to talk only of the practical, the present day, to avoid contentious and painful memories.

Late one February afternoon, they walked along the beach, following the lacy edge of the shore. The sea sucked at the pebbles, rolling them round, spitting them out.

'Sometimes there are seals,' she told him. 'They look like mermaids, I always think. Sea-green girls with great, dark eyes.'

'You like it here, don't you?'

'I love it.' Georgie and Freya ran ahead, stooping to pick up a frond of seaweed, a bone-white length of driftwood. 'We lived in such awful places before we found Samphire Cottage. You wouldn't believe how awful.'

'Worse than Beckett Street?'

'Much worse. Beckett Street had a kitchen sink and a bath and an inside loo.'

'And silverfish and mould.'

She laughed. The wind had picked up, throwing grains of sand in their faces. Georgie leaned back against the gale, her arms outstretched, roaring with laughter.

'At first,' Liv said, 'I thought it would be best never to live anywhere for more than six months – never to *settle* – but you can't do that with children, can you? Then I wondered whether to go and live with my mother in Crete – she asked me, you see – but that's no safer, is it? Stefan would find me there. You think that the world's a big place, but then you realize that it's all bound together with planes and boats and phones and things. And, besides, I had to learn to manage on my own.'

'So you settled for Samphire Cottage?'

'Yes. Anyway, I began to understand how impossible it is to remain anonymous. You have to register children at schools and playgroups, don't you, and with doctors? So your name goes on lists.' She frowned. 'If Stefan looked for us, he could find us, Felix, I know he could.'

'Perhaps he no longer wants to.'

She remembered Stefan's arm curling around Sheila's neck. Sheila's taut, flung-back throat. *I'll do anything to get you back, Liv, anything at all.*

She heard Felix say, 'Will you get a divorce?'

'I can't. Not yet. Unless both of you consent, you have to live apart for five years. Stefan and I have only been separated for three and a half.'

'But after that?'

'I don't know.' She looked out to sea. 'What I do know is that I'll never marry again.' She twisted her fingers together. 'The greatest lesson Stefan taught me is the importance of independence. Of having my own money. Without that, you don't have choices.' She turned to him, and on impulse, she hooked her cold hand through his arm. 'That's why I'm so grateful for what you've done for me, Felix. To be able to earn money from something I enjoy – what could be better?'

'What would you think of a partnership?'

She glanced at him. 'You and me?'

'Yes. It's not a hobby any more, is it, Liv? You've made money from it. Time to move on, go on to the next stage.' He looked down at her briefly, and then his gaze shifted back to the waves, crashing against the shore. Suddenly there was passion in the green-gold eyes. 'I've been thinking about it for some time. There's a huge market for the sort of textiles you design, Liv. I know there is. It's just a question of tapping into it.'

Above her, seagulls shrieked as they glided on the updrafts. She felt a bubble of excitement inside her, a premonition of change, of possibility.

'We'd have to have a name,' he said. 'Galenski and Corcoran ... Corcoran and Galenski ...'

'No.'

'Stefan,' he said, understanding instantly. 'Of course.'

'And, anyway,' she said, 'Corcoran and Galenski is far too long and cumbersome. Something shorter, simpler, would be better.' She hugged her arms around her, looking up at him.

'Something that sums up our image ...'

'*Image*.' She wanted to laugh. 'Will we have an image, Felix?'

'Of course we will.' The corners of his mouth curled. His long lashes were beaded with seaspray. He looked ahead, to the long strip of pebble beach. 'I see us as romantic ... nostalgic ... rural ...'

'Fields of buttercups ...'

'Waves on the seashore ...'

'Hedgerows,' she said, delight in her voice.

'"Briar Rose",' said Felix. 'What do you think, Liv?'

'Briar Rose ...' She spoke the words softly, smiling as she repeated them over and over. 'Briar Rose.'

*

The disturbing recollection of her conversation with Henry Wyborne drifted to the back of Katherine's mind, put aside but not forgotten. The present preoccupied her. The evenings she spent with Jordan, which had once been her private delight, seemed to be going wrong. Often, they quarrelled. They had quarrelled before, of course, but had always made it up, the passion of their reconciliation erasing the memory of the quarrel. Now the bad feelings lingered and grated.

In late spring, Jordan suggested that they go out for a day. A whole day all to themselves, he said. They could drive to the countryside, to the New Forest, perhaps, and dine somewhere before returning to London. He looked pleased with himself, proud of himself, as he offered her the gift of his company, a special treat to keep her content for the next few months. It had not, Katherine thought, occurred to him that she might refuse. A spirit of contrariness made her want to say, 'No, sorry, Jordan, I can't.' Just to see the expression on his face. But she did not, of course, and he arranged to pick her up the following Saturday.

The day started badly. Jordan was late, and did not arrive at her flat until midday. Constituency business, he explained. He looked cross. Katherine suggested they abandon the New Forest and head for somewhere nearer. 'Certainly not,' he said. He had promised her the New Forest, so they would go to the New Forest. He pressed his foot on the Jaguar's accelerator, and they roared out of town.

An hour or so up the road, they both began to feel hungry. Because it was already early afternoon, Jordan didn't want to make a detour into a nearby town. They would find somewhere on the road, he said. The succession of pubs and cafés that, until then, had been quite frequent seemed to peter out. The few remaining places Jordan dismissed for one reason or another. 'Too grim' – a Copper Kettle with red gingham curtains. 'Too public' – a large roadhouse with a dozen expensive cars parked outside. 'Unspeakable' – a tea-stall in a lay-by surrounded by rows of motorbikes. In the end, they bought cheese and pickle sandwiches and tea in styrofoam cups from a garage, and ate as they drove. The sandwiches curled at the edges, and the tea tasted metallic.

They reached Lyndhurst in the mid-afternoon. It had been drizzling on and off all day, and as they walked beneath the trees, the rain thickened. Their shoes squelched on the muddy ground, and drops of water plummeted from the overhanging branches of the oaks. They should cut their losses and dine early, Jordan suggested. Make up for the awful sandwiches.

The restaurant was a few miles out of Ringwood. 'Terribly discreet,' Jordan said, as he parked the Jaguar in the wide, gravelled drive. Katherine wondered how he knew. Was that the sort of thing he and his colleagues talked about in the bar, in their clubs? *Found a quiet little place in the country. Won't spill the beans, if you know what I mean, old chap.*

Katherine tidied herself in a ladies' room scattered with bowls of pot-pourri and boxes of pink tissues. The restaurant, with its pillars and porticoes and flights of stone steps, was designed to impress. Jordan had ordered champagne. The alcohol, the food, relaxed her a little. She found herself laughing at Jordan's scurrilous anecdotes about his colleagues; she in turn told him about the more awful typescripts sent to her publishing house.

They were finishing their pudding when he said, 'You won't stay there, Katherine, will you?'

She looked up at him, surprised. 'I don't know. Why?'

'I assumed that it was a stepping-stone. I mean, feminist books, it's rather a minority interest, isn't it?'

'Half the population,' she said crisply.

'Not all women read that sort of thing.' He shrugged. 'Some of them are rather extreme, aren't they?'

'Books that are by women for women. I don't call that extreme, Jordan.'

'You know what I mean. Lesbianism . . . obscure memoirs of eighteenth-century diarists—'

'Why shouldn't women who prefer women be able to read about others who share their feelings? And why shouldn't unknown writers be lifted out of obscurity?'

'Perhaps,' he said, 'they are deservedly obscure. Because they are second-rate.'

She put down her spoon. 'They are obscure because they are written by *women*.'

He touched her hand. 'Don't be cross with me, darling – I was only trying to understand.'

'And some of the memoirs are wonderful,' she said furiously. 'So touching.'

'It just seems to me that when there are so many more pressing problems in the world, you're wasting your talents on – on sidelines.'

'*Sidelines*,' she repeated, so loudly that the diners of the adjacent table turned to stare at her. She made herself speak more quietly. 'What can be more pressing than the right of one half of the population to be equal to the other?'

'Oh, come on, darling.' He signalled to the waiter to bring the coffee. 'Your little publishing house can't solve the problems of the whole world.'

'We don't try to solve the problems of the world. I'm not that naïve. We try and do what we can to make things a bit better in our own corner of the world.'

'The vote ... changes to the divorce laws ... legal abortion ... the Pill ... equal pay ...' He ticked them off on his fingers. 'Surely all the battles have been won?'

She took out her cigarettes. 'When there is a woman chief constable ... or when half the High Court judges are women ... or half the Members of Parliament ... then the battle might be *won*, Jordan!'

He lit her cigarette. He said, 'My job's not that enviable, you know. Unsociable hours, too much travelling.'

'Why do it, then?'

He gave a crooked smile. 'To serve my country?'

She thought of Henry Wyborne. 'That's not *all*, is it, Jordan?'

He caught her hand. 'Of course not.'

'You enjoy power, don't you?'

'I admit it, I do.' He signalled to the waiter, who brought him

351

the bill. Writing the cheque, he said softly, 'Do you condemn me for that, Katherine?'

'Of course not.' She found herself studying him. He was forty-one now, and his brown hair was greying at the temples. There was a mesh of fine lines around his heavily lidded eyes. None of the metaphors for their colour were ever quite right, she thought. Steel ... iron ... granite ... All were commonplace and inaccurate. Their grey reminded her of the pale, opaque ice that lingered in winter at the edges of pools and lakes. She wondered whether that was what had attracted her to him, the challenge of that cool, controlled exterior; her private knowledge of the passion that lay beneath it. Whether that was what brought her back to him, time and again, despite their differences, despite the limitations of their relationship.

He said, 'What are you thinking of?' and she said, 'Nothing. Nothing at all.' She did not know why she felt so sad. They went out into the foyer, and he helped her on with her coat. Outside, the cold evening air took her breath away.

In the car, he started up the ignition, and said, 'There, that was nice, wasn't it?'

There, that was nice. As if the evening had been a treat for a difficult child. A sop to a nagging wife. She wondered whether he was the same with Tricia. Gifts and outings to compensate for the gaps between. She wondered whether he could not see the aching gaps that had yawned between them throughout the day.

She had the sudden irresistible desire to hurt him, to jolt him out of his complacency. She said, 'You never answered my question, Jordan. What matters are more pressing than the equality of women?'

He put the car into overdrive as they headed along a long, straight road. He liked to drive fast. He said, 'The appalling state of the economy, obviously. Inflation's still out of control.'

'You're the politician, Jordan,' she taunted him. 'You're the one with the power. Shouldn't you be putting things right?'

'We're in opposition, darling, remember. At the moment, all

we can do is to complain a little. Which is infuriating and frustrating, like wading through treacle.'

'Though things weren't exactly hunky-dory when the Conservatives were last in, were they?'

'Heath hadn't the right ideas. Too weak and shilly-shallying. We needed a change of leader. A stronger leader.'

'And you think Margaret Thatcher's the right person for the job?'

'I don't know. I must admit, I had misgivings at first.'

'Because she's a woman?'

'I suppose so.'

'You don't think women can be strong?'

He said, exasperated, 'Katherine, someone's going to have to take some very difficult decisions. Just now, the country's going to Hell on a handcart.' His brow was furrowed. 'We need a change of air,' he muttered. 'Things have been too easy for too long. We've become lazy and comfortable and soft. I don't care whether the Party's led by man, woman or beast, as long as whoever it is is prepared to be ruthless. As long as they'll do what has to be done.'

'Another Social Contract?' she said derisively.

'Of course not. The only cure for inflation – the only way to damp down the power of the unions – is to have higher unemployment.'

It was quite dark now. They were heading down a narrow country road. The branches of the trees met overhead, shifting in the wind, blocking out the inky sky.

She said, '*Deliberately* raise unemployment? You can't mean that, Jordan.'

'Why not?'

'Frighten people, so that they don't ask for higher wages?'

'It's the only way, Katherine.'

'That's immoral, Jordan.' Her voice shook with anger. 'Cruel and ruthless and immoral.'

'Then what do you suggest?' He was contemptuous. 'Go on as we are now?'

'There must be another way.'

'I don't think so. People have become too greedy, too grasping.'

She thought of the restaurant: the porcelain and the silver-ware, the silent, unobtrusive waiters. She said angrily, 'Putting men out of work means condemning their wives and children to poverty as well.'

'They won't be begging on the streets, Katherine. We have a benefit system.'

'Subsistence level, Jordan, and you know it. *You* couldn't live on unemployment benefit, could you?'

The car swerved, too fast, around a corner. She needed another cigarette; her bag was on the back seat. She unbuckled her seat-belt to reach it.

He said, 'I don't put myself in the position where I might have to.'

'Because of Tricia.' She searched for her lighter. It seemed to be out of fuel; she flicked it over and over again. 'You couldn't afford your flat in London, your house in Hertfordshire, your holidays in Tuscany, this car, without Tricia, could you?' She knew that she was about to say something unforgivable, but could not stop herself. 'You couldn't afford *me* without Tricia, could you, Jordan?'

'What the hell do you mean?' One of his hands slipped from the wheel as he shot an angry glance at her.

'The presents ... the jewellery ... Do you pay for them, Jordan, or does Tricia?'

'For God's sake, Katherine!'

She was shaking. The lighter still wouldn't work. She felt as though something long suppressed was boiling over inside her. Then, glancing out of the windscreen, she saw the fallen branch that lay across the road. She heard herself cry out. Jordan wrenched at the steering-wheel as he jabbed his foot on the brake. There was a squeal of tyres and she was flung against the dashboard.

When the car came to a halt she was in the footwell, her head wedged against the door. Sky and trees, glimpsed through the window, were at an odd angle. Her chest hurt, as though there was a weight on it, but when she looked down, there was only her handbag, its contents strewn around the inside of the car.

She heard Jordan say, 'Katherine? Katherine, are you all right?' She could hear the fear in his voice. 'Katherine, darling—'

'It hurts . . .' It hurt to speak; it hurt to breathe.

He had switched on the interior light and unbuckled his seat-belt. 'Katherine . . .' he whispered. 'I'm so sorry . . .' He reached across to her, but when he tried to help her out of the footwell, she cried out.

'Where does it hurt?'

'Here.' She touched her ribcage. She remembered undoing her seat-belt so that she could get her cigarettes.

Very slowly and gently, he helped her out of the footwell. She was weeping with pain by the time she was back in her seat. She gasped, 'The car . . .'

'I think the nose is in a ditch.' The Jaguar had come to a halt diagonally across the road. 'I'll have to try and push it out.'

'There was a pub back there . . . you could call a garage . . .'

'I can't do that, darling,' he said sharply. 'You know I can't do that.'

Her brain seemed to be working at half its usual speed. 'Why not?'

'I'm over the limit. The champagne – the claret. I can't involve anyone else. It's too much of a risk. If the police or the press—' Jordan pressed the heel of his hand against his forehead. 'I think it's best if you sit on the verge, darling, while I try to push the car out of the ditch. If you've broken ribs, you shouldn't be joggled about.'

He helped her out of the car. Every movement hurt. She sat on the tartan rug he laid on the grass, his overcoat wrapped around her shoulders. She breathed shallowly, so as not to disturb the pain. She was aware of the silence of the countryside, and the drip of the rain, and Jordan's bowed figure as he struggled to push the car back on to the road.

It seemed to take for ever, but then he was beside her, helping her back into the passenger seat. She could see the relief in his eyes.

'The wheels don't seem to be damaged ... There's a dent in the bonnet, but she should still be driveable, thank God.' He put the Jaguar into gear, and they started up the road. 'Seems to be OK ...' He glanced at her. 'I'll take you to one of the London hospitals. Guy's – somewhere decent. They'll take care of you, you poor darling. You'll be all right, I promise you.'

Katherine closed her eyes. Every time she dozed off, she was jolted awake by the pain in her ribs. She could not stop shivering, and that, too, hurt. At length she became aware of the smooth, fast flight of the motorway, and then the buildings crowding around them as they entered the city. The last bit was awful, as the car stopped and started at traffic lights, gathered up speed then slowed down again. She wanted to lie down. She wanted something to kill the pain. She wanted to be warm again, to be able to sleep, to blot out the remembrance of this day.

She heard him say, 'Here we are.' He was stooping beside her, gathering up her things and putting them into her handbag. He took out his wallet. 'Here's some cash, for a taxi.' He tucked several notes into her purse.

She stared at him. He said patiently, 'I can't come in with you, you know that, don't you, sweetheart? I'm so sorry, but I just can't. You do understand, don't you?'

He drove to the entrance to the hospital, and she climbed out of the car. She did not look back as she walked alone into the hospital. She heard the purr of the engine as he drove away.

Two hours later, an exhausted-looking junior doctor told her that she had three cracked ribs. 'You can take painkillers, but otherwise it's just rest and time, I'm afraid. I'll see if I can find a bed for you, Miss Constant.'

'I'd rather go home.'

'We should keep an eye on you. There may be shock.'

'Really, I'd rather go home.'

He sighed. 'Very well. If that's what you prefer.' He looked down at his notes. 'Have you someone to take care of you?'

'My mother,' she lied.

'And you said you received these injuries falling downstairs?' He looked embarrassed. 'Are you quite sure about that, Miss Constant? One would expect more general bruising with a fall. Were you alone when you had the accident?'

'Quite alone,' she said firmly. It was only when she was in the taxi, going home, that she understood the implication of his questions. The battered wife ... the abused woman. Katherine closed her eyes, shutting out the city, sick with pain and humiliation.

Jordan telephoned the day after the accident. Katherine lied to him, as she had lied to the doctor, telling him that she was going home to her parents. 'Well,' he said, 'if you're sure you'll be all right?' She thought he sounded relieved.

She kept to her bed for the first couple of days, getting up only for slow, painful journeys to the kitchen and the bathroom. She took the painkillers that the doctor at the hospital had prescribed, and was thankful that they allowed her to sleep at night and doze much of the day. She didn't want to think yet: she knew she must do so soon, that she was only putting off the moment, but she needed the brief respite.

Hector phoned on Tuesday evening. 'You didn't come to supper,' he said. She usually went to Hector's flat after work on Monday evenings.

'I couldn't make it.'

'Oh.' There was a silence. Then he said, 'Are you all right, Katherine? Only you sound a bit funny.'

'I was in an accident,' she said. 'A car accident. But I'm all right now.' She replaced the receiver and went back to bed.

The following morning the doorbell rang. At first she ignored it, but the ringing persisted so she hauled herself out of bed. 'Who is it?' she called down the entryphone.

'It's me. Hector.'

She let him in. His eyes widened when he saw her. '*Katherine*.'

'I wasn't wearing my seat-belt. Hit the dashboard. Two lovely black eyes.' She tried to smile. 'And three broken ribs.'

Hector's glasses had steamed up; he took them off and polished them with his tie. 'I thought you might need things – food, aspirins.' He squinted at her. 'I could bring them round after work.'

'I'm all right. I don't need anything.'

'Lucozade . . . magazines?'

'I told you, Hector, I don't need anything.'

'Right.' He replaced his glasses. 'Then I'll go.'

She sat down on the sofa. When she thought he had gone, she dabbed at her eyes with the corner of her dressing-gown. Then she heard him say, 'Katherine, you're not really all right, are you?'

He was standing in the doorway. She squeezed her lids together, shutting him out. She heard the door close, and knew he had come to sit beside her. 'A car accident, you said? Horrible things. Shake you up. You think what might have happened. Was anyone else hurt?' She shook her head.

'Were you driving?'

Tears were streaming down her face, but she did not bother to staunch them. 'No.' She swallowed. 'I was with a friend.'

'And is your friend all right?'

'I think so.'

'You *think* so?'

'I haven't seen him since the accident.'

There was a silence. She opened her eyes, caught sight of the expression on his face. She thought how shallow, how *tacky* her relationship with Jordan must seem to someone like Hector. To someone who had loved openly, passionately, completely. She thought of all the deceptions, all the moral evasions that she and Jordan routinely practised, and felt bitterly ashamed.

She whispered, 'I don't want to talk about it just now.'

'Of course. Not now. Not ever, if you don't want to.' His voice was gentle, which made her want to cry again. He took a handkerchief from his pocket, and very carefully wiped the tears from her bruised face. Then he stood up and said, 'I've got to go to work now, but I'll come and see you again later, I promise.'

At half past seven that evening Hector reappeared, his arms full of carrier-bags. Mrs Zwierzanski was sitting with Alice, he explained. Mrs Zwierzanski was the widowed Polish lady who owned the flat above his. He emptied the carriers, putting the chocolates and grapes beside Katherine's bed, arranging flowers – irises, daffodils and narcissi – in a jug. He made her soup and toast, brought them to her on a tray, and sat on a chair beside the bed, telling her about the events of his day while she ate.

He came the next evening, and the next. He brought her orange squash and special ginger biscuits from Fortnum's, and tapes for her cassette player, and wonderful, crumbling old books from his shop. When her temperature shot up, and she ached, restless and miserable, unable to find any comfortable position, he helped her on to the sofa while he remade the bed. When she settled back among the smooth, clean sheets, she smiled for the first time that day. 'Hector, you are wonderful.'

'Would you like anything to eat?'

'I couldn't. But I think I might be able to sleep now.'

She closed her eyes, and when she woke the next morning, her temperature was back to normal. She rose and showered, and attempted to wash her hair. It was a slow and messy procedure, but she felt better for it. She dressed in jeans and a loose jersey, tied back her hair with an elastic band, and sat on the sofa throughout the day, reading the pile of manuscripts she had had sent to her flat.

When Hector arrived that evening, she said, 'Look. Real clothes.'

'You look better.' He smiled, and kissed her cheek, and glanced at the manuscripts. 'Good stuff?'

'A couple.' She had finished the memoir of a woman imprisoned in a Japanese camp after the fall of Singapore; and had just begun the diary of a young girl who had been subjected to years of abuse by her father. 'Haunting, some of them,' she said, with a small shiver. 'Horrifying.'

He made Welsh rabbit and a tomato salad, washed down with a glass of orange juice. She had almost finished her supper, when he said, 'Penny for 'em.'

She glanced at him, and smiled crookedly. 'My thoughts aren't worth even a penny, I'm afraid.' She took a deep breath. 'I have to learn to do without someone, you see. I know that I must – I've known for ages, I think – but I'm not sure whether I'm brave enough.'

'The driver of the car?' She nodded. Hector frowned. 'I guessed there was someone, of course.'

'I met him at your wedding,' she said, and swooped suddenly back through the years, to the bright, heady summer of 1968. 'Married, of course. He has a child.' She looked at Hector as she spoke, anticipating disapproval and censoriousness.

But he said only, 'And you fell in love with him?'

'Yes.' She bit her lip. 'Rotten luck, don't you think?'

'A year ago, I'd have agreed with you. But now . . .' He shrugged.

'"Better to have loved and lost", you mean?' she said sharply, cynically.

'I think so, don't you?'

On the spur of the moment, she said, 'I went to see Henry Wyborne last Christmas. I wanted to ask him whether they'd quarrelled. Rachel and her parents. I thought that could have been why she left Fernhill Grange early.'

He looked unconvinced. 'They always got on so well, though. Never a cross word.' He went into the kitchen. 'And it was just Rachel and Henry, of course. Diana was away that week. Some sort of reunion. Something to do with the war.'

There was the sound of coffee being made, plates being washed up. After a while, he came back into the room.

'Anyway, what I wanted to tell you was that I don't feel bitter any more. At least I've known love, known happiness. Not everyone can say that, can they? I do still have my memories of Rachel – and there's Alice, of course. So just because a thing doesn't work out in the end doesn't mean it shouldn't have happened.' Hector grimaced, and ran his hands through his untidy hair. 'Oh, God, I'm beginning to sound like Patience Strong. What I meant was . . .'

She patted his hand. 'It's all right, Hector. I know what you meant.'

Katherine endured another fitful night. Not because of fever, but because of the relentless, repetitive thoughts that circled through her head. Of Jordan, of Hector, of Rachel. When she did eventually doze off, she dreamed of Rachel. Her old dream: that she had woken up, and Rachel was standing at the foot of her bed, trying to tell her something. Though she strained to hear, Rachel mouthed silently, guarding her secrets. For the first time she noticed that, though she herself had been changed by the years, Rachel was unaltered, her chestnut hair still caught back in the ponytail of her girlhood, her clothes and makeup unmistakably of the previous decade.

Katherine woke up. Sitting up, glancing at the foot of the bed, she half expected Rachel to be there. But there was nothing, of course, so she fumbled for the switch of the bedside lamp, and sat, hugging her knees. Rachel's presence seemed to pervade the room. Suddenly Katherine longed for the easy, uncomplicated friendships of her girlhood. For Liv and for Rachel, and for the shared experiences and common need that had once bound them together. Then the longing dissolved into anger. My life's a mess, an utter mess, she thought, and you've both left me to sort it out on my own. Rachel, Liv, where are you when I need you?

She got out of bed. It was cold, so she wrapped the duvet around her and went into the kitchen. She wanted a cigarette, but smoking made her cough, and coughing hurt her ribs; she wanted a drink, but the doctor had told her not to mix alcohol with the painkillers. There seemed, she thought self-pityingly, no comfort available to her. She put on the kettle and found a tea-bag.

She was pouring boiling water into a mug when she remembered what Hector had said. *Diana was away that week. It was just Rachel and Henry, of course* ... Katherine rubbed her forehead with the back of her hand.

She knew that she wouldn't get back to sleep so she found the abused daughter's manuscript she had begun the previous day and took it back to bed with her cup of tea. Curled up in the duvet, she began to read. Such an ordinary life it must have seemed to outsiders, she thought, this tale of power and degradation and twisted love. An ordinary English family in an ordinary English house in an ordinary English village. A father and daughter who had kept their terrible secret for decades ...

The tea slopped from the cup on to the sheets. Katherine sat very still, staring out into the darkness.

It was just Rachel and Henry, of course ...

Slowly but steadily the business was taking over Samphire Cottage. Felix had built a newer, bigger silkscreen, which occupied most of the lean-to. The highest shelves of the kitchen were crammed with jars of dye. Rolls of cotton, which Felix had bought from a supplier in Lancashire, jostled with buckets and dustpans in the broom cupboard. Squares of drying material were suspended from wires slung across the ceiling of both the kitchen and the lean-to. In the living room, a trestle table bearing pencils, crayons and paper fought for space with the children's toys. The sewing-machine was on another trestle table in the corner of Liv's bedroom. The house smelt of dyestuffs and the chemicals used for fixing them. Pans bubbled on the Aga, and there was often the scorched scent of cured cloth. Offcuts and strands of cotton clung to every surface.

Often, Liv worked until past midnight. Every moment of every day was busy. When there was too much work for her to do on her own, the others helped. One weekend, when Toby placed an order for twenty tablecloths, Liv prepared the dyes and hemmed the finished pieces, Felix operated the silkscreen, and Mrs Maynard ironed the dry cloth and minded the girls. They worked through the night, and when on Sunday evening the order was complete, they celebrated with a bottle of red wine.

She gave up both the bar work and the cleaning job. For the next few nights she woke in the early hours of the morning, sleepless with terror, convinced she had made a dreadful mistake. All the things that might go wrong rushed through her mind in terrifying procession. Freya or Georgie might fall ill and she'd be unable to keep up with the orders. Toby's customers might take an inexplicable dislike to her latest designs, and refuse to buy them. Floral prints might go out of fashion. Worst of all, she might one day simply run out of inspiration. She imagined herself sitting at the trestle table in the front room, her mind blank, her pencil still. She would not be able to pay the rent, and the children would go hungry. The security she had so painstakingly acquired over the past few years would be destroyed.

Felix, calling at Samphire Cottage one evening *en route* to his father's house, was dismissive of her fears. 'If Toby's customers stop wanting our textiles, then someone else will.' He was kneeling in front of the Aga, dismantling the oven, which had given off an ominous smell of burning during the last few days. 'I had a couple of enquiries earlier this week. A place in Richmond, and somewhere in Bath.'

Liv was sitting at the kitchen table, trimming seams. She paused. 'Bath? You mean, just out of the blue?'

'Mmm. I'm going to drive there next week.' His voice was muffled by the cavernous interior of the Aga.

In spite of herself, she was impressed. She looked at him. 'Felix, your *shirt*.'

He had driven to Norfolk straight from work, and was still wearing a suit, and collar and tie. He backed out of the oven.

'Hell.' There were black sooty streaks across his white shirt..

'There are some rather awful things that Mrs Maynard's

brother, who had the cottage before us, left behind. I meant to give them back to her, but I keep forgetting. You could borrow a jersey.' From the back of the airing cupboard she unearthed a man's jersey, greenish-brown and knobbly. 'I don't know what it's made from.'

'Hedgehog spines,' said Felix, eyeing it.

She giggled. 'It's quite clean, though.'

He unknotted his tie, and pulled his shirt over his head. Brown skin, slim waist, well-muscled shoulders. Her mouth was suddenly dry. She had to turn away, to pretend to search through a cupboard for Lux flakes. At first she couldn't think why she felt so odd, and then, of course, she knew, and dropped the packet on the floor in her embarrassment. It was as though a switch had been flicked on, reminding her of feelings she had hidden away, had left disused for so long she had almost believed herself no longer capable of them. Physical desire: dear God, she thought, I'd forgotten all that. She went to the broom cupboard, ostensibly to find the dustpan and brush, in reality to press her hot face against the cool, tiled wall. She seemed to have lost her balance, her equilibrium.

She swept up the soap flakes. Emptying the dustpan into the outside bin, she took a deep breath of cold air to steady herself. Back in the kitchen, she picked up Felix's discarded shirt, and ran water into the sink.

'You don't have to do that.'

'I might as well.'

'Then that's very sweet of you.' His hand rested on her shoulder. She wanted to tilt her head, to press her face against it, but he had moved away, returning to the oven.

'And as for all your other worries,' he said, 'well, Freya and Georgie seem as fit as fiddles, as far as I can see. And if they went down with measles or mumps or something, then Mrs Maynard would help out, wouldn't she?'

'I suppose so.' She plonked the washed shirt on to the draining-board.

'And,' he added, 'there's always a place for florals, isn't there?' His voice echoed against the sides of the Aga. 'And if for some extraordinary reason the flower prints didn't sell, then you could do something else, couldn't you?' He emerged from the oven, something clutched in his hand. 'Squirrels,' he said vaguely. 'Lizards ... snails ...'

She began to giggle, pressing the back of her knuckles against her mouth.

'What?'

'Snails ...' She could hardly get the word out.

'What's wrong with snails?' He came to stand beside her.

'On *curtains*. It's not really—' She leaned against the table, helpless with laughter.

He grinned. 'I don't see why not.' He held out a piece of blackened cloth to her. 'This was causing the problem with the stove.'

She made an effort to get hold of herself. 'It's a cushion cover.'

'It must have fallen down the back when you were drying them.'

'I thought I was one short. I thought I must have counted wrong.' She wanted to laugh again. She wiped her eyes with the back of her hand.

He said, 'I'd almost forgotten,' and went outside. As he unlocked the boot of the car, her eyes traced the contours of his body. She thought, Even in the hedgehog jersey ... even with soot beneath his fingernails and dark shadows around his eyes from a long week's work ... She shivered, and wrapped her arms around herself.

He came back into the house. 'I bought this to celebrate.' He gave her a bottle of champagne. 'Selfridges have promised to place a regular order. Terrific news, don't you think, Liv?'

'A guaranteed income.'

'For the next few months at least.' He was easing the cork out of the bottle. 'Unless you radically alter your designs.'

'*Snails.*'

365

'We could start a new trend. We could specialize in molluscs.'

Champagne bubbled over the rims of the tumblers, and trailed over the table. He handed a glass to her. 'To Briar Rose.'

The dry, sharp bubbles tickled the back of her throat. She'd have a drink or two, she thought, and then perhaps she'd forget all these exhausting, inconvenient thoughts, and she'd go back to thinking of Felix as a business partner, or a friend. She drained her glass. She knew he was watching her. She said, 'What?' and he said, 'You look happy. It's a long time since I've seen you look really happy, Liv. Not since...' He smiled. 'Do you remember the first time we met?'

'Toby's house.'

'He was having a party. And you came with Katherine.'

'I was staying with her for the weekend.' Katherine's bedsit: posters of Che Guevara, and Marmite sandwiches. 'I was recovering...'

'From what?'

'From a broken heart.' Again, she smiled. 'What was his name? Charles... Carl. That was it. Carl.'

'Your first love?'

'Twentieth, I should think. I was always falling in love then. It wasn't the real thing, of course.'

'How do you tell?'

She had to look away, to escape the intensity of his gaze. He would read her mind. He would see her desire written in her eyes. She said, 'You just know, don't you?'

'You see, I once thought it was the real thing, but then...' He shrugged.

Again, she thought of Katherine, a sharp stab to the heart. 'Who, Felix?'

'A girl called Saffron. She lived at Nancy's place.'

She watched him carefully. 'No one else?'

He shook his head. She sensed evasion.

'And you...' he said.

'Oh – just Stefan. Stefan was the real thing.' Again, she

drained her glass. 'And with him, it was like ... it was like drowning.'

Her hands trembled, spilling champagne as she poured herself another glass. He said, 'Steady ... I'll do that.' His fingers brushed against hers as he took the bottle from her.

She gave a short laugh. 'I'm not used to drinking any more. Not with the girls. I always worry that I'll have to get up in the night.' She shivered.

'Are you cold?'

'The Aga ...' She had let the coal burner go out so that it was cool enough for Felix to repair.

'I could light it.'

'No need. The fire's laid in the front room.'

He picked up the bottle and glasses, and took them through. In the living room, he put his lighter to the heap of kindling and newspaper. Flames flared. He was kneeling on the hearth in front of the fire, and she just knelt beside him and pressed the side of her face against his shoulder, and closed her eyes. The back of her hand brushed against his short, silky curls.

And then he took her in his arms, and kissed her face, her neck, her mouth. There was a small rending sound as one of the buttons of her blouse ripped itself from its moorings and leaped to the far side of the room. His palms brushed against her naked skin as he fought the hooks and eyes of her bra. 'This bloody jumper,' he said, tearing Mrs Maynard's brother's jersey over his head. Her lips pressed against the hollow of his collar bones, and she tasted the saltiness of his skin. So long, she thought hazily, since she had not cared about consequences, so many years of being careful.

Being careful. She pulled away, sat up.

'Felix.'

'What?' He was tousle-haired, urgent-eyed.

'I'm not on the Pill.'

'It doesn't matter.' He was rummaging in the back pocket of his trousers. 'I mean, I'll take care—'

'*Felix*,' she said, slightly shocked, and then she didn't say any more.

It was midnight before Felix arrived at his father's house. Parking the car, he sat for a moment, remembering. Liv's image was pinned on to the night sky and on to the flat silver face of the moon, and her scent lingered on his skin. He had a sense of something miraculous having happened, of suddenly, unexpectedly, having recovered the good fortune he had thought he had lost.

Eventually, he got out of the car and let himself into the house. There was a light on in the kitchen. Mia was sitting at the table. There was a glass in front of her, and a packet of cigarettes and an ashtray.

'Felix,' she said, and smiled at him. He thought she looked tired. Her eyes were red-rimmed. Some of his elation died away.

'What's wrong?' His voice was sharp. 'Is Dad . . .?'

'Bernard's fine. He's asleep. And nothing's wrong.' The tenuous smile still hovered around the corners of her mouth; she took a cigarette from the packet, and flicked her lighter over and over. 'Damned thing.'

'Let me.' He lit her cigarette.

'Thank you, Felix darling.' She pushed the Player's packet towards him. 'And the gin's in the larder, if you want to help yourself.'

He shook his head. 'Is there anything to eat?' He hadn't eaten since lunch-time: the drive up to Norwich . . . Liv . . .

'There's some sausages, I think.' Mia made as if to get out of the chair.

'It's all right, Mia, I'll do it.'

She sat back. 'Probably a wise decision – I am rather squiffy, and I've never been the best of cooks, have I?'

'Nonsense.'

'Oh, come on, Felix, you don't have to be kind. We've known

each other long enough, haven't we?' There was an edge to her voice.

He said, 'Well, it's possible that Dad loves you for attributes other than your culinary skills, Mia.'

He put the frying-pan on the hob, and lit the gas. Then he heard her small, stifled sobs. He turned round. 'Mia?' He was appalled. 'I didn't mean – I'm so sorry.'

'It's not *that*! Not my bloody cooking!'

Tears poured unchecked down her cheeks. He searched in his pocket for a handkerchief, but if he had started the day with one, he had abandoned it on Liv's living-room floor, flung to the four winds with the rest of his clothing.

He handed her a tea-towel, and crouched beside her, his arm around her shaking shoulders. She gasped, 'I thought – when we left that place – I thought – it would be different!'

'When you left what place?'

'Wyatts.' She was scrubbing her face with the tea-towel. 'Bloody Wyatts.'

He was bewildered. 'You didn't like it?'

The tears paused. She stared at him. 'Oh, Felix. I *hated* Wyatts. It wasn't *my* house, was it? It was *her* house.' Her voice was savage. 'Tessa's house. A *shrine* to her. A shrine to a *saint*.' Mia blew her nose on the tea-towel, and said, more calmly, 'I'm sorry, Felix. I shouldn't be saying these things to you. I know Tessa was your mother, and you loved her dearly, and that her death was such a tragedy for you and Rose and Bernard. It's just that –' and she took a deep breath ' – I could compete with a real, live woman. I mean, I'm not bad for my age, am I? I haven't let myself go. But I can't compete with a *ghost*.'

There was smoke issuing from the frying-pan; he rose and extinguished the gas. He said, 'It's not about competition, surely, is it?'

'Isn't it?' She glared at him fiercely. 'I thought when we came here that it would be different. A new start – a new house, a second chance. But nothing's changed. I went into Bernard's study this evening, and he was looking at her photographs. A whole album, full of pictures of Tessa. And I saw the expression on his face.' She closed her eyes tightly, and whispered, 'I'm not sure how much longer I can go on being second-best. I thought I was used to it, you see. But it hurts, Felix, it hurts!'

He thought of Liv. *I'll never marry again*, she had said. *Stefan was the real thing.* He turned away from Mia, scraping the black bits out of the frying-pan into the sink.

He heard her say more calmly, 'Oh, you learn ways of protecting yourself. Strategies to defend yourself. So that you don't put your entire self to ransom. At Wyatts I had the animals to look after, and to love. Here, I have my job. It's not much of a job, but it takes my mind off things.' Her voice dropped. 'But it's not enough. It's not enough. Perhaps if there'd been a child . . .' She sighed, and said once more, 'I'm sorry. I shouldn't have dumped all this on you, Felix. The moment you walked through the door, as well. But I do love Bernard, you see. I love him very much.'

He gave her a hug, and said, 'And Dad adores you, I know he does,' but the words were mechanical. There was now a heaviness in his heart.

'I know. In his way. And, most of the time, I'm content with that.'

Felix remained in the kitchen for another half-hour, talking to Mia, and then he went up to the guest room. He lay on the bed, his hands cushioning his head, the curtains open, looking out at the night sky. He wondered whether he, like Mia, could be content with not being loved as he loved. *You learn ways of protecting yourself*, Mia had said, *so that you don't put your whole self to ransom*. When his thoughts drifted inevitably to Saffron, he remembered the depth of jealousy and misery that had accompanied his endless, exhausting certainty that he was not, would never be, first with her.

After a while, he drew the curtains and snuffed out the light. But he did not immediately fall asleep, but lay awake, thinking of Liv, almost frightened by the depth of his need for her.

Chapter Sixteen

The latch on Fernhill Grange's front gate had broken; Katherine could not close it, and it moved slowly back and forth in the breeze, the clang of metal on metal providing a mournful accompaniment to her ascent up the drive.

She pressed the doorbell, and after a few moments heard footsteps. Henry Wyborne opened the door.

'May I come in?' She made herself meet his gaze.

'Is there any particular reason for this visit? Or have you fallen into the habit of visiting lonely widowers?'

'I wanted to talk to you about Rachel.' His eyes became wary. 'Can I come in?'

There was a silence. Then he said, 'I have a suspicion that if I refuse you, you'll set up camp on my doorstep.' He stood aside, letting her enter. 'You have a remarkable tenacity, don't you? Even as a child, I seem to recall. Whereas Rachel could always be distracted – appeased.' He preceded her into the drawing room. 'Sit down, Katherine. A drink?'

'Not for me, thanks.' It was early afternoon. The air in the room was cold and stale, as if no windows had been opened for weeks. Henry Wyborne poured a large measure of Scotch into a cut-glass tumbler as Katherine slid thankfully into a chair. It was two weeks since the accident, but her ribs still ached after exercise.

'Hector told me,' she said, 'that you and Rachel were alone together in the week before she died.'

'Yes.' His back was to her as he restoppered the decanter. 'What of it?'

'So whatever happened, you knew about it. You knew about it and Rachel knew about it, and no one else did.'

He sighed. 'I told you. Nothing happened.'

'Rachel phoned me, you see.' As he turned to her she saw the flicker of expression across his face. Surprise. Vigilance.

'Phoned you?'

'On the Saturday. I was out, unfortunately. But Liv was in.' She wished now that she had accepted his offer of a drink. 'Rachel phoned both Liv and me the morning after she went back to Bellingford. The day before she died. As I told you, I didn't take the phone call, but Liv did. Rachel wanted Liv and me to go and see her that day.'

She saw how white his knuckles were as he gripped the glass. He said, 'And did you?'

'No. I was out, and Liv was busy.' Katherine imagined Rachel, alone and frightened at Bellingford. Guilt still lingered, dark and ingrained. 'Rachel wouldn't tell Liv what was wrong. All she said was that something awful had happened and she didn't know what to do about it. Liv tried to persuade her to say more, but she wouldn't. Rachel insisted that she come and talk to her in person. She was very distressed, Liv said. Frantic ... frightened. Liv thought she was crying.'

She watched Henry Wyborne carefully as she spoke. She could not read his expression. But the colour had drained away from his face, so that he appeared yellowed and old.

'Ever since Rachel died it's haunted me,' she said. 'Not knowing what it was she wanted to tell us.'

He licked his lips. 'The baby,' he said. 'The baby was born that day. That's why she was frightened, I expect. The ordeal of childbirth ...'

'It wasn't the baby. Liv asked Rachel about that. And it wasn't anything to do with Hector.' She looked up at him. 'I've thought about it and thought about it, Mr Wyborne, and I've come to the conclusion that it was something to do with you.'

He gave a short laugh. 'And would you like to share with me how you came to such an extraordinary conclusion, Katherine?'

'You tried to stop Rachel and Hector marrying, didn't you?

You told Hector she'd chosen to go to Paris early. But that wasn't true, was it? You forced her to go.'

'That's one way of looking at it, I suppose.'

'What other way is there?'

'That I was trying to protect her.'

'Protect her!' Katherine almost wanted to laugh.

'Yes. From doing something she'd later regret.'

'No. You wanted to keep Rachel to yourself, didn't you?'

His eyes narrowed. 'What on earth are you implying?'

'That you tried to stop the marriage because you didn't want to lose her.'

'Is that so unreasonable? I *loved* her.'

She heard the anguish in his voice, but she persevered. She said, 'There are different sorts of love, aren't there?'

His eyes were hard, dark arrow-slits against his pale face. She thought of Graham, and of Stefan, and said, 'Love can be destructive, can't it? To some men, love means ownership – possession. Possession of a woman, body and soul.'

He took a step towards her, and she flinched. 'You are suggesting . . .' and he paused, the words brittle, about to snap '. . . that my love for my daughter was inappropriate . . . that it was . . . unnatural?'

'Wasn't it?'

For a fraction of a second she thought that he might hit her. Then the moment seemed to pass, and she saw his shoulders slump.

'No,' he muttered. 'No, you're quite wrong.' He shot a glance at her. 'You are obsessed with sex, like so many of your generation.' The corners of his mouth twisted. 'How did we bring you into the world, we for whom procreation – and pleasure – was such a furtive, unspoken thing? You are quite wrong, Katherine. And there are other obsessions, you know.'

She wasn't sure whether she believed him. But she found herself thinking of Jordan. How his wife, child and mistress existed as peripherals to his ambition, and to his need for power.

'But something had happened, hadn't it?' she whispered. 'Something awful, which made Rachel leave Fernhill Grange early. I'm right, aren't I?'

She knew, looking at him, that she had struck a nerve. She went on remorselessly, 'You have to tell me the truth, Mr Wyborne. For Hector's sake. Have you any idea how guilty he still feels?'

'Dear God. *Guilt.*' His tone was savage. 'Why do you think I gave him the child? Why do you think I did that?'

'I don't know. I hadn't thought—'

'To begin to make things right, of course.' Henry Wyborne closed his eyes. 'Not that one can ever put right the past. You think you're safe, don't you, and then, out of the blue—' He stared at her. 'You have no idea what I'm talking about, have you, Katherine? Your generation has so little understanding of the experiences of mine. What do you, who have not lived through a war, know of love or of loss?'

'I've read about it,' she faltered. 'I suppose it must have been awful – the Blitz, the battle of Britain. All that.' Even to her own ears, her stumbling words sounded naïve and schoolgirlish. 'But I don't see what that's got to do with Rachel.'

'Of course you don't. Why should you?' Henry had gone to stand by the window, looking out at the neglected garden. There was a long silence. Then he said, so softly she had to strain to hear it, 'But it doesn't matter now, does it? Nothing matters, because I have nothing left to lose.' He swung round to face her again. Then he said, 'Rachel was distressed, Katherine, because she'd just met my wife.' The anger had drained from his voice, and he sounded very weary.

'Your wife?' It was her turn to stare at him. 'Diana was your wife.'

Henry Wyborne shook his head. 'No. That's the thing, you see. She wasn't.'

*

374

After a while, she rose and went to the sideboard and poured herself a drink. She heard him say, 'Dear me, Katherine, have I succeeded in reducing you to speechlessness? Such an achievement.'

She sat down again, and took a sip of whisky. Then she said again, 'Diana was your wife.'

'Diana *believed* she was my wife. As Rachel, of course, also believed her to be. But she wasn't, I'm afraid.' His gaze rested on Katherine. 'You reminded me that I tried to stop Rachel marrying Hector. You're quite right, I did. But not because, as you so delicately put it, I wished to keep Rachel to myself. No, I simply wanted to stop Rachel repeating my own mistakes.'

'What mistakes?' she whispered.

'Rachel was only eighteen when she met Hector. Too young to know her own mind, I believed. After all, I was twenty when I went to France. I was twenty-one when I married.'

She tried to do the arithmetic. The numbers stumbled and fell. He said softly, 'I married Lucie Rolland on the tenth of May nineteen forty.'

She stared at him mutely. He gave her a bitter smile. 'Shall I satisfy your curiosity, Katherine? Shall I tell you about Lucie? I met her in the spring of that year.'

'The war—'

'I'd been stationed in France for several months with the British Expeditionary Force. There was nothing much doing – the Phoney War, they called it. A lot of the other chaps were chummy with the French girls ... something to do, better than sitting around, kicking their heels. Not me, though. I was very young, I suppose, not much more than a year out of public school. No sisters – not much experience of girls at all, in fact. I met Lucie when I was cycling back to the camp one day. She was sitting on the verge at the side of the road. Her shoelace had broken.' Henry Wyborne's eyes were unfocused, and it seemed to Katherine that he was looking back into the past. 'She wasn't wearing any stockings. She had such lovely feet – small and slender. It was the first time I'd felt like *that* about a woman. A real woman, I mean, not a film star, or a pin-up.'

He took his cigarette case from his inside pocket, and offered it to Katherine. She shook her head. He went on, 'Anyway, she told me that her name was Lucie Rolland, and that she lived with her widowed mother on a farm near Servins. She hadn't any English, and my French was only schoolboy stuff, but that didn't seem to matter. I'd always found it hard going, talking to girls – couldn't seem to think of the right things to say – but it was easy, somehow, with Lucie.' There was the snap of his lighter. 'Anyway, we arranged to meet the following evening. And the evening after that. I couldn't think of anything but Lucie. There I was, stuck in the dullest corner of France, miles from home, marooned in a war that wasn't a real war, and I was happier than I'd been in my entire life.'

'You fell in love with her?'

He exhaled a cloud of blue smoke. 'I was infatuated with her. And I wanted her, my God, how I wanted her. But she was a good Catholic girl, and good Catholic girls did not generally, at that time, jump into bed with men they weren't married to. So,' he paused, 'I asked her to marry me.'

She blinked. 'She consented?'

'She pointed out, very sensibly, that we were young, and that we were of different nationalities, different religions.'

Katherine struggled to imagine Henry Wyborne at twenty-one years old. Young and inexperienced in a strange land. In love for the first time.

'Did your parents know about Lucie?'

'No. I had great intentions, though. Great plans.' His words were short, clipped, sardonic. 'After we had won the war – and I envisaged a brief, glorious encounter in which I would, of course, distinguish myself – I would take Lucie back to England. I'd introduce her to my parents, my proud, straitlaced, impoverished parents, and they'd fall in love with her, just as I had. They'd see how beautiful, simple and charming she was, and it wouldn't matter a jot that she was Roman Catholic, that she had been born a Jew, that she was a foreigner, that she was a peasant.' She could hear the rancour in his voice. 'That was what I told myself, anyway. The optimism – the foolishness – of youth ...'

He was silent for a while, smoking and drinking, and then he said, 'Only it didn't quite work out as I had planned. History doesn't tend to go according to plan, does it? In May, Hitler invaded Holland, and suddenly it wasn't a phoney war any more. It was the real thing. And in the midst of all that, my main concern was not my country or my regiment, or the fate of all the poor sods who'd found themselves caught up in war, but Lucie. We'd been given our marching orders, you see. Again, I asked her to marry me. Told her that I didn't know when we'd see each other again.'

Katherine whispered, 'And this time ...'

'She said yes. And found a sympathetic priest.' Henry Wyborne smiled. 'I suppose he thought that if he refused to wed us, we'd simply not bother with the ceremony.' He looked sharply at Katherine. 'I wasn't the only one, you know. There were other involvements. One chap managed to take his French wife back to England through Dunkirk – togged her up in battledress, smuggled her on to a boat.' He stubbed out his cigarette. 'Anyway, we were married. Man and wife. A friend of mine called Roger Bailey was best man, and Lucie's mother attended her. And then, the next day, we said our goodbyes, and I marched into Belgium with the rest of the BEF.' He glared at Katherine. 'You must understand that I hadn't entertained the possibility of defeat. As far as I was concerned, it was all going to be easy. We were heading towards the river Dyle, where I assumed we'd rout the Germans. Then, I thought, we'd return to Arras, and I'd claim Lucie and bring her back to England in triumph.' He gave a sour little laugh. 'I can even remember thinking that would make it all right with my parents, if I came home a hero. That they'd forgive me the other thing. But it didn't turn out like that, of course. The campaign was a disaster. Neither the French army nor our own was ready for what was flung at them. The bloody Maginot line, which we'd all put so much faith in, was worse than useless, and the French generals were squabbling amongst themselves. So we ended up with little option but to retreat.'

She said, 'And Lucie?'

He glanced quickly at her. 'I went back for her. Roger and I – we went back for her. But she'd gone.'

'Gone?'

His eyes glittered. 'The Rollands' farmhouse was deserted.'

'Where? Where had she gone?'

'I don't know. South, I suppose. Everyone was going south. The roads were full of them – refugees from Holland and Belgium and France. They were on foot, in cars, herding their cattle. I remember an old chap pushing his crippled wife in a pram ... I remember children's faces pressed up against the windows of cars ... they'd put the mattresses on the roofs of the cars because they thought that would protect them from the bombers.' A single tear shone like a diamond in the hollow beneath his eye. 'That was when I began to grow up,' he said savagely. 'That was when I knew it was real. That was when I began to see that, compared to all this, I was nothing, and Lucie was nothing. When you see entire nations fleeing for their lives ...'

She had to look away, unable to bear the expression in his eyes. After a while, she heard him say more calmly, 'Roger and I searched for Lucie, of course. We scouted around – asked for her in cafés and shops in Arras and Servins – but it was hopeless. Then Roger pointed out that she might be trying to find me. So we went back the way we'd come, and tried to rejoin our regiment. But that was hopeless, too. They were scattered to the four winds, in bits and bobs all over the place. Every man for himself. So we got along as best as we could, and ended up at Dunkirk with the rest of the BEF.'

Again, she said, 'And Lucie?'

'Not a whisper. At first, we asked everywhere, but after a while ...' His voice faded away. Then he looked at her defiantly, and said, 'In the end, all you want to do is to stay alive. And get home. All the other things become unimportant.' Clutched between his fingers, his cigarette had burnt down almost to the filter. 'And when I saw the beach,' he added softly, 'when I saw Dunkirk – the queues of men going into the sea, the bombers, the sunken ships – well, my God, nothing in my life had prepared me for that. Nothing. What in home or school or all the idiocies of an upper-middle-class English upbringing could have made me expect *that*? It was like Hell, I thought. Like a medieval painting of Hell.'

He fell silent again. Katherine remembered his earlier words. *Your generation has so little understanding of the experiences of mine.*

Eventually he said, 'I got away. Picked up by a Channel steamer on the last day. Roger didn't make it. A Stuker shot him while we were waiting on the beach.'

She said softly, 'I'm sorry.'

'Anyway, I made it back. And after Dunkirk, everything was different. Fewer illusions, you see. And Hitler just over the Channel, thumbing his nose at us. Though I still hadn't quite got the message. If you'd told me – if you'd told me it would be more than four years till France was free again, then I'd never have believed you. And as for Lucie,' his face clouded, 'well, the first leave I had, I went to see my parents. I did try to tell them, I honestly did. But I couldn't bring myself to do it. The newspapers were full of stuff about the fall of France, and there was my father railing about what a useless shower the French were – had let the Germans walk into their country twice, and expected us to bail them out, that sort of nonsense. I told myself I'd wait till he calmed down, wait for a better time. Only there never was a better time. The longer I waited, the more impossible it became. And then—' He broke off.

Katherine prompted gently, 'And then?'

'And then I met Diana. Diana Marlowe, as she was. It was in a club, in the West End, in the Blitz.' He spread out his hands in a gesture of defeat and acknowledgement. 'And once I met Diana, I didn't think of Lucie any more.'

She said softly, '*Oh.*'

'That first night, a bomb hit the adjacent building. The shock made the club's ceiling crack. Lots of the girls screamed and made a fuss, but not Diana. We were dancing at the time, and she just giggled, and wiped the plaster dust off her nose, and said, "Well, I was almost out of face powder." I thought what a great girl she was, to be able to make a joke at a time like that.' He stared fiercely at Katherine. 'I suppose Diana was of a type that your generation likes to make fun of. A brick. A good sport.'

Katherine said honestly, 'I was always very fond of Diana. She was such a happy person, wasn't she? I always thought how lucky Rachel was, having Diana for a mother.'

He bowed his head then, biting his lip. When he spoke again, his voice had thickened. 'She took my breath away, you know. People say that, but they don't really mean it. It's just a cliché they use. But it happened to me. I saw her, and my breath caught in my throat.' When he looked up at her, Katherine saw the tears in his eyes. He said, 'You mustn't think it was just because of ambition – or just for power. It was for love.'

Tears stung at the back of Katherine's own eyes. 'Did you tell Diana about Lucie?'

'No. Never. At first because it would have seemed . . .' he paused ' . . . *improper*, almost. An interruption of something that was quite perfect. And then, as time passed, I couldn't bear to tell Diana, I just couldn't. I knew what it would do to her, how disappointed she'd be in me. She was such an honest, straight-forward person, you see. So every day that passed, the more difficult it became. Every day that passed, the deception became greater. Every day that passed, my complicity, my silence, became more wrong.' Henry's eyes were anguished. 'And then I began to think—' He stopped, but after a while seemed to recover himself. He looked at Katherine. 'Then I began to think that perhaps I wouldn't have to tell her.'

'What do you mean?'

'That Lucie might not survive the war.'

'*Oh*,' she said again, and he went on, grimly, 'Lucie was of Jewish birth, as I told you. A Roman Catholic convert. And as the war went on, it became obvious that, as a Jew in occupied Europe, her chances of survival were poor. So I said to myself, Why upset Diana by telling her of a marriage that might no longer exist? Why not wait until the end of the war, and find out whether Lucie's alive or dead?'

'And did you?'

'I went over with the Third Army at D-Day. Had my chance later in the year, after Paris was retaken, and we were back after all those years in northern France. There wasn't much left of the Rollands' farmhouse – it had been burned out at some point during the war. But I made enquiries. Someone told me that Lucie and her mother had been taken from their homes, and sent to Germany.' He glanced at her. 'To a concentration camp.'

The harsh words echoed in the Wybornes' luxurious drawing room. Katherine heard Henry Wyborne say softly, 'The terrible thing is that then I began to hope.'

'Hope?'

'Yes, God forgive me. Hope that it was over. That history had given me an easy way out of a marriage that had become an embarrassment – no, worse, a guilty secret – something I had learned to regret deeply. If Lucie was dead, I'd be able to marry Diana, who would be, in my parents' eyes, an infinitely more suitable bride for their only son than poor Lucie. You see,' and once more, Henry Wyborne smiled his unsettling smile, 'though my family had birth, Diana's had birth *and* money.'

'Whereas Lucie had neither.'

'Exactly. Marriage to Diana would give me a huge step up the ladder. Acknowledging my marriage to Lucie could do me only harm.' He frowned. 'I do remember disliking myself, for a while, at least, for seeming to welcome another's suffering. But I learned to rationalize it. I told myself that it was not the possibility of Lucie's death that pleased me, but the possibility of marrying the woman I loved. And I told myself that my marriage to Lucie might not even have been legal. That it'd been a rushed job – a youthful aberration – and that I'd been only twenty-one years old, and I'd had neither the consent of my parents nor of my commanding officer. And when, after the end of the war, I made further enquiries – rather sketchy enquiries, I have to admit – and still found no trace of Lucie, I told myself that I'd tried, I'd done my best, and now the most honourable course would be to marry the woman who had loved me for more than five years.' His lip curled. 'How we deceive ourselves, Katherine. How we twist morality to suit our own convenience.'

I can't come into the hospital with you, Katherine. You do understand, don't you? She had to look away.

'So you married Diana?'

'Yes. A society wedding, as much as such a thing was possible at the time. A bigamous society wedding.'

She shivered. 'Lucie was still alive?'

'Yes.'

'When did you find out?'

The expression in his eyes altered, shutting her away. 'Oh, not for years. Not for years and years.' He fell silent for a while, then seemed to rouse himself. 'Another drink?'

The decanter was almost empty. She said, 'I'll make some tea.'

He smiled. 'Of course. Sensible girl. A cure for all ills, isn't it, a nice cup of tea?'

She went into the kitchen. Dirty crockery littered every surface, and there was cold, stewed tea in the pot. She washed it out, and searched through the cupboards for a packet of tea. Boiling the kettle, spooning sugar, her hands trembled, and her cracked ribs ached, somewhere in the region of her heart.

She took the cups into the drawing room. 'There wasn't any milk, so I had to use lemon,' she said. 'I hope that's all right.'

His gaze drifted around the untidy room. 'I should clear up . . . Not much of a memorial to Diana, is it now, this place?' He stirred his tea. 'Diana's family helped us buy Fernhill Grange,' he said. 'Diana's father helped me with my political career – he had a lot of influence in the Party. When Rachel was born, I thought I had everything I wanted. Diana would have liked more children, but they never came. I didn't mind – to me, Rachel was perfect.' He put the cup and saucer on to the window-sill, and lit another cigarette. 'I began,' he said, 'to believe that I had made my own good fortune. That I *deserved* it. My family ... my home ... my career.' He glanced at Katherine. 'I know the folly of that now. Rachel's death taught me that.'

She murmured, 'Lucie?'

He closed his eyes for a moment. 'She came here,' he said despairingly. 'That week. She just – turned up – when Rachel was staying here, collecting baby things. I'd gone to the garage to fetch my car – they were servicing it. Rachel was having a rest in the garden. Lucie spoke to her, said she was looking for someone. Rachel had good French, remember. She introduced herself to Lucie as Mrs Seton. Lucie told Rachel she was looking for her husband. For Henry Wyborne.'

His lids were squeezed tight. She thought he would not say any more, but then he whispered, 'Whatever guilt Hector endures, it is nothing compared to mine. Since that day, I have not known a moment that was free of remorse. Not one single moment.'

Later, as she made ready to leave the house, he said, 'What will you do now?'

'Do?' She stared at him blankly. She longed to be outside, breathing in the cool, clean air.

'You could sell my story to the papers. A scoop, don't you think?'

She shook her head. 'I won't do that. I promise you I won't do that. I must tell Hector, though. He deserves to know what happened.' She saw him bow his head, as if in assent. 'And you, Mr Wyborne? What will you do?'

'Oh, I shall resign my seat, of course. And I shall try to find Lucie.' He smiled thinly. 'Try to put things right, as far as one is permitted to. Make sure she's comfortable in her old age, at least.' He was silent for a moment, and then he said, 'When Rachel died, I thought that God was punishing me. Is that what you think, Katherine?'

She thought of Philip. She thought of Lucie Rolland, taken from her country to imprisonment and suffering in a foreign land.

'I think,' she said slowly, 'that a God who hurts people to punish other people wouldn't be much of a God. But, really, I think that these things are random. That they just happen.' Then she offered him her hand. 'Goodbye, Mr Wyborne.'

When Felix didn't return to Samphire Cottage after his weekend with his family, Liv told herself that his father must have needed him in Norwich. When the days passed and he did not write, she thought that he must be waiting for her to phone – after all, he had a telephone, but she did not. She phoned his flat on Monday evening, and again on Tuesday, but there was no reply. She remembered that he had told her he was going to Bath. He would send a postcard. The days passed. No postcard arrived.

She recalled that she had made the first move, not Felix. Her fingers, running through his hair, her lips, pressing against the back of his neck. Her doubts altered the tenor of her days, casting a shadow over them. After all, she had been mistaken about Felix before. In London, all those years ago, she had thought he cared for her, and then she had discovered that he loved Katherine. She remembered the night she had seen them together. The affair had been short-lived, presumably. It occurred to her that she had not changed as much as she had believed she had. In spite of everything that had happened to her – two children, a disastrous marriage, the years of surviving on her own – underneath it all she was still the same old naïve, romantic Liv. She had not, it seemed, moved with the times. She still looked for love, for enduring love, in an age when most seemed content with sex.

She had had too much to drink and she had thrown herself at him, and he – kind, obliging Felix – had not had the heart to refuse her. He had felt sorry for her: the sex-starved single mother, the lonely ex-wife. The best thing to do, she concluded miserably, was to pretend it had never happened. There must be no awkwardness, no recriminations. Her stupidity must not threaten the business they were building up together. When she telephoned on Friday evening, Felix was at home. She came straight to the point. Mrs Maynard had offered to rent them her barn. Felix himself had suggested they look for new premises and, conveniently close to Samphire Cottage, the barn might be the perfect solution. If he wished to, he could drive up at the weekend and they could look at it together. It would have to be a quick visit – she was busy, and didn't have much time to spare. When she put the phone down, she felt pleased with herself. She had made clear to him, she thought, that he was under no obligation to her. That what had happened was not important; that their relationship could continue as before, friendly and practical.

And yet, walking back from the phone-box to the cottage, she felt particularly low. All the signs of spring were around her – buds on the may bushes, brimstone butterflies like scraps of yellow silk – but just now they failed to spell out their usual optimism. A week ago, just a week ago, she had felt happy. Love had worked its miracle, transforming everything. All that was mundane had seemed brighter, and full of promise. She tried to dispel the feeling of flatness, taking the children's hands in hers and running up the lane, but it persisted.

She met Felix at the farm the following midday. They left the children with Mrs Maynard, and went to look at the barn. It was a huge old building with a cruck roof. Felix's torch illuminated the arching rafters overhead.

'Like a cathedral.'

'Perhaps it's too big,' she said doubtfully.

'Better that than too small or we'd have to look for somewhere else in six months' time.' He swung the torch around the perimeter of the floor.

'What are you looking for?'

'Damp. It's quite low-lying. The river's not far away. Seems OK, though.'

She hugged her arms around herself. 'It's cold.'

'Damned difficult to heat, I should imagine. It'll be all right in the summer, but in the depths of winter it'll be perishing.'

'We could use oil heaters.'

'Expensive ... We might have to, though. I'll take some

measurements so I can work out how we can make best use of the space.'

He sounded, she thought, as though he had already made up his mind. 'Do you think we should take it, then, Felix?'

'Of course.'

'I thought we were just looking.'

'Did you?'

'I hadn't imagined,' she said huffily, 'that we'd make up our minds today.'

'I don't see any point in hanging about.' He glanced at her. 'Unless you're having doubts.'

'Doubts?'

'It's cheap and it's convenient. A very good price per square foot. What's the problem?'

He had hardly even discussed it with her. So arrogant, she thought furiously. So like a man, steamrollering through the big decisions. She said, 'It's just that it's a big commitment.'

'And you're not keen on commitment, are you, Liv?' She only just caught the muttered words.

'What did you say?' But he had turned away from her. She wanted to shake him. 'Felix, what did you say?'

'If you're not keen ... if you're having second thoughts about the business, then for God's sake say so now, before we both get in too deep.'

'I didn't say I was having second thoughts.'

'Didn't you?' At last, his cold gaze met hers. 'But you've been giving me the brush-off ever since I arrived, haven't you?'

'I thought,' she whispered, 'that we were talking about the barn.'

'Amongst other things.' His eyes were as chill and hard as onyx.

She clenched her fists. 'It's you who's having second thoughts, Felix, not me. And as for blowing hot and cold ...' She thought of Katherine. 'Well, you're not exactly *consistent*, are you? You say one thing and do another – I never know where I am with you.' It infuriated her that she could feel tears stinging at the back of her eyeballs. 'I suppose it's my fault – I suppose I always think these things have to *mean* something – I suppose I've never been much use with men—' Her voice wobbled, and she turned on her heel and ran out of the barn.

She did not go back to the farmhouse, but headed across the field, to the road that led to Samphire Cottage. She needed to be on her own. She knew that she had deceived herself, telling herself that she and Felix could return to their former friendship. You couldn't unpick the past; however briefly, they had been lovers, and that altered everything. She wondered whether it would get easier in time, and thought that it probably would not.

Walking up the lane to the cottage, she saw the unfamiliar car. Then the woman sitting inside it. It took a moment or two, blinking away the tears, to realize that the woman was Katherine.

Katherine climbed out of the car. 'You all right, Livvy?'

'Fine. I'm fine.'

Katherine was wearing jeans and a coffee-coloured peasant top. Her apricot hair was cut in a pageboy bob, brushing her shoulders. She took off her sunglasses. 'I know it's been ages, Liv, but I had to talk to you. Toby told me where to find you.'

It was hard to think of anything she wanted less than a conversation with Katherine. Her eyes ached. But she said reluctantly, 'You'd better come in. I haven't got long, though. The children . . .'

'Freya and Georgie.' Katherine smiled. 'How are they? Freya must be five – no, six.'

'And Georgie's four.'

Indoors, Katherine looked around the kitchen. 'So lovely. You always were good at rural idylls, weren't you, Liv?' She buried her face in the vase of wild roses on the centre of the table. Then she said, 'Toby told me that you and Felix had gone into business together.'

'For the time being.'

'It's not a permanent arrangement?'

'I don't know. I haven't decided.' As soon as Katherine had gone, she thought, she would go and find Felix, and explain to him that it wasn't going to work. It was impossible to keep up the pretence that what had happened between them was unimportant to her. It would be hard, at first, surviving on her own without the income from the business, but she would cope. She had coped before.

Yet the thought of not seeing him any more made her feel utterly forlorn. She wanted to fling herself on to her bed, to kick her heels and howl, as Freya did when she was unhappy.

'I wanted,' Katherine said suddenly, 'to tell you about Rachel. I spoke to her father, you see.'

She couldn't think what Katherine was talking about. Then Katherine said, 'Do you think I could make a cup of coffee, or something? Only it was a long journey, and I'm trying to give up smoking.' Her long, pale fingers pleated and unpleated the folds of her blouse. For the first time, it occurred to Liv that Katherine, too, was finding this conversation difficult. 'And I wasn't sure about coming here and bothering you when we've been out of touch for so long, but Hector said I should and—'

'Rachel's Hector?'

'We've been friends for years.'

'Hector? A friend?'

'Yes. A friend. You don't think he'd ever be anything else to me, do you, Liv? Hector's still in love with Rachel, you know. Hector will always be in love with Rachel. That was why I went to see Mr Wyborne. Because of Hector. I wanted to know what had happened. That weekend she died, I mean. I thought it might help.'

It seemed a long time ago, Liv thought, the day she had looked out of a window and had seen Stefan walking across the grass towards her. Yet she still remembered the miracle of the moment, and how Rachel's pleading voice had become suddenly unimportant.

She put the kettle on the hob. Her hands were clumsy, as she spooned coffee into mugs. She heard Katherine say, 'Rachel had found out that Henry and Diana weren't properly married, you see.'

Grains of sugar scattered over the work-surface. Shocked, she stared at Katherine. 'They were living together?'

'In a way.'

'That's not so awful. My mother lives with Richard.'

'It wasn't like that. They'd married, but it was a bigamous marriage.'

She swung round, teaspoon in hand. '*God.*'

'Henry Wyborne had been married before, in nineteen forty. He thought his wife – his first wife – was dead, but she wasn't.' Katherine twisted her fingers together. 'I am dying for a cigarette.' She looked at Liv. 'You haven't . . .?'

'No.'

'Oh, Liv. Always so *good*. You always made me feel such a *slut.*'

She realized that, just for a moment, she had forgotten Felix. She put the mug of coffee in front of Katherine. 'Tell me,' she said. 'Tell me everything.'

Katherine told Liv about the day Henry Wyborne had met Lucie Rolland, sitting on the verge, broken shoelace in hand. About their love affair and their hasty marriage, and about Henry Wyborne's escape from Dunkirk without his new wife. And about the night he had met Diana Marlowe in a London club: they had danced as the bombs had fallen around them. And about Henry's attempts after the war to find out what had happened to Lucie. His belief that she had died in Germany, and his marriage to Diana. Lucie's reappearance, more than twenty years later, at Fernhill Grange.

Lucie had introduced herself to Rachel as Henry Wyborne's wife. 'Rachel didn't believe her at first,' said Katherine, 'but then, as Lucie told her about the marriage, the war, Rachel began to accept that she was telling the truth. She'd always known her father had escaped from Dunkirk, after all. Then Henry appeared. Rachel was extremely upset by then, of course. And then, Mr Wyborne was vague about this bit, but I think this is what happened. He must have been horrified at first, of course, that his secret had been found out after all these years, but then I should imagine that his instinct to survive took over. He bundled Lucie into another room, and spoke to her on her own. Then he went back to Rachel. At first, he tried to deny Lucie – claimed she wasn't telling the truth, that she was a madwoman – but then, when he saw that it was no good, he switched to trying to justify himself.' Katherine was silent for a moment, and then she said, 'He told me that he'd never realized that Rachel could be so unforgiving. That everything was so black and white to her. But I can remember being like that, then. Seeing what a mess grown-ups made of things, and believing I'd never be like them. Thinking that things were right or wrong, and that there was nothing in between.'

'They quarrelled?'

'For the first and only time. Rachel wanted it all put right, you see, Lucie acknowledged and pensioned off, something like that. Well, Henry wasn't having any of that, of course. So he pointed out to Rachel what it would mean to Diana if the truth came out. How awful it would be.'

'Oh.'

'Exactly. And then he went off to get a drink or something, and then the next thing that happened was that he heard the car starting up, and saw Rachel heading off down the drive.' Katherine frowned. 'I think that at first he felt he'd done the right thing. Maintained the status quo. He thought that Rachel would eventually calm down, see things his way, forget about it. So he gave Lucie some money, and sent her back to France. And he thought, or hoped, that was that.'

'And the next day, Rachel phoned us.'

'Yes. Well, you can imagine what was going through her head, can't you? Everything, absolutely everything the Wybornes possessed, was dependent on her parents' marriage. The lovely house, the servants, the foreign holidays, her private school, her clothes, her riding lessons, even Rachel's own legitimacy, the whole bloody lot. Bellingford, too. Henry had given Rachel money on her marriage to Hector so that they could do up Bellingford. I think Rachel must have seen that everything she had, everything she was, was dependent on a lie. She had seen that Lucie Rolland was poor, sick and perhaps a little deranged, and she had contrasted Lucie's life with her own. And perhaps Rachel began to think that everything that was hers should have been Lucie's.' Katherine looked up. 'I think that's why she phoned us, why she wanted to talk to us. I think that she was facing an impossible decision. Bigamy's a crime, after all. She must have worked out that she could tell the truth and ruin her mother's life as well as her father's, or she could keep quiet and live with the knowledge that everything she had had been gained through a deception.'

Rachel's voice echoed. *You have to come, Liv. I need you. I don't know what to do.* Liv whispered, 'Poor Rachel.'

'I suppose she chose to talk to us because we weren't involved,' Katherine went on. 'Which Hector was, in a way, because of the money and the house. She couldn't make up her mind on her own, and she had no brothers or sisters to talk to, so she phoned us.'

'Blood sisters,' said Liv softly.

'Yes. And in the end, of course, she didn't have to make the choice, did she? She went into labour, and then . . .' Katherine's voice faded away. 'I felt sorry for him, you know. For Henry Wyborne. I didn't think I would, but I did. To have quarrelled with Rachel like that – to have blackmailed her into silence by pointing out to her what the truth would do to Diana – and then for Rachel to die.' She shook her head. 'How do you live with memories like that? He was convinced, you see, that the shock had contributed to Rachel's death. That it had caused the embolism. That was why he didn't argue when Diana told him that she wanted to bring up Alice. He felt that as he'd been responsible for Diana losing her daughter, he couldn't possibly deny her the consolation of her granddaughter. He knew it was wrong, though, just as he knew it was wrong for Diana to blame Hector for Rachel's death. But he couldn't tell Diana that, could he? Not without telling her the truth. Just as he couldn't take from her the little she had left after Rachel's death – her position in society, her belief in her marriage.'

'And was it Henry Wyborne's fault? Did the shock kill Rachel?'

'I don't think so. I talked to my father about it. He told me that embolisms are very rare, and that they just sometimes happen for no particular reason.'

Liv went to the window. The sun had come out, and the pale green slits of the willow leaves glittered. She said, 'But why? Why did she turn up *then*?'

'Lucie? Oh, because she'd seen Henry Wyborne's picture in the newspaper. *She*'d assumed *he* was dead. Back in nineteen forty, he'd said he'd come for her, you see. He'd promised that, whatever happened, he'd come for her. And she'd lost so many people she loved that it was easy for her to believe that she'd lost one more. So when he didn't turn up, she assumed the worst. And then, in nineteen sixty-eight, she saw his photo in a French paper – an article on up-and-coming European politicians, something like that. Lucie herself was at a low ebb at that time. Short of cash, afraid that she might lose her home. So she went to England to find him.'

'And Lucie – had she remarried?'

'No. Apparently she'd spent the last year of the war in a concentration camp. Something like that – you wouldn't be the same afterwards, would you? I suspect that Henry found her quite easy to deal with. She was rather in awe of him – the big house, the important man. She was nervous and frightened. She hadn't come to cause trouble, or to blackmail him.'

'What did she want?'

'To pick up where she'd left off, I think. To go back to the bit of her life where she'd been happy.' Katherine rose from the table, and went into the lean-to. There was a silence. Liv heard her blow her nose. After a while Liv said, 'Have you told Hector?'

'Yes. I think it helped.' Katherine's voice was slightly thickened. 'At first he was upset, of course – and angry with Henry for not having told him the truth – but since then, I think it's helped. Laid things to rest a bit.' She blew her nose again. Then she said, 'Did you make these?'

Liv went into the lean-to. Katherine was running a length of cloth through her fingers. 'It's lovely. So lovely. You mustn't give up. How can you think of giving up?'

'Because of Felix.' Katherine looked blank. 'I'm not sure I can work with him.'

Katherine made a face. 'He's *picky*, of course. I noticed that when we worked for *Frodo's Finger*. And he can be horribly single-minded – but most men can be like that, can't they? But that's hardly enough reason—'

'It's not *that*.' There was no need, she saw suddenly, to hide the truth. Secrets corroded and destroyed. 'It's not just a business relationship, Katherine,' she said baldly. 'I mean, it was till recently, but last Friday – well, I didn't mean to, but—'

'You went to bed with him?' Katherine shrugged. 'Felix has been in love with you for years and years, so what's the problem?'

'You don't have to say that, Katherine. You don't have to *lie*.'

'I'm not lying. Why should I? It's true.'

'But that time . . .' Liv took a deep breath. 'I *saw* you, you see. You and Felix. The night Stefan was arrested.'

Katherine's expression altered. 'Oh. I did wonder. When you left London so suddenly. I told myself it was because of Stefan, but I did wonder.'

'I'd thought he cared about me,' said Liv wearily, 'but then, when I saw you, I knew that he didn't.'

'No, you've got it all wrong, Liv.'

'I know what I saw,' she said angrily.

'Felix and I made love once,' said Katherine. Her eyes met Liv's. 'Just once. And that was enough to show us that though we'd been fine as friends, we'd never do as lovers.' Katherine flung out her hands, palms up. 'I seduced him, if you must know. I was feeling awful about something – far too long a story to go into just now – and he was feeling miserable because he'd just found out they were going to lose the family home, and because he believed you were going back to Stefan. So we comforted each other.' She looked across at Liv. 'When he told me that he was in love with you, I hated you. You had everything, and I had nothing. I thought, Felix is *my* friend, why should he love you and not me? I was jealous. It's not very nice to admit it, but I was. And I've always had a bad habit of wanting what other people have got, haven't I? Anyway, he was drunk, and I was drunk, and we ended up in bed together, and the minute it was over we both knew it was an awful mistake.'

Katherine ran her hands through her hair. 'For Heaven's sake, Liv,' she said exasperatedly, 'even *Toby*'s noticed that Felix loves you, and he's never been the most observant person.' Her dark eyes focused on Liv, and she repeated, 'Felix loves you, Liv. He's loved you for years.'

Felix's car was still parked in the courtyard. Liv looked in the barn, but it was empty. Then she glimpsed him, standing by the gate on the far side of the field.

She thought about Lucie Rolland. How, after decades, a person you had believed gone for ever could come back into your life. And she thought of the pink house beneath the sea, and the waves that ebbed and flowed through its empty windows.

She walked across the meadow. Tall grasses and golden buttercups brushed against her legs. Hearing her footsteps, Felix turned round. He smiled fleetingly. 'I'm sorry, Liv. Ordering you about like that. Only I thought – I thought even if the rest of it meant nothing to you, we still had Briar Rose.' He paused. Then he said, 'I don't think I could bear to have nothing.'

She stood beside him, leaning her arms on top of the gate. 'You haven't got nothing, Felix. I'm here, aren't I?'

'After I left you last week,' he said slowly, 'I thought that I'd never be first with you. That I'd always be second best. The thing is, you see, that I love you.'

'You're not second best, Felix. Never second best.' She leaned her head against his shoulder. 'Stefan was the first man I fell in love with. Before that, I often thought I was in love, but once I met Stefan, I knew that nothing had come close to what I felt for him.' She gazed out across the road and marshes, to where the misty grey-green sea merged into the horizon, and she said quietly, 'But I don't *want* to feel like that again, Felix. I thought that was what I wanted – passionate, all-encompassing love – but I was wrong. It didn't bring me happiness. It almost destroyed me.'

He stroked her hair. 'I desire you,' she said, 'and I like you, and I enjoy your company. And I don't want anyone else. I don't know whether that adds up to love, but even if it doesn't, could it be good enough for you?'

'Oh, I should think,' he said, just before he kissed her, 'that it'll just about do.'

Katherine met Jordan by the aviary in the centre of the park. As she told him it was over, she watched the birds flutter from perch to wire. 'I'm sick of sharing,' she said. 'All my life, I've had to share. I'd rather be on my own.'

She saw in his eyes a mixture of pain and relief. They had come too close to the wire, and it had frightened him. She knew that, had she not put an end to it, the affair would have drifted on, their meetings gradually becoming less frequent, their passion slowly seeping away. She told herself that she should be proud that it was she who had had the courage to put an end to something that was already dying, but she felt no pride, only desolation and emptiness.

He kissed her before he left her; closing her eyes, she smelt feathers, and decay. Leaving her, he paused once. 'Oh, by the way,' he said, 'Henry Wyborne has resigned his seat. Did you know?' Then he walked away.

The months passed. The relentless summer of 1976 seemed an inappropriate backdrop to the chill that had settled around her heart. Fine day followed fine day. The sun glared in a Mediterranean-blue sky, and the drought dried up the reservoirs and cracked the riverbeds into jigsaws of dried mud. Dust greyed the cars parked alongside the road, and flowers wilted in gardens. Dutifully, Katherine placed a brick in the cistern, and watered her pot plants with her bathwater.

At the end of August, Hector and Alice took a cottage in Lyme Regis for a fortnight. Katherine went to stay with them for a few days. The cottage had blue pebbledashed walls, and ceilings so low Hector had to stoop. In the evenings, they played board games and watched television; each morning, they walked along the flat umber rocks that edged the shore. Reddish-brown sea-anemones glistened in the pools, and crabs the colour of onyx scuttled over the rocks. The fragments of limestone that fell from the cliffs revealed their secrets: ammonites and sea-urchins, and the delicate wands of belemnites.

As the morning went on, Katherine took shelter in the shade, hiding her pale limbs from the sun. The sea rolled against the shore, and she was content to sit for hours watching the curve of the waves and the glitter of the sunlight on the water. Her heart, which had felt as dry and desiccated as the empty streambeds, seemed to swell a little, as if coaxed back into life by the sea's rhythmic beat. She thought, in six months, I shall feel better. In a year, I shan't think of him all the time. In five years' time, I'll hardly think of him at all.

Shading her eyes, she could see Alice dipping her net into a rock-pool. Hector's hand was on her shoulder, steadying her. Alice drew the net out of the water; peering into it, she jumped up and down, laughing.

Katherine reached into her bag and took out a postcard. Writing Liv's address, she smiled to herself. If it hadn't been for you, Rachel, thought Katherine, I'd never have made it up with Liv. Wherever you are, I hope you're pleased with yourself.

Chapter Seventeen

Felix screened off part of the barn to make a small office and design studio for Liv. Another area was set aside as a workroom to mix dyes. Soon after they moved in, Felix bought a continuous printing machine, to speed up production. Liv worked each day after taking the children to school; at half past three, she broke off from whatever she was doing and dashed out to collect Freya and Georgie. The barn echoed with the hiss of the driers and the rattle of the printing machine's rollers. After the cloth was printed, it was baked in an oven, washed to remove the excess dye, and then steam-dried. The air was always thick with the scent of dyestuffs, and cloudy with steam. Liv loved it. She loved the noise, the smell, the colours. Most of all, she loved the moment when she first saw her design appear on the newly printed cloth: a field of scarlet poppies against pale gold ears of wheat, or a trellis-work of tiny rambling roses.

Felix gave up his job in the bank to work full time for Briar Rose. He sourced the raw cloth and dyestuffs, kept an eye open for more efficient machinery, and travelled throughout Britain, looking for new outlets for their textiles. Liv created the designs, mixed the dyes, and oversaw the printing process. Daphne Maynard helped care for Freya and Georgie when Liv was busy, and turned her hand to help with whatever was necessary when they had to fulfil a rush order.

In December 1976, Thea and Richard returned to England to live in Richard's house in Fernhill. Richard's arthritis, brought on by the injury he had received at Monte Cassino during the war, had worsened; he would probably need an operation. Felix, Liv and the girls visited at Christmas. Thea's huge Cretan pots shared the pale, elegant rooms of the Queen Anne house with Richard's books and First World War memorabilia. Thea had begun to reupholster the faded sofas and *chaise-longues* with fabrics that brought to mind the colours of the Mediterranean: sand, azure and turquoise.

The evening before they were due to return to Norfolk, Thea drew Liv aside. She told her that because Richard's deteriorating health had meant that they had not known when they would be able to travel again, they had taken a circuitous route returning to England from Crete, visiting all the places they had not yet got round to seeing: Malta and North Africa, Portugal and Spain. In a small hotel in Marrakesh, the proprietor had commented on Thea's surname. 'Fairbrother,' he had said, frowning. 'We had a gentleman of that name not long ago.' He had shown Thea the entry in the register. *F. Fairbrother*, the signature had said, in handwriting that had made Thea's heart pause for a moment before reassuming its usual steady beat.

'I couldn't be certain,' Thea said, looking at Liv. 'Handwriting changes as people grow older and, besides, I haven't seen Fin's signature in years. But it is possible that was your father's writing.' She had made enquiries, Thea added, but had found out nothing more. 'I wasn't sure whether to tell you, Liv,' she said, 'but you seem so happy, these days, that I thought even if it's just another dead end, another disappointment . . .' Thea hugged her daughter.

At night, lying in bed with Felix asleep beside her, Liv imagined Fin winding his unending path around the earth. The unanswered questions that had haunted her since childhood had lost the power to gouge away at her self-assurance. He had not left her because he had not loved her, or because she had not been a good enough daughter. It had been a twist of Fin's own character that had prompted him to leave, and not some failing of hers. She had learned too much about love and the failure of love either to blame herself for her father's absence, or to continue blaming him for leaving her. After a while, she turned in bed, wrapping her arms around Felix, and then she closed her eyes and slept.

In the New Year, they took on a girl from the village to help part-time with the paperwork. There was now a telephone at Samphire Cottage and, to Freya and Georgie's delight, a television. Liv had learned to drive, and had bought herself a small car. Both the telephone and the car gave her a sense of freedom. For the first time in her adult life, she was free, too, of anxiety about money. Though she knew that the success of the business was still precarious, she was nevertheless more financially secure than she had ever been. Though Felix insisted on reinvesting as much of the profits as possible, Liv was able to afford to buy the girls the clothes, books and toys they needed. Once a month or so, the four of them ate out at a restaurant. Freya had started ballet lessons in the village hall, and Liv had promised Georgie that she could learn to ride as soon as she was old enough.

Felix continued to live in London. When, in the New Year, he had suggested they live together, and she had refused him, they had almost quarrelled. 'On a good week,' he said, 'we spend two or three nights together. On a bad week, we're lucky if we've half an hour to ourselves.' Liv pointed out to him that even if they set up house together, they still wouldn't see much more of each other. He spent half of the week travelling, and besides, he had responsibilities of his own, didn't he? His father and his vow to recover the family home. Wyatts. It was not, she said, as she kissed him, that she did not want to see more of him. It was just that the present arrangement suited both of them. Freya and Georgie were settled in their schools, and she did not want to repeat the disruptions of their early years by moving them. She was near the barn; he was near Toby and the big London shops. He drew her to him, cradling her head in the curve of his shoulder. 'It's just that I miss you, Liv,' he said. 'That I want to be near you.'

Later, alone, she acknowledged privately that she continued to treasure the isolation of her cottage by the marsh. It was her retreat, her sanctuary. After the noise and bustle of the barn, the cottage's silence was welcome. At the end of a long day, she would sit in the lean-to, drinking a glass of wine as the last rays of the sun dipped below the horizon. If she concentrated, she could hear the distant murmur of the sea. Her life seemed to have drifted at last into a settled, happier phase. She sensed the fragility of her contentment, and was reluctant to make any change that might disrupt it. She told herself that her independence had been too hard won to hand over lightly. And if a part of her knew that her reluctance to put her relationship with Felix on any permanent footing was due to the lack of trust that the years with Stefan had bred in her, then she pushed the thought away, unwilling to face it.

Freya was now seven, and Georgie was five. Both attended the primary school in the village. Both, to Liv's relief, easily accepted Felix as a frequent overnight visitor to the house. When, on rare days off work, the four of them went out to the cinema or for picnics by the seaside, Liv knew that they looked, from the outside at least, like a proper family. Yet she also knew that she must not build her daughters' lives on a deception, so she searched out an old photograph of Stefan, and framed it and put it in the girls' bedroom.

Georgie glanced at it fleetingly then went back to bathing her pink plastic piglets in a cup; Freya stared at the black and white image, tracing Stefan's features with the tip of her forefinger. Liv searched for the words that might explain Stefan to his bright, lanky, restless seven-year-old daughter. The words that might explain to her that though, Stefan had always loved her, he had not been able to live with her. Freya's eyes – Stefan's dark, opaque blue – gazed at her, curious, hungry, expectant.

Throughout the first half of 1977, the business prospered. Liv designed a series of fabrics inspired by the Corcoran's blocks, adapting the old wallpaper patterns for use with textiles. One of the fabrics, 'Rose Red', was an instant success, and Liv only began to appreciate how great a success when it was featured on the front cover of the May issue of *House and Garden*.

At the end of June, Thea offered to look after the girls while Felix and Liv had a long weekend away. They tagged a few days in a guest-house in the Lake District on to visits to customers in

Edinburgh and Glasgow. The guest-house was beside Lake Windermere. The bliss, Liv thought, of not having to get up early in the morning. The bliss of someone else doing the cooking. The bliss of being able to read a novel uninterrupted, and being allowed to make love to Felix without worrying about the patter of small feet in the corridor.

They headed back down the M6 on Sunday afternoon. Liv was glancing idly at the map when the place names caught her eye. Lancaster ... Caton ... Littledale ... She glanced at Felix. 'Have we time for a small detour?'

'Should have. Where to?'

'Holm Edge.'

She felt his gaze. 'Are you sure?'

She nodded. They turned off the motorway at the exit to Caton. Driving through Caton, she recognized the shops and houses. If she blinked, surely she would see in the shadows her former self, hauling the heavy pram up the kerb, rushing round the shops so that she would not be late home to Stefan.

She gave Felix directions. Heading along the Littledale road, she looked up, searching for the house on the hill. She remembered following the map Stefan had drawn on the back of her hand, and seeing Holm Edge for the first time.

'There,' she said, pointing.

'I thought it would be bigger.' Felix focused on the house. 'I always imagined some great Gothic pile.'

They headed up the track. 'The holly tree,' she said. 'It's gone.' A stump was all that remained of the holly tree that had once stood by the gate. The gate itself was rusted, its hinges broken. Though a part of her half expected, peering over the drystone wall, to see Stefan's Citroën, the garden was, of course, empty and overgrown. The windows of the house gazed back at her, black and blank and unseeing.

She struggled to open the gate, but it had jammed in the mud. Felix put his weight against it, pushing it wide enough to allow them into the garden. Thistles and nettles caught at their legs as they crossed the grass. Looking down the valley, Liv saw that the clump of brambles, where they had once picked blackberries for jam, had doubled in size, its snaking suckers clawing into the stony ground.

The house looked as though it had been uninhabited for years. Part of the roof had collapsed, and grey splinters of slate scattered the grass. Some of the windows were broken, others were curtained by dust and cobwebs. Paint had peeled from the front door. It was unlocked; opening it, Liv saw the chunks of plaster that had fallen from the crumbling ceiling. Inside the kitchen, the cupboard doors swung drunkenly from their hinges and the floor was covered with a thin glaze of brown water. Encircling the house, Liv peered through a grimy window into the room that had once been Stefan's study. Now, the dirty glass cast a greyish gloom, hazing the interior, so that if she half closed her eyes she could imagine it just as before: Stefan's desk, the towers of books and, sprawling over the walls, the brightly coloured spider's web of diagrams. The smallness of both kitchen and study – their low ceilings and cramped dimensions – took her by surprise. The rooms, the house, even the landscape itself seemed to have been diminished by the years.

She went into the barn. 'We had to burn the doors,' she explained to Felix. 'We'd run out of coal because of the miners' strike, so Stefan chopped up the doors.' Something caught her eye and, stooping, she picked up a fragment of red paper: a Kit-Kat wrapper.

'There's the remains of a bonfire.' Felix kicked at a heap of grey ash. 'And look at this.' A few empty tins, mineral bottles and a matted blanket were heaped in a corner.

'Kids playing, probably.'

'Or a tramp.' He glanced at her. 'Seen enough?'

She nodded. They went outside. A cloud passed over the sun, casting a shadow on the grass. She turned and looked up at the fell. The heather rippled and moved: the wind, she thought. Cold suddenly, she hugged her arms around herself.

They walked back to the car. 'We could head back cross-country, if you like,' said Felix. 'Through the Trough of Bowland. It might take longer, but it'll be beautiful at this time of year.'

She watched him for a while, as he bent his head to read the map. She knew that the house, and the landscape that surrounded it, had lost the power to hurt her or to confine her. What had taken place there was over, finished with. She remembered what she had said to Felix the previous summer. *Felix, I desire you and I like you and I enjoy your company, but I don't know whether that adds up to love.* What an idiot she had been, she thought. She knew now.

It was an unseasonably cold, wet summer, yet twice during those grey, dank months, Felix experienced a feeling of triumph. The first time was when, driving out of Bristol, he saw curtains of 'Rose Red' fabric hanging in the windows of a stranger's house. The second was the day he paid off his father's bank loan. He would have liked, on that occasion, to throw a wad of notes on to the bank manager's desk and grind his face into it, but he managed to confine himself to a cheque sent through the post.

Bernard's thanks were profuse, but there was an air of defeat beneath the gratitude that troubled Felix. Even during the worst days, Bernard had never given up. He had fought to regain his health after the heart-attack, and had endured the house sale and the bankruptcy proceedings with unfailing dignity, and had made valiant efforts to adapt to a changed lifestyle. Now, Mia confided to Felix that, when she wasn't at home, Bernard ate only bread and cheese because he couldn't be bothered to cook. He had stopped buying a newspaper, and spent hours sitting in front of the television. Mia had tried to encourage him to join a club, or at least visit the local library, but though Bernard made the effort once or twice, he didn't persevere.

To Felix, it was more obvious than ever how greatly his father missed Wyatts. How much he *needed* Wyatts. Once, Wyatts had occupied all Bernard Corcoran's spare time. His weekends had been spent making small repairs to the house and maintaining the grounds. Bernard was a practical man, and the cramped Norwich house allowed him little scope for his former pleasures. He had never seemed to fit the small rooms and narrow garden. Felix recalled the disturbing conversation he had had with Mia the previous year, but brushed the memory aside. Mia couldn't really have meant that she hated Wyatts; that had just been a low moment in a bad day.

Returning to London from the barn, he always took the route that passed Wyatts. One day, amid a flicker of beech leaves, he caught sight of a blue and yellow board. He braked, his heart pounding, his mouth dry, and got out of the car. 'For Sale', the board said.

He walked down the drive. A woman answered his knock at the door. She was fortyish, and wore smart slacks, a navy blue blazer with brass buttons, and a pink cotton shirt. There was a downward twist to the corners of her mouth. 'By appointment only,' she reminded Felix sharply, as she struggled to restrain the German shepherd dog at her heels. 'It says so on the board. You'll have to contact the estate agent.'

He gave her a friendly smile. A few complimentary remarks about the house and its location, voiced in his best public-school accent, and she seemed to unbend a little. She introduced herself as Mrs Darnell, and told him the asking price of the house. Sixty-five thousand pounds. Felix's heart gave an odd little bounce. Four years ago, they had sold Wyatts for forty thousand. The house had been on the market for three weeks, said Mrs Darnell, but they hadn't had much interest yet. That sour turn to the mouth again. They'd bought it as an investment, she explained, but now they needed to free up some capital. They were looking for a quick sale. Her husband's business ... She gave a little shrug.

He went back to the car, and drove to the pub in the next village, where he bought himself lunch. Sixty-five thousand pounds ... He drank a single whisky to steady his nerves, then began to make calculations. Mrs Darnell would probably agree to knock off a few thousand for a quick sale. He had bought his London house at a good time in an up-and-coming area, and it should raise twenty-five thousand or so. He'd cash in the few remaining stocks and shares his mother had left him, and he was sure that, if he asked her, Rose would do likewise. He'd have to borrow the remainder. No building society would lend to him – he was self-employed, the part-owner of a business that had only recently become successful – so he'd have to look elsewhere. As soon as he got back to London, he'd look up some of his former colleagues from the investment bank. He'd call in favours, work the networks that were the lifeblood of the City.

He loosened the collar of his shirt. He felt hot, and his pulse was racing as though he had a fever. Glancing at his watch, he saw that he had time enough to call into Norwich on his way to London. Give his father the good news. As he drove, anxieties raced through his head. The investment that the business still badly needed, and from which he would have to divert funds . . . the worrying fact that Briar Rose's profits lurched wildly from one month to the next.

Yet, he thought savagely, they needed Wyatts; it belonged to them. He found himself imagining Liv there. Freya and Georgie playing in the garden . . . A child of their own, perhaps, in the nursery . . .

As he neared the street in which his father lived, he heard the ambulance siren. The blue light flared its warning in his rear-view mirror, and he pulled over to the side of the street to let it pass. The howl of the siren echoed as the ambulance swerved around the corner. He thought, Which of the neighbours? and then, for the second time that day, his heart lurched, and he fumbled with handbrake and gearstick, the day's optimism utterly erased by a dreadful suspicion as he followed in the vehicle's wake.

Philip Constant died that summer. He had had more frequent fits during the past year and then, towards the end of July, he suffered a massive seizure. Katherine took time off work and went to Cambridge, to Addenbrookes Hospital. At first, Philip was garlanded with tubes and wires, but after a couple of days, her father came into the room and removed them, moving gently and carefully, as if it were still possible to disturb his youngest son's quiet composure. Katherine knew what the removal of the tubes meant: that Philip would not recover.

She took turns with her mother, sitting beside her brother's bed. She knew that Philip had gone a long, long way away from her; she sensed that he had just a final step to make, a last crossing to a different shore. Every now and then she would emerge from the hospital, blinded by the sunlight, dazed by the way in which the rest of the world continued its complacent turning. Sitting on a bench in the botanical gardens, she had to fight the impulse to call out to the carefree strangers that surrounded her and tell them that, not far away, a twenty-year-old boy was dying.

When it came, the moment of death was just a slow lessening of breath, a final stilling of the stumbling workings of a damaged body. When she knew that it was over, Katherine left her mother alone with Philip, and went out into the corridor. Simon was standing by a window. Her face must have told him what had happened, because he just put his arms around her and hugged her while she wept into his jacket.

Throughout the funeral service a week later, Katherine took turns to hold Michael and Sarah's son, Tristram. Tristram was a large, dribbly, complaining baby, for whom Katherine could find little auntly feeling, but at least mopping saliva from the lapels of her black jacket provided a distraction. Looking round the crowded church, Katherine thought, So many people ... She hadn't known that so many people cared about Philip. Several of the staff from the home in which Philip had lived as an adult had attended, as well as teachers and pupils from the special school he had been to when younger. Friends and neighbours, and colleagues of her father filled the intermediate pews, and to one side of the church Katherine glimpsed Liv and Thea and Richard. Then, as the organ music began to play, she saw Hector slip into the back of the church, and her heart gave a little leap of recognition and relief.

Leaving the church, the white, overcast sky glared down at her. The air seemed hot and wet, as though compressed between sky and earth. The burial was followed by a buffet at the Constants' house. Katherine passed round sandwiches, made tea, and spoke to aunts and cousins she hadn't seen in years.

She was in the kitchen, among the stacks of dirty crockery, prising ice cubes out of a tray, when the door opened. Looking up, she saw Hector. The last remains of her fragile composure slipped away, and she heard herself say, 'So good of you to come, Hector. I didn't expect it. All this way. The shop—' Her fingers slipped, and an ice cube hurled itself across the floor.

'Let me,' he said. He took the tray from her and up-ended the ice neatly into the jug. 'You didn't think I'd put the bloody shop before coming here, did you, Katherine?'

She said weakly, 'You hardly knew Philip.'

'That's not the point. I know *you*. I know what he meant to *you*.' There was a silence, and then he said, 'I'm sorry – I don't mean to be cross. That's the last thing you need. You look exhausted. Sit down.' He pulled out a chair.

Katherine stood still for a moment, pressing her cold, wet hands together. 'The lemonade . . . and people want more tea.'

'I'll do all that. Sit down. I insist.'

She smiled weakly. 'So masterful, Hector.'

He gave a crooked grin. 'I have my moments.'

She sat down. It was true, she felt exhausted. Her legs ached, and a muscle to the side of her head had been pulsing all day. She closed her eyes, and heard Hector leave the room.

When he came back, he said, 'That's done, they're all refilled with tea or whatever. And I looked for Scotch for you, but there doesn't seem to be any.'

'There's brandy under the sink. Medicinal purposes.'

Hector hunted among the packets of Daz and bottles of bleach for the brandy. He poured a large measure, and placed the glass in Katherine's hands. 'Can I get you anything to eat?'

407

'No thanks. I couldn't.'

'Then . . . do you want to talk about it?'

'Philip? No. There's really nothing more to say, is there?' She felt drained, squeezed dry by the events of the week. 'To be honest, I'm sick of talking. I feel as though I've spent the last few hours saying the same things over and over again. That it was a mercy, and that at least it was easy in the end, and that he didn't feel any pain – all that.'

He was filling the sink with hot water. 'And that's not what you think?'

'Hector, I feel so *angry*!' She stared out through the french windows at the garden. 'I say all those things, and inside, I'm just *raging* at the unfairness and the pointlessness of it.' She struggled to get hold of herself. 'I'd like to be able to think about something else – to do something else – but I can't, and it just makes me feel tired as well as angry.'

He plunged dirty plates into the sink. 'We've missed you, Alice and I. When will you come back to London?'

'Soon. I've missed so much work.'

'Then I'll think of some distractions. I'll get a babysitter. We'll go to the theatre. And see some films . . .'

'I don't think I'd be very good company.'

'Katherine, you put up with me for years and years and years. God knows why. I can't have been any company at all. At the very least, I owe you a few evenings out. And also, I've been wondering . . .'

'What, Hector?'

'Whether to take Alice to Bellingford.'

She glanced at him. 'I suppose it would mean . . . facing up to the ghosts.'

'A final exorcism.' He put another glass on the draining-board. 'I can't have Alice go on thinking her family's just a heap of old photos in a scrapbook, can I?'

'When will you go?'

'I don't know. When it fits in with school and the shop. It would take a weekend – it's too far to travel up and down in the same day.' He turned to her. 'When we go, would you come with us, Katherine?'

'Moral support?'

'Partly. And also—' He broke off. Then he said, 'Also because I'd enjoy your company.'

'Of course I'll come, Hector.'

'Then thank you.' And he leaned forward, and touched her mouth with his lips. She gave a little laugh.

'I don't think I've ever,' and she was unsure whether she was laughing or crying, 'been kissed by a man wearing rubber gloves and a pinny before.'

Waking one night, Liv heard the footsteps. Then a small, muffled snap: a twig breaking, or a match striking. She sat up in bed, listening, and seemed to hear the soles of shoes crushing the clumps of wet grass, but could not quite separate their faint, regular beat from the pounding of her own heart. Then, unmistakably, there was the click of the gate closing. In the silence that followed, she interpreted every sound – the wind rustling in the willow leaves, the creaking of the floorboards in the old cottage – as evidence of an intruder. Pulling aside a curtain, she peered out of the window. The garden was still and empty, bathed in moonlight.

She curled up in bed, but was unable to sleep. Her thoughts turned inevitably to the events of the summer. To Felix's father's death, and, just six weeks' later, Philip Constant's. Several times during the month that had passed since Philip had died, she had held Katherine while she had wept for the loss of her brother. It hurt her that Felix had not yet let her do the same for him.

The second heart-attack had been massive, killing Bernard Corcoran instantly. Since his father's death, Felix had immersed himself in work, spending all his energies on the business. He had spoken little of his father, and had rebuffed any attempt by Liv to bring up the subject. Lying awake in the darkness, Liv reminded herself yet again that Felix needed to work out his grief in his own way. Most of the time, she managed to believe that. But alone in the comfortless centre of the night, all the haunting thoughts that by day she managed to suppress came to the forefront of her mind. That Felix had not permitted her to share his grief with him. That he would not accept the solace she offered. That what they felt for each other was a second-rate sort of love, suitable only for easy times.

She slept badly and, waking early in the morning, went into the garden, looking for signs of an intruder. But there was nothing: no convenient scrap of material, snagged on the brambles, no footprints impressed in the damp earth at the edge of the verge. She told herself that she had imagined it, that she had misinterpreted the normal sounds of the night as something more sinister.

Yet three days later, coming home from the barn in the late afternoon, she saw that the garden gate was swinging open. The gate had a complicated catch that Georgie had only just learned to master, and insisted on closing by herself each time they left the house. She could clearly remember Georgie shutting the gate that morning. The postman, she told herself, or the vicar, delivering the parish magazine. Yet nothing had been put through the letter-box.

That night, she drifted in and out of sleep, her dreams confused with reality. A dark figure walked the summit of the shingle ridge. A shape shifted beneath the willow branches. Eyes – a dense, opaque blue – glittered in the tall reeds.

A hand slipped the latch of the gate. In her dreams, he waited, crouched by the ditch. He bided his time.

Before she went to bed each night, she walked around the house, checking bolts and window latches. Once, in the middle of the night, she climbed out of bed and looked out. The moon was full, and she thought she saw, silhouetted against a navy blue sky, a figure.

The rain began in the early morning, rattling against the

window-pane, startling her out of sleep. She spent the morning at the barn, going through the paperwork with Janice, the part-time secretary, and the afternoon at the cottage, working on a new design. Puddles sheened the potholes in the road, and the grass around the house was like a quagmire. Water brimmed in the ditches and streamed down the roof of the lean-to. Later, clearing up the kitchen, she heard in the distance a crack of thunder. Through the kitchen window, a sudden movement caught her eye, and she started, but it was only the branches of the trees, bending in the wind.

Once, she had treasured her solitude; now, the cottage's isolation frightened her. The evening stretched out before her, with only the television for company. She found the remains of a bottle of wine in the fridge, and curled up in bed, reading a novel and drinking, and dreamed of strange creatures that emerged from the sea, slithering across the pebbles and the marsh, to wait for her, hidden in the undergrowth.

The telephone rang early the next morning, jerking her out of a fitful sleep. One of Mrs Maynard's labourers told her that the river had burst its banks during the night and had flooded the barn. She bundled Freya and Georgie into the car in dressing-gowns, pyjamas and wellingtons. Driving to the barn, the tyres of her car cast up curls of muddy water. At the entrance to the farm, the car wheels jammed in the thick mud, spinning impotently. With a sense of dread, she caught sight of the brown, swollen river, and the slick of dark water that lapped over the meadow and circled the footings of the barn.

She guessed the scale of the disaster as soon as she opened the door. It felt wrong, sounded wrong, smelt wrong. The scents of cotton and dye had been erased, replaced by the dank odour of muddy water. When the daylight illuminated the bright swirls of fabric bobbing in the water, she wanted, just for a moment, to weep.

She worked throughout the day to salvage what she could. All the stock stored at ground level was ruined, the bales of raw cotton as well as the printed textiles. The water had got into the filing cabinet, reducing order books and headed notepaper to papier-mâché. The printing machine had been swept against the dividing wall, and was badly damaged.

She left messages at Felix's flat in London, and with Toby. Then she carried the undamaged bales of cloth to a dry outhouse beside the farm, and telephoned Janice, and between them they rescued what paperwork was salvageable. As the river ebbed, she swept the brown, soupy water out of the barn doors on to the grass. As she worked, she found herself reminded of that other flood, at Holm Edge, the day before Freya had been born. Though she tried to suppress the terrible recollections – Stefan's abandonment of her, and her own isolation and fear – every now and then the memories would come rushing back.

Sternly, she told herself that every bucketful of muddy water swept out was one bucketful less in the barn, and that each ruined bale of cloth or broken jar of dye taken away meant that the heap of detritus grew smaller. She made herself work on, though all her muscles trembled with exhaustion, though her clothes were cold and wet with mud, and she longed to go home, and fall into a hot bath.

Janice offered to take Freya and Georgie home at six, and to sit with them until Liv came back to the cottage. At seven o'clock, Liv heard a car draw up in the courtyard. She went outside, and saw Felix.

He said, 'Toby told me, when I called in at the shop.' She saw him pale as he looked inside the barn. Walking around the room, he reached out to touch a sodden length of cloth, a mud-soaked reel of thread. He stopped beside the broken printing machine. 'Just as things were starting to take off,' he muttered. 'Just as we were beginning to turn the corner.' He drew back, shoulders hunched, staring at the devastation. Then he said, 'Well, that's it, isn't it?'

Liv had sat down on an upturned tea-chest. Her head ached. 'What do you mean, that's it?'

'We've failed, haven't we?' Savagely, Felix seized a length of wet cloth and hurled it against the wall. 'You find the money . . .

you work every hour of the bloody day ... and in the end, the bloody *weather* finishes you off.'

She rubbed her muddy fingertip along the furrow between her eyebrows. She was tired and hungry and her nerves jangled. 'It's awful, I know, but it doesn't mean that we're *finished*, Felix.'

'Look at it, Liv. Just look at it.' Stooping, he picked something out of a puddle. It was a label: the words *Briar Rose* were embroidered in fuchsia pink on a navy blue background. 'What do you think this is, Liv? Some sort of minor setback – a small hiccup on our road to success?' His gaze swept around the barn, and he said bitterly, 'There's nothing left. Nothing.'

Her temper, brittle all day, snapped. She hissed, 'We've a full order book, and there's still some cloth in stock in your place in London. All my designs are safe at the cottage. And we've somewhere to live – and even some money in the bank.' Her voice was shaking. 'That's not *nothing*, Felix. I had nothing when I lived at Holm Edge. I had nothing when I left London. This isn't *nothing*.'

'The printing machine's damaged. Almost our entire stock of raw cloth is ruined—'

'You could repair the printing machine, couldn't you?'

'Possibly. But it would take time.'

'Then you can work all night, can't you, Felix? As for the cloth, we'll just have to buy more, won't we?'

'With what?' He flung out his hands.

'We'll borrow, if we have to.' She hugged her arms around herself. She knew that she was on the verge of tears. 'Don't you dare give up on me, Felix Corcoran,' she said fiercely. 'Not after all we've been through. Not after all our hard work. This was your idea in the first place, remember. Don't you dare give up on me now.'

There was a long silence. Then his shoulders seemed to droop, and he looked around the barn. 'I'm just not sure what I'm doing it for, any more, Liv,' he said. 'And I'm not sure that I care enough any more.'

She stared at him, unable to believe what she was hearing. 'So you're going to give up, just like that? Our first real difficulty, and you're throwing it all in? Isn't that a bit ... *feeble*? A bit ... *cowardly*?' Her words resounded against the muddy walls of the barn, harsh and accusing.

There was a quick flare of anger in his eyes. Then it died as suddenly as it had been born, and he said quietly, 'I was trying to make things right for my father, you see. And now that he's dead, well, what's the point?' Then he turned on his heel and walked out of the barn.

As he crossed the grass, her voice followed him. 'I'll tell you why you're doing it, Felix! You're doing it for me. And you're doing it for Freya and for Georgie. Because we love you, and we need you!'

Yet the wind whipped her words away, and she was unsure whether he had heard her. Tears streamed down her face, tears of anger and of grief. 'Think about it, Felix,' she shouted, as he unlocked the door of his car. 'Make up your mind once and for all what it is that you really want!' But her voice broke, and she fell silent, and the rear lights of his car blurred into twin scarlet stars as he headed down the drive.

He couldn't bear being alone, so he bought a bottle of Scotch and an eighth of grass and looked up half a dozen old friends, from his student days, who were living in a squat in Bethnal Green. Bengali children with brightly coloured clothes and flashing dark eyes played in the street, ducking out of the way of passing cars. The air was thick with spices and traffic fumes. The doors and windows of the squat were boarded up, so Felix made his way through the back garden, clambering across overflowing dustbins, old mattresses and a gnarled Russian vine, which embraced the house in its sprawling green grasp. Indoors, the rooms were dark and cold, the nailed planks and the vine allowing little access for the sun. The kitchen was a nightmare of black mould and unidentifiable things bobbing in grey opaque water. Felix's friends were in the front room, lying on tattered floor cushions, smoking. A Grateful Dead track swamped the traffic noises from the street.

At first, he had a sense of homecoming. The music, the psychedelic paintings on the walls, and the pungent aroma of the grass reminded him both of the shared houses in which he had lived as a student, and of the parties at Toby's place in Chelsea. Lounging on the cushions, closing his eyes, letting it all flow over him, Felix felt his responsibilities fall away. The business, his family, the futile years he had spent trying to reclaim what they had lost: he forgot them all. He felt free again, young again. Some time before he drifted off to sleep, he resolved to dig out his old rucksack and go travelling again. He'd go further afield this time – the Far East, perhaps.

Though he had meant to sleep in the following morning, he woke early. Sunlight seeped through the cracks between the boards that covered the window. His friends slept on, draped over cushions, curled up on the floor. He went into the kitchen, and rifled gingerly through packets of ancient food in dingy cupboards, and made himself a cup of coffee. Wandering out to the shops, he bought a loaf of bread, some cheese and pâté and sat in the cave-like embrace of the Russian vine, eating. If his mind drifted to Liv and the devastation in the barn, he pushed those thoughts ruthlessly away. He told himself that he'd spent too long forcing himself into a mould that simply didn't fit. He had burdened himself with possessions, with commitments. He needed to put himself first, to do his own thing again, to reclaim the ideals he had lost.

Yet his contentment seemed to seep away as the day went on. Talking to his friends, he realized that none of them had worked since leaving college. They had bummed off their parents or friends; they had claimed social security. They had lived rent free in squats; they were expert in sliding a can of beans or a packet of tea beneath the folds of their coats as they wandered around the supermarket. Felix found himself thinking of Liv, of the years she had spent taking whatever work she could find so that she could feed and clothe her children. When he attempted to voice his disquiet, his friend told him to be cool, and pointed out that their way of life was, in itself, an attack on the capitalist system. Yet Felix's unease remained, and though he stayed another couple of nights, he found himself walking out of the house one morning, and not going back.

After he had gone home and showered and changed, he made his way to a pub in the City. Several of his colleagues from his days in the investment bank were there, propping up the bar. They welcomed him like an old friend, bought him drinks, offered him cigarettes. Around midnight, he found himself in a club in Soho, watching a bored girl take off her clothes to Shirley Bassey singing 'Big Spender'. Then a part of the night seemed to go missing, because the next thing he knew he was unpeeling his eyelids inside the familiar walls of his own house. His head pounded, and his mouth tasted foul. Eventually, he crawled off to the bathroom and was horribly sick. He spent the day in bed, with the phone off the hook, ignoring the doorbell. He ate nothing but aspirins and drank only water.

He woke the following morning with his headache gone, and his limbs no longer shaking. He had a long shower, but could not wash away his sense of self-loathing. He made himself coffee, and sat for a while, staring at the headlines in the newspaper, but none of them seemed to make sense, so after a while he grabbed his jacket and his keys and left the house. He drove aimlessly at first, with no particular direction in mind, only a longing to leave London behind him. Eventually he found himself surrounded by the pleasant woodland and valleys of Berkshire. Villages, hills and turnings in the road became familiar. And he knew, at last, where he was going.

He arrived at Great Dransfield at midday. He walked around the side of the house, ducking beneath the overgrown buddleias and lilacs, opening the green door and catching his breath, just as he had on his first visit, years ago, as he saw how the gardens, orchards and lake spread themselves out before him. He did not immediately go into the house, but wandered around the grounds.

Everything was just the same, he thought. Memories flickered in and out of his tired brain, ignited by the familiar scenery. Claire, sitting on the terrace, surrounded by hanks of dyed wool drying in the sun. Justin and India, shrieking with laughter as they swung from the tree beside the lake. And Saffron, of course, floating across the still water in the moonlight, a pale, ethereal Lady of the Lake.

He heard a voice call his name. Nancy was walking down the terrace. He asked her the same question he had asked when he had first visited Great Dransfield. 'Do you think I could stay for a few days, Nancy?'

Her reply echoed back through the years. 'Of course you can, Felix. Stay as long as you like.'

Hector took Saturday afternoon off from the bookshop, and drove Alice and Katherine up to Northumberland. They were to stay in Alnwick overnight and drive on to Bellingford the following morning. As they approached Alnwick, Hector explained that an agency had been looking after Bellingford during the last eight years, checking for burst pipes and leaks in the roof, and that he had put the furniture and the paintings in storage before he had gone abroad. 'So it'll be rather bare, rather depressing, I'm afraid.'

They left their luggage at the hotel, and drove to Alnmouth. The sun was sinking through the sky as they walked along the beach. Alice ran ahead, letting off her pent-up energy from the long car journey. Black pebbles of sea coal scattered the pale sand, and the North Sea was liquid gold in the sunset.

Back at the hotel, after Alice had gone to bed, Katherine and Hector ate in the hotel dining room. Over chicken chasseur, Katherine told Hector about her mother.

'She's got a job – a part-time job, working in a shoe shop in Cambridge. And she's planning a weekend in Paris with a friend. *Paris!* She hasn't been abroad since before she got married.'

'She's spreading her wings,' said Hector. 'Sowing her wild oats . . .'

'I suppose so. A bit late, don't you think?'

'Better late than never.' He frowned. 'I suppose I've never really got round to it.'

She looked up at him. 'Wild oats?'

'The sixties . . . doing your own thing. It rather passed me by.'

She smiled. 'No hippie trails to Marrakesh, Hector? No acid-fuelled years in a commune?'

'I'm afraid not. I was never particularly . . . *alternative*.'

'I can't quite imagine you in beads and a headband.'

He was wearing a sports jacket and polo shirt. 'I suppose I am rather *straight*. Rather old-fashioned.' He looked rueful. 'Rather dull.'

She touched his hand. 'Not dull. Never dull. I was teasing.' Katherine put aside her knife and fork. The chicken was rather chewy.

'I went from school to the City, you see. No halcyon years between.'

'Do you regret that?'

'Sometimes.'

'Are you attracted to the unconventional?'

He said again, 'Sometimes.' He was looking at her. Her face felt hot: the wine, she thought.

'Shall we have pudding?'

He glanced at the menu. 'Trifle, spotted dick, or ice-cream. I think not. Katherine?'

'No thanks. A drink, perhaps.'

'I'll just check on Alice.'

'I'll go, if you like. I've left my cigarettes in my room.'

She went upstairs. Alice was asleep, her thumb in her mouth, her fair hair spread out on the pillow. Katherine watched her for a moment, then kissed her, careful not to disturb her. In her own room, she checked her makeup and hair, and found her cigarettes.

Hector was waiting for her in the bar. French windows looked out over a wide lawn, bordered with roses. He stood up when Katherine came in, and handed her a glass. 'Whisky and ginger, I assumed.'

'Tell me about your family, Hector. Have the Setons lived in Northumberland for ages?'

'Oh, centuries and centuries,' he said. 'Origins lost in the mists of the past.'

'Do you know much about them?'

'The ancestors? A fair bit. Especially the mad and the bad.' He grinned. 'Black Johnnie Seton was supposed to have dabbled in witchcraft. And Margaret Seton left her dull but respectable husband and ran off with a gypsy.'

'I can't imagine what it must be like to belong somewhere,' said Katherine. 'I mean, really belong. I don't even know much about my grandparents.'

'When I was a child, I loved all my nanny's stories about the house. Wonderful place for a child to grow up, Bellingford. But the history didn't interest me at all. I thought it was as dull as ditchwater.'

'And now?'

'Oh, I don't feel like that now. Because of Alice, I suppose. After all, it's her past as well as mine, isn't it?' He had finished his whisky.

'Another drink?' she asked.

'I'll get them.'

'*Hector*. It's my turn.'

'I told you.' He stood up. 'Old-fashioned. Straight.'

While he went to the bar, Katherine rose and tried the doors of the french windows. They were open, so she walked outside on to the terrace, and lit a cigarette. Only five today, she thought. Not too bad. The air was perfumed with the scent of the late roses. The garden looked out over fields and woods, to the distant hills. The leaves of the roses glittered in the moonlight, and the flowers were like rich grey velvet.

Hector came to stand beside her. 'You see,' he said softly, 'this is what I miss in London.'

'Yes,' she said, teasing him, 'but where are the theatres, the cinemas? The shops, the restaurants? I mean, what do people *do* here?'

They walked down the terrace steps to the lawn. Damp blades of grass licked at Katherine's ankles. She ducked to avoid the branches of a rambling rose.

'Oh,' said Hector, 'out in the sticks we make our own amusements.'

'Chew straws.'

'Brew cider.'

'Country dancing.'

'Sleep with the sheep.'

Katherine giggled. Behind them, a voice called out, 'Time, please!'

'I suppose we should go back,' said Hector reluctantly.

'I can't,' she said. 'I'm caught.' The trailing frond of a rose had hitched itself to her skirt.

'Let me.' He knelt on the grass beside her, and released the tiny thorns. He said, 'It's cut you.' There was a ball of blood just above her ankle.

'Just a little scratch.'

'In Victorian times,' he said, 'a glimpse of ankle was thought terribly erotic.'

She laughed. 'And what do you think, Hector?'

'I told you,' he said, 'I'm very old-fashioned.'

Katherine woke the next morning feeling happy, an unaccustomed emotion since Philip's death. The bright, sunny morning, she thought. The recollection of a delightful evening, and the prospect of a whole day in the company of Hector and Alice.

After breakfast they drove to Bellingford. Hector explained to her, 'Bellingford's not really a castle. It's a pele tower with some not particularly tasteful Victorian additions. That's why the National Trust has never been interested – neither fish nor fowl, you see. So you mustn't expect anything distinguished.' He pointed. 'There.'

Katherine looked out. From the sheer walls of the square stone tower, arrow-slit windows glared down like meanly narrowed eyes. The adjoining Victorian house was a feast of Gothic revival turrets and decorative crenellations. Bellingford's setting was as uncompromising, Katherine thought, as the pele tower itself: there were no other houses in sight, and the hills circled the building like ramparts.

They explored the grounds first. Alice ran ahead, darting up and down terraces and ducking beneath the low, overhanging boughs of the copper beeches. As they walked, Hector fell silent. Glancing at him, Katherine said tentatively, 'This must be rather awful for you. Because of Rachel.'

'It does bring back memories, yes.' Hector looked down the long slope of the garden. 'Rachel hated the pond. Called it the bathtub.' There was an oblong ornamental pond on the terrace. 'She wanted to get rid of it, replace it with something more natural-looking, but we never got round to it.'

They wandered through shrubberies and parterres, straggling and overgrown after years of neglect. 'Come and see the house,' said Hector. He called to Alice, who scampered across the grass towards them.

'I'd rather play outside, Daddy. Please, please, can I play outside?'

'On your own, Alice?'

'I'm not a baby. I'm eight. Please, Daddy.'

Hector sighed. 'Oh, very well.' Alice clapped her hands together, and ran back across the lawn. 'But don't go near the road, and don't play by the pond, and you mustn't climb the trees and . . .'

They went into the house. As they walked from room to room, Hector said little, replying only monosyllabically to Katherine's questions. After a while, she too fell silent. Did he, she wondered, glimpse spectres flitting through these empty passageways? Did he still see, hanging on that peg, Rachel's coat? Did he still hear, echoing against those walls, Rachel's laughter? Climbing the stairs, exploring dark, gloomy chambers, Katherine found herself looking for evidence, searching for traces. A turn of the head, and surely she'd glimpse Rachel's red cashmere scarf, thrown carelessly over the banisters. A deep breath, and she'd catch a waft of Joy, Rachel's scent, imprisoned all these years in the enclosed rooms of the castle.

But there was nothing, of course. Long ago, someone had packed up Rachel's clothes, had tidied away her hairbrushes, jewellery and wristwatch, all those small objects that seem to gather to themselves the essence of a person, and had put away the magazines, the novels, the sewing-boxes and paintboxes, everything that once held clues to character and pastime. Now, Katherine tried to remember Rachel's interests, Rachel's preoccupations. Had she sewed, like Liv? Or had she preferred to read, or to ride? She could not now recall.

Returning from Fernhill Grange for the final weekend of her life, Rachel must have walked through these rooms and corridors, struggling with her impossible dilemma. From here, she had made her phone calls, and in this house, she had waited for the friends who had never arrived. Alone within these walls, she might even have greeted the onset of labour with something like relief. Pain, and the knowledge that the birth of her child was imminent, might have offered, at least, a distraction. The forces that had taken over her body would have had the compensation of allowing little room for thought.

Yet there was no trail of that last anguish. No record, etched into the stones, of loneliness or a sense of betrayal. Here, perhaps, Rachel's tragedy was not diminished, but took on a different perspective, becoming just a moment in time, a bright flame that had flared briefly, taking its place in centuries of human passion. The dark, empty rooms guarded their secrets.

They went out into the courtyard. Hector looked up at the high walls. 'This was where I asked Rachel to marry me,' he said. 'Or, rather, she asked me. I'd been meaning to all day, of course, but I couldn't seem to get round to it. Couldn't find the words.' He smiled ruefully. 'A failing of mine.'

Shadows slid across the weathered walls. Katherine saw Hector frown. 'I did wonder,' he said, 'whether Alice might find it all a bit overwhelming.'

'She seems in her element.'

'Good. That's good.' He was pacing around the courtyard. He seemed edgy, nervous. Suddenly, he said, 'I'm thinking of giving up the bookshop, Katherine.'

She stared at him. 'Are you?'

'Rents are going up again ... This last year we've barely broken even. And with Alice's school fees to pay, and the agent's fees for this place, I've had to eat into my capital.' He rested his shoulder against the wall, looking at Katherine. 'And, to be honest, my heart's never really been in it.'

'What will you do? Work in a bank again?'

'Good God, no.' Once more, he looked around the courtyard. 'Rachel had an idea that we could make money out of Bellingford. Tea-rooms, riding stables, that sort of thing.'

'And did you?'

'No. Never got round to it. But I think it might be worth having a go.'

She was sure she had misheard him, misunderstood him. 'Hector . . .?'

'It would make sense, Katherine. If we came back here, it would mean I could dispense with the agent, and sell my London flat. I'd save a fortune. And, besides, I've been thinking for some time that central London isn't the ideal place to bring up a child. The traffic ... and a couple of weeks ago, some chap was hanging about outside the school. Asking the little girls to come and see his puppies, that sort of thing. They sent letters to the parents. It made me think. Something like that, it makes you think.'

There was a sudden cold twist to Katherine's heart, as though icy fingers had reached out and squeezed it. She said, 'So you're thinking of living here again?'

'It's a possibility.' He ran a hand through his untidy hair. 'Not straight away, of course. There'd be a lot to sort out.'

'I thought,' she tried to keep her voice light, 'I thought you were just showing Alice her history. That's what you said, Hector. So it wasn't just photos in a scrapbook.'

'Partly that. There were other reasons for coming here, Katherine.'

She turned away before she could meet his eyes. He had already told her his other motives for returning to Bellingford. *Facing up to the ghosts. A final exorcism* ... She did not know at first why she felt so dreadful, and then, quite suddenly, she did.

Hector had taken off his glasses, and was polishing the lenses with his handkerchief. 'I wasn't sure,' he said. 'About Rachel. She was so young. And I've never been good at being certain about things. I wasn't sure whether she loved me. Or whether it would last. I remember telling her that I'd love her in ten years' time and in twenty. That I'd be hers till I died. But—'

Alice's voice, some distance away, interrupted him. She was shouting something. Hector blinked, focusing on Katherine. 'I haven't ... I mean, what I wanted to say was—'

'*Daddy!*'

'I wanted to tell you, Katherine—'

'Daddy! Daddy, you have to come here *quickly*!'

He said, once more, 'Katherine,' and then, when she did not reply, she heard his footsteps, fading as he walked away from her. Alone in the shadow of Bellingford's high stone walls, she was thankful for the brief respite. She understood now why Hector had taken her here. He had intended to warn her, to break the news of his going away gently. He had tried – kind Hector – to be gentle because he had glimpsed in her a dependence. Or worse (and she shuddered) – a need.

Some time in the future – in six months, perhaps, or maybe a year – Hector would leave London for Northumberland. Alice, whom she had come to love, would go with him. The thought of their absence appalled her.

Katherine saw Hector reappear at the entrance of the courtyard, holding Alice's hand. 'Don't you dare let him see that you mind,' she muttered fiercely to herself. 'Don't you dare.' There could be nothing more humiliating than to look into his eyes and see fear: fear that she might weep, make a fuss, make a scene.

So she smiled, and held her head high, so that she could at all costs keep her pride. It wasn't, she thought, with something akin to desperation, as though she had much else. She heard herself begin to talk, the fast words almost tripping over themselves, her misery hidden beneath their bright, glassy veneer: 'Brr ... it's getting a bit chilly, isn't it? And I'm famished. Do you think we could find a pub or something? Though there probably isn't anywhere for miles. This place really is in the middle of nowhere, Hector. So cut off ... When you think of London, it's as though we've gone back *decades*.'

Chapter Eighteen

Only a few of the original community at Great Dransfield remained. To Felix, Nancy seemed unchanged, but Claire's dark hair was now peppered with grey, and Justin and India had become tow-haired, sullen teenagers. Rose now occupied the attic bedroom in which Felix had once slept. A tall, gangling youth called Jason had Saffron's old room, and a couple and their twin infant sons occupied the bedroom that Bryony and Lawrence had once shared. And there seemed to Felix to be swarms of children, from babies in prams to ragged, noisy creatures who swooped down the banisters and hurled themselves across the garden, and swam in the ice-cold waters of the lake.

Felix's emotions, which had lurched exhaustingly between anger and numbness and guilt, seemed at last to begin to find an equilibrium. One evening, a few days after his arrival at Great Dransfield, he was sitting at the top of the terrace steps when Nancy came to join him.

She sat down beside him. 'You look lost in thought, my dear Felix.'

'I was thinking how *easy* everything used to be.'

Her long cobalt dress fell in folds around her ankles. 'Easy?' she repeated. 'Bryony's colicky baby ... those awful house meetings when everyone argued ... that dreadful time Justin nearly drowned ... *Easy?*'

'I was thinking of myself, I suppose. Everything seemed to be clearer then.'

She said gently, 'Tell me, Felix,' and he smiled and said, 'You are the most tactful woman I know, Nancy. I turn up on your doorstep, vagrant for the second time, and you don't even ask questions.'

'The trickier thing,' she said, 'was persuading Rose not to ask questions.'

He smiled ruefully. She looked at him. 'Why did you come here, Felix?'

'Because I couldn't think where else to go.'

'But you don't mean to stay, do you?'

'No. Not this time.'

She waited for him to go on. He heard in the silence the soughing of the trees in the wind. 'Coming here was ... self-indulgent,' he said. 'Selfish. I've left someone in the lurch, you see, Nancy. Someone I love very much. It was very wrong of me, but I was desperate. Everything seemed such a mess.'

He looked out towards the lake. Some of the children were playing on the bank. There was a dark, skinny little girl who reminded him of Freya.

He turned to Nancy. 'Doesn't it scare you sometimes, all this? The responsibility that you've taken on for these people's lives, for making this place work? I mean, I know it's supposed to be shared equally, but it never works out that way, does it?'

Nancy pulled her shawl around her shoulders. 'I used to wake up in the night, wondering whether I'd be able to pay the rates and the electricity bill. Or afraid that a spark would fall from one of the open fires and we'd all be burned in our beds. And, what was almost worse, wondering whether the whole idea of a self-sufficient community wasn't just a piece of self-deception. Wasn't just the silly, naïve dream of a middle-aged, middle-class spinster who just couldn't get the hang of the real world.' She smiled. 'But after a while I stopped worrying. There didn't seem to be any point. I came to the conclusion that the most that any of us can do is to muddle through, trying to do our best.'

He looked out towards the lake. 'After my father was bank-rupted,' he said, 'I tried, Nancy, I really tried to be a good son. I got a proper job. Saved money in the bank. All that.' The children were running across the lawn, back to the house. In his mind's eye, Felix saw the for-sale sign outside Wyatts. He whispered, 'I wanted to make things right again. I almost did it. It was as if I could reach out and touch it.' He remembered following the ambulance along the street. Seeing it park outside his father's house. Dread becoming certainty. The bitterness of knowing that all his efforts had been in vain.

He picked up a pebble from the steps, letting it fall from one palm to the other. 'And I thought, That's it, I'm through with responsibility. I've had enough.'

He had not been able to bear anyone to come close to him. He remembered Liv's angry words, flung at him across the stretch of meadow between barn and farmyard. She had told him she loved him. He had waited years for those words. But he had walked away.

He heard Nancy prompt, 'And have you changed your mind?'

'The thing is,' he said, 'that I miss them. So much. Not only Liv, the children as well. I've got used to them.'

Muddling through, he thought. He wondered whether that would be good enough. They sat in silence for a while, watching the dying sun paint the lake with crimson.

He drove to Wyatts for the last time. It was late September, and the leaves were turning. He remembered that his mother had always liked the autumn best, had said that the browns and golds matched the weathered shades of the house.

The for-sale sign had gone. He parked the car and walked up the driveway. There was a skip in the courtyard; a man was emptying a wheelbarrow into it. Seeing Felix, he straightened. 'Can I help you?'

'I've lost my way.' He looked up at the house. 'Lovely old place.'

'Isn't it?' He was young, only five years or so older than Felix himself, red-headed and cheerful-looking. 'We've just moved in. Hell of a lot of work to do.'

'Is there?'

''Fraid so. The previous owners only used it at weekends, and before that it was in the same family for years. They didn't keep up with the times. All that dreary old panelling . . .'

The skip was heaped with shattered lengths of oak. Felix remembered the warm, welcoming entrance hall, with its oak-panelled walls.

'Putting up a nice bit of woodchip,' the red-headed man added. 'Some bright colours'll cheer up the place.' He smiled. 'Oh, yes, hell of a lot to do. The kitchen's like something out of the Ark. Chap's coming to fit the new units next week.'

Felix let his gaze drift around the house and garden, from the pergola to the meadow and box hedges, from the twin gables that embraced the courtyard to the dormer windows in the low-pitched roof.

'As I said, though, plenty of scope. And I like a challenge. And it's a nice old place underneath.'

'It is, isn't it?'

'You said you were lost. Can I help you? There's a map in the car.'

Felix said, 'Actually, I've just remembered my way. But thanks all the same.' Then he walked back up the drive.

He drove to the barn. He saw that, in the week that had lapsed since they had quarrelled, the river had receded to its customary shallow flow, and that Liv had dragged all the ruined cloth and materials out of the barn, piling them in a heap on the meadow.

He went inside. She was sitting at her desk, her head bent over a sheaf of papers. He said her name, and she turned.

'Felix.'

He recognized the wariness in her eyes. He could not, for a moment, find the words. He glanced around the barn. 'You've done a terrific job.'

'I have, haven't I?'

'The floor. You've cleaned all the floor.'

'I was once a professional Mrs Mop, remember,' she said,

trying to make a joke of it. But her eyes watched him guardedly, and she remained seated.

'I came to say that I'm sorry.'

There was a silence. Then she said, 'For what, exactly, Felix?'

'For leaving you with all this while I go off and have a little *crise de nerfs*.'

There was a pause. Then she said, 'I don't mind you going. I could understand that. That's what I wanted to do when I saw it. Just go away, chuck it all in.' She was twisting her pen between her fingers as she spoke. 'But I do need to know whether you're coming back. And, if so, I'd like to know how long you mean to stay.'

He said, 'For ever, if you'll have me,' and he saw her close her eyes very tightly.

Opening them, she looked up, and said in a choked sort of voice, 'I don't think I've much of an alternative. I think I need you, Felix. I can't manage the bloody maths without you.' The invoice book, with its rows of figures, was open in front of her.

'I went back to Wyatts,' he said. He thought of the jolly-looking man, and the skip, and the drifts of copper-coloured leaves on the driveway. He looked down at his hands. 'I thought I'd hate to see someone else living there. Hate to see them making their mark on the place. But it's funny, I didn't really mind. In a way, it almost helped, seeing that it had changed. Drew a line, made a full stop.' He glanced up at her, and said, 'Houses are just bricks and mortar, aren't they? It's people who matter. I've remembered that now. Rose and Mia matter. And you and Freya and Georgie. You matter most of all to me, Liv.'

He went to her, then, and she pressed the side of her head against his thigh as he buried his fingers in her thick, black hair. Stooping, he kissed away the tears.

After a while, he looked round the barn. 'Do you think this is salvageable?'

'Janice helped me put together the records.' She blew her nose. 'I've phoned most of the customers, told them what happened.'

'Any cancellations?'

'Half a dozen. Could have been worse.'

'We'll have to go cap in hand to the bank, I'm afraid.' Gently, he drew the balls of his thumbs along the dark shadows beneath her eyes. 'You look tired, love.'

'I haven't been sleeping.' She wrapped her arms around herself. 'I've been afraid—' She broke off.

'Of what?'

'That someone's watching me.'

'Tell me, Liv.'

'There's really nothing much to tell. Just . . . oh, noises in the night. And the gate left open when I was sure that I shut it. And I thought I saw someone on the shingle ridge.'

'A birdwatcher?'

'At night?' Her eyes darkened. 'I thought of Stefan, you see.'

Not fear, he thought. Terror. He said gently, 'Are you sure?'

She shook her head. 'Not at all.'

'This man you saw—'

'He was too far away. Just a silhouette.'

'Have you been to the police?'

'I don't think there's any point. There's nothing . . . solid.'

'Is it possible,' he chose his words carefully, 'that you're tired and anxious, and putting two and two together and making five?'

'Yes,' she said, and gave a watery smile. 'Perfectly possible. And, besides, if it was Stefan, I'd know, wouldn't I? That's what I keep telling myself. He'd come to the house – he'd make himself known. He'd speak to me or something – he'd try and persuade me to come back to him. Wouldn't he?'

He put his arms around her again. 'It'll be all right, Liv,' he whispered. 'It'll be all right.'

'Do you think so?' She looked up at him. 'Do you remember the first time we met? In London, after Toby's party? The dinosaurs? Running from the dinosaurs?' She shivered. 'I can still feel them sometimes. Just round the corner. Bloody dinosaurs.'

*

Hector phoned Katherine.

'You didn't come to supper last night.'

'Sorry. I've been busy. I meant to let you know, but I forgot.'

'Alice missed you.'

She could hear the bewilderment, and the hurt, in his voice. She gathered together all her resolve, and said, 'Actually, Hector, there's been something I've been meaning to tell you.'

'Yes?'

'I'm applying for a new job.'

'Oh.' He sounded relieved. 'Time-consuming things, job applications. Distracting. Is it something exciting?'

'Wonderful. Just what I want.' Yet even to her, her tone sounded bleak. 'An old friend of mine, Netta Parker, wants to talk to me about it. It's a magazine,' she said. 'Rather a prestigious magazine. If I get the job, I'll be the features editor.'

'That's marvellous. Congratulations.'

'It would mean a move.'

'A move?'

'To America,' she said. 'New York.'

There was a silence. Then he said, 'Oh . . . I didn't realize . . .'

'Such an opportunity.'

'Of course.'

'It's not something I can turn down, Hector.' Her eyes stung.

Another silence. 'I'm very pleased for you, Katherine.'

Suddenly, she couldn't bear it any longer. 'I have to go. Someone's at the door. I'll speak to you later . . .'

She put down the receiver, and stood still for a long time, pressing the palms of her hands against the sockets of her eyes. Then she went to the wardrobe, and began flinging her best clothes – her Betty Jackson suit and her Bill Gibb dress – on to the sofa, ready to take to the dry-cleaner's the next morning.

Visiting London on Friday, Liv made a detour to Katherine's flat. She had spoken to Katherine on the telephone the previous evening. With studied casualness, Katherine had mentioned that she was going away for a few days. She had a job interview, she explained. She had then made some unconvincing excuse and put the phone down. Liv had been left with a sense of unease, a suspicion that something important had been left unsaid.

She reached Katherine's flat just before midday. She thought that Katherine looked flustered, edgy. On the living-room floor there was an open suitcase, and a great many clothes were strewn about the chairs and sofa.

'It's a bit of a mess,' Katherine said apologetically. She glanced at Liv. 'What are you doing in London?'

'Felix and I had an interview with the bank manager. We need a loan.'

'*Oh*. Coffee?'

'Please.' Liv moved aside several jackets, and collapsed into a chair.

'How did it go?'

'I don't know. The bank'll send their decision in due course.' Liv made a face. 'It was awful, actually. They were so condescending. So supercilious.'

Katherine made the coffee. 'Where's Felix now?'

'Sweet-talking some friends in the City.'

'And you and Felix?'

'Better,' she said, and smiled. 'Much better.' She looked around the room. 'Rather a lot of stuff for a job interview, isn't it, Katherine?'

'It's in America. New York.'

Liv's eyes widened. 'You didn't say.'

'Netta told me about the job ages ago, and I wasn't keen then. But now . . .' Her voice trailed away. Then she seemed to pull herself together. 'It's the chance of a lifetime.'

Katherine looked, Liv thought, utterly miserable. Not how a person going after the job of their dreams ought to look. 'What made you change your mind?'

Katherine had lit a cigarette. 'This and that.'

'*Katherine*.'

'The thing is that I've done something stupid,' said Katherine suddenly. 'Really stupid.' She was standing at the window, her back to Liv. 'The thing is that I've fallen in love with Hector.'

'It's not stupid to love someone,' said Liv gently. 'Not stupid at all.'

'It is,' said Katherine, 'when there isn't the smallest chance that they'll feel the same about you.'

'Are you sure? Are you sure that Hector doesn't—'

'Absolutely sure.' Katherine's voice, interrupting her, was brittle. She swung round. 'Hector's going back to Bellingford, Liv. He means to live there. We went up last weekend. I thought he just wanted Alice to see it. It never crossed my mind that he was thinking of *living* there again. But he is. And when he told me,' she shrugged, 'well, I just knew. Knew that he'd become more than just a friend. To me, anyway.' She paused. 'I think that it was after the accident that I began to feel differently about him. He was so kind to me. It's very beguiling, isn't it, kindness? And then, when Philip died . . .' Liv saw the tears in Katherine's eyes. 'When we were at Bellingford, and he told me that he was going to leave London, I suddenly saw how awful it would be, him not being there any more. I knew that I'd rather be with him than anyone else. I love him, Liv. And not only him, but Alice as well. I shall miss her so much.' Katherine tried to smile. 'A substitute for one of my own, I suppose. I must be feeling broody. Pathetic, isn't it? Another woman's child . . .' Katherine was furiously twisting a lock of hair around her forefinger.

'You see, we had a lovely evening the day before we went to Bellingford. We had dinner together at a hotel in Alnwick. And I found myself wanting him. And I thought that evening that he wanted me too. But the next day, when we went to Bellingford, it was different. He was so quiet, so on edge. As though he was afraid he'd got himself into something he didn't know how to get out of. As though he was regretting the things he'd said the night before. Of course,' once more Katherine smiled humourlessly, 'I could *make* him love me. I know that I could, because I'm good at that, aren't I, Liv?' Her voice was savage. Then her expression changed. 'But I won't,' she said softly. 'I won't because of Rachel.'

'Rachel? I don't see—'

'Do you remember, ages ago, when we were still at school, that Rachel told us that she was afraid that she would be left behind?' Katherine lit another cigarette from the butt of the last, and sat down on the window-sill. 'It was the spring term. We'd skived off school. We were auditioning...'

Liv smiled. 'For a film.'

'You and I were going to go to university, and Rachel was going to go to her awful finishing-school. And she told us that she was afraid we might forget her.' Katherine glanced at Liv. 'The thing is, when I was at Bellingford, I found it hard to remember anything about her. I mean, *really* remember. Not just, oh, facts – what she looked like, where she lived, that sort of thing. I mean, what sort of person she really was.'

'But she didn't have much of a chance to *be* anything, did she?' said Liv slowly. 'After all, she died so young. Think how much you and I have changed since we were nineteen.'

'We have forgotten her, though, haven't we? We promised not to, but we have. Hector hasn't. When we were at Bellingford, he was thinking about her, I know he was. *Hector* hasn't forgotten Rachel. And if that's all she's got – if Hector's memories of her are all that remains – then who am I to take that away from her?'

Liv almost said, 'But Rachel's *dead*.' But, glancing at Katherine's pale, set face, she bit the words back.

'Does Hector know?'

'That I love him? No. I almost made a fool of myself, but then Alice appeared, thank God, and distracted him.' She gave a crooked smile. 'I know that I've always had a bad habit of wanting what other people have got, but, well, someone else's husband and someone else's child, even I can see that's a bit much.'

Someone else's child ... Liv said firmly, 'Alice needs you, Katherine.'

'She's got Hector. She'll be fine.' Yet Katherine's voice was strained.

'Alice has already lost her mother and her grandmother. You can't just walk out on her. Think what it would do to her.'

Katherine slid off the window-sill, and began to hurl skirts and trousers into the suitcase. 'I have to go, Liv. My plane—'

'Let me talk to Hector.'

'*No*.' Katherine glared at her. 'You're not to say a word to him, do you understand? You're to promise.' She glanced at her watch. 'I have to be at Heathrow in a few hours. I'd better get a move on.'

'You're flying today?'

'Six o'clock.'

Liv made one last attempt. 'Katherine, this is madness. You can't just go.'

'Can't I? Just watch me.' Then Katherine's shoulders sagged, as though the anger had drained out of her. She said more quietly, 'I have to.' She sat down on the arm of the sofa.

'I went to America before, didn't I, after Rachel died, and after that awful man tried to rape me? It let me make a new start. It was the right thing to do then, and it's the right thing to do now. I couldn't bear to stay here, you see. I couldn't bear to be nothing to them. I don't know how I shall manage it, but I have to start again, don't I?'

Walking away from the Islington flat, Liv remembered what Katherine had said to her. *You're not to say a word to Hector. You're to promise.* She paused, irresolute for a moment, and then she thought, Oh, damn you, Katherine, for a bossy cow. Some promises were better broken. She hailed a taxi to take her to Bayswater.

The secondhand bookshop was dark and musty, as secondhand bookshops usually are. Shelves grew from the floor to the ceiling. A young man with spiky bleached-blond hair was behind the cash desk. Liv asked for Hector.

'Hector!' the young man bawled. 'Visitor for you!'

Hector emerged, blinking, from a back room. 'What is it, Kevin?' Then he saw Liv.

'I need to speak to you, Hector.'

'I'm with a customer.'

'Then get rid of them. We have to talk.'

'About what?'

'About Katherine.'

His face seemed to close in. 'I don't think there's much point, do you?'

'*Hector!*' she hissed furiously.

Kevin said, 'I'll deal with Mr Potter, if you like,' and disappeared into the back room.

Liv glared at Hector. 'Do you know that Katherine's going to America?'

'Yes,' he said coldly. 'She told me.'

'Did she tell you that she's going today?'

'*Today?*' His gaze dropped, and he began to tidy up around the till. 'No. She didn't tell me that.'

'You've got to stop her, Hector.'

'And how do you propose that I do that?'

'Phone her.'

'She's made up her mind, Liv.' He was sorting through the heap of papers and pens beside the cash desk. 'She was very clear about that.'

'Don't you *mind* that she's going?'

Papers fluttered from Hector's hands to the floor. He disregarded them. She heard him say, very softly, 'Of course I *mind*.'

'But not enough,' she said angrily, 'to do something about it?'

'It's not that—'

'She loves you.'

'No. That's the thing. She doesn't.'

'*Hector*. I've just come from Katherine's flat. She *told* me she loved you.'

'I think you've made a mistake, Liv.'

'There's no mistake.'

'I really think you must have—'

She wanted to shake him. 'But perhaps *you* don't *care* about her.'

'Liv, I—'

'After all she's done for you,' she said furiously. 'All these years, being a friend to you, helping you with Alice—'

'Liv—'

'If it's because of Rachel, then that's ridiculous. Absolutely ridiculous. You have to start thinking of the living, not the dead—'

'Liv,' he shouted, 'I *love* Katherine!'

There was a silence. 'Oh,' she said, after a while. Kevin re-emerged from the office.

Hector said, more quietly, 'I love Katherine. I adore Katherine. And I want to marry Katherine.' Several customers, browsing among the bookshelves, had turned to stare at him. Kevin, who was gathering up the papers from the floor, looked up.

Hector sighed. 'I wasn't sure what she felt about me, and then last weekend, the weekend we spent in Northumberland, I began to think that she cared for me. I was going to ask her to marry me, Liv. I was on the verge of it.'

'What happened?'

'She just made it clear that she wasn't interested.'

Liv thought of Hector – cautious, diffident Hector – and touchy, fiery Katherine. 'Did you tell her you loved her?'

He shook his head. Exasperated, she said, 'Did you say anything at all to her?'

He took off his glasses, and began to polish them with his tie. 'We were talking about the house, mostly. I was nervous. Trying to pluck up the courage.'

'Did you talk about Rachel?'

His blue eyes widened. 'Yes. Yes, I suppose we did.'

'Hector, Katherine thinks you're still in love with Rachel.'

Kevin had risen from the floor and was standing unmoving behind Hector, the papers clutched against his chest. The browsers had shuffled within earshot, turning the pages of their books, unseeing, ears pricked.

Hector said, very quietly, 'There'll always be a part of me that loves Rachel. It wouldn't be right to forget her, would it? But you have to move on. It took me a long time to understand that, and I wouldn't ever have managed it without Katherine and Alice, but you do have to move on.' He pressed the tips of his fingers against his forehead, and screwed up his eyes. Then he groaned. 'Oh, God, I can see how it must have seemed to her ... Taking her to the house, telling her I was thinking of living there again ... Talking to her about Rachel ... I told Katherine the plans we'd made ... that I'd said to Rachel that I'd love her till the day I died. You see, I was trying to explain to Katherine that though, in a way, that was still true, it didn't mean that I couldn't love someone else. That I couldn't love her. Oh, God,' he said again, remembering, as he ran his fingers through his hair. 'Alice called out, Liv, and I had to go to her, and by the time I came back, Katherine was different. She'd seemed to be enjoying herself, but then she changed. She was *spiky*. Defensive. Avoiding me. Wanting to get away from Bellingford as soon as possible. So I thought it was hopeless.' He looked up, and for the first time Liv saw his eyes brighten. 'Do you really think—'

'Katherine loves you, Hector. She told me so herself. And she doesn't want to go to America. Not really.'

'Her plane?'

'Six o'clock, she said.'

'I'll phone her flat.' He went into the back office. When he came out again, he said, 'There's no answer. She must have already left.' He stared at his watch. 'I'll drive to Heathrow.'

A muttered chorus of approval from the browsers. Then he said, 'Alice.'

'I'll pick her up from school,' said Liv.

'And the shop?'

'I'll hold the fort,' said Kevin.

*

439

Driving out towards Hammersmith, Hector kept glancing at the clock on the dashboard. Snaking through the busy traffic, jumping every amber light, his mood veered constantly between optimism and despair. That she loved him. That he might be too late.

He became wedged in a long queue of traffic at the Hammersmith flyover, and sat drumming his fingers on the steering wheel as he inched forward. After Hammersmith, the traffic eased a little but, looking once more at the clock, he saw that it was almost half past three. She'd check in at four, perhaps, then head for the duty-free area. He pressed his foot on the accelerator. The needle of the speedometer climbed: fifty, sixty, seventy. Overtaking on the inside lane, swerving around lorries and buses, he muttered a quick prayer that all traffic police should today be otherwise occupied.

At Chiswick, he turned on to the A4. Pushed to eighty miles an hour, the frame of his ten-year-old MGB rattled in protest. He disregarded it; disregarded also the fuel gauge, dipping dangerously into the red.

He could not, from the haze of memory, recall the first time he had seen her. Not like Rachel, who would remain for ever that first bright silver flame. Katherine had become a part of him gradually, almost insidiously, an accumulation of images and memory that had led him away from a life of grief and self-absorption to a new optimism and hope for the future. He thought of Katherine sitting in his flat after the bomb scare on the tube, trying to disguise the shaking of her hands as they gripped her cup of coffee. He thought of Katherine alternately coaxing and bullying him out of his self-imposed isolation during the early days of their friendship. Katherine cradling Alice on her knee. Katherine at the seaside, stretching out her long, pale limbs in the shadow of the cliffs.

And Katherine wounded and bruised after the accident. He had seen the vulnerability in her eyes then, and he had wanted to protect her, to defend her, to seize her wretched recalcitrant lover by the scruff of his neck and ask him what the hell he thought he was doing to her. And, lastly, Katherine in Northumberland, surrounded by roses, with a bead of blood like a single ruby just above her ankle. He had longed to kiss it away, to taste her skin and the blood that ran through her veins, to know her intimately. He had lain awake that night, hot and aching for her.

He knew her courage, and he knew her temper. Her awkward, lanky grace; her sensuousness. Her fierce bright intelligence, and her capacity for love. He knew all these things about her.

He was within a few miles of Heathrow. Above him, the solid shapes of the jets hovered like vast raptors. Glancing at the clock, swearing under his breath, he turned the steering-wheel sharply, swooping down the sliproad that took him off the A road. Lanes fed him towards the airport. He thought, If I'm too late, then I shall follow you across the ocean, if necessary. I shall kneel outside your door, Katherine, and I shall howl like a wolf till you come to me.

The check-in queue had thinned out a little, but she still waited, pushing her luggage trolley aimlessly around the aisles of the newsagent's. She did not know what she was waiting for: some sort of sign that she had done the right thing, made the right decision, she supposed. 'It's in the bag,' Netta had said conspiratorially, 'if you want it, Katherine.' She'd be leapfrogging over the shoulders of her colleagues, both male and female. It was all she had ever wanted, she told herself. An exciting and prestigious career, an apartment in New York. Netta would be her introduction to a new circle of friends. The salary she would earn would secure her future and allow her to enjoy the present. Even if Hector had wanted her, why should she turn such a prospect down in favour of domesticity in the form of a ready-made family and a draughty castle in the middle of nowhere?

She picked up a magazine she wouldn't bother to read, and took a paperback at random from the bestsellers. It was four o'clock. Once she'd checked in her luggage, and gone through passport control, there could be no going back. With a sense of fatalism, she began to push her trolley towards the check-in desk.

Then she heard him call her name. She stood quite still for a moment, half convinced that she had imagined it. Looking up, she saw him.

He was weaving between the crowds. Standing in the middle of the concourse, she waited for him. 'Katherine—' he said. He was red-faced, out of breath.

'What are you doing here, Hector?'

'Liv—' he gasped, 'Liv told me you were leaving today—'

'I told her not to,' she said tightly. 'I made her promise.'

'Katherine, you mustn't go. Please don't go.'

She said, 'I've made up my mind, Hector,' and tried to shove her trolley forward. But it had a wonky wheel, which wedged stuck, refusing to permit her passage.

As she wrestled with it, she heard him say, 'You can change your mind.'

'And why on earth should I do that?' Glaring at him, she tried desperately to push the trolley forward.

'Because I don't want you to go,' he said simply. 'Because I love you.'

She paused, looking straight ahead. His words were the only sound in the noise and bustle of the airport.

'I love you, Katherine,' he repeated. 'And I want you to marry me.'

She whispered, '*Rachel* . . .' and he took her hands in his, easing them away from the handle of the trolley.

'Rachel was then, and you are now, Katherine. The thing about the past is that it stays frozen, doesn't it? Rachel will never grow older than nineteen. Rachel and I will never know what it is to be married for five years – or for twenty-five, or for fifty. I don't know what it would have been like if we'd had longer together. Maybe it would have been wonderful. Maybe it wouldn't. But I'll never know. But I'd like to find out with you, Katherine. I'd really like to.'

She closed her eyes. She said, 'But Bellingford . . .' and her voice shook.

'I know you hate the country,' he said quickly. 'Stupid of me

442

to take you there. And I know you love your job. We'll stay in London. Anywhere, my darling. Anywhere you like.'

She looked up at him. 'I thought you didn't care, Hector. I thought you'd taken me there to break it to me gently. To tell me that you were going away.'

'Oh, Katherine,' he said softly. 'I took you there to ask you to marry me.'

She gave the trolley one last futile shove with her hip, and then she said, 'This *fucking* thing,' and then her voice broke, and he took her in his arms and hugged and kissed her.

Eventually, she said, 'I suppose we'd better go back.'

'I've got the car.' He made a face. 'Though it's probably been towed away by now.'

'Where did you leave it?'

'In an unloading bay.'

'*Hector*,' she said, wide-eyed. 'The police will find it. They'll think there's a bomb in it.'

'Dear God,' he said, horrified. 'I hadn't thought.'

'Heathrow airport will grind to a halt.' She wanted to giggle.

'Our first proper night together,' he said, 'and I'll probably spend it in prison.' He swung her suitcase off the trolley.

'I'll visit you in Strangeways.' They were heading out of the concourse.

'Even if I'm wearing one of those stripy get-ups with arrows?'

'I think,' she said, as they hurried along the pavement, 'that sort of thing went out with Dickens.'

There was a policeman standing beside the MGB, making notes in a pad. 'Oops,' said Hector, and then he took her hand in his as they began to run.

443

Chapter Nineteen

The sounds of the autumn seeped into her dreams. At night the marshes were alive with rustlings. Voices whispered in the gently moving reeds, but she could never make out the words. Branches rubbed against each other, making small clickings and grindings. To their echo, she'd dream of bones rising from the sea, as dry and pale as driftwood, forming into men who walked with a discordant tap and scrape towards the house. Skeletal feet marked birds' footprints in the muddy ground, and grey fingers tapped at window-panes. Sometimes, half-awake, she'd imagine she glimpsed him standing by the window. Or, just as she drifted back to sleep, he'd slide into bed beside her and reach out to her his cold hand.

She'd tell herself that she had heard only the cry of a gull, or the distant murmur of the sea. 'All's well,' she'd whisper, and close her eyes. Yet her skin was chilled, and she could feel the beating of her heart. She'd picture the cottage, seeing clearly how the marsh and the trees hid it from the road and the sea, cutting it off from the rest of the world.

Awake at night, she'd try to distract herself with the events of the last few weeks. Felix's so far fruitless attempts to find an investor to rescue the business; Freya's problems with her school work; Richard Thorneycroft's slow recovery from his hip operation. Richard and Thea's house had been burgled: there had been shards of glass on the floor where the french windows had been broken, and footprints on the carpet. 'He didn't take anything,' Thea had said, 'but that's not the point, Liv. The house doesn't feel like it belongs to us any more. I imagine him going through my things, picking them up, throwing them aside. I didn't think this sort of thing happened in Fernhill. All the years we were in Crete we never used to lock our door . . .'

A sea of troubles. She turned in bed, trying to concentrate on happier things: Katherine's engagement to Hector, and the new certainty and security of her own relationship with Felix. Sharing her life with another person no longer seemed synonymous with a loss of independence and freedom. She had discovered that it gave depth and dimension to her days. An intellect for hers to sharpen itself against. Strong arms to cradle her when she was tired. Someone to share her fears.

Yet she did not tell Felix about the dreams. She could not quite understand the dreams. She had never been happier, so why should she dream? The shadow of the watcher in the summer, she thought, lingered.

She was walking along the beach. She could hear the scratch of the pebbles beneath her feet, see the smooth polished glass turned to jewels by the push and pull of the tide. She looked out to sea and saw Freya. She was floating beneath the waves, her upturned face a few inches beneath the surface of the water. She looked as though she had been encased in glass, like a storybook princess. Her black hair swayed in the current like bladderwrack, and her eyes were open. Though she stretched out a hand to touch her, to pull her daughter from the waves, she could not reach her. The pebbles were sucked away from beneath her feet, so that she struggled to keep her balance, and the force of the waves prevented her wading forward. Her tears mingled with the spume from the waves.

She woke, staring into the darkness, her face wet. Though she dozed intermittently throughout the remainder of the night, her dream lingered. Her head ached, and she recalled that pale, still face, its familiar maps and contours altered by the shifting pattern of the water. Her inability, in her dream, to save her child haunted her, tainting the day.

Freya was unusually quiet that morning, eating her breakfast quickly, and dressing herself with untypical speed and obedience. She disappeared up to her bedroom while Liv brushed Georgie's hair. She loved to do Georgie's hair. Thick and curling, it sprang and gleamed at her touch like a wild animal.

At twenty to nine Freya came downstairs. Liv glanced up at her. 'You don't need that heavy coat today, darling.' Freya was wearing last year's winter coat. 'It's not cold.'

'I like this coat,' said Freya obstinately.

'And it's too small for you now – you've grown out of it. Go and put your anorak on.'

'I want to wear this coat. I can wear what I want.'

Liv glimpsed the light of battle in Freya's eye. Arguments just before school always seemed worse than other arguments; she was about to concede when she noticed a bulge beneath the heavy folds of the coat.

'What have you got there, Freya?'

'Nothing.'

'*Freya.*'

Reluctantly, Freya produced a large carrier-bag. Liv looked inside it. It was full of dolls and dolls' clothes.

'You can't take that many toys to school, darling. Mrs Chambers won't like it. Go and put them back in the bedroom.'

Freya said, 'They're not for *school*.'

'What are they for, then?'

Freya was wriggling from one leg to the other. Eventually she said, 'I'm going to have a stall.'

'A stall?' Liv glanced at her watch. Ten to nine.

'Like Daphne does, only she sells vegetables. A stall by the road. I'm going to sell my dolls. I hate dolls, anyway.'

Liv stared at her daughter. 'By the road?'

Freya's expression was mulish. 'While you're working. You're always working. It's boring.'

'Where, Freya? Where were you planning to have your stall?'

'Outside the farm. I told you, like Daphne does.'

Liv glanced into the bag again. 'Some of these things belong to Georgie.'

'I don't want her silly dolls in my bedroom.'

Her temper, already fragile that day, snapped. 'You can't sell your sister's toys. You must put them back in the bedroom, Freya.'

'Don't want to.'

Liv searched for her house keys, her car keys. 'Just do it.'

'You can't make me.' Freya's voice trembled.

Five to nine. She grabbed the bag from Freya's hands and dumped it on the sofa. Freya yelled. Liv found her house keys in her mackintosh pocket, her car keys under a cushion.

'Get into the car.'

Georgie scuttled; Freya wailed. As Liv drove the mile and a half to school, her head pounded in rhythm with Freya's howls. Outside the school gates, she made a last-ditch effort to retrieve things. 'Freya, if you want to get rid of your dolls, you can do, of course. Perhaps you could give them to a jumble sale, or to a charity shop.'

But Freya said angrily, 'I wanted the *money*. You don't get *money* from a jumble sale,' and then she ran across the courtyard into school.

Without a goodbye kiss. The first time, thought Liv sadly.

Felix had been in London overnight. He telephoned the barn at mid-morning. Liv told him about Freya.

'She has an entrepreneurial spirit,' he said.

'It's not *funny*, Felix. She was going to set up her stall on the road outside the farm.' She shivered, envisaging her small daughter, who had not yet lost the innate trustfulness of childhood, seeing a stranger beckon to her from a passing car. 'Anyone could have come along,' she said. 'Anything could have happened.'

He said reasonably, 'Liv, you or Daphne or Janice would have noticed that she'd gone. Or you'd have seen her dragging a table or God knows what down to the road. I mean, Freya's not exactly a *quiet* child, is she? Everything she does involves a great deal of commotion. You'd have noticed, honestly. And, anyway, you nipped it in the bud, didn't you?'

'Yes.' She was doodling on a scrap of paper.

There was a pause. Then Felix said, 'Liv, what's wrong?'

'Oh . . .' She sighed. 'I didn't sleep well. And there was something Freya said.'

'What?'

'That I work all the time.' Her head still ached; she rubbed her eyes with her clenched fist. 'And she's right, isn't she?'

'It won't be like this for ever,' he said gently. 'We're just going through a bad patch. We'll have a holiday soon, I promise you. All four of us.'

'Yes.' She made an effort. 'Yes, a holiday would be lovely.'

'I'll be with you by late afternoon. And I'll have a word with Freya about her business plans, if you like.'

It was, Freya thought, one of the most horrible days she'd ever had in her whole life. First, Mummy had been so mean about the dolls. Just because some of them were Georgie's, even though Georgie's dolls were always all over the floor of the bedroom that she, Freya, had to share with her, which meant, thought Freya, that she had the *right* to sell them. Then, at school, she discovered that Mrs Chambers was ill, so there was a new teacher called Miss Pritchard. Miss Pritchard was thin and yellow-haired and some-how sharp-looking, and told Freya off for being late. And then she made them do maths, which Freya hated. She had reached the bit in her maths book where she was supposed to share things out between people, which she could just about do if there weren't too many things to share between too many people. But Miss Pritchard glanced over Freya's shoulder, and said that she was rather behind, wasn't she, and she'd better skip a few pages, hadn't she? A new and terrifying set of problems stared back at Freya as Miss Pritchard moved on to her next victim.

The numbers muddled up in her head, worse than they usually did, and when she had to show Miss Pritchard her book, she knew that she was in for another telling-off. 'You'd better look at this page again at afternoon break, hadn't you, Freya?'

said Miss Pritchard crisply, after scoring through most of Freya's answers with her red pen.

Throughout the rest of the day she felt cross and miserable. She hated school; she wanted to run away. She imagined taking the train to the seaside, or getting on to a bus and going to a big town. But she hadn't any money because Mummy hadn't let her make the stall. At afternoon break, she had another stab at the hated maths, and managed, more by luck than anything else, some right answers. Miss Pritchard glanced at the clock, and told her to go outside with the others for a few minutes and let off some steam. Freya wandered around the playground in front of the school, and then the bell rang. She didn't want to go back indoors to horrible Miss Pritchard, so she dragged her heels, running her fingers along the iron railings that fenced in the playground. Beverley Baverstock, whom Freya hated, shouted, 'You'll be in trouble, Freya Galenski!' but Freya ignored her.

When the playground was empty, she felt suddenly relieved, as though, by herself, all her cross thoughts would ebb away and she might feel better. Then she heard someone say her name.

She looked up and saw the man standing by the railings. She recognized him instantly from the photograph in her bedroom. 'Are you my daddy?' she said, and he held out his arms to her.

One of Briar Rose's most important customers phoned up at ten past three, asking a series of complicated questions, so Liv was late leaving the barn to fetch the girls. Georgie was already in the playground when Liv arrived at school; she chattered about her day while they waited outside the gates for Freya. After a few minutes, Freya's classmates began to tumble out into the playground. Liv, remembering the quarrel that morning, guessed that Freya would come out last, feet dragging and coat trailing on the ground, a visual statement of protest. Iced buns from the baker, she resolved, would put Freya into a better mood and then they'd have a long talk. She'd take the phone off the hook, and forget about the business for the rest of the afternoon.

But at half past three there was still no sign of Freya. Liv looked around, convinced that she'd spy her, thumb in mouth, skulking by the climbing frame, or, her troubles forgotten, talking excitedly to one of her classmates. But the playground was empty, and most of the other mothers and children had already drifted away. Liv walked alongside the railings, Georgie's hand clutched in hers. No Freya. Not in the playground, not on the road. There was a sensation of unease in the pit of her stomach. The same sensation she always had when the children were in danger: if they played too close to the river, or if they darted across a country road without first looking.

She went into the cloakroom. There was nothing hanging from Freya's peg: no coat, no schoolbag. Liv recalled the image from her dream: Freya's face, enclosed within its glassy prison. Or that other picture from this morning's nightmare: Freya walking to a stranger's car, seeing his smile, listening to his words, climbing in . . .

She was being silly, she told herself. She would find Freya in the classroom, talking to Mrs Chambers. But when she opened the door of the classroom, there was only an unfamiliar fair-haired woman, stacking books back on the shelves.

She looked up at Liv. 'Can I help you?'

'I was looking for Mrs Chambers . . . well, for my daughter, really. For Freya.'

'I'm Miss Pritchard. Mrs Chambers is unwell, Mrs Galenski, so I've taken her place today.' A frown. 'Freya's father collected her early. A dentist's appointment, he said.'

Just for a moment, she was relieved. Everything was all right. Felix had taken Freya home. Yet she recalled that she had taken both girls to the dentist at half-term. She felt confused. Why should Felix tell Freya's teacher that he was taking her to the dentist?

'A dental appointment?'

'Yes.' Another book was snapped neatly on to the shelf. 'You really should provide a note, Mrs Galenski, if Freya has to miss school time.'

She thought, *Freya's father collected her early. A dentist's appointment, he said.* A dentist's appointment that didn't exist. And *Freya's father*. She never referred to Felix as Freya's father. She had always been honest both with her daughters and with their teachers about the family set-up.

A black cloud seemed to be forming somewhere in the middle of her head, and a strange buzzing noise threatened to swamp her thoughts. She heard Miss Pritchard say, 'Mrs Galenski, are you all right?' and she struggled to pull herself together.

'What time did they leave?'

'A quarter past two. At the end of afternoon break.' For the first time, Miss Pritchard's brisk efficiency lapsed a little. 'There's no difficulty, is there? No mistake?'

She said, 'Was Freya's father tall and dark ... blue-eyed?'

A nod. 'Mrs Galenski—'

'His voice?'

'Well-spoken. Charming, actually. A slightly foreign accent...' Miss Pritchard looked up. Liv saw the fear in her eyes. 'He was Freya's father, wasn't he?'

'Oh, yes,' said Liv. The buzzing sound had become a roar. She blinked to clear her sight. 'Oh, yes.'

She drove first to the cottage, then to the farm. Crashing the gears, swerving too close to the kerb. Turning into the farmyard, the brakes screeched and the tyres slipped as she headed up the track.

Felix's car was parked in the courtyard. He was coming out of the barn, crossing the grass to her. She gasped, 'Freya – she's here?'

'I thought you were picking her up. Daphne said ...'

The last fragment of hope crumbled. If he had not caught her, she would have fallen. She heard his voice, as if from a long way off. 'Liv, what's happened?'

'Stefan,' she said. 'Stefan's got Freya.'

*

He took her inside the farmhouse, made her sit down. Daphne made tea that she cradled in her hands; with a sense of detachment, she watched her fingers judder, as though they were not really part of her.

'She's with Stefan,' she repeated. Her voice was flat, expressionless. 'He came to the school and said he had to take her out early. There was a supply teacher, who didn't know Freya's background, and she let him take her.'

She heard Daphne mutter softly under her breath, 'Dear God,' and saw her draw Georgie to her side.

Felix crouched in front of her. 'Are you sure, Liv? Are you sure it was Stefan?'

She understood what he meant. He meant, 'Are you sure it was Stefan and not some nameless monster who happened to spy an unhappy and solitary little girl?'

She nodded. 'I'm certain. I described him to the teacher. And Freya said that he was her daddy. Well, she wouldn't have said that about any man, would she? She has Stefan's photograph in her bedroom, doesn't she, and—' She could hear her voice rising higher and higher. She clamped her hand over her mouth.

Felix said, 'I'll phone the police.'

'No.'

He paused, his hand touching the receiver. 'Liv—'

'No, you mustn't.' She forced herself to gulp a mouthful of tea. 'We have to find her. Not the police.'

He rubbed his forehead with the back of his hand. 'I really think we should tell the police, Liv. They have the resources. Perhaps they can trace Stefan's car.'

'He won't be afraid of me, but he would be afraid of the police.' She was beginning to think more clearly. She put aside the mug and knotted her hands together tightly. 'If we involve the police, he might be frightened into doing something rash.' She remembered the struggle in the café in London: the expression on Stefan's face when he had heard the police siren. She looked up at Felix. 'He doesn't mean to hurt her, I'm sure of that. He loves her.' *Freya, my little goddess.* 'He won't hurt her unless something frightens him, unless he thinks he's cornered.'

Reluctantly, Felix moved away from the telephone. 'Where do you think they've gone?'

'I went to the cottage, but there was no sign of them.' She pressed her fingertips against the bones of her forehead, closing her eyes. Once, she had known intimately the irrational workings of Stefan's mind. Why had he taken her? And where?

Images formed behind her eyelids. A red Kit-Kat wrapper on the floor of a barn. The ashes of a bonfire. A heap of discarded tins and bottles. She opened her eyes.

'He's gone back to Holm Edge. I'm sure of it, Felix. Stefan's taken Freya to Holm Edge.'

Stefan had a head start of an hour and a half. Driving west through Norfolk, heading for the A1, Liv prayed. Please, God, don't let anything bad happen to Freya, please, God. Don't let her be frightened, and don't let her be hurt. Let her be safe at Holm Edge, and let me find the words to persuade Stefan to give her back to me.

It had begun to rain. Grey drops slid down the windscreen. She made a bargain. If it's me he wants, then that's all right. I'll do that. I'll stay with him so long as he lets Freya leave. Anything. She turned away from Felix, looking out of the side window at the fast greyish-brown blur of the traffic, as though afraid that he might read in her eyes the promise she had made.

She thought of Stefan standing beside the bedroom window, the shotgun in his hands. Whatever he wants, she repeated silently, just as long as it's me and not Freya.

Freya had fallen asleep in the car, and had not woken until they reached the house. It was a funny house, half-way up a hill. She told her daddy that it was a funny house, and he smiled at her, and said, 'It's like a house in a fairy-tale, isn't it?' and she smiled back, pleased that he understood her so well.

He didn't take her into the stone house, but to the barn beside it. It was a much smaller barn than the one at Mrs Maynard's farm, and it wasn't full of boring old machinery and bits of cloth. There were bales of straw and a sleeping-bag and a wobbly table with only three legs. And lots of books: Freya had a look at one of the books, but it was very boring, with no pictures.

Her daddy said, 'I expect you're hungry, aren't you, Freya?' and she nodded.

'Starving.'

It was the sort of supper Freya liked best. Chocolate biscuits and crisps and apples and lemonade. When they had eaten, Freya asked her daddy whether he had a television.

He shook his head. 'I don't like televisions. There are a lot of bad things on television.' He looked at her. 'Would you like to do some drawing, Freya?'

She drew for a while, but he only had plain white paper and a pencil, no felt-tips, so after a while she began to feel rather bored. She wanted to pee, so she asked where the lavatory was.

'Just use the grass,' he said. 'Take my torch, Freya.'

She went out into the garden. It didn't feel right, she thought, peeing in the garden. The garden was very big and dark and, even with the torch, rather scary. There were all sorts of awful noises, like monsters coming towards her. She missed her mummy. She even missed Georgie.

She went back into the barn. Her daddy beckoned to her. 'What's wrong, Freya?'

'I want to go home.' Her voice wobbled.

'Tomorrow, sweetheart,' he said. Gently, he took her hands in his.

'I want my mummy.' She knew she sounded like a baby.

He said, 'Your mummy's coming for you, Freya,' and he smiled. His smile frightened her even more than the garden had.

She put her thumb in her mouth and began to suck, not caring if it looked babyish.

She said, 'You're to wait at the top of the track, Felix. I don't want Stefan to see you.'

He turned off the ignition. 'I'm coming with you.'

'No.' She put her hand on his arm. 'No, Felix.'

'Half an hour, then. Half an hour, and I'm coming.'

She got out of the car. As she walked down the track, she switched off her torch. In the complete darkness she could see the chinks of light between the wooden walls of the barn, and her heart lifted. Freya was there. She knew she was.

She opened the gate. The soles of her shoes slipped on the wet, tussocky grass as she crossed the garden. At the doorway to the barn, she paused. 'Stefan?'

A light illuminated the interior of the barn. She saw him, sitting on a hay bale. Her gaze flicked quickly around, and then she saw Freya, curled up in a sleeping-bag on the floor. Her eyes were closed, but she could see the rise and fall of her chest. She felt dizzy with relief.

Stefan said, 'I was afraid the light might keep her awake, but I think she's properly asleep now.' He looked up at her. 'You came, Liv.'

'That was what you wanted, wasn't it, Stefan? That was why you took Freya, wasn't it?'

He had placed the torch on top of a straw bale. The pale light picked out the interior of the barn. She looked round. She saw the picnic table, the rows of tins and bottles, the cardboard box full of crisps and tissues and apples. The bottled water, and the washing-up bowl, with a plate, knife and fork placed neatly beside it. The paper and pen placed exactly parallel to the stack of books.

He said, 'I've made it nice for you, haven't I, Liv?' and her heart seemed to miss a beat.

'You've done this for me?'

'Do you like it?'

'It's very – ' her voice faltered ' – very tidy.' She looked at him. He was wearing jeans, a T-shirt – not warm enough for this weather, surely – and a mackintosh. There was a rip in the sleeve of the mackintosh. She saw that he had lost weight over the years, that dark shadows gouged the hollows of his eye sockets and cheekbones, and that she could trace the lines of the bones in his long, thin hands.

'How long have you been living here, Stefan?'

'Oh . . . months,' he said vaguely. 'A long time.'

'Why did you come back?'

He smiled. 'This is where I was happy.'

She turned away from him for a moment, closing her eyes. When she could speak again, she said, 'Weren't you happy in Canada, Stefan?'

'They put me in a hospital. Or was it a prison? I didn't like it. It frightened me.'

She said softly, 'Poor Stefan,' and her gaze drifted once more around the room. She saw the shotgun, then, on top of the stack of hay bales.

He must have followed her glance, because he said, 'There's still rats. Do you remember the rats, Liv? I still hear them at night.'

She pressed her hands together. 'Do you shoot them, Stefan?'

'Sometimes.' He licked his lips. 'They twitch when they die. I can't bear that. I hate them, but I can't bear to see the way they twitch when they die.'

There was a silence. After a while, she said, 'How did you find me?'

Again, he smiled. 'I found a letter in your mother's house. A letter you'd written to her. Your address was in it.'

Exhausted, she tried to take in what he was saying. 'You went to my mother's house? In Fernhill?'

'Clever, wasn't it?' He looked pleased with himself. 'I don't know why I didn't think of it sooner. I wasn't well when I first came here, Liv.' His smile faded. 'My head was bad. I saw things.

456

They did things to me in Canada – shock treatment – and it made my head bad.' He was rocking gently backwards and forwards as he spoke, like an unhappy child. Then he said, 'But then I went to Fernhill. I asked about your mother and Richard Thorneycroft. Someone told me they'd come back to England, and were living in the village. It was easy getting into the house. I cut my hand, though, breaking the window.'

'It was *you*. *You* broke in . . .' The confusion persisted. 'So you've only just—'

'I told you, Liv, I was ill.' For the first time, he sounded angry.

'Yes. I'm sorry, Stefan. I understand.' She thought of the footsteps in the night, and the silhouetted figure on the pebble ridge. 'Only I thought you'd found my house before, in the summer.'

He shook his head. 'I'd have come to you before, then, wouldn't I?'

'Yes, Stefan.' Her voice echoed in the barn. 'You would.'

'You weren't at home,' he said. 'So I thought I'd go to the school, see if I could see the girls. And then she came out into the playground.' He glanced at Freya. 'She's a beauty, isn't she? A beauty.'

Another silence. She looked at Freya, curled up in the sleeping-bag. She wanted to take her in her arms, and never let her go. Yet Stefan stood between them, and she remembered the feeling of impotence in her dream as she had fought against sea and sand to reach her daughter.

He said, 'Would you like a drink?'

'Please.'

Carefully, he filled a cup with lemonade. She thought how pathetic it all was: the mismatched collection of crockery, the bottles of minerals and tins of spaghetti.

She drank the lemonade. He said, 'It's so good to see you here, Liv. Just like old times,' and then he smiled, and just for a moment, she saw him as he had once been, young and strong and sound.

She put down the cup. 'Why did you want me to come here, Stefan?'

'I just wanted to see you again.' He stood up, and she closed her eyes as he ran his fingertips along the contours of her face. 'I love you, Liv,' he said. 'I'll always love you. I've never loved anyone as I love you.' And then he quoted softly:

> 'O! when mine eyes did see Olivia first
> Methought she purg'd the air of pestilence.
> That instant was I turned into a hart,
> And my desires, like fell and cruel hounds,
> E'er since pursued me.'

His palms cupped her face. 'I can't forget you,' he said. 'I did try, but I can't. I can't just start again.'

'Stefan—' she whispered.

'I just had to see you again. That's all I wanted. And afterwards ...'

And afterwards, she thought. 'What, Stefan?' she said. Her voice shook.

But in the silence that followed, something in his eyes seemed to alter. 'Nothing.' He smiled. 'I won't trouble you again.'

'You know I have to take Freya home, don't you?'

'Not yet.' His voice pleaded.

'It's not warm enough for her, you see. She'll catch cold.'

She took a step towards the sleeping-bag. Now, she thought, now he'll reach for the gun.

But he did not move and, glancing at him, she saw the tears in his eyes. She knew then that he would not hurt her, would not hurt Freya. Whatever in the past had driven him to control, to be violent, had long ago left him. She had no reason to fear him any more. She thought, I'll phone a doctor tomorrow, find someone to look after him. I'll find somewhere decent for him to stay, somewhere that'll make him better.

'Do you mind if I take the sleeping-bag, Stefan? Only I don't want to wake her.'

'Take it. I won't need it.'

She scooped Freya up in her arms. Her cheek brushed against

her daughter's, and she cradled the child's heavy warmth. And then she walked out of the door.

His gaze darted from the track to the clock. Twenty-four minutes, twenty-five. Another five minutes, and he'd drive back to that farmhouse they had passed on the road, tell them to phone the police. And then he'd go and get her himself.

Sitting in the darkness, waiting all that unendurable time, he had learned once more how precarious happiness was. All his old agonizings about trust and commitment had seemed irrelevant, compressed into a nutshell by the enormity of the moment. He did not pray, because he had long since given up making bargains with God, but he continued to look through the darkness, waiting for the light of her torch. Lurching between fear and hope, he seemed at last to reach a plateau, a stillness in which there was only the clock, and the night.

Thirty minutes. He turned the ignition. Caught in the head-lamps of the car, he saw her, walking down the track, the child in her arms. Just for a moment, he bent, and leaned his head against the steering-wheel, weak with relief.

Then he heard the gunshot. And it seemed to Felix that it went on for ever, reverberating against the fells, filling the valley, clouding even the stars in the sky.

Liv never went back to the cottage by the marsh. Those first few weeks, when the nightmare images persisted, she stayed with Thea and Richard. Thea dealt with the police, and fended off the press. To do the smallest task exhausted her; for the first time in years she let herself be looked after. She took sleeping pills at night, and was thankful of the haze they imparted to her days. People regarded her as if she was a curiosity: she could see pity in their eyes. She wanted to say to them, 'But it's all right, I don't feel anything really. I've stopped feeling.'

After the inquest, after the funeral, she went to live with Felix in London. Slowly, she began to pick up the pieces. The noise and bustle of the city reassured her; she needed busyness and immediacy. She began to work again. In the light, bright attic at the top of the house that Felix had made into a studio for her, bold geometric patterns and bright abstracts flowed from her pen. She had done with her florals, her old-fashioned flower prints. She knew now that the countryside was cruel and unforgiving, and that the dreams it offered were false dreams.

Always, always, she feared for her children. She knew that it was a fear that would never leave her. She might put it away in a distant cupboard and lock the door, but still it would seep out in her darkest moments, haunting her. She fought the impulse to keep Freya and Georgie permanently by her side, knowing that if she gave in to it, they would suffer a different sort of damage. Yet to let Freya walk alone the hundred yards to the local shop frightened her, and each day, collecting the girls from their new school, fear hovered around her tense shoulders until she saw them run into the playground.

She knew that she had moved to the city for Freya's sake, too, because she saw in her elder daughter the capacity to dream that had destroyed Stefan, and had almost destroyed her. She would have her daughters' feet firmly on the ground. They would be doctors, lawyers, teachers, professions rooted in fact. She feared the genes that must be a part of their make-up, the double-edged inheritance of dreamers like Fin, like Stefan, like herself.

She noticed him first one morning when she was working in the studio. She looked out of the window and caught sight of him on the opposite side of the road, standing on the pavement, looking up at the house. She didn't recognize him as one of the neighbours, and assumed that he was lost, checking the house numbers.

That afternoon, she saw him again. They stopped most days after school at the small park opposite the house to feed the ducks and walk round the circular pond. He was sitting on a bench, crumbling what looked like the remains of a packet of sandwiches and throwing them to the ducks. He had a dog with him, a large, shaggy creature of indeterminate breed. He must be staying nearby, Liv thought. He was tall and broad-shouldered, sixtyish, she guessed. As they circled the pond, he smiled and wished her good afternoon. He had a craggy, weatherbeaten face and nice eyes, dark and friendly.

The following morning, the streets were silvered by the first frost of winter. A pale blue sky arched overhead, and there was a sharpness in the air. Liv took the children to school and hurried home. An idea for a new design was forming in her mind. For the first time since Stefan's death, she was impatient to reach her desk, excited by the prospect of creation.

The stranger had taken up his place of the previous morning, standing on the pavement on the opposite side of the road to the house. She gave him a quick nod, and hurried up the steps to the front door. She was fumbling with her key in the lock when she heard him say, 'Olivia.' She glanced back over her shoulder and saw that he was crossing the road to her. Her heart hammered, and she shoved open the door, her fingers slippery and nerveless, slamming it behind her. She sat on the stairs, shaking, staring at the closed door. She'd phone Felix. She'd phone the police. Not another stalker, she thought irrationally, not more footsteps in the night.

She had picked up the receiver when an extraordinary idea crossed her mind. She never knew what had sparked it: memory, recognition, or a fleeting glimpse of her own image in his. She put down the phone, and opened the door. He was heading up the street, the dog at his side, away from her. Yet as she watched, he turned and looked back, as if for one last glance, and seeing her, paused. Then he walked back to her.

'I'm sorry,' he said. 'I didn't mean to frighten you. Stupid of me.'

She said, 'It's all right. You're Fin, aren't you?' and he nodded.

*

She let him into the house. In the kitchen, she made coffee while he stood, a large, restless sort of man, with a presence that somehow seemed to fill the smallish room.

'It was you, wasn't it?' she said. 'At the cottage.'

'You saw me?'

'Once. And I heard . . . noises. At night.'

'Oh.' He looked crestfallen. 'I used to be good at that sort of thing. Covert operations.' He smiled ruefully. 'I must be losing my touch.'

She put a cup of coffee on the table. He said again, 'I'm so sorry, I didn't mean to frighten you. But I wanted to know that you were all right.'

'Twenty years,' she said. She was suddenly hot with anger. 'You've been gone almost twenty years.'

'There's nothing I can do or say to make that up to you, Olivia.'

'Liv,' she said furiously. 'Everyone calls me Liv.'

'Then, Liv, I could spend the whole day apologizing to you, and it wouldn't compensate for what I did, would it?'

'All those years . . . wondering where you'd gone . . . always thinking you were going to come back.' She swung round to him. 'Believing that it was *my* fault. Believing that *I* hadn't been good enough.'

'Never that,' he said. She could see the pain in his eyes. 'It was never that, Liv.'

She went to stand by the window. A part of her wanted to shout at him, to tell him to go away and never come back. After all, she had got through the last twenty years without him, so why shouldn't she manage the next?

But she felt tired, and the anger drained away, and she said instead, 'I got your postcard. The one you sent on my eighteenth birthday.'

There was a silence. 'Sit down,' she said. 'And drink your coffee. And tell me why you went. And why you came back.'

She watched him stir sugar into his coffee. The dog lay on the floor beside him, his head between his paws. 'I went,' he said, 'because I thought that if I didn't, I'd die here.' He looked up at her. 'Have you ever felt like that, Liv? Trapped somewhere you shouldn't be? Caught up in a life that isn't right for you?'

She thought of Holm Edge. She said tightly, 'You were able to live where you chose. You were able to go out to work. You had money of your own. No one was hurting you.'

'And I'd chosen that life, after all, hadn't I? Say it, Liv,' he said gently. 'Because you're right, of course – I chose to return to England after the war, and I chose marriage and fatherhood. Why should I complain about what I'd got through my own free choice?'

Yet so had she also chosen to marry Stefan. No one had forced her. She said stiffly, 'We make mistakes, I suppose.'

'*You* were not a mistake. Nor was Thea. I was the mistake. I couldn't fit in.'

She glanced at him, not understanding.

'War suited me,' he said, with a shrug of the shoulders. 'I'm ashamed to admit it, because it destroyed so many millions. But it's the truth, it suited me. Gave me an outlet for my talents. I was never so happy. I never felt so alive. I was in Norway at first, and later on in the Far East. I saw things I'd never seen before, did things I've never done since.' He patted his pockets. 'Do you mind if I smoke?'

She found him an ashtray. He struck a match, inhaled his cigarette. 'And then,' he said, 'the war ended and I came back to Britain. And there was no place for me. I was a leftover, a relic from another era. I couldn't fit in.' He looked up at her. 'I did try, Liv. I really did try. But I couldn't do it. I couldn't make myself be something I wasn't.' He sighed. 'It was Suez that did for me, I think. Such a spectacle we made of ourselves, trying to delude ourselves that we were still a great nation, that we still had influence.'

She said, 'So you went abroad?'

'Yes. We had a lot of arguments, Thea and I. I don't know if you remember that. Lousy thing for a kid, to have to listen to their parents yelling at each other.'

She remembered walking along the beach, while their angry words frayed like rags in the wind. She had tried to shut out their voices by concentrating on finding the pieces of coloured glass.

'So I thought,' he said, 'that it might be better to make a clean break of it. Better for you, as well as for me.'

She knew that he was asking for absolution. Twice, she had fled from Stefan. She said carefully, 'It's hard to know what's best, isn't it, when you have children? It's not always clear.' She looked at him. 'You haven't drunk your coffee. It'll be cold. I'll make some more.' She put the kettle on. 'Where did you go?'

'Oh, anywhere and everywhere. South America. The Pacific. The Far East. I worked on boats, mostly. I've always liked boats.'

She spooned coffee into the jug. 'But you came back. Why did you come back?'

'Because I nearly drowned.'

She thought of the pink house beneath the sea, and the dream she had had of Freya, her black hair like fronds of weed beneath the waves. 'Drowned?'

'I'd been lucky for years. Then I chose the wrong boat, the wrong skipper, and ended up drinking too many mouthfuls of the South China Seas. They fished me out, but I was ill afterwards. Pneumonia. I was in hospital for weeks.' Fin stubbed out his cigarette. 'I had no visitors. Not one. All the other patients had most of their extended family around their beds, and there I was, on my own. It made me think. It made me think that I was getting on a bit. That I was too old to go on charging around the globe like a twenty-year-old. And it made me think that before I died, there were things I should do. Visits to make. Debts to pay.' He looked up at her. 'I felt guilty about you. I wanted to make sure you were all right.'

She bit her lip. Her back to him, she poured boiling water on the coffee. 'So you came back to England?'

'Yes. Six months ago.' He smiled. 'For some reason I thought you'd still be living in the same house.'

'The pink house?'

'Yes. Part of me knew that you'd probably have moved on, of

course, but it seemed as good a place to start as any. Anyway,' he ran his fingers through his silvery hair, 'it had gone.'

'Washed away by the sea.'

'I couldn't believe it. I was stumped, at first. I saw what a fool I'd been, expecting things to remain unchanged while I played my idiot games. But then I had a piece of luck. I asked in the post office about the house, and the postmistress remembered you.'

She recalled it clearly: fleeing to the coast to escape Stefan, and the crushing disappointment she had felt when she had discovered that the house had gone.

'I stayed there for a few weeks,' she told him. 'A few years ago, after I left London.'

'The postmistress told me I was the second person to ask about the house. She remembered your name. Olivia Galenski, she said, but I knew it was you.'

'My family allowance,' said Liv. 'I cashed my family allowance there.'

'She told me you'd had two little girls in tow. But no husband.'

'I'd left Stefan by then.' It was still hard to say his name.

'And I thought,' he said, 'that it sounded as though things had been difficult for you. I was worried about you. Two small children, managing on your own. So I set about tracing you. Followed you up the coast.' He looked at her. 'I thought you'd probably been escaping from something, you see. That's what you do, when things aren't working out, don't you, you go back to the place where you were happy? And I guessed you hadn't much cash – a single woman on her own with two little kids – so I asked around the summer lets and caravan sites.' He made a face. 'Dreary places, some of them.'

She smiled, remembering. 'Once, we lived in a caravan that shook whenever the wind blew.' She put the coffee in front of him. 'So you found us – you found Samphire Cottage?'

'Eventually, yes. Took me a while, I can tell you.'

'But you didn't tell me you'd found me. You didn't tell me you'd come back.'

'I didn't think I'd the right,' he said simply. 'I could see that you were happy. Those two pretty little girls, that steady-looking chap. Oh, I wanted to go to you, Liv, I wanted to knock on your door, to say, "Here I am," the prodigal father, take you in my arms, get to know the grandchildren, all that. I even kidded myself for a while that that was what I was going to do. I hung around a bit, trying to pluck up the courage. But in the end, I hadn't the nerve.' He looked sad. 'Funked it. Told myself that you didn't need me, and left the area.'

'Where did you go?'

'Cornwall,' he said. 'Lots of boats in Cornwall. I've saved up a fair bit of cash over the years, and I found a cottage to rent, and bought myself a boat. And I found Eric.' He patted the dog. 'Or, rather, he found me. Followed me home one day, and wouldn't leave.' He was silent for a moment, and then he said, 'And then I found out what had happened. Your husband. I don't read the newspapers much or listen to the radio – got out of the habit somehow – and I've never really got on with television, but one day I was sitting next to a chap on the bus, and he was reading the paper, and I caught sight of your name. It was in an article about the inquest into your husband's death.'

It had been in all the papers. *Suicide in Deserted Farmhouse* in the broadsheets; *Love Triangle Husband Abducts Kiddie, Shoots Himself* in the tabloids.

'So I went to your cottage in Norfolk, but you'd gone. Thought I'd lost you all over again. But then I remembered that the newspaper had mentioned the name of your business – Briar Rose. That gave me a start. Anyway, to cut a long story short, eventually I found out you were living in London.' Fin paused. 'Bloody awful thing to happen,' he said. 'Just bloody awful.' He looked up at her. 'Knew a chap in Malaya who did the same thing. Knew he was going off his head, but I couldn't seem to find a way to help him.'

She turned away from him, and blew her nose. He said, 'Sorry. Shouldn't have mentioned it. Change the subject.'

She shook her head. 'At the coroner's court, they said that

Stefan had committed suicide while the balance of his mind was disturbed. As though a mind is a precise thing, like a pair of scales. But it isn't, is it?'

Fin said gently, 'What was he like?'

'Stefan?' Tears ached behind her eyes but she did not let them fall. 'Oh, he was handsome and clever and it was wonderful to be with him. And he was violent and cold and possessive and controlling, and in the end, I knew that I had no choice but to leave him.'

He patted the chair beside him. 'Come and sit down.'

She sat. He said, 'How's your little girl?'

'Freya? She's fine. Well, almost fine. She still has nightmares.'

'And the other one? The little plump one?'

'Georgie?' She smiled. 'Georgie will always be all right. She's that sort of person. I don't know how she manages it when you think of her parents, but she is.'

'She's that sort of person,' he said firmly, 'because she has a wonderful mother.'

'Hmm,' she said, disbelieving. 'I'm not so sure. A great deal of the time, I seem to get it all wrong.'

'Well, that's parenthood for you, my dear Olivia,' he said. 'That's parenthood for you.'

She told him about the day she and Thea had left the pink house, and how Diana Wyborne had helped them find a home. And about Katherine and Rachel, and about Hector, and about Alice. They went for a walk in the park, and he asked after Thea, so she told him about Richard Thorneycroft. He dug his hands into the pockets of his coat, and stood looking out at the pond, unspeaking. After a while, she looped her hand through his arm, and suggested they go to a café for lunch.

It was odd, she thought, having a father again. It took her a while to get used to it. 'My father,' she'd say, practising it. She'd watch him playing with the girls, and wonder whether one day he'd just walk out of the door, and not come back. Yet the months passed, and Fin and Eric travelled regularly from Cornwall to London to stay for the weekend. After a while, she began to realize that he needed her. That he chose to be with her. That, sometimes, dreams did come true.

Katherine and Hector were married in the spring of 1978. Alice, Freya and Georgie were bridesmaids. Liv made their sapphire chiffon dresses and Katherine's cream-coloured gown. There was a wedding breakfast in Bellingford's Great Hall, and then the male guests wandered off to see the drains that Hector had recently installed. The women remained – Barbara, Thea, Freya, Georgie, Daphne, Rose, Alice and Netta – filling the gloomy hall with shrieks of argument and laughter.

Katherine, plate in hand, came to sit beside Liv. 'All these *women*,' she hissed. 'The *noise*.'

'You'll have to have boys, Katherine.'

'*Well* . . .' Katherine looked pleased with herself. Almost smug. 'I thought I was going to throw up this morning. When we got to the bit where the vicar asked whether there's any lawful impediment. Just as well I had to keep my mouth shut, or I might have remembered all the reasons why marriage is a simply terrible idea.'

Liv was momentarily distracted from the spectacle of Georgie feeding her bridesmaid's posy to Rose Corcoran's dog. She hugged Katherine. 'A new baby! That's wonderful, Katherine. Congratulations.'

Katherine made a face. 'I seem to be doing everything I always said I wouldn't do. Getting married. Having a baby. Living in the middle of nowhere. Oh, and I've signed up for the Open University. Well, I have to do something to keep my brain working, don't I, living out here in the sticks?' Katherine ate another vol-au-vent. Then she said, 'I had a letter from Henry Wyborne.'

The posy's ribbon was now being knotted around the dog's neck. Liv beckoned to Freya, and glanced distractedly at Katherine. 'Henry Wyborne?'

'He's managed to trace Lucie Rolland. He told me that he's made sure she's all right. Financially, I mean. He hasn't fallen in love with her all over again, anything like that.'

'So,' said Liv, 'almost a happy ending.'

'Mum,' whispered Freya loudly, 'how much longer do I have to wear this awful dress?'

'Your dungarees are in the car, darling. Tell you what, if you take Georgie outside and keep an eye on her while she runs around for a while, I'll go and get them in a minute.'

Katherine had moved away to talk to Netta. Liv said meaningfully, '*Freya*,' and Freya sighed, grabbed Georgie's hand and hauled her out into the garden. Liv glimpsed Felix, standing outside the door. She rose and went to him.

She kissed the back of his neck. 'Had enough of drains?'

'They have,' he said, turning to her, 'only a limited appeal.'

'Katherine's pregnant,' she said.

'*Oh*.' He looked at her. 'Does it make you think ...?'

'When the business takes up less of my time,' she said firmly. 'When Freya and Georgie are easier. Then ... maybe.'

He looked around. 'Where are Freya and Georgie?'

'In the garden. Georgie was torturing Rose's dog. I told Freya to keep an eye on her.'

He looked sceptical. 'Coming for a walk?' He held out his hand.

'In a moment.' She kissed him again. 'There's something I have to do.'

She walked back through the hallway to the door that led to the pele tower. When she had closed it behind her, shutting out the roar of conversation and laughter, she climbed the narrow, winding stairs. At the top of the tower she stood, her palms propped on the parapet, looking out across the gardens to the hills. Looking down, she saw that the wedding-guests had left the Great Hall for the garden. Three little girls in sapphire blue dresses were running across the lawn. Alice, who was Rachel's legacy, and Freya and Georgie. Definitely a happy ending, she thought.

Then she moved away from the parapet, and outstretched her arms. She began to spin round. Faster and faster, until everything blurred together: her own dark-eyed girls and Rachel's, Katherine and Thea, until, stopping at last, opening her eyes, she looked out and saw it, there on the distant horizon, the shining silver ribbon of the sea.